C0-ALR-113

THE SAVAGE

Arriving in California to join the fight against crooked politicians in the Indian Ring, Sundance learned of a plot to kill his old friend General Crook. The enraged half-breed swore that blood would be spilled—enough to make a desert bloom.

GOLD STRIKE

Sundance and a band of die-hard prospectors and drifters faced off millionaire miner Jackson Selby's marauders in a life-or-death battle over the ownership of the richest gold mine in Nevada territory. Before they were through, the mine would be salted with bones and blood would pool in the deepest shafts.

PETER McCURTIN

DOUBLE-BARREL SUNDANCE

THE SAVAGE and GOLD STRIKE

Book Margins, Inc.

A BMI Edition

Published by special arrangement with Dorchester Publishing

If you purchased this book without a cover you should be aware that this book is stolen property. It was reported as "unsold and destroyed" to the publisher and neither the author nor the publisher has received any payment for this "stripped book."

THE SAVAGE Copyright © MCMLXXIX by Dorchester Publishing Co., Inc.

GOLD STRIKE Copyright © MCMLXXX by Dorchester Publishing Co., Inc.

All rights reserved. No part of this book may be reproduced or transmitted in any form or by any electronic or mechanical means, including photocopying, recording or by any information storage and retrieval system, without the written permission of the Publisher, except where permitted by law.

Printed in the United States of America.

THE SAVAGE

Chapter 1

The huge Baldwin locomotive, bell clanging, came to a halt at the Los Angeles railroad depot. Crowds still cheered, though this was the third train to come in from El Paso. Pistol shots rang out, and a brass band began to thump its way through a martial tune. The depot, an ambitious-looking structure, was so new they hadn't painted it yet. Smells of raw wood and escaping steam rose up into the clear blue sky. An enormous banner in gold and blue proclaimed: WELCOME TO THE SOUTHERN PACIFIC.

The boxcar door was pushed open and Jim Sundance jumped down, motioning the great horse Eagle to follow him. More accustomed to lonely places than wild boom towns, the big stallion looked to his master for reassurance.

"Easy, horse," Sundance said softly.

For once, Jim Sundance, with his copper skin, yellow

hair and Indian clothing, was in a place where his unusual appearance caused no surprise, for this once-sleepy Mexican village was now a growing city teeming with men from every race: Mexicans, Chinese, Negroes, Italians, Germans, and Irish! The smell of money brought them there, just as it brought the land speculators, gamblers, whores, pimps, bunco artists, outlaws, army deserters, and escaped convicts from Australia. They came across the plains, across the Isthmus of Panama, over the mountains, and around the Horn.

Some, like Sundance, came by the new Southern Pacific railroad. He could have traveled in a coach with the other passengers, but he preferred the company of horses to the stink of tobacco smoke and the babble of voices. In the coaches there would be sweat smells, nonstop poker games, the strident cries of candy butchers, and the mean-eyed pickpockets waiting for men to fall asleep.

Leading his horse through the excited crowd, Sundance saddled Eagle in a freight yard and rode toward *Calle de los Negros*, where there was a wagonyard for travelers who couldn't afford hotels and boardinghouses, or didn't want to stay in them. The streets he rode through were jammed with people and horses and yelping dogs. Saloons were everywhere, and more were being erected as fast as carpenters and builders could work. Drunken men snored in the gutter outside the saloons from which they had staggered or been thrown. A team caliope blared and two Mexicans were fighting with knives while a crowd cheered them on, making bets on the outcome. A city policeman, with buttons missing from his uniform and stubble on his face, watched without too much interest from across the street. Sundance knew he would arrest the winner.

Calle de los Negros, a long narrow street, now called Nigger Alley by the Anglos—the whites—hadn't changed much since Sundance had seen it nearly ten years before. A few Negroes lived there now, but they hadn't given the street its name. It simply meant the street of the dark-skinned people.

A few Mexicans glanced at him as he rode to the wagonyard at the far end of the street, but it was just casual curiosity, for he was nothing out of the ordinary in a colorful, reckless town. He reached the gate of the wagonyard, and there was old Gabriel Feliz, dozing in a cane chair in front of his mud-walled house, as if he hadn't moved for ten years. He wore a loose white shirt and a red sash and his straw hat was tilted over his eyes. The butt of an old percussion Colt stuck out of the sash. Years before when the town was smaller but just as wild, Sundance had seen him use the Colt on two drunken Russians, holdovers from the old Russian forts up north, who were threatening to burn his wagonyard to the ground.

Both men were armed. They had their guns in their hands, but Gabriel Feliz shot them dead without getting out of his chair. Sundance had been ready to give him a hand, but it wasn't necessary. The Colt was a percussion-type, and Sundance advised Feliz to have it converted to take metal cartridges.

"I am used to the old ways," the old man had said.

Now he pushed his straw hat back as Sundance rode in. He smiled broadly and got up quickly for a man of his girth. Sundance dismounted, and they shook hands. The wagonyard was thick with the smell of horses and the smell of cooking that came from the cabins on all sides.

"You have been away a long time, Sundance," Feliz said formally. "And how has your life been since last we met?"

9

Sundance said it had been all right. "And yours, Gabriel?"

The Mexican shrugged. "I do the best I can in my poor way."

Sundance knew that Gabriel Feliz was a very rich man in spite of his broken chair and tattered sandals. In his youth, in Mexico, he had been a bandit, and Sundance knew that he was still deeply but safely involved in smuggling and the purchase of stolen goods. One of his many enterprises was a butcher shop where even the Anglos came to buy their meat—the best in the city, it was said. It was the best because the old thief's suppliers stole only the best.

Sundance and Gabriel Feliz had been friends for a long time.

"I see you have many customers," Sundance said, nodding at the horses and wagons and buggies that filled the yard. "Do you have a place where I can stay? A corner of the stable will do if you don't have an empty cabin. I'm here to see General Crook."

"Ah, your old friend." Feliz looked puzzled. "Then why do you not stay with him?"

"He wants me too, but I don't want to leave my horse. This is a city of horse thieves."

The Mexican nodded gravely. "So it is said, but please do not speak of sleeping in the stable. Yes, my friend, I have a cabin for you. I do not like the look of the man who occupies it now. I think he is ready to leave."

Sundance said, "You don't have to throw him out on account of me. The stable will do fine."

"He was leaving anyway," Feliz lied, hitching up the sash on his wobbling belly. "I will go now and remind him. He will be gone before you have finishing putting up your fine horse."

Sundance watered Eagle, and was leaving the stable when he saw an angry looking man in a leather cap hitching up a buckboard. Feliz stood nearby with his hand resting casually on the butt of his gun.

"*Vaya con Dios!*" Feliz called out as the buckboard clattered out of the yard.

Sundance followed the Mexican into the cabin. It was a one-room cabin with nothing in it except a bunk bed, a table, two rickety chairs, and a cook stove. A sheet of tin had been nailed to the wall beside the stove, and pots and skillets hung from pegs. A film of gray dust clung to everything.

"You have provisions?" Feliz asked, turning toward the door. Sundance knew the fat man wanted to get back to his chair.

"Everything I need," Sundance said. "No need to fuss over me, my friend."

Feliz went out and came back in a few minutes with a bottle of tequila. "I can send a boy for whiskey if you like."

Sundance thanked the old man for the bottle of fiery rotgut. He blew dust from a glass and poured a short drink. Feliz had left a lemon and a spoon of salt. He didn't bother to use either. Tequila, he always figured, was bad enough by itself.

He was having his second drink—his limit was two—when he heard somebody coming to the door. Then a middle-aged man with a carefully trimmed beard and humorous eyes, stood in the doorway. His black bow-tie was as neatly tied as his beard was trimmed. If Sundance hadn't immediately spotted the shoulder holster under his arm he might have taken him for a prosperous merchant.

"Mind if I come in, Mr. Sundance?" he asked, taking off his flat-crowned gray hat.

Setting down his glass, Sundance told him to come ahead.

"I'm Sheriff William A. Rowland," he said. "No thanks, I'd rather stand. I have to be somewhere in an hour. Do you happen to know an old Indian who goes by the name of Charlie Cooper. Or maybe it's Kupa."

"How did you know my name, Sheriff?"

"Charlie Cooper told me. The old man is dying in a shack out back of Cleary's Saloon. He asked me to send you to him. There's nothing anybody can do for him, not after years of drinking everything he could beg, borrow or steal. I don't rightly know where he came from, what tribe he is, but he's been a swamper at Cleary's for years. Lived in a little shack where they stored empty beer barrels. He's been dying for months, couldn't work, but Cleary let him stay on. If you care to go there you'll find Cleary's on Downey Plaza. Ask anybody."

Sundance was thinking. "Did he have any other name besides Charlie Cooper?"

Sheriff Rowland tugged at the point of his beard. "Well, yes. Sometimes when he got very drunk he said his true name was Many Horses. Does that mean anything to you?"

"It might," Sundance answered, "if he's the same Many Horses I knew many years ago. You're taking an awful lot of trouble for a drunken old Indian?"

Rowland said, "An act of Christian charity. I've seen him around Cleary's for years, and took pity on him. But now I have to be in the Mayor's office."

Sundance walked to the door with the sheriff. "You're the man who brought in Tiburcio Vasquez, aren't you?"

Vasquez had been one of the most wanted outlaws in California. Many men, lawmen and others, had died under his guns.

12

"That was my job," Sheriff Rowland said mildly. "It seems to me I've heard of you, too."

"I'm not here to kill anybody, if that's what you mean."

The two men grinned. "That's good to hear," the sheriff said.

After Rowland had gone, Sundance left all his weapons, except for the Colt .44, in the cabin. He closed the door. There was no lock on it. Gabriel Feliz tilted back his hat when he heard Sundance coming.

"You are on your way to General Crook? They say he lives in much splendor at the Bella Union Hotel."

Sundance knew what George Crook would think of that. "Not yet," he said. "I left my other weapons in the cabin. Keep an eye on them, will you?"

Feliz said proudly, "I will guard them with my life. The man who touches them will die where he stands."

Sundance knew that was true.

An old colored man holding a horse outside a store told him where he could find Downey Plaza. Cleary's Saloon was a three-story building with deep-set arched doors and windows, and the brick face was stuccoed and painted in imitation of light blue granite. The roof was tin, and it looked like business was booming.

Sundance went through the alley that separated the saloon from the hotel next door. A well dressed drunk was vomiting on his shoes. Out back, half hidden by wagons and stacked lumber, Sundance saw a small shack without a door. There were no windows, and the stink of stale beer and rotting fruit was everywhere.

Standing in the doorway, Sundance called out, "Many Horses?"

He had to say it several times before a faint voice answered him from the semi-darkness of the shack.

"Sundance!"

Sundance had to stoop to get through the door, and when his eyes became accustomed to the gloom he saw a withered old man lying on a pile of sacks in the corner. He was covered up to the chin with a dirt-encrusted blanket. On a barrel stood the stub of a candle in a rusty tin can.

Light flared as Sundance struck a match and the wick took hold. He moved the light closer to the bed and his face blanched as he saw the ruin of what had once been a brave Cheyenne warrior. It took an effort to see behind the filthy clothes and ravaged face. The shack stank of sweat and whiskey.

"Sundance! You came. I knew you would." Many Horses tried to raise his hand, but it fell back limply on the foul-smelling blanket.

"You have to leave this place, Many Horses," Sundance said. "I have a place where you can get well. Gabriel Feliz will give me a wagon. I will take you there."

Sundance knew there was nothing anybody could do for the dying man who had once been a Cheyenne warrior, loved by his friends and feared by his enemies.

"I will die here, Sundance. Here, where I have lived in disgrace." Many Horses' voice grew slightly stronger.

"How did you know I was in Los Angeles?"

"Because Crook was here, I knew you would come."

"How did you know he was here?"

Many Horses turned his face to the wall. "I know, Sundance."

Sundance wondered how the old man knew. He guessed that few men spoke to Many Horses except to curse and kick him.

He said, "If you don't want me to help you, why did you send for me? To sit with you while you die?"

Many Horses' voice had a hopeless, muffled sound. "I

14

do not need help to die. I sent for you because Crook is to die. Let me speak, Sundance. A man has been paid to kill him. He is growing too powerful for what you call the Indian Ring."

Sundance suddenly felt cold, because he had come to Los Angeles to be a part of the convention that was being held in support of General Crook's impending nomination as Secretary of the Interior. If nominated and confirmed as Secretary, Crook would have complete control over the Bureau of Indian Affairs. Like Sundance, Crook had been fighting the crooked politicians of the Indian Ring for many years, and now he had a chance to smash them for good. They had tried to kill Sundance many times, but they had been afraid to touch General Crook because he was too well known, too respected. But now, with millions to lose in graft and outright theft, the Ring might be just desperate enough . . .

"You must tell me how you know this, Many Horses," Sundance said. "You're sure what you say is true?"

"I give you my word as a Cheyenne. I am shamed in their eyes, but I am still a Cheyenne. I tell you it is true. A man has been paid to kill Crook. I do not know when he will do it or how, but it is to be done. You must stop him. Crook is the one great hope for all Indians. You must give him his life."

"What is the name of this killer?"

Many Horses didn't answer.

Sundance asked the question again. "His name, Many Horses! If I am to stop him I must know who he is."

"I cannot tell you that. Do not ask my reasons." The back of the old Cheyenne's head was turned toward Sundance. His thick, once black hair was completely gray now, chopped off short, matted with dirt.

"You must tell me, Many Horses. General Crook was your friend, and he still is. Just telling me he is to be killed is not enough. You don't want to die knowing that a few words would help to save him. That is not death with honor."

"I have not lived with honor, Sundance. My honor died in a bottle of white man's whiskey. I was a chief, but I was a drunkard, too. I was crazed with whiskey when I led my men against the soldiers. Because of me they were slaughtered. I was the only one to escape. I have wandered many places since then."

"That's all in the past, Many Horses. Buried with all our mistakes. Now you are to die, so let it be as a man. For your lost honor, tell me this man's name."

It took an effort for Many Horses to turn and face Sundance. "I am old and I am dying," he said. "You must leave me in peace for a while, so I can think on what you have said. That is the way it must be. I know when I am to die, and I will not die before we have spoken again. Come back today after you have talked to your general. I will know what I must do by then."

Knowing it was useless to ask any more questions, Sundance stood up. At the door he turned and said, "Think well on it, Many Horses. The knowledge that you helped to save a great man's life will spread far beyond this miserable place. That is what you will be remembered for, and not the disgrace of so many years ago."

Walking back to the wagonyard, Sundance wondered if years of lonely wandering and soaking his brain in rotgut whiskey had driven the old Cheyenne chief crazy. And yet there was nothing crazy about the way he talked. He had once been a brave man, and he had given his word that he was telling the truth. Why had he refused to name

16

the killer? Everything else made sense except that. It figured that the Indian Ring would want to kill General Crook, and this would be the best place to do it, among crowds, in a city filled with desperados from all over the world.

Riding to the Bella Union Hotel on Eagle, he looked at the men crowding the sidewalks.

It could be anyone.

Chapter 2

General George Crook, ill at ease in a starched linen collar and black frock coat, clapped Sundance lightly on the arm, and said in his brisk military voice, "Nonsense, man, you'll stay with us. We have a whole suite all to ourselves. Two rooms are empty. Take your pick."

The general looked to his wife for support. "Isn't that right, my dear?" Crook's wife was the former Mary Dailey, the pretty Irish girl he had married in Maryland during the Civil War. She was somewhat younger than her husband, but there was no other man in her thoughts.

"Yes, Jim, why don't you stay. That wagonyard is no place for a special guest of the guest of honor at the convention."

Crook looked embarrassed, then they all laughed.

"Thanks again, Mrs. Crook," Sundance answered, "but I'm already settled in. The wagonyard suits me fine."

Crook's bearded face cracked in a smile. "It would suit

18

me better than this place. There's no way Mary—or Washington—will ever make a gentleman out of me. You know how hard it is to get plain steak and potatoes in a place like this? They keep trying to get me to eat some of their fancy French food. Who in Hades wants to eat that slop!"

General George Crook was a simple man who didn't swear, didn't drink, but he smoked like a chimney. The parlor of the hotel suite was blue with the smoke of expensive Havana cigars, the only luxury he allowed himself. He lit one now and puffed vigorously.

"I'm going to hire a special steak and potatoes chef for George when we get to Washington," his wife said.

The general, noticing the tense look on Sundance's face, turned to his wife. "You have things to do, Mary?"

Mary Crook looked from her husband to Sundance. The hint wasn't lost on her. They had been man and wife for too long. "The offer is still good, Jim. Now I have to see to the guest list for tomorrow night."

After she left, Crook said briskly, "Well, spit it out, Jim. I always know when you have something important to tell me. What is it you couldn't say in front of Mary?"

The two friends sat down in facing armchairs. "I have word that somebody is going to kill you, Three Stars." That was what the Indians called Crook, always with respect. Sundance considered it a good name for this man who had killed so many Indians, and yet was the best friend they ever had when the killing stopped. All the Indians looked up to George Crook, even those crazed with sorrow for their dead and hatred for the white man.

"Who's going to kill me, Jim?" The general might have been asking the time of day. He crossed his legs and continued to send cigar smoke spiraling toward the ceiling.

"I don't know the man's name, but I think I'm going to get it. I'll know for sure this afternoon. Do you remember Many Horses, a chief of the Cheyenne?"

"I ought to remember him. He fought me long and hard before liquor destroyed him. Don't tell me he's still alive. After his men were wiped out at Branch Crossing he disappeared. He didn't wait to be banished by his people."

"He's alive but he's dying," Sundance said. "Many Horses is right here in Los Angeles, has been for years. A swamper in a saloon."

"Well, I'll be blasted. *He* told you?"

"Yes. He knew you were here in the city, so he figured I'd be along."

"How would he know where I'd be?"

"That's what I thought, Three Stars. None of it makes much sense except the part about the Indian Ring. Many Horses says the Ring has hired a man to kill you. The odd thing is that I believe him."

"A man craving whiskey will say anything, Jim. Did he ask you for money?"

"No. I think Many Horses is past whiskey. He doesn't need whiskey to die."

"Few men are past whiskey, Jim. That's why I never drank it myself. I knew I might get to like it too much. Then where would I be?"

"Probably President, like Grant. You don't believe what Many Horses told me? He gave me his word as a Cheyenne that what he said was true."

"It's been many a year since Many Horses was a true Cheyenne, but we'll let that go. My point is, what would a drunken, dying saloon swamper know about any plans the Ring might have for me? I doubt if Many Horses knows for sure what year it is. And why wouldn't he give you this hired killer's name, if the story is true and such a killer exists?"

Sundance said, "He seems to know who the killer is, but he refused to tell me. I know it all sounds crazy, but there it is. He said he would have to think about it. I am to talk to him later today."

Crook got up and began to pace the ornate room. "It's crazy all right, and if Many Horses could read I'd say he'd been delving into dime novels. Now I don't say the Ring wouldn't like to see me in my grave, but all they've done so far is try to get me kicked out of the army. Grant may be a fool as a politician, but he isn't a backstabber. Anyway, Sheridan and Sherman would never let him get away with it. Remember, Jim, us four fellers saved the nation in its time of need."

Crook's loud laugh was sarcastic. "That's what they used to say about us. No, my friend, I'm afraid poor old Many Horses uncorked one too many bottle. Now why don't we forget this rubbish and have some lunch?"

Sundance persisted. "But what if his story is true? You've always trusted my judgment, Three Stars. I get the feeling that your life is in danger."

"Then so be it. You know how many times I've been shot at and wounded, how many men have threatened to take my life. A lot. You and Simon Tolliver were there the night those diehard Rebels tried to kill me. They didn't get me, thanks to you and Simon. Have you seen Simon these past years?"

"Just recently, Three Stars. I just came up from Texas where I helped him to fight off a murdering landgrabber. Simon is fine, and the landgrabber is where the dogs won't bite him."

Crook sat down again and reached for another

21

Havana. He was still laughing when he struck a match to light it. "Knowing you, I don't doubt it for a minute."

Sundance smiled tightly. "You keep trying to change the subject, sir."

Waving the lighted cigar with some annoyance, Crook said, "All right! All right! You're going to spoil my lunch with all this talk of murder and plots of murder. Now take this damn fool story Many Horses spun you. You're half Cheyenne, but I know the man better than you do. When you fight a man for so long, you get to know a lot about him. Many Horses was a brave man. He was also a weak man, and frankly I don't believe him. Oh, I don't say he might not have heard *something*. A man hears all sorts of rubbish when he hangs around a saloon night and day. Lost gold mines, stock ventures that can't fail. Yes, and maybe even some whiskey-inspired plot against yours truly, George Crook. In some crazy way, Many Horses may be trying to pay me back for what I did for his son after his disgrace. I felt sorry for the boy, thought he was gifted and intelligent. That was why I got him the appointment to the Gillespie Indian School in Pennsylvania."

"I heard something about that," Sundance said. "How did he do?"

The general frowned. "Fine at the beginning. I asked after him from time to time. I asked him to write to me, and he did, but there was no warmth in his letters. Judson—Colonel Judson—at the school told me the boy was aloof, with no friends among the other Indian boys. He excelled in all the sports, as if he wanted to prove that he was better, stronger and smarter than anyone else. Now it was the other boys' turn to be unfriendly. Judson said he didn't seem to care. Of course his father's disgrace could be the cause of that."

"I can understand that," Sundance said.

Crook continued. "As you know, the Gillespie School is primarily agricultural, though it does give the boys a good education in the general sense. After they graduate, it is expected that the boys will return to their tribes, to demonstrate the skills they have learned."

"He didn't go back to the Cheyenne?"

"How did you know?"

"Just guessed. It's hard for a man when he's caught between two worlds. I've always managed to handle it, but I can see where somebody else might not."

Crook pulled a cuspidor close to his chair and spat in it. "He wrote to me in the Northwest after he graduated. Asked me to get him some job with the Bureau of Indian Affairs. You know as well as I do that there are no Indians in the Bureau, more's the pity. Maybe he thought he would be the first. However, policy is policy, and there was nothing I could do. I wrote back, urging him to go back to his people. I didn't get a reply. I didn't know what became of him till four years later when I was leading one of the Apache campaigns. We crossed the border with the consent of the Mexican government, but they sent a troop of cavalry to keep an eye on us. Well, sir, one of the young lieutenants in that troop was Many Horses' son. He tried to avoid me, but I knew who he was, and when I spoke to him I sensed bitterness. I remember one thing he said: 'I'm here because the Mexicans don't care about the color of a man's skin.'"

"You have to say that for them, Three Stars."

"Don't I know it, Jim. Again, I urged him to return to his people, to go home where he belonged. He said he had no home, and then he walked away. The campaign ended quickly, and I never saw him again. I've often wondered if he's still in the Mexican army. He had the air of a man who would go far, yet there was a cruel streak in him I didn't like. I remember one day we captured five Apache hostiles, and since he was in authority we handed the prisoners over to him. Later I heard he tortured them cruelly to get information. I don't know if he got it—probably not. He shot those five men, didn't order it done, but did it himself. Shot them in cold blood, their hands roped behind their backs. I've been a soldier all my life and never saw the need to do that."

"Not all soldiers are like you. Now, sir, I'd like to remind you that we're off the track again. I wish you'd take this threat seriously."

"I'd like to ask you a question, Jim. How many times have you heard some hothead say I'm going to kill this or that man, and how few of them do it?"

"A few is enough. One is enough. One is all it takes if he's determined enough. How many men thought a broken-down actor like Booth would kill President Lincoln? Booth could hardly shoot a gun or stay on a horse. But he went around telling people he was going to kill Lincoln, and then he did it. What you have to remember is that Many Horses said this man who wants to kill you has been hired to do it, and that rules out some madman with a personal grudge. So it isn't some officer you cashiered, some Rebel still brooding about the War. A man like that would do it himself. Try anyway. Again, my guess is the Indian Ring is behind this plot."

"They always did hate me, I'll grant you that, but you really think they'd go that far?"

"With millions to lose they would do anything they had to. I know for a fact that they hired an expert rifleman to murder an honest Indian agent up in Montana. Anyway, you've been saying all along how hot you'll make it for them if you get to the Department of the Interior. You always have a way of speaking your mind, Three Stars."

"I'm too old to change my ways, Jim. Yes, by the Savior, I'll make it hot for them. The first day I take office I'll scourge that gang of scoundrels out of Washington the way Jesus ran the Pharisees from the Temple. And if I can put some of them in jail where they rightly belong, I'll do that, too."

"All the more reason why they'd want to kill you. If you had millions to lose, how would you feel?"

Crook laughed and dropped his cigar stub in the cuspidor. "I better air this place out." He got up and opened two windows. Then, turning back to Sundance, he said, "I don't have millions and I don't want millions. All I want is a decent life for the Indians, and if I have anything to do with it, that's what they'll get. To Hades with the Indian Ring!"

Sundance said, "With all respect, Three Stars, I have to remind you that there may be more involved here than the Ring. Right here in southern California the Ring has many important friends. At least men with the same interests. Here they stole the land from the Mexicans as well as the Indians. They're still doing it, and now the state supreme court has ruled that most of the old Spanish land grants have no legal standing. You said publicly that you were going to investigate that. I read it in the El Paso newspaper."

"I said I'd look into the matter, Jim. I said that as Secretary of the Interior I would look after the interests of all men."

The last remark made Sundance smile. Here was a lion

25

of a man. "That isn't how politics works, sir. A smart politician says a lot without saying anything. He waits until he gets into office before he says what he intends to do, and then does it."

"Then I guess I'm not a smart politician. I know you're trying to look out for me, Jim. I know that and appreciate it, but even if this threat is real, what am I supposed to do?"

Sundance said, "Stay here in the hotel as much as possible. Lots of good men from your old commands are here, officers and enlisted men. Let them post a guard over you while I go after this killer. I talked with Sheriff Rowland today. He looks like a good man. He has deputies."

The look the general gave Sundance was sour. "Why don't you call on the Navy for help while you're at it? I'm not about to skulk no matter who's out there planning to kill me. Now, Jim, we've been friends for a long time, but that's the end of it. If you catch this so-called murderer I'll appreciate it. Otherwise . . ."

Mary Crook came into the room carrying a newspaper. "Are you two talking about whatever it was you didn't want me to hear? Never mind that. George, this is the Los Angeles *Express*, the only newspaper that supports you for the nomination. You want to hear what they say about you?"

"Absolutely not."

"Well, I want you to hear it just the same." Mrs. Crook began to read while the general fumed:

This newspaper heartily endorses Lieutenant General George Crook of the United States Army for Secretary of the Interior. No better choice is available in all the length and breadth of this great nation. General Crook was born near Dayton, Ohio, in 1829, and graduated from the United States Military Academy at West Point, N.Y., in 1852. During the late War he distinguished himself in many decisive battles...

Looking extremely pained, Crook held up his hand. "Mary, my dear, I know all that. Now kindly stop."

"All right, George, I'll skip to the last part."

As a soldier General Crook is fearless both morally and physically, shunning neither responsibility nor personal danger. Of a kindly and sympathetic disposition, he makes friends in all classes of society. He thoroughly understands the Indian character. Realizing their hopelessness to hold their land against encroachment, he is more prone to pardon than to punish. In his recommendations on the subject of the Indians, he is far in advance of his time. He believes that they should be granted equal rights with the whites in courts of law, and all privileges of citizenship. It is expected that General Crook will resign from the Army immediately following the nomination.

Sundance got up to go. "Did you really say all that, Three Stars?"

"A good part of it, and what are you grinning at?" Crook walked out to the stairs with Sundance.

"No wonder they want to kill you," Sundance said. "Citzenship for the Indians. That's enough to do it right there." He nodded. "You don't want to hear anymore about it, and you won't for now. But I can't let them kill a man who is 'fearless both morally and physically, not to mention his kindly and sympathetic disposition.'"

"You heathen!" Crook was grinning as he held out his hand. "When will we see you? The convention's not far off."

"I'll be back when I clear up a few things. Will you listen?"

"Well, I just might," General George Crook replied.

Chapter 3

On the way back to Cleary's Saloon Sundance stopped at the wagonyard to borrow a wagon and an old straw mattress from Gabriel Feliz. The old Mexican looked at him with curious eyes, but didn't say anything.

Sundance had no way of knowing whether Many Horses would name the killer. Even so, he wasn't about to let him die in his own filth. The honor of his mother's people was at stake. Sundance would take the dying Cheyenne back to the wagonyard, wash him, dress him in clean clothes, and let him die with some dignity.

When he got to the big saloon on Downey Plaza, he backed the wagon into the alley. He got down to move two barrels out of the way. He maneuvered the wagon around the back of the saloon and jumped down.

"Many Horses!" he called out as he stooped and went into the darkness of the windowless shack. There was a sudden flash of danger in his mind, a feeling more than

29

knowledge that something was coming at him in the darkness. He felt a sinister presence, but it was too late, and even while his mind was rushing to preserve itself, something hard smashed him across the back of the head. A light flared briefly behind his eyes, and then there was nothing. It was sometime later when he felt the sensation of cold and realized that somebody was pouring water over his head. He tried to jump to his feet, but he was already up off the ground, sitting in a chair with his hands roped around the back of it.

Another glass of water was thrown in his face. "Wake up, you bastard!" a rough voice commanded. The order was followed by several backhand slaps across his face.

In his skull there was a pain like a nightmare, and when he opened his eyes he found himself surrounded by angry faces, curious faces, faces with no expression. A big, red-faced man in a broadcloth coat and silk hat came up close and caught him by the throat. The smell of whiskey gusted in Sundance's face.

"Why did you do it, halfbreed?" the big man wanted to know. "What reason did you have to kill the old man? What reason would anybody have?"

The big man turned to a boy with a bartender's apron tied around his waist. "Tell your story again, Jimmy, so our halfbreed friend here'll know we have him dead to rights."

The boy said, "It's like I told the others before you came out, Mr. Cleary. I was rolling an empty keg out here and saw the halfbreed's feet sticking out of the door. First I figured he was just drunk and stumbled in there to sleep it off. Then I saw the wagon by the alley and wondered what was going on. I lit a match and looked in the shack and there was old Charlie Cooper with a knife sticking out of his chest. The halfbreed was lying on his back. I grabbed his pistol before he had a chance to do any more harm. That's right, Mr. Cleary, I took away his gun."

"Good work, Jimmy," Cleary said. He grabbed a fistful of Sundance's hair and twisted it. "I'm going to ask you again, halfbreed. Why did you do it? Was it because you thought the poor old rumpot had money hidden away?"

"I didn't kill him," Sundance said, knowing that the crowd was getting edgy. While Many Horses had been alive most of them had treated him like a dog; now that he was dead they could afford to be sentimental about the degraded old savage.

The pain in his skull was now just a painful throbbing, but Sundance couldn't remember having ever been hit so hard in his life, and yet there was no blood.

"Old Charlie Cooper committed suicide, is that your story, halfbreed?" Cleary asked. "And you were just lying there to keep him company."

Sundance tried to sit up straight in the chair, and one of the men hit him in the face.

"Let him have his way," Cleary ordered. "Then we'll decide what to do with him."

"Hang him!" somebody at the back of the crowd yelled out.

Sundance talked to Cleary. "Sheriff Rowland knows who I am. Send for the sheriff and he'll clear this up. Talk to Gabriel Feliz who has the wagonyard at *Calle de los Negros* and he'll tell you Sheriff Rowland came to see me this morning. The sheriff said the man you knew as Charlie Cooper was dying back here. Charlie's name—his Cheyenne name—was Many Horses. I knew him many years ago. That was why I wanted to help him. You see the

31

wagon with the mattress in it! But all this doesn't mean anything if you don't send for the sheriff."

Sheriff Rowland came out the back door of the saloon and pushed his way through the crowd. "What's going on here? I walked in the front door and the place was all emptied out." He looked at the blood leaking from the corners of Sundance's mouth. "What are you doing to this man?"

Cleary said gruffly, "It looks like he murdered the old Indian. Charlie's lying in there with a knife in his heart. Jimmy here found the halfbreed laying not far from the corpse. The halfbreed says you know him."

Sheriff Rowland was a politician, and probably a smart one, Sundance figured. He tugged at the end of his neat beard before he answered. "I know who he is. Charlie asked me to send him over here, for what reason I don't know. What was the reason?"

The question was for Sundance. "No special reason," Sundance answered. "We're both Cheyenne, that's all."

"How would a drunk like Charlie know where you were?"

"Sheriff, I'd be obliged if you'd free me of these ropes. Maybe it's better we say the rest of what has to be said at your office."

Sheriff Rowland took out a pocket knife and cut the ropes. "I'll take his gun," he said to the young bartender, who looked as if he didn't want to give it up. "Fetch that knife out of Charlie's chest and kindly wipe off the blood before you give it to me. I guess the county will have to bury him."

"No," Sundance said, rubbing his rope-burned wrists. "I'll bury him. What about the wagon? It belongs to Gabriel Feliz."

32

"Leave it here until after we talk. No point going all the way across town to my office. We'll go down to the other side of the Plaza. I'd just as soon not talk in Cleary's. Too many peep holes and speaking tubes for my taste. Besides, Matt Cleary and I don't see eye to eye politically."

Rowland led the way to a small Mexican bar that served nothing but mescal and beer. At a table in the back by the wall, they both ordered beer. In the middle of the cantina four men were bellowing their way through a noisy card game. The semi-darkness of the low-ceilinged room was pleasant after the harsh sunlight of the plaza. There were flies, but then there were flies everywhere in Los Angeles. Outside, a water cart went by, wetting down the dust of the street.

A waiter brought the beer, and it was warm. Rowland said, "I might as well tell you, Sundance. I've been making inquiries about you. It appears that you are a close personal friend of General Crook."

"I know General Crook."

"You went to visit him at the Bella Union today. That's right. I had you followed. After you left there you borrowed the wagon from Feliz and went to the shack behind Cleary's."

"If your man followed me, why didn't he find me unconscious instead of the bartender?"

Rowland sipped his beer. His flat-crowned gray hat lay on another chair. "He always reports back to me first. My point is, you went straight from a private meeting with the man who may be the next Secretary of the Interior to a stinking little shack behind a saloon. You're trying to make up your mind about me, aren't you, Sundance?"

That was true. Sundance had been thinking about this man who had brought in Tiburcio Vasquez. That meant he was tough and determined, but it didn't prove anything else. Some of the bravest lawmen in the West were its biggest thieves and grafters.

"How long have you been in Los Angeles?" he asked Rowland.

"Most of my life."

"How long have you been Sheriff?"

"Fifteen years."

"Then you know this town better than most people. You know what goes on here, especially the politics."

"I'd have to say yes to that. What are you getting at?"

The waiter brought two more bottles of beer. In the center of the cantina the card game was noisier than ever. An Anglo boy with red hair came in and said to the Mexican, "I hear there's a cockfight today." The bartender yelled at him to get out.

"I'd better tell you," Sundance began. "Many Horses sent for me to tell me there is going to be an attempt on the life of General Crook. He said certain politicians in Washington had paid a killer to murder him while he's here in Los Angeles."

Sundance quickly sketched in the details. "General Crook will have to believe there's a plot, now that Many Horses has been murdered. Obviously he wasn't killed for money. Many Horses didn't have one cent to cross another. He had no enemies. What enemies could he have?"

Rowland said, "The man who killed him."

"I don't see him as what you would call an enemy," Sundance said. "He murdered Many Horses before he could reveal his name. That was just practical. Sheriff, I want to ask you something. When I told you about the plot to kill General Crook you didn't look so surprised.

Does that mean you know something you're not telling me?"

Sheriff Rowland shook his head. "No, and that's the truth. I was just thinking it had to happen some day. You saw that editorial in the *Express* today. Equal rights for the Indians, citizenship for the Indians! You should have heard the talk over at City Hall, and in the saloons. Of course, there are a lot of people who agree with him; a lot more who don't. I do and I don't agree with him myself. No offense, Sundance, but I'd just as soon not give Los Angeles back to the Indians and Mexicans."

"Then you haven't heard any talk about a plot to kill the general?"

"Not exactly talk, but there are plenty of people who wouldn't mourn over it if it happened. There are people who would like to get rid of Crook, but aren't ready to get involved in a murder scheme."

"Sympathizers?"

"That's the word. Just like during the war, people are taking sides. In a way it's not too different than during the war years. You've got to remember that Los Angeles is like no other city in this country. It's half wild and it's half civilized. Take Mayor Downey, for instance. We get along some of the time. His Honor was born in Ireland and worked his way up to Governor of California at one time. You'd think his background, the school of hard knocks, would make him a Union man during the war. Not so. Downey was so pro-Confederate they pushed him out of office."

"What you're saying is a lot of important people in Los Angeles are lined up against General Crook."

"I'm not saying it the way you're saying it, Sundance. It's one thing to disagree with a man, even hate him for his opinions, but it's something else again to plot to kill him."

Sundance said, "Sometimes it's not such a big step, Sheriff."

"Damn it, why did your friend have to pick Los Angeles for this convention! If he gets assassinated here, one of our biggest Civil War heroes, it's going to set the city back years. The Eastern paper'll be saying we're still a bunch of savages, though you say this killer is from the East."

Sundance shook his head. "Nobody said that, not even Many Horses. He said the Indian Ring hired this man."

Rowland, once again, returned to the most puzzling point of all. What would a drunken saloon swamper, an illiterate old Indian, know about the all-powerful Indian Ring?

"We'll have to let that pass, Sheriff. Walk around it for the time being. We keep looking at it as an obstacle in the middle of the road, and we keep stopping. Let's just buy the idea that Many Horses somehow learned of this plot. Then we go on from there."

Sheriff Rowland said quietly, signaling for another bottle of beer, "If this man killed Charlie Cooper, or Many Horses, as you call him, then he knows what you look like. And if he knows what you look like it's just one more step to knowing who you are and what you're doing in Los Angeles. Well, maybe that's the best thing that's happened thus far. If he figures Charlie told you about the plot maybe he'll call it off."

"He already knows I know, Sheriff. That's why he killed Many Horses. Many Horses told me everything he knew except the killer's name. I tried to get it out of him, but he said he had to think about it. I was to come back. I did, with the wagon. I told you the rest. No, he won't call it

36

off. We know about the plot, but we don't know who he is. You can swear in a hundred extra deputies, but they won't know who they're looking for."

·"Then the general will have to remain under heavy guard." The sheriff looked hopeful, then dejected again when Sundance shook his head.

"You say that because you don't know General Crook. I kept pressing him on the matter of posting a guard. He said finally he had heard enough. And when the general tells you that you know he means it. What we have to do is post a guard he doesn't see while we go looking for this man."

"That won't be easy."

"It'll be better than nothing. My thought is this: if the Ring has hired a Los Angeles man to kill the general, maybe you already have something in your files. It isn't likely that they'd do such a thing, but you never know. Are you going to be in your office later in the day?"

"We can go now if you like." Sheriff Rowland put coins on the table and picked up his hat. The waiter came to take the money. Rowland threw him a coin for himself.

"No," Sundance said, "I have to bury Many Horses, if you don't want an inquest."

Rowland said, "We know how he died." The sheriff held up the knife. "With this."

The knife was fairly short, with a plain bone handle and a thick blade. Both edges of the blade were razor-sharp. Rowland tapped the blade on the table and it gave out a high, clear note. "Well tempered, very hard steel," he commented. "Don't know as I ever saw one like it before."

Sundance had. "It's handmade, a combination throwing and stabbing knife. You mind if I hang on to it for a while?"

37

"It's evidence."

"Yes, I know. And maybe it isn't evidence."

"Oh, all right, here it is, but I want it back, mind you. I have a whole collection of knives and guns. Come on over any time you want. My house is right behind City Hall."

Gabriel Feliz got up from his chair and took off his hat while Sundance drove the wagon with Many Horses' body in it through the gate of the wagonyard. Sundance reined in the horse and said, "I need a quiet place to prepare my friend for burial, and then if you will tell me where I can bury him..."

Feliz, moving slowly because of his fat, led the way past the stables to what had once been a carpentry shop. All the tools were gone; only the bench and vice remained.

"No one will bother you here," the Mexican said. "I'll send the hot water and clean clothes you need. The poor man, he is so very dirty."

Sundance said, "And a blanket to bury him in."

"You do not want a coffin? It is not trouble to send for one."

"No need."

Sundance carried the withered body from the wagon to the carpenter's workbench. It seemed to be already mummified, dried up, as if left for years in the desert. With no sense of disgust Sundance cut the filthy shirt and pants away. Then when Gabriel Feliz and one of his sons came with two buckets of hot water and strong yellow soap, he scrubbed the body clean. He washed the grime from the dead man's hair and combed it down each side of his face.

He was putting the clean shirt and pants on the body

when he heard a sound behind him. The Colt came out fast and he found himself pointing it at George Crook.

Sundance eased down the hammer and put the gun away. The general was in full uniform. He walked over to look at the dead face of Many Horses. "So that's what he looks like now."

"What are you doing here, sir?" Sundance asked Crook, knowing that the killer could be anywhere.

Crook wasn't accustomed to being questioned in so sharp a tone. He gave Sundance that look that made even other generals quake in their boots. "What do you think I'm doing? I'm paying my respects to the dead." Crook's face then softened. "Sorry, Jim, after you left I decided I ought to go and see what I could do for Many Horses. I wasn't thinking about that story of his. But, you know, it was a detachment from my command that wiped out his force at Branch Crossing. When I got to Cleary's they told me you had already gone. Now I'm here."

Sundance started to say something, then changed his mind.

Crook was stripping off his uniform coat. "I'll wrap him in the blanket and carry him to the wagon."

"All right, sir."

Sundance went to talk to Gabriel Feliz, and the Mexican said, "Up on the hill there is where the old Mexican cemetery is. *Negros* too." Feliz smiled. "I own the cemetery. Every week I get offers from Anglos who want to buy it. I could get a good price, but I can't sell the resting place of the dead."

By the time Sundance returned to the wagon, the body of Many Horses was already in it, wrapped in the blanket, and Crook was doing up the buttons on his coat. "Are we ready?"

Sundance wasn't ready to have George Crook shot down while he walked through the streets behind a wagon with a dead man in it. He wasn't ready at all, yet there was nothing he could do. "Ready, sir," he answered.

One of Gabriel Feliz's many sons climbed up in the wagon seat and shook the reins, urging the horses to a steady walk. Sundance and General Crook took their places behind the wagon as it moved across the wagonyard and out through the gate. Men and women came out of the cabins to look at them as they passed.

"My God! It's the general himself," an old man said. "It can't be, but it is." He limped up close to Sundance and asked, "Is it somebody he served with in the Civil War?"

Sundance answered. "Yes, in a war."

People came out of the houses on *Calle de los Negros* as they climbed the hill toward the old, neglected cemetery. The gate had long since rotted away, and the whole place was overgrown with weeds. Crook and Sundance followed the wagon inside. Sundance felt the trickle of sweat on his body, as he glanced at the man walking beside him with a measured military step. At any moment now a shot might ring out and Lieutenant General George Crook, after all his great campaigns, would be dead.

No shot rang out, yet Sundance knew they were being watched. His eyes swept the line of brush and weeds at the far side of the cemetery. The branches moved in the wind, so there was no way to be sure. Now the wagon was more than halfway through the cemetery; there was still no shooting. Sundance thought he knew why: the killer had never expected to be given such an opportunity.

Sundance knew he was there, could feel his eyes boring relentlessly into both of them "This place looks all right," he decided before they got too close to the line of brush. He took the pick from the wagon and began to break ground. Crook put his coat and hat on the wagon seat and began to shovel dirt. The Feliz boy stood around smoking a brown-paper Mexican cigarette.

They were just about finished with the grave when Sundance looked up and saw a man in his thirties in a city suit standing not too far from the gravesite. Sundance drew the Colt in one easy motion. The man's eyes bulged as the hammer went back and the muzzle looked him straight in the face.

"Open your coat," Sundance ordered. "Hold up the tails and turn around."

"But I'm a reporter. The New York *Herald*. Dobson's the name. I have a letter from the publisher to General Crook."

Sundance climbed out of the grave and looked at the letter. His fingers made smudges on it. It looked all right. "You ought not sneak up on people," he said, handing the letter back.

Crook shoveled out the last of the dirt and Sundance helped him to climb back on top. He dusted off his hands and shook hands with the reporter.

"It's an honor and a pleasure, General," the reporter said. "I had gone to your hotel requesting an interview, but I was told you had gone to Downey Plaza. You might say, sir, that I trailed you here." The reporter gave a high-pitched laugh that made Crook frown with annoyance. "What about the interview, General?"

"Not now, sonny," Crook snapped. "Can't you see you're at a funeral."

Dobson, the reporter, looked from Crook to Sundance and then back to the blanket wrapped body. "Do you

41

mind telling me the name of the deceased, General Crook?"

Crook talked while he and Sundance lowered Many Horses' body into the grave with slip ropes. "His name was Many Horses and he was once a great chief of the Cheyenne. He is not as well known as other chiefs because he lasted only a few years as a warrior, but I never had a finer enemy. His life was destroyed by white whiskey sellers who had no right to be where they were. I have hanged any number of whiskey sellers in my time. I can only hope that among them were the men who sold Many Horses his first bottle of rotgut."

Crook and Sundance began to shovel in the dirt on top of the body. The reporter was writing down Crook's words.

"The way we have treated the Indians in this country is a disgrace to all we stand for. But when it comes to the Indians we don't seem to stand for much. We have murdered their men, or degraded them like Chief Many Horses. We have raped and abused their women. We have taken everything from them and given them nothing in return but disease and death. It is time that this otherwise fine country of ours took a good look at itself. I have nothing more to say, Mr. Dobson."

The reporter was reluctant to leave. "General," he said, "did you know that some newspapers are calling you 'The John Brown of the Indians'?"

Sundance thought Crook was going to hit the reporter with the shovel. He got between the two men in time.

"Don't press your luck, Mr. Dobson," he said. "There's the gate. The interview's over."

Chapter 4

Sundance liked and respected George Crook more than any man on earth, but there were times when the general could be downright exasperating. That was the way of the man, and there was no changing him. Walking back to the wagonyard from the Bella Union Hotel, along the teeming nighttime streets of Los Angeles, he wondered what to do.

They had gone to the hotel after Many Horses' funeral; Crook had conceded very little: "Look, Jim, I won't walk around with a target on my back and a sign on my chest telling the world who I am, if that's what you mean. And I won't wear the uniform again while I'm here. I had no intention of wearing it. I put it on to show my respect for Many Horses. As for the rest of it, I'll just have to take my chances. I won't skulk."

Sundance had said, "A lot of people will lose their chances if you get killed, Three Stars."

43

Crook's response to that was irritable. "I don't need a lecture on duty from you, old friend or not. I have no intention of getting shot."

"Will you carry the double-action .38 I just gave you?"

"Damn bean blower! All right, I'll carry it. More than that I can't promise. Now if you won't stay for supper—how many times do Mary and I have to invite you?—will you get the blazes out of here."

Crook bit the end off a long black Havana and poked tobacco shreds from his teeth with a fingernail. He smiled at Sundance through a cloud of fragrant cigar smoke. "This will probably be the only chance you'll ever get to take supper with Helen Hunt Jackson, celebrated author of *Ramona*, a true tale of our American Indians. It's been selling like hotcakes, they tell me. I tried to read it. Mrs. Jackson is a good woman—her heart is in the right place where the Indian is concerned, but Lord how she talks. John Greer, who is handling my campaign, says we need her support in California. You sure you won't stay?"

Sundance had said, "I'd like to pass this time. Gabriel Feliz has promised me the best stolen steak in Los Angeles. Of course, Gabe didn't say it was stolen."

"Wish I could go and share it with you, Jim. Instead, I have to sit around and look wise while Mrs. Jackson talks and talks...and talks. I want you Indians to know how much I suffer on your behalf."

Now, walking back to the wagonyard, Sundance knew there was nothing to joke about. He wondered if the general knew how serious the threat was. He guessed the general knew. The facts provided by the killing of Many Horses were too much to ignore. The costly handmade knife used to kill the old man was the strongest evidence of all. No ordinary thief and murderer would be likely to carry a knife like that.

It was a beautifully handcrafted weapon, and even Sundance had seen few like it in his time. Earlier in the day he had tested it on a fencepost in the wagonyard. He threw it at the post, and it flashed from his hand, straight and true. He dug it out of the rotting wood and moved back another ten feet. Thrown again, it buried itself in the same place. It was so well made, so well balanced, that it seemed to aim itself, if you threw it right. There was no maker's name on the blade, no initials or other markings, nothing to indicate where it came from.

Sundance wondered how many others like it the killer had. It was a killer's knife, and the man who had ordered it made knew his killer's trade. Was that how he planned to kill the general, with a knife silent and deadly in a crowd? Or would he come up close in a hand-shaking crowd of well-wishers and shoot the general in the stomach with a greased and dirtied dum-dum bullet, inflicting a terrible wound from which there could be no recovery? Or would he lay back at long range with a high-velocity rifle and shoot at a target no bigger than a man's hand? You could do that, too, if you were a good enough shot.

Passing a saloon, one of four in the same block, Sundance stepped around a drunken blind man, crawling on his hands and knees, begging for money. The beggar cursed him as he went by, and Sundance knew it could even be a man like that: a killer made up to look like a piece of human trash. That was the hell of it; it could be anybody.

One thing was sure: the Indian Ring would hire the best man they could find. With millions at stake, this killer would be no big-talking saloon braggart, his mind twisted by liquor and laudanum or mad dreams of a small but certain place in the history books because he had assassinated a famous man. He wouldn't shout any Latin words about the death of tyrants while Crook was bleeding his life away on some floor.

No, Sundance decided, the man who had been hired to kill George Crook would be a professional. A man who was good at his dirty trade, a man who planned his every move.

He was on Pico Street now, a narrow, twisting street named after the last Mexican governor of California. It led down to Calle de los Negros, where the wagonyard was. The air was rank with the smells of human filth, greasy cooking, and poverty. It was dark, but the heat of the day still beat down on the city. The street ran downhill from where he was, and the open drain, choked with dead mongrels and other rubbish, had backed up in this dry season. In one of the low-roofed houses a woman was screaming while a man roared at her to be quiet. A bottle broke a window and the screaming stopped.

Sundance's moccasined feet sloshed through a pool of dirty water from the backed-up drain. There was no way to get around it, and when he got to the other side he stomped the muck from his feet. More than anything he wanted to get away from this wild city; he longed for the clean heat of the desert, the cold of the high country, with the wind whistling down from snow-covered peaks.

Then he heard them. They were coming up the hill in his direction, sounding drunk and happy, men going home filled to the brim with wine or tequila. Instinctively, he touched the butt of his long-barreled Colt. They were singing an old Mexican love song, and it didn't seem more than that, if you didn't listen too hard. Whoever they were they were trying too hard to sound drunk and carefree.

Now the pool of fetid water was behind him. He turned

46

quickly, but nobody was sliding through it, sneaking up to kill him. His eyes went from the water to the top of Pico Street. Nothing! The singing came closer.

It sounded like three men; one was louder than the others. He had a high, tenor voice, very soulful, and it gave a sincere wobble when it came to the hard notes. There was a twist in the street, and Sundance couldn't see them yet. He slowed his pace and let them get closer.

He could see them now, three men who looked like Mexicans, with the big hats and the unconscious swagger. They seemed to fill up the street, their arms linked, staggering as they came. The tenor let out a yell, and the song started all over again.

Sundance looked for cover; there was none. All the doors on the dark street were closed and no doubt barred. He would have to face them head-on.

When the three men pretended to see him for the first time, they stopped singing and unlinked their arms and moved apart. The only light in the street came from the candles and oil lamps in the houses that lined it. Some of the lights were starting to go out.

The three men wore dirty white shirts and pants; it was hard to see their faces under the floppy sombreros. Sundance didn't see any guns, but he knew they were there, stuck in waistbands, covered by shirts. That would give him a small edge. He knew the man in the middle was the leader of this wolf pack. Bigger than the others, there was something catlike in the way he moved. He spat a cigarillo from his mouth and called out, "Buenos noches, señor, what are you doing in this part of town? You are looking for a woman maybe? You have money, or you would not be looking for a woman. You would like to give us money? We are poor men and need some money. I

47

think you would like to give us money."

It would come in seconds, Sundance knew, and he wasn't to wait for them to start it. Mexicans liked to talk, to stage things in their own way. Sundance had killed more than a few Mexicans who talked too much.

"If you want money, why . . ." Sundance drew and fired and killed the man in the middle. The bullet struck him in the face. Sundance swung the Colt and shot the man on the right. The heavy pistol boomed and flashed in the dark silence of the street. He fired again, and the man went down, screaming and cursing. Now the third man was firing, pulling the trigger as fast as he could. but his aim was bad and all the bullets went wild. Sundance had to shoot him three times before he went down.

For an instant there was dead silence, then Sundance whirled as something splashed softly in the pool of dirty water behind him. A fourth man was coming at him with a pistol in his hand; he dropped to one knee and aimed it as Sundance's hand flashed down to the throwing knife in his belt. He fired and missed. Sundance threw the knife with tremendous force; it buried itself to the handle in the killer's chest. He staggered backward, screaming and shuddering, both hands trying to pull the knife free. Then the screaming stopped abruptly and he fell with a heavy splash.

Reloading quickly, Sundance went into the pool of water and took off the dead man's hat, and even in the poor light he could see the man wasn't a Mexican. The hat and the clothes were Mexican, but the dead man's face was narrow, long-jawed and white, not a Mexican face at all. His hair was bright red.

Sundance groped in the water for the gun, and found it. A Remington .44, single-action, well cared-for by the look of it. Gun oil glistened through the water on the cylinder. Sundance stuck it in his belt.

A search of the dead man's pockets turned up nothing but a wad of greenbacks and a handful of coins. There wasn't even a scrap of paper to say who he was.

After pulling the knife from his chest, Sundance went to look at the three other men. They were Mexicans, and one of them was still alive but going fast. Blood bubbled from a hole in his chest, and the only sound in the street was his labored breathing. Sweat beaded his face and dripped from his chin; his entire body trembled with pain and fear.

Sundance bent down beside the dying man. "Who hired you to kill me?"

The Mexican's eyes rolled crazily in his head; he grabbed at Sundance's wrist. Sundance let him do it. It was a feeble grip. "Please! I want a priest," he moaned. "I do not want to die without a priest."

Sundance had no pity for this man. "You'll get a priest when you tell me who hired you. Tell me or you will die with a stain on your soul. You will burn in Hell for all eternity." He knew the man would never live to confess his sins.

The Mexican's breathing was becoming rapid and shallow; he would be dead in minutes. "I do not know the man, a gringo with red hair. He never spoke to me but only to Luis. You were pointed out to us when you left the cantina with the sheriff. We were to wait until it was dark, then we were to kill you. I do not know the reason. Luis did not know the reason. The gringo gave Luis money, and Luis gave some to us. That is all I know, I swear it. Now please, the priest. For God's sake . . ."

"Sure," Sundance said. By the time he stood up the Mexican was dead.

He drew his gun when he heard men coming up the hill;

they could be more of the scavengers who worked for the big Mexican named Luis, now dead in the middle of the street. Easing into the shadow of a doorway, he thumbed back the hammer of the Colt.

He let the hammer down and smiled when he saw Gabriel Feliz coming up the hill at a waddling run. Sundance had never seen him move so fast. The fat old Mexican had the percussion Colt in his hand; four of his sons were with him, and they all carried guns.

Sundance stepped into the street so they could see him. For all his years, Gabriel Feliz was a deadly shot, and Sundance didn't want to die at the hands of an old friend.

The old Mexican staggered to a halt, gasping like a spent horse, all of his three hundred pounds quivering with excitement. Sweat coursed down his mahogany-colored face. He mopped at it with a bandanna the size of a small tablecloth.

"Ah, Sundance, you're all right, they didn't kill you!"

"Rest, Gabriel," Sundance said. "You'll kill yourself running like that."

Without turning his head, the old man reached out and one of his sons put a bottle of tequila in his hand. He uncorked it with his few remaining teeth and offered it to Sundance.

"You first," Sundance said.

Still gasping, Gabriel Feliz drank a third of the bottle and passed it to Sundance, who took two swallows and gave it back. The old man finished it, and his breathing became easier.

"Those mangy dogs!" he said. "To try to kill a man like you!"

"How did you know they were shooting at me?" Sundance asked. He knew they must have heard the shots, but then shooting was nothing special in a wild town like Los Angeles, especially in the Mexican quarter.

"Word came to me that Luis Melendez and his jackals had been paid to kill you. In my business I hear many things. Many of them are untrue, but I knew this was true. Is that the dog lying over there?"

"His name is Luis."

Gabriel Feliz waddled over and spat in the dead man's face. "This is the dog. I am glad you are alive, my friend, but I am sorry you killed him. I have always wanted to kill him myself. For a long time he boasted that some day he would be king of Calle de los Negros. Of course, there is no king of Calle de los Negros. It was a foolish boast from a stupid man."

"Of course," Sundance agreed.

Gabriel Feliz went over to inspect the other Mexicans sprawled on the greasy cobblestones. He turned one over with the toe of his sandal. "I know these dogs, but who is that in the water. I can see he is not of my people."

Sundance said, "He's the gringo who paid these men to kill me. I've been thinking about the way he shot at me."

"In what way was that?"

"He dropped down on one knee when he aimed the pistol at me. That's how they train them to do it in the army. That is not to say that he is in the army, or ever has been. But it's a thought."

The old man looked quickly at Sundance. "You don't know who he is, or why he tried to murder you? All this, of course, is your own business." Gabriel Feliz shrugged and his voice was apologetic.

"I never saw him before in my life," Sundance said, then decided to tell the old man the whole story.

"Whatever you say, my friend. Is there anything else I can do for you?"

Sundance nodded. "I am very much in your debt,

51

Gabriel, and now I must ask for more help."

"Gladly given, Sundance. My sons and I are as one. They know of past favors."

In minutes Sundance finished the story about Crook, the plot to kill him. "Now you know as much as I do, Gabriel. You know this town as well as any man. As you say, you hear things. I want you to pass the word among your friends. Yes, even your enemies. Tell them General Crook is a good and great man, a friend of the Mexican as well as the Indian. If they hear anything, anything at all, I'd like to know about it. Will you do it?"

The old Mexican said, "I will do anything you say. Many men owe me for past favors, and now is the time to call for repayment. My sons will go into the streets and the cantinas to see what can be learned of this plot against your friend. I cannot promise they will succeed, but they will try very hard. Is that not so, my sons?"

There was a chorus of agreement, and Sundance had to fight back a smile. Old Gabriel and his sons were a dirty, dangerous bunch; and he was glad to have them on his side.

"But what a foolish man your friend the general is," the old man said, "not to listen to your good advice. I say that with good will." He smiled. "If it is your wish, my sons and I can keep him safe at my rancho in the hills. This convention is not of more importance than a good man's life. At my rancho he would be safe until this danger has passed. I pity the man who would try to harm him there. His death would not come quickly."

Sundance had no doubt of that; in his time Gabriel Feliz had been, as the Mexicans say, a man of great ferocity. But he knew that was not the way to handle it. "The general would never agree to that, Gabriel, but I

52

thank you for the offer. I know it was made with kindness."

"The general could be persuaded, for his own protection, of course. At first he would be very angry, as I am sure you know, but later he would come to understand. Your friend would enjoy himself at my rancho. Good food, sunshine, music." Gabriel Feliz winked at Sundance. "A pretty señorita or two."

Sundance wondered what Mary Dailey Crook would think of the pretty señorita or two. "You mean, kidnap the general?" He knew that was exactly what the old Sonoran bandit had in mind.

"Oh, nothing like that, Sundance. I do not even like the word. It could be done with great discretion. Your friend the general would be a guest, never a prisoner. His lady could accompany him. In time he would thank you for it."

Sundance could just imagine the Crooks penned up in the old man's rancho, stolen beef in the corrals and wild-looking riflemen patrolling the hills.

"In time he would roast me alive for it," Sundance said. "That's the least he would do. No thanks, Gabriel, I can't go along with your plan."

The old man persisted. "The general would not have to know you had anything to do with it. We could pretend to hold him for ransom."

"It wouldn't work. General Crook is as smart as you are, Gabriel. He'd figure it out. He'd know. I see the sense of it, but I have to say no."

"A pity," Gabriel Feliz said. He gestured toward the dead men. "You want to leave these dogs in the street. That is where they lived and died, like dogs!"

"No," Sundance said, "I'd better cart the bodies over to

the sheriff's office. He may have an idea who the dead gringo is."

"I would not count on it, Sundance," the old man said after sending one of his sons to fetch the wagon. He waded into the pool and dragged the dead man out by his long red hair. Then he struck a match and held it close to the dead face. "You see this man has had not much sun. See how white his skin is. I would say he comes a long way from this city."

Sundance knew he was right.

Chapter 5

Sheriff William Rowland was eating a late supper when Sundance knocked on his door. The sheriff's white frame house looked more New England than southern California, and it stood on a quarter acre of land behind city hall. Once there had been a vegetable garden, but now it was choked with weeds. Sundance guessed Rowland was a busy man.

The sheriff came to the door with a napkin tucked inside his collar. He had his coat off; he looked like a man with a lot of worries; the plot against Crook would loom larger than all the others. He was muttering angrily when he opened the door.

Light flooded out onto the porch. "Oh, it's you, Sundance," he said, opening the door wider. "I was about to stuff cotton in my ears and turn in for the night. A man has to get some sleep. When you knocked I thought it was that fool chief deputy of mine. I told MacPhail to use the brains God gave him, such as they are, and not come running to me every time something is wrong. But does he listen to me? Like hell he does."

"I know it's late, Sheriff," Sundance said.

"What's the difference! I'd rather see you than MacPhail. I'd kick him out tomorrow if he wasn't related to the mayor. I tell you I'm going crazy trying to keep the peace in this town. The Southern Pacific celebration is bad enough by itself without having to worry about the General Crook convention. Not to mention the Captain Jack Crawford Wild West Show. They're sleeping three men to a bed in the hotels and boarding houses, those who are lucky enough to get a bed. I can only guess how many strangers are in town."

The sheriff laughed and started to wave Sundance into the house. "I got that off my chest, didn't I? You had your supper yet?"

"What about yours?"

"I've had what I want of it. These days I do my own cooking. I had a Mexican woman but what she dished up was slow poison. I don't think I've had one decent meal since the missus died." Rowland paused. "But you didn't come here to talk about my stomach."

"No, I didn't," Sundance said. "I have four dead men out there in a wagon."

"Judas Priest! Did you say four? Did you do it?"

Sundance said he did, then told how it happened, adding, "One of them is a white man, an American, I guess, though we didn't trade any words. One of the Mexicans said this man hired them to kill me. He didn't have a name he could give me. The white man could be the man they sent to kill General Crook, but I doubt it."

Rowland said, "I don't know enough to doubt

anything," and while Sundance waited on the porch he went into the house to get a lamp.

They went out to the wagon with the four corpses in it. "That's Luis Melendez sure enough," he said. "It'll be a pleasure to strike his name from the books. But what would a sneaking killer like Melendez have to do with killing General Crook?"

"Melendez wasn't hired to kill the general; he was hired to kill me, and didn't even know why."

Rowland looked long and hard at the red-haired American, then straightened up, shaking his head. "Never saw him before. I'd remember if I had. Definitely not from Los Angeles, not lately anway. You were talking about looking through the files. I guess you want to do it now."

Sundance said yes.

"Might as well," Rowland said, picking up the lamp from the bed of the wagon. In the yellow glow of the lamp the faces of the four dead men had a ghostly look. "I'd like to get this Crook business over with, if that's possible. You know, Sundance, when I came here from Ohio twenty years ago this town wasn't hardly a town; more a village, the only sound was the sound of the lemon trees growing. Now we got a railroad celebration, a political convention, and a goddamned Wild West Show. Just about every crook and lawbreaker west of the Mississippi is in town, looking for easy pickings. Finding them, too. Dodge City in its wildest days was never like this."

They left the wagon with the four dead men and walked the short distance to City Hall. Rowland used a key to open the back door that led into the basement. There it was cold and musty-smelling, though it was a warm night outside. A coal oil lamp burned dimly in the

57

hallway; Rowland kicked at a plump rat with a bald tail that rushed at them from a dark corner.

"The hell with Mayor Downey," the sheriff said. "He's got my department buried down here."

Rowland led Sundance into an office and lit two lamps. One of the wicks was badly trimmed and the flame had blackened the side of the globe. Beyond the sheriff's desk two golden oak cabinets stood against the wall.

"If your dead American isn't in there I don't know what to think," Rowland said, opening a drawer stuffed with wanted posters and circulars, letters from police departments and detective agencies in other cities. There were photographs, even some old daguerreotypes.

Rowland said, "I'm trying to work out a system like they have back in New York. Chief Inspector Tom Byrnes is photographing every crook he lays his hands on, right down to the cheapest tinhorn bunco artist and pickpocket. I don't have the budget for that, thanks to Downey. I do the best I can. I try to concentrate on the big fish: the killers and the bank robbers. Here it is!"

Rowland produced a thick, leatherbound book that looked like an oversized bank ledger. Each page was devoted to the record of one man; to many pages a small photograph was fastened with a pin.

"You think you're looking for a man who might have been in the army?" Rowland asked, turning the pages slowly. "A red-haired man about forty, is that it? Tall and thin, an inch or two over six feet?"

Sundance was studying the faces in the rogues' gallery. There were only a few men described as having red hair, but each time he read the words he asked the sheriff to stop. So far none was over six feet and there was no mention of any army service.

"It's just a guess," he said. Another red-haired man turned up in the book, but he was only five eight, of "stout build," and his occupation was listed as "cowboy." There was no photograph. It didn't matter; he was too young.

"Still and all it isn't a bad guess," the sheriff said, continuing to turn the pages. "A few years back I killed a deserter who murdered a whole family out in the valley. He did the same thing as your man—got down on one knee to shoot at me. I never went after another man who ever did the same thing."

The middle-aged lawman smiled with grim satisfaction. "Of course, when all was said and done, his army-style shooting didn't do him any good. He got off one shot before I drilled him right between the eyes."

"Stop there," Sundance said, feeling a surge of excitement.

"Stop where?"

Sundance pointed. "That man with the beard. Look! The book says he's red-haired and six feet two. Occupation: former cavalry officer, first lieutenant. Courtmartialed and cashiered from the army for 'gross brutality' following the Battle at Branch Crossing, Wyoming Territory. John Jacob Cass was later convicted of murder in Fremont, California, but escaped from custody two days before his execution. A year later he was convicted of manslaughter in Fresno under an assumed name, served ten years, and was released before his real identity was revealed. He is still wanted for the Fremont murder."

Sheriff Rowland looked closely at the bearded face in the photograph. "By the living Christ, it looks like him, if you can see him without the beard. I think I can. Wait a minute while I get a piece of white chalk."

Sundance waited while the sheriff looked in the cluttered drawer of his desk. He watched while Rowland blotted out the beard. As he worked, Rowland asked, "Do you know who this man served under at Branch Crossing?"

"General Crook was in overall command there," Sundance answered, "but the general's main force was engaging a larger force of Cheyenne about five miles away. Crook took hundreds of prisoners after he won the fight; there was nobody left alive at Branch Crossing."

Sheriff Rowland was still working with the piece of chalk, wetting his finger and wiping it away here and there. He cleaned his fingers on the napkin that was still stuffed in his collar. He was almost finished. "Then Crook, as commander, would be the one who ordered Cass's military trial?"

"That's right," Sundance said. "One of Crook's subordinates might have recommended it; finally, it would be up to the general to approve it. A colonel could approve it if the general wasn't available at the time. I never heard about it. I'll have to ask General Crook."

"It's him all right," the sheriff decided, holding the picture of John Jacob Cass close to the light. "Even allowing for my handiwork, it looks like the same man. He was in his twenties when this picture was taken. Probably some travelling photographer came to some army post and took pictures of all the officers and their wives. I think we've found your killer, Sundance."

Sundance wasn't so sure. "We've found one killer, Sheriff, but I don't think he's the man they sent to kill Crook. A real professional killer wouldn't risk getting himself killed with a big job coming up."

Sheriff Rowland put the picture back in the book and

closed it with a bang. His eyes were red-rimmed from lack of sleep and his beard fairly bristled with anger. He threw the book in the drawer and kicked it shut with his foot.

"Damn it, man, what more proof do you want? He was kicked out of the army in disgrace, and he blames Crook because he was in command at the time. He couldn't get at him before now because he spent ten years in Folsom Prison. I'll bet he's been looking for Crook ever since they let him out. Then when he heard or read that Crook was going to be here in Los Angeles . . . I tell you it all makes sense."

"Some of it does," Sundance said, "but what about Many Horses? How did he hear about the plot and why was he killed?

"You said it yourself: he was going to give you the killer's name."

"If it had been Cass, Many Horses would have told me the first time. Many Horses would have absolutely no reason to protect Cass, of all people, not after what he did to the Cheyenne at Branch Crossing. That's the part that bothers me. Many Horses was killed with a specially made throwing knife. That doesn't fit with Cass. They don't teach knife throwing at West Point, and neither does Folsom Prison. Besides, Cass tried to kill me with a gun."

Sheriff Rowland picked up the lamp so abruptly he nearly knocked it over. "I don't know what you're going to do, but I'm going to bed. I still think we've found our killer. When you've been a lawman as long as I have you learn to accept what you've got. Who knows what goes on in the mind of a killer! A man who's been rotting in jail for ten years. Maybe he knew that you and Crook were friends and figured you'd get in his way. He could have

61

been watching you ever since you got to town. You led him to Many Horses, then later he came back and killed him. You happened along and got knocked on the head. Cass got panicky, left the knife and ran away."

Sundance said, "That's a lot of maybes, Sheriff, but there's no use arguing about it. I've got to go on believing there's another man out there waiting for a chance to get Crook."

"Believe what you like," Rowland snapped as he locked the door and led the way back to the wagon. "I'm going to stop worrying about Crook unless you can show me I'm wrong. Help me dump the bodies over the fence and I'll cover them with a tarpaulin. MacPhail can bury them in the morning. I guess he can manage to do that right."

"Come on in, Jim," George Crook said at seven o'clock the next morning when Sundance arrived at the hotel. He was in his shirtsleeves and wasn't wearing a tie. He patted his trousers pocket and smiled. "Yes! Yes! I'm carrying that little gun all the time."

Crook had finished breakfast, but there was some coffee left in the silver pot. "You want anything besides the coffee? I can order it right up."

Sundance said just coffee. Crook poured for both of them. "Do you recall a young first lieutenant named John Jacob Cass? He was tried and cashiered after the slaughter at Branch Crossing. 'Gross brutality' was the charge."

Crook lit a cigar and blew smoke at the ceiling while he thought about it. "Seems to me I do. Sure, I remember now. A young fellow with red hair. I don't know that we ever had reason to speak. Colonel Magruder was presiding judge at the trial. Another young lieutenant, can't recall his name, brought the charges against Cass. Cass was convicted of killing what was left of Many Horses' men after they surrendered. That was more than ten years ago. Why bring it up now?"

"I killed Cass last night, Three Stars," Sundance said, and explained how it happened while the general chomped silently on his cigar. "Sheriff Rowland thinks Cass came to Los Angeles to kill you."

"He sure waited a long time to get around to it."

"Cass was in prison for ten years. Did you ever get a threat from him in all that time?"

"From Cass? Not that I recall. I've had more than a few threats in my time. But wait a minute. There was one letter that came not long after Cass was booted out of the army."

"What did it say, do you recall?"

Crook said, "It sort of rambled on about white men turning on other white men when they ought to stick together in the face of the enemy. That would be the Indians, of course. We weren't fighting any other enemy at that time. No, there was no direct threat, but a threat was there. The letter writer said I had done 'something nice' for him so it was only fitting that he should do 'something nice' for me someday. He said that was a solemn promise. It was signed 'A Sincere Friend.'"

"Do you remember where the letter came from. This is important, Three Stars. Try to remember."

"Somewhere in California, I believe. I can't be sure, Jim."

"Was it Fremont?"

"It might have been. Yes, I believe it was. I didn't pay

63

much heed to the blamed thing. Are you trying to tell me that Cass sent the letter?"

"It's beginning to look like it. Whoever, sent it obviously had a grudge against you, and Cass was in Fremont about that time. That part about 'white men turning on other white men' fits Cass."

Crook rubbed his hands vigorously. "Then it's finished—it's over and done. Now why don't you stop sipping that lukewarm coffee and eat a real breakfast. Steak and eggs, that's the ticket. How about it?"

"It's not finished, Three Stars. I have a gut feeling that it's far from over."

"Fill your gut with a hearty breakfast and maybe the bad feeling will go away. No wonder the sheriff lost his temper with you. You know, Jim, you may be half white and half Indian, but there's some mule in there, too. Next thing you'll be looking under the beds. The convention is only a few days off. For now why don't you ease up, and after the convention is done with maybe we'll go hunting in the Sierras, provided Mary doesn't object too strenuously."

Sundance pushed his chair back and got up to go. "I'd like that, Three Stars. That's fine country up there."

The general always became excited when he talked about hunting. "You bet it is. It's got black bear, black-and white-tailed deer, mountain lion, ninety kinds of fish. Tastiest panfish in the world. I can just about smell a mess of yellow perch frying on a frosty morning. If I ever get out of this man's army I'm going to build a lodge up there in the high country. Then you'll see some hunting. You know, they still got eagles up there."

Sundance picked up his hat and put it on. "I'm going to keep on looking, Three Stars, and don't leave that .38 in a drawer when you go out."

Crook got so mad that he stuck his cigar in his coffee cup. It went out with a loud hiss. "Here I am talking about fried perch and you're still talking about murder! That's the big difference between you and me, Jim. You don't know when to ease up."

"Just habit, sir."

"Oh, go to blazes!" Crook said, but he smiled when he said it. "I'm still looking forward to a good hunt."

"So am I," Sundance said. He didn't add that he wasn't sure they would ever hunt the high country again. In spite of what the facts seemed to prove, he knew that it would get worse before it got better. That was the Indian side of his nature, and he always followed it when the feeling was strong enough. It was very strong now.

"I could stay with you until the convention is over," he suggested to Crook. "You invited me to stay. All right, I accept the offer."

Crook took Sundance by the arm and led him firmly to the door. He was laughing as he did it. "Oh, no you don't, you crafty halfbreed. I won't have you dogging my tracks every place I go. Can't have you doing that, not after what that newspaper scribbler, that New York fellow, Dobson, said about you in the morning edition of the Los Angeles *Star*. He didn't like the way you pulled a gun on him at the funeral. It looks like Mr. Dobson's employers don't like me one bit. Apart from condemning me for my stand on Indian rights, Mr. Dobson said I had hired a professional gunfighter to intimidate people who don't like my ideas. That would be you, Jim."

Crook opened the door, still smiling. "Personally, I'd like to consign him to Hades. On the other hand, you're the one who said I had to play politics. If you follow me around, Mr. Dobson will keep harping on it. I'll bet right now he's trying to dig up every bit of dirt he thinks he can find on you. Renegade gunfighter, the rest of it. Believe me, he'll get plenty of help from your enemies in Washington."

The two men shook hands, and Sundance went out of the hotel.

When Sundance got back to the wagonyard one of Gabriel Feliz's sons came running to the gate. It was hot and quiet in the yard; no noise at all except horses stirring restlessly. There was nobody around, but the Feliz boy, after looking this way and that, spoke in a low, conspiratorial voice.

"We have found the assassin," he whispered, looking very proud of himself. "My father and my brothers are with him in the carpenter's shop. He is a very fierce-looking man. It is easy to believe he is the killer. All the time he remains silent, but"—the young Mexican smiled—"my father will make him talk. My father knows all the ways of how it is done. Come, I will show you."

Well, anything was possible, Sundance decided, and followed the boy to the far end of the yard. So far he hadn't done any better, and he wasn't about to rule anything out.

Gabriel Feliz came out of the carpenter's shop when he heard them coming. His smile was wide, full of satisfaction. "Ah, Sundance, my good friend, my son has told you the good news?"

Sundance said, "He told me you had found a man."

The old man refused to be hurried; this was his great moment and he wanted to wring it dry. "Not just a man, my friend, but the man you are looking for. Last night after you went to the sheriff I sent my sons out into the city. My sons, I said, you can sleep after you have found this man. All night they searched through the saloons and cantinas. They spent much time, much money. Very early this morning they came across a fierce-looking white man in a cantina. He was very drunk and talking to himself, but loud enough for my sons to hear. This man sat at a table by himself, and on the table before him was a picture of the general. It had been torn from a newspaper. It was as if this man could not take his eyes away from it. Over and over he said, 'You are going to die! You are going to die! I will rid the world of you forever!' Words like that, words of hate. My sons struck him from behind and brought him here. You had already left by then. Yes, my friend, he had a gun. Here it is."

Sundance took the Smith & Wesson .44 caliber revolver. It was in good condition. He thumbed back the hammer and pressed the latch that opened the hinged cylinder. It was loaded.

He gave the gun back to Gabriel Feliz. "I don't know," he said. "Has he said anything?"

"So far, not a single word," the man answered. "Last night he talked all the time. Now he is sober and silent, but he will talk. I was getting ready to make him talk when you arrived. Let us go in."

A lanky man with a wild black beard was roped to the carpenter's bench. An old frock coat hung loosely from his gaunt frame; his thin lips were cracked and swollen. One of the Feliz boys was pouring a pitcher on the floor, doing it very slowly. The gaunt man's bloodshot eyes stared longingly at the clear cold water as it soaked into the ground. A brazier full of glowing coals stood a few feet away; there was a poker in it and the tip was turning white.

After wrapping a rag around the handle, the old man took the poker from the fire. The gaunt man looked at it without expression, though it was now only inches from his face.

"You will find your tongue or lose it," Gabriel Feliz said mildly. "Then one eye and then the other."

"Wait," Sundance said, pushing the old man's hand aside. "Let me talk to him. If that doesn't work you can use the torture."

Gabriel Feliz shrugged and stuck the poker back in the fire. "One way or another he will talk."

"Who are you?" Sundance asked the gaunt man.

There was no reply, just a narrowing of the bloodshot eyes. He tried to lunge at Sundance, but the ropes held him firmly.

"You are wasting your time, Sundance," Gabriel Feliz said. "I have asked him the same question many times." The fat old Mexican laughed and his sons joined in. "Of course, it is possible that he has a hatred for Mexicans as well as the general."

"I think he hates everything," Sundance replied, suddenly thinking of the worn Bible his English father had carried with him through all his years on the plains. Nicholas Sundance, the name the Cheyenne gave him, had taught his son to read with the help of the Bible. That had been many years before, but Sundance still remembered everything he had learned.

He spoke quietly: *And the mean shall be brought down, and the mighty man shall be humbled, and the eyes of the lofty shall be humbled. Woe unto them that call evil good, and good evil; that put darkness for light, and light for darkness; that put bitter for sweet, and sweet for bitter.*

Without warning a maddened scream tore from the gaunt man's twisted mouth. He began to babble in response to the words from Isaiah 5: *Therefore as the fire devoureth the stubble, and the flame consumeth the chaff, so their root shall be as rottenness, and their blossom shall go up as dust: because they have cast away the law of the Lord of Hosts, and despised the word of the Holy One of Israel* . . .

Spittle dribbled into the gaunt man's beard as his words became incoherent. He lurched against the ropes, kicking and screaming. Gradually his voice died away and he began to sob.

Sundance turned to Gabriel Feliz. "You see he is not the man I seek. He is mad and for some reason; his mind has fixed itself on General Crook. Better take him to the sheriff and get him locked up."

"So we must keep on looking, keep on asking questions," Gabriel Feliz said.

Sundance nodded. "That's what we have to do."

Chapter 6

"Maybe we should let Captain Dent know what we're doing," Collinson said to Sundance.

They were sitting at a table in Cleary's Saloon on Downey Plaza. Collinson was Major Raymond Collinson; the man with him was Sergeant Major Hanley; both men belonged to one of the cavalry regiments under Crook's command. Collinson was in his late forties, Hanley was a few years older. On the table there were two beer mugs and a bottle of whiskey.

Sundance finished his first drink and corked the bottle. "That wouldn't work," he told the two men. "Dent has been the general's aide for a long time. He'd feel obliged to tell him what we were doing. Then the general would run all over us like an old bull buffalo."

Major Collinson signaled the waiter to bring two more beers. A grin creased his weatherbeaten face, burned a deep brown by more campaigns that he remembered. "I'd hate for that to happen. I well recall the dressing down he gave me years back when I turned in what he called a sloppy report. Come to think of it, I guess it was kind of sloppy. I don't recall what the report was about, but I'll never forget the dressing-down he gave me. He's a funny man, Crook. After he got through yelling at me he gave me a cigar."

"That's the way he is," Sundance said.

"We can't let him get killed." Collinson pushed a beer across the table to Hanley. "If I could get my hands on the son of a bitch that wants to kill him..."

Hanley growled, "Not if I see him first, Major. I wouldn't use a bullet on him. I'd kick him to death. There isn't a better man or soldier alive than George Crook."

"That's why we have to look out for him," Sundance said, "seeing as he won't do it himself. Find a handful of men you can trust and post a guard on him night and day. If the killer is close by he'll be bound to spot you, and maybe that's good. At least he'll know that he can't just walk in and kill him."

"What bothers me, after hearing what you've said, is why he hasn't tried to kill him by now." Collinson made a wet ring on the table with the bottom of his glass, then rubbed it away with his finger. "The general has been here for days, and he's been all over town. Why hasn't the killer taken advantage of that?"

It was just past noon and the ground floor bar in Cleary's was jammed with drinkers. A man from the kitchen had to restock the free lunch counter every few minutes. In a circular cage among the potted palm trees a clockwork bird twittered shrilly.

Sundance poured his second drink and looked at Collinson. "I wish I had an answer for your question,

Major. The killer had plenty of chances, but he passed them up. It's as if he's waiting for something. It could be that he's even trying to make it harder for himself."

Hanley said, "You're getting ahead of me, Sundance. Why would he want to do that?"

"Look at it this way. He could have killed the general the first days he was in town. But he didn't. The way I see it—he's defying anybody to stop him from doing what he came to do. If that's true, then we know we're dealing with an arrogant man with great confidence in himself. He knows we know about his plan to kill Crook. Far from stopping him, I think it's going to make him more determined. I have an idea how this man thinks, but that isn't much good when we don't know what he looks like."

"It's a hell of a thing," Hanley growled. "Those bastards in Washington, all slobbering at the same trough. If Crook gets killed they're going to find some dead politicians floating in the Potomac."

Major Collinson said sharply, "I don't want to hear talk like that. We're here to protect General Crook and, by God, that's what we're going to do. If you don't have anything further to say, Sundance, we'd better be getting back. I want to talk to Lieutenant Hammer. Now there's a man we can count on."

The two soldiers stood up and shook hands with Sundance.

"He'll be all right," Collinson said.

Sergeant Major Hanley bunched his hairy fists. "He'd better be."

After they left, Sundance told the waiter to bring him a steak and a pot of coffee. While he was waiting for it a girl with dyed red hair and a beauty spot on her face came over and sat down without being asked. "Anything I can do for you, mister?"

"No offense," Sundance said. "Maybe some other time."

The girl's eyes flared but the fire went out of them when Sundance gave her a silver dollar. She went back to the bar and began to pester an old man with a white goatee and a varnished straw hat.

He was starting on the steak when a big man, very wide in the shoulders, came in the front door, pushing people out of his way. Anger showed in his eyes; his jaw muscles, thick as ropes, were clenched and unclenched. He wore a wool shirt and old army pants; the knees were patched with cloth of a different color. His yellow, uneven teeth gnawed at a stubby brown mustache. He had a newspaper in his hand.

The newspaper, thrown hard, landed on the table with a whack. Coffee splashed from Sundance's cup. He lifted the pot and filled the cup again. Looking up at the big man, he asked quietly, "Something I can do for you?"

"I'll be the judge of that," the big man said. "First I want everybody to hear what I think of you. You're Georgie Crook's hired gunman. That's what it says in the paper. Why don't you gun me down like you did John Cass! I'm not wearing a gun, so why don't you go ahead."

Sundance put down his knife and fork and saw Cleary, the dudishly dressed proprietor, watching from the stairs. He wondered why he didn't interfere; there were plenty of shotgun guards and bouncers in the place.

"Go away before you get hurt," Sundance told the big man.

It didn't scare him. "Get shot you mean, or stabbed like John Cass. Done in by Georgie Crook's halfbreed in a dark street. But it's not so easy in front of witnesses, is it, halfbreed. I told you I wasn't wearing a gun. You gun me down, and you'll hang for it in this town."

Sundance's thick steak was getting cold. "Maybe you better get a gun. A man who talks like you do ought to have something to back it up. Anyway, what have you to do with Cass?"

The man took a step toward Sundance and yelled, "See the way his hand moved toward his gun. I don't have a gun, but he's ready to kill me. You heard the halfbreed ask me about John Cass. I'll tell you what. I served under Lieutenant Cass, and a tougher soldier you never met. They kicked him out of the army for killing a bunch of dirty, stinking Injuns. Now, is that any reason to destroy a man's career. No wonder he went bad and took to stealing and killing. Georgie Crook, the god-damned hypocrite, could have gone easy on him, but no he said it wasn't up to him to interfere with the findings of the court. Bullshit! Georgie Crook could have saved this man's career with the stroke of a pen."

Sundance didn't like to hear General Crook bad-mouthed in a public place. Cleary was still standing on the stairs; he tried to avoid Sundance's eyes when he looked at him.

Sundance stood up and faced the man. "Since I can't eat in peace I'd best be going. Step out of my way."

"Or you'll kill me, is that it? I guess what it says in the paper is true. You'd be nothing without a gun. I'm just one man, a poor man, but I ain't afraid of you, just like I ain't got no respect for your Injun-sucking general."

Sundance came close to killing him where he stood, then he remembered what Crook had said about playing politics. "It looks like you're going to pick a fight with me, mister, whether I want or don't want it. All right, you'll get your fight, but there's just one more thing."

Sundance's voice was quiet and deadly. "Don't

74

mention General Crook's name again."

Cleary came down from the stairs and followed them outside. Before they went into the center of the plaza, Sundance unbuckled his gun belt and handed it to an elderly man who looked like a storekeeper. Once again, he wondered what Cleary had to do with this. Maybe Cleary didn't like Crook's politics. Maybe he just liked to watch a fight as long as it didn't take place inside his fancy saloon.

The big man turned suddenly and threw a left and a right at Sundance's head. Sundance ducked and punched him solidly in his wide, flat belly. There was no fat there; it was banded with muscle; it was like punching a rain barrel. All he did was grunt and show broken teeth in a vicious grin. "You'll have cause to remember who I am, halfbreed," he roared, swinging a massive right fist at Sundance's head. "Jack Clagett is who I am, and if I don't stomp you to death you'll wish I had." The wild swing missed Sundance's face, but stone-hard knuckles grazed the side of his skull. Sundance backed off, knowing he didn't have the weight to stand there and slug it out. He had faced men like Clagett before, though Clagett was one of the biggest men he had ever seen. It was obvious that Clagett was a bully and a brawler, and maybe he even punched sandbags and soaked his hands in brine to make them as hard as they were.

"Stand and fight like a man, halfbreed," Clagett bellowed as Sundance began to circle him. Suddenly he rushed forward, clumsily like a bear, but just as dangerous. Sundance reached out with a long left jab and caught him in the mouth. Then he feinted with his right and punched him again in the same place. This time the blow drew a thin trickle of blood. Clagett didn't seem to notice it. He thought Sundance's attempt to outbox him was downright foolish. He started a loud laugh, but didn't get to finish it as another left hit him in the jaw. All Sundance's strength was behind the punch; it barely rocked Clagett's head.

The laughing stopped. Clagett began to come in slowly, swinging his fists from side to side. His fists were out about fifteen inches from his body and eight inches apart. This was his idea of a guard, and it wasn't a bad one for a man of his size. Sundance knew that Clagett had always depended on his ability to take punishment as a means of getting him through anything. This wasn't a bad method either, provided the other man didn't wear you down, because no man can take punishment indefinitely.

Sundance sidestepped and hit Clagett a short-armed right over the heart. His arm was hinged and rigid as he did it. He gave it everything he had, and it brought a loud grunt from the gap-toothed mouth. Knowing there was no use punching the belly or the face, not unless he could smash the other man's thick, flat nose, Sundance went after the heart and the throat. He looped a right to the jugular vein, then hit it again. If you hit the side of the neck often enough the vein would begin to swell.

Clagett came in, pretending to be cautious, but Sundance knew he was preparing for a rush. It came. Lowering his bullet head, Clagett tried to get Sundance in the belly. Sundance sidestepped and kicked Clagett in his wide behind as the momentum carried him past. Some of the spectators began to laugh. When Clagett turned back to Sundance, his coarse features were twisted with hate.

He didn't try any more rushes; he bored in slowly, fists swinging like sledges, eyes glittering with hate. There was no more laughing from the crowd. Clagett caught Sundance with a savage blow on the upper arm. The pain, replaced by numbness, ran down into his right hand. He knew that if Clagett got him in the same place the arm wouldn't be much good for awhile. Flexing his arm to restore the circulation, he stood sideways, his left weaving back and forth.

"Not feeling so cocky now, are you, halfbreed!" Clagett said. "Dance around all you want, you red nigger, and it won't make a damn bit of difference. I can wait you out and beat you down. 'Course you can always run. That's it, why don't you run while you got the chance. No, you don't get your gun back. All you get to do is run."

Clagett's tongue was between his teeth when Sundance smashed him with a left uppercut. The big man screamed with pain as his ragged teeth snapped together and half an inch of his tongue was severed. It began to bleed profusely; blood ran out of Clagett's mouth, soaking his shirt. He rubbed at his mouth with the back of his hand; it came away slick with blood. He tried to yell something at Sundance, but the words were unintelligible. Now there was no attempt at guard or defense. Clagett bulled his way through the flurry of blows that Sundance threw at him. Any one of the blows would have dropped an ordinary man. Clagett just whipped his head this way and that; a wild bull bothered by gnats.

Now he tried for a kick at Sundance's groin. He tried for a backward kick, a mistake because Sundance grabbed his foot, twisted it and threw him on his back. He landed hard in the dust of the Plaza, but scrambled to his feet and launched another fierce attack. Now Clagett's arms were out straight, the fingers clenching and unclenching like claws. Sundance knew he was going to try to get at his eyes, and he realized, too, that if Clagett got him in a grip he would use those dirty broken teeth. In

77

the wild frontier towns you saw more than one man missing an eye, a nose, an ear as the result of a vicious fight.

Sundance was tiring in spite of all his efforts to conserve his strength. If he didn't do something soon the fight might go to Clagett; and the other man wouldn't just knock him unconscious and settle for that. If Clagett got him down he would finish him for good.

Sundance circled again, making the big man come to him. Clagett turned awkwardly, blood still streaming from his mouth. Sundance was getting set to try for another punch in the bleeding mouth, when somebody in the crowd threw a rock and hit him hard behind the knee. His leg buckled without warning, and then he was lying on the ground and Clagett was all over him, smothering him with his immense weight. Clagett's hands were buried in his hair, trying to rip it out by the roots. Sundance's eyes watered with the terrible pain. Clagett's bloody teeth snapped like those of a mad dog. He was trying to drag Sundance's face up toward his own.

Using his last ounce of strength, Sundance let go of Clagett's arms and punched upward at the nose. He felt bone and cartilage crunch beneath his knuckles, then something warm sprayed over his arm. Clagett gasped, his crushed nose streaming blood. This was the most effective blow in any fight; nothing hurt worse or bled the most or demoralized an opponent more than a broken nose. Clagett rolled away, trying to shield his ruined face with his hands. Hardly able to breathe, Sundance went after him. It was time to get it over with.

He staggered to his feet, pausing unsteadily for a moment, then kicked Clagett in the side of the head. The big man's body shuddered and went limp; blood bubbled from his nose and mouth.

Sundance, still dizzy, strapped on his gunbelt and walked over to Matt Cleary who was turning to go inside the saloon. Cleary's fat face was red and angry. "What do you want?" he said. "You know you just about killed that man."

"If I wanted to kill him he'd be dead now," Sundance said. "You saw the fight coming. Why didn't you stop it?"

"I don't know what you're talking about. Anyway, you more than took care of yourself."

The saloonkeeper was turning to go.

"Wait a minute," Sundance said, eyes narrowed. "Who is this man Clagett?"

Cleary gave Sundance a bland smile. "Sometimes he drinks in my saloon when he has money. Other than that, I don't know a damned thing about him. I mind my business; that way I stay out of trouble."

Cleary walked away.

Like hell you mind your business, Sundance decided, looking at the fat politician. It was plain as day that Matt Cleary, saloonkeeper and powerful Los Angeles politician, was lying through his teeth.

The question was—why?

Chapter 7

Sundance climbed the stairs to the second floor of the Bella Union Hotel and was about to knock on the door when a voice behind him said, "Who might you be, mister?"

Turning slowly, Sundance saw a hard-faced man in his thirties holding a Winchester repeating shotgun, a lever action. He was in civilian clothes, but Sundance immediately recognized him as a soldier. The repeater was steady in his hands, and the pockets of his canvas coat bulged with extra shells. A six-shooter, an Army Colt .45, stuck out of the waistband of his pants. From the tip of his ear to the jawline an old scar ran in a jagged line. He came out of a room at the end of the hallway, and his eyes were not friendly.

Sundance gave the soldier his name, keeping his hand well away from his gun. The Winchester 10-gauge repeater was a fearsome weapon; it took five shells and was the fastest-firing shotgun available in the world. In some cities the police used it to break up riots when they really got out of hand. They called it an "alley sweeper" because nobody ever lived in the face of a direct blast.

"Major Collinson knows me," Sundance said. "I'm a friend of General Crook."

"You sure look like the way he described you," the soldier said, not budging the shotgun an inch from Sundance's belly. He didn't try to get any closer: there was no need with the Winchester. "Did the major give you the password?"

"I gave it to him, soldier. 'Yellow perch.'"

The soldier lowered the shotgun and grinned. "Can't be too careful, can we. Go on in, Mr. Sundance. My name is Sam Eldredge, Sergeant, U. S. Cavalry. I hear the general thinks a lot of you."

"No more than I think of men like you."

"Don't you worry, Mr. Sundance. Nobody's going to get Old George, not while I'm here."

Sundance smiled. "I don't doubt it for a minute, Sergeant. His own name for Crook was Three Stars, but the men who served under Crook and liked him—and most of them liked him—called him Old George, though he really wasn't that old.

Eldredge went back to the room, but kept the door ajar. Sundance didn't knock on the door of Crook's suite until the bodyguard was out of sight.

It was locked from the inside; he heard the key turning in the lock and knew that the general was taking at least a few precautions.

Crook's aide opened the door and shook hands with Sundance after locking it again. The big elaborate room was blue with cigar smoke, though all the windows were

81

open. That didn't matter because the suite was in the back of the hotel, away from the noise of the street, and there were no tall buildings facing it from where an assassin could fire a shot.

A bar had been set up and a Negro bartender in a fancy hotel uniform was busy serving drinks. Conversation buzzed like a swarm of bees. Mrs. Crook was talking to four women, all elegantly dressed; she waved to Sundance as he came in. The four ladies gave Sundance puzzled looks, then turned back to hear what Mrs. Crook was saying.

General Crook spotted Sundance and hurried over to shake hands. The general looked uncomfortable in his high starched collar; it had made a red mark on his neck, and he tugged at it irritably.

Taking Sundance by the arm, Crook said, "By Gosh, Jim, it's always good to see you." Crook's language was always mild; the strongest word he ever used was "damnation!" "I often think we're the only two sane men in a crazy world. If these people don't leave soon I think I'll start shooting out the lights."

Sundance understood. He didn't like crowded places either, and he knew the general longed for the chill solitude of the high country as much as he did.

"You can't do that, Three Stars. The Eastern newspapers would start calling you a wild man from the West. Like me."

"Sometimes I envy you your life, Jim. Come and go as you please." Crook used his cigar like a pointer. "You see that swag-bellied gent over there, the one with the waxed mustache and the tall Sazerac cocktail in his hand. That's John Greer, my campaign manager. Used to be a newspaper editor in Chicago and later worked for a mail-order house, writing up their catalogues. Now he arranges lecture tours for people like Mark Twain, and manages political conventions for fools like me."

Sundance nodded. "I see him. What's he done to you? He must have done something, or you wouldn't be so riled."

Crook's voice came out, no doubt louder than he had intended. The four ladies with Mrs. Crook turned to look. Mrs. Crook frowned and shook her head. The general ignored her disapproval, but lowered his voice.

"Greer is trying to fob a blamed Wild West show off on me. Not only that but he arranged it months ago without telling me." Crook gestured again with his smoldering Havana. "The old faker he's talking to is Captain Jack Crawford, so-called King of the Indian Scouts. He's the one with the Buffalo Bill hat and beard. Noble-looking as blazes, isn't he?"

"He looks noble, sure enough," Sundance agreed. "Maybe not as noble as Buffalo Bill Cody, but he'd pass in a crowd. I remember Jack Crawford when he was shooting meat for the Union Pacific."

Crook looked for a place to get rid of his cigar; not finding it, he kept on smoking. Once again his wife was giving him discreet hand signals, but he looked the other way, back at Sundance.

"Jim, you ever know Jack Crawford to do much of anything except kill buffalo from a good stand, in a safe place?"

"Not much, Three Stars. Tell me about this circus."

"I'll tell you. Greer wants to bring in Crawford's blasted wild west show on the final night of the convention. Greer wanted to get Bill Cody's show instead of Crawford's, but Bill is touring England and Europe right now. I hear the Queen of England asked Bill to come over, Lord knows why. So instead of Bill Cody I get Crawford. You want to know why Greer wants a Wild West show?"

"Sort of, Three Stars. No better place than a Wild West show to display a lot of tame wild Indians."

"Right on the head, Jim. Greer says my campaign has been dull and needs a boost. He says I give them too many facts and figures. He says we have to dramatize this campaign. That comes from being an ex-newspaperman, I guess, but I hate to cheapen the cause. Damnation! Tepees, tomahawks, peace pipes! It's a wonder Greer doesn't want to show off a few scalps. I'd like to take his scalp for hiring Crawford on the sly."

Sundance said, "Just so long as you win. I guess Greer knows his business as well as any man."

"I guess so," Crook said reluctantly. "Well, you better come over and meet the King of the Scouts himself."

Sundance shook hands with John Greer, then with Captain Jack, who had a booming, tent-show voice and a false, hearty manner. For an old man he had clear blue eyes and an unlined face. He looked every inch the great scout, Sundance decided, that is if you didn't know any real scouts. Obviously he had patterned himself after Bill Cody, right down to his beautiful snowy beard. He had a very large glass of whiskey in his hand.

"Well, Mr. Sundance," he bellowed, "it's an honor and a privilege to meet such an old friend of the general's. Let me say that I have heard of your exploits, sir. Indeed, your fame has spread throughout the West." Captain Jack fixed Sundance with an appraising eye while he gulped his whiskey. He brushed his mustache right and left. "Mr. Sundance, if you ever decide to retire from your present hazardous profession, please be assured that there will always be a place for you with my Wild West show." Captain Jack waved his hands in the air, sketching what he saw there. "It takes no imagination to see you on one of my posters, sir." Captain Jack's loud voice grew louder: "CAPTAIN JACK CRAWFORD PROUDLY PRESENTS JIM SUNDANCE..."

"No thanks, Captain Jack," Sundance said, smiling at the genial old fraud.

"Think about the possibilities, my good friend," Captain Jack boomed in a voice that threatened to shatter the chandeliers. "They tell me your father, Nicholas Sundance, was a graduate of Oxford University. Why not bill you as the only Cheyenne who ever graduated from Oxford? All over the nation I can see the newspapers picking it up."

Sundance shook his head. "I'd be no good at it, Captain Jack. Why don't you tell me about the show you're going to put on at the convention."

"A small show," General Crook cut in while Captain Jack drank off the rest of his whiskey and waved at the bartender to pour another.

Captain Jack gave a loud, practiced laugh. His clear blue eyes shone with good fellowship, the love of being a showman, and the greed for money. He said, "My dear general, no show is ever small where Captain Jack Crawford's Wild West Show is concerned. In my time I have entertained kings and presidents and the captains of industry. In the field of showmanship I take my hat off to no man save my old and dear friend, Buffalo Bill Cody."

Captain Jack paused to take off his white Stetson. He put it on again at a rakish angle and smiled with pleasure at the sound of his own voice after putting away a huge drink of whiskey. "Many's the time Bill Cody and I hunted together on the high plains. Yes, gentlemen, fought together side by side, slept under the same blanket."

The old fraud gulped the rest of his whiskey and said solemnly, after he hiccuped, "Yes, gentlemen . . . and died together."

Crook looked at Sundance. "Oh, for God's sake!" he growled.

"In a manner of speaking, of course," Captain Jack put in hastily, realizing that he had gone too far, even for a windbag like him. "And now, my dear friends, it's time that an old scout got his rest." Captain Jack hiccuped again, then followed the hiccup with a windy belch. "My humble apologies, ladies and gentlemen, but now I must bid you adieu."

Captain Jack went out unsteadily, and after he had gone Crook turned to Sundance. "You see what I have to put up with! Cody is bad enough, but Crawford is worse. The great Indian fighters! Those two fakers have fought more booze than Indians."

It was time to tell Crook about the fight in front of Cleary's Saloon. "I tried to walk away from it, Three Stars, but he kept pushing it. I wanted you to know before somebody gave you the wrong side of it. That man Dobson is sure to make something out of it. I just couldn't let it pass."

Crook spoke slowly and deliberately, frowning at the noise of the party. "I think I know it happened, Jim. Don't worry about it. To blazes with Dobson and his newspapers. He would have attacked me anyway."

A wide grin spread across Crook's weatherbeaten face. "I guess you didn't think I'd know about those fellows you

86

have posted in the room at the end of the hall. No use trying to deny it, Jim. All right, I give in. If it makes you feel better I won't go against it. Just warn them not to shoot any prominent citizens just because they look suspicious. That goes for most politicians, I guess. You're still clinging to your idea of a plot and not just one cashiered officer with a grudge?"

"Afraid I am, Three Stars. There's something going on, and it's far from simple." Quickly, Sundance told Crook about Cleary, the saloonkeeper, and how he did nothing to stop the fight. "In fact," Sundance went on, "I got the feeling that he had something to do with it. Of course, I have no hard proof of that. It was just the way he behaved. Does what I'm saying make any sense to you, sir?"

"None of what's been happening lately makes sense to me, Jim. I thought, hoped anyway, that we had set this thing to rest when you killed Cass. Now you're throwing the eye of suspicion on Matt Cleary, the biggest saloonkeeper and speculator in the city, not to mention a powerful political figure."

Sundance said, "I'm only telling you what I saw and how I feel. That doesn't say I'm right."

Crook spoke hastily because his annoyed wife was bearing down on him. "You're seldom wrong, Jim. That's the hell of it. Well, here comes the missus."

"Hello, Jim," Mrs. Crook said, then turning to her husband, told him, "George Crook, you're neglecting our guests. How you carry on! I think everybody in the room heard what you said about Captain Jack except Captain Jack himself. What you said was most unkind."

Crook laughed. "It didn't make any difference, my dear. Captain Jack never hears any voice but his own."

"You come along, too, Jim," Mrs. Crook said.

"That's right," Crook growled, chomping on his cigar. "Why should you get off scot free? A little suffering will do you good. Mayor Downey hasn't arrived yet, but there are two people I want you to meet. I guess you already know John Clum. You can't see him because he's behind that very large lady with the pearl fan in her hand. That's California's most famous lady writer, Helen Hunt Jackson. I already told you about her."

"You said she talks. That makes it even, because John Clum hardly talks at all."

"A shame what the Indian Ring did to that man," Crook said. "He was the best Indian agent in the West. That agency of his was a model for the whole country."

Sundance knew all about John Clum, how he had fought the Indian Ring every step of the way, resisting threats and bribery; how, finally, he would have been murdered if he hadn't organized a heavily armed bodyguard of Apache scouts. But what they couldn't do with guns they did with political influence. Clum, a melancholy man who always wore a Mexican sombrero for reasons known only to himself, knew it would be useless to fight the false charges they brought against him. He quit the agency a defeated man.

Crook and Sundance steered their way around the large woman. She was talking so fast, with so many extravagant gestures of her beringed hands, that she didn't notice them at first. She had thick red hair that had obviously been dyed, and it sat on top of her head like a hen on a nest. Her thin mouth was determined; she was a woman used to having her way. A glass of port was dwarfed by her meaty hand; she had a way of running all her words together, breaking off one thought and rushing straight into another.

"Oh, General Crook, I was just telling Mr. Clum here . . . oh, this must be Mr. Sundance. . . . I've heard so much about you, Mr. Sundance. . . . Is it true that you . . . do you know Mr. Clum? . . . I was just telling him about my new novel. . . . They intended to publish it in three volumes. . . . Where did Captain Jack run off to?"

Sundance and John Clum shook hands, then Clum stood back a few paces. "You haven't changed much, Jim. How long has it been?"

"About six years," Sundance answered. "You look all right yourself."

"Damn liar! You know I look like an old man and feel like one, too."

"We'll change all that when and if I get to Washington," George said fiercely, his gray eyes glinting with anger. "That gang of pariahs in Washington will be sorry they did down a decent man. You won't be just an ordinary Indian agent if I get the job. I have bigger plans for you than that."

Clum said, "A good agent is all I ever wanted to be. I'd surely like to go back to my Apaches. I hear the last two agents have been starving them to death, reselling the supplies and blankets and medical things they get. Every few months they increase the number of Apaches on the reservation, on the records anyway. They claim more and more Apaches are drifting back from northern Mexico. So they keep getting richer and richer at the Apaches' expense. No wonder the Indians go to war."

"We'll see about changing all that when the time comes," Crook said, nodding to his wife. "Now friends, I have to go and greet His Honor, The Mayor of Los Angeles, John Downey. Better come along with me, Mrs. Jackson. I'll see you two fellows later."

There was a surge of people in the direction of Mayor Downey, who had once been Governor of California and might soon be a U.S. Senator. He was a benevolent-looking Irishman with hard, calculating eyes. Sundance didn't much like what he saw of him.

John Clum went to the bar and got two drinks, a big one for himself, a small one for Sundance. They sat down on an overstuffed sofa in a corner of the long room. Out in the center Mayor Downey was shaking hands and slapping backs. Mrs. Helen Hunt Jackson seemed to be giving him a piece of her mind. All he did was smile broadly, the case-hardened politician.

Clum's eyes were melancholy as he looked at Sundance and sipped his drink. "You think anything is going to come of all this, Jim. I like to keep on hoping, but there are times when it seems a waste of time. I thought I could buck the Ring and get away with it. Sure I was able to defy them for a while. They couldn't get close enough to kill me because of my Apache bodyguard. Day and night I was guarded by a dozen riflemen, men I trusted with my life. No, the Ring couldn't kill me, so they put on the political pressure and broke me like a rotten stick."

"Don't be like that, John. You fought a good fight and lost, but the war isn't over yet. If anybody can turn this thing around it will be George Crook, if he's alive to do it."

Sundance explained quickly while Clum's face took on an increasingly shocked look.

"I fell like I want to be sick," Clum said. "I can see them wanting to kill me. I'm nobody—but a man like General Crook, who by all rights ought to be the President of this country..."

"That's why we all have to help," Sundance said. "If

anything happens to the general it will set us back years. I guess you know that."

Clum nodded. "Only too well."

"You got any of your Apaches with you? I hear you've got a bunch of them working for you since you started the ranch."

"Cicatrice and Gray Wolf are with me. They wanted to come along because they think the Ring still wants to kill me. So I didn't argue about it. Why do you ask?"

"I don't rightly know. It's just that Apaches seem to know things even other Indians don't. We need all the help we can get. Maybe I'll talk to them later, if you don't have any objections."

"I don't control my Apaches. You know that." Clum smiled. "Except when it's for their own good. Talk to them all you want."

"Maybe I will." Sundance explained that he guessed the killer would try to get Crook in front of the convention crowd. "It's a hunch but it's a powerful one. You've lived among the Apaches most of your life and know there are things that can't be accounted for in a commonsense way."

"I grant you that."

"Did you ever have a really strong hunch that you tried to go against?"

Clum said, "I had one I won't ever forget. Early one morning I woke up with the feeling, a very strong feeling, that I'd die if I tried to go to San Carlos that day. There was nothing to account for it, but there it was. This was before the trouble started with the Ring, so it wasn't that. Well, I said the hell with it and hitched up the buckboard. The bad feeling stayed with me all the way to the river. It was running low and I could have been across in no time.

91

Just then, something made me hold back. A good thing I did, because the next moment a flash flood came roaring down like an express train. It would have caught me right in the middle of the river. Is that the kind of thing you mean?"

"In a way. I don't know why, but in my mind I see the convention as the place."

"The problem is that anything is possible," Clum said. "There's no way, not yet, maybe never, how Many Horses got word of the plot . . . if there is a plot. Maybe whoever it is was just making a tool of the old man. Maybe he just wanted to build up an atmosphere of danger, get people all jittery, and then when nothing happens everybody will get careless, especially the general. That would be the time to strike, maybe long after the convention is over."

"I've considered that," Sundance said, "but my hunch still points at the final night, the big closing night. All the important people will be there on that final night. Leland Stanford to boost his new line on the Southern Pacific, Mayor Downey to show himself to the voters, the Governor of California so as not to be left out. Not to mention congressmen and senators. That would be a mighty tempting audience for the kind of man I'm thinking about."

"You mean crazy?"

Sundance said no. "Not the way you mean. I'm trying to put a picture, a sketch of this man together in my mind. No, not crazy. More like arrogant; full of pride."

"I don't know what to think, Jim. You said Many Horses told you this man had been hired. That means hired for pay, so where does all this other stuff fit?"

"You have a point there, but I still think I'm on the right track. Men are complicated animals, full of twists and turns. There's no accounting how a man will behave if something drives him to it."

"It sure is crazy," Clum agreed. "I don't want to ask you this, but I have to. General Crook tried to help me fight the Ring, and I'm beholden to him for that, among other things. So I want to keep him alive as much as you do. But what happens if you don't turn up this killer before the convention? It won't be like a hotel suite where you can guard the doors and identify everybody who comes in and out. A convention is like a madhouse. Noise, lights, brass bands, hundreds of people milling about. There's no way to control it. I was at a Democratic convention in St. Louis one time, and I know what I'm talking about."

"I can't give you an answer, because I don't have one." He had been thinking while Clum talked. Why not, he decided. It was better than nothing. "I'd like to talk to your two Apaches," Sundance said.

Chapter 8

John Clum and his two Apaches were camped five miles from the city on the banks of the clear-flowing Los Angeles river. The sun had almost dipped low behind the hills by the time they got there; the sky was mottled with red and orange; the campfire was brighter than the other colors.

Three horses were tethered to a rope strung between two trees; the wagon horses were in another place, down by the banks of the river. An iron stewpot was bubbling over a fire held together by a ring of stones. It smelled good in the clear air of the early evening; it was starting to turn cool.

Sundance knew the old man stirring the pot was Cicatrice because of the deep, puckered scar that ran across his face, even across the bridge of his nose. Cicatrice was the Spanish word for scar, and the old man was a Mescalero Apache, fiercest of all Apaches; and in days long gone there had been a big price on his head. In his way he had been an oddity among the Apaches: a medicine man as well as a warrior. It was rumored that he was a "witch," as the Mexican Apaches said. In his time many men had feared him, even the white missionaries who came to the reservation after the Apaches had finally surrendered, because there was something silent and remote about him. His wife and five children had been murdered by the Mexican soldiers while he was still in his twenties, and it was said that for many years after he talked to his dead family while he was under the influence of peyote, the religious drug of the Apaches.

Cicatrice's war against the whites had been one of religion, not of plunder. He counseled his warriors to forsake all they had ever learned of the white man's Christ. By returning to the ancient religion of their people, they would at least drive the whites from their lands.

Cicatrice had failed, had retreated into the dark recesses of his mind, and stopped fighting for ever. Now he was a very old man, wrinkled and stooped; only his dark eyes showed fire. He kept on stirring the pot of stew while Sundance and Clum dismounted.

"Cicatrice, this is Sundance," John Clum began. "He is a true friend who always speaks the truth. Treat anything he says as if it came from my own mouth. I ask you to trust him for my sake. Do you understand?"

Cicatrice nodded slowly, raising his eyes from the ground to look squarely at Sundance. These were not an old man's eyes, Sundance realized with something of a shock; and they peered at him strangely from the withered face. "I understand, John."

"Good," Clum said. "We'll talk later. I'm as hungry as a cougar. Let's dig in."

Gray Wolf, the other Apache, came up from the river with a small barrel of water. He was about half the other Indian's age; hostile eyes regarded Sundance from a very wide, very dark-skinned face. Gray Wolf was short, getting fat from ranch living, but once, like Cicatrice, he had been a feared Apache warrior.

Sundance had never encountered the two Apaches before; he knew who they were.

After Clum told Gray Wolf who Sundance was the Apache scowled.

"What's the matter?" Clum asked him. "I have said this man is my friend."

"I am not so sure," Gray Wolf answered. "He was a scout of Crook's in Mexico. I saw him once from a peak. He is the same man. Because of this man the soldiers nearly caught up. But we got away to the far south where they dared not follow."

Ladling deer stew onto his plate, Clum said, "I know all that. Sundance worked as a scout for General Crook, as many Indians did. Apaches, as well. He is a friend of Crook."

"He is a friend for money," Gray Wolf sneered. "I have heard of this Sundance, and everything he does he does for money."

"Listen," Clum said angrily, "I don't care what you think of Sundance. He needs help and I'm going to give it to him. Somebody is going to kill General Crook."

After Gray Wolf heard him out he said to Clum, "It is no matter to me what happens to Crook. You have always been a better friend to the Indian than the three-star general. It is said that he is generous to us. Why not? It is easy to be generous when so many of our people are dead—massacred by Crook's soldiers. If you do not like

96

what I say I will go back to the reservation."

"Eat your stew, for Christ's sake," Clum said. "If you don't want to help, just keep out of it."

Gray Wolf, despite his hostility, began to eat noisily, glaring at Sundance over the top of his plate.

Sundance noticed that Cicatrice had eaten almost nothing, just slices of dried apple and a few sips of water. He had cooked the stew, but had absolutely no interest in it. That was often the way of the old, Sundance knew, but wasn't sure it was only that.

Cicatrice sat with his back against a rock, staring into the fire. Except for a dull glow in the west it was almost completely dark.

Without warning, Cicatrice said to Sundance, "You still mourn for your lost family, your father and mother?"

"Yes, I think of them every day I live. A man who does not mourn his family dead is not a man."

Cicatrice nodded gravely. "I too lost my wife and children when I was a young man. Like you, I think of them every day I live. Soon I will be with them."

"Will you help me, Cicatrice?" Sundance asked the old man. "I know that white soldiers murdered your family, but..."

Cicatrice held up his hand, giving a command to stop. "It no longer matters how they died. It happened so long ago I sometimes forget how they died. All I remember now are their faces. Now tell me about this man you seek. Do not leave anything out. Tell me how you think you see him in your mind."

When Sundance finished, the old man nodded again. "I must contemplate what you have said. But before that I must ask you, do you have anything that belongs to this man, something he dropped in his flight."

"A knife, nothing else," Sundance replied, handing the weapon to the old Apache medicine man. "See, there are no markings, nothing to say where it was made."

"We will see," Cicatrice said. "You will wait while I reflect on this knife and other things. Be patient, Sundance."

Gray Wolf finished eating and took his plate and Clum's down to the river to wash them. He left Sundance's where it was. After Clum heaped more wood on the fire, he leaned back and lit his pipe. In a few minutes Gray Wolf came back from the river and said he was going to sleep. He wrapped himself in a multi-colored blanket, crawled under the wagon, and began to snore.

"Gray Wolf is a sorehead," Clum said. "He still dreams about the so-called great old days. Of course it looks great to him because it's all so long ago. I'll bet if he had a choice he wouldn't go on the warpath. Those three big meals he eats every day must look better and better as the years go by."

For once in his life, John Clum talked a blue streak. Sundance said something now and then just to let Clum know he was there, but his eyes were fixed on the dim outline of Cicatrice, standing silently in the darkness.

Suddenly the old Apache began to chant so softly that the sound was carried away on the night wind. Clum looked quickly at Sundance. The two men remained silent while the chanting continued, and there in the glow of the fire it had a ghostly, lonesome sound like the cry of a lost soul.

A few minutes later Cicatrice returned to the circle of light and held out the knife to Sundance.

Clum rushed in with a question. "What is it, Cicatrice?"

Sundance cut in. "Let him talk."

Cicatrice's voice was high and thin. "I cannot see the man who owns this knife. That will come later. I hope it will come later. But the knife itself was fashioned in Mexico, in the city of Vera Cruz. At this time I cannot tell you more than that...."

The old man's voice began to fade.

"Rest, Cicatrice," Clum said. "If there is anything more to tell when you have finished your sleep, you will tell me."

The old Apache went to wrap himself in his blanket.

Clum took the knife from Sundance and looked at it. "Mexico!" he complained. "He might as well have said South America or Europe. What the hell use is that?"

"Maybe a lot of use," Sundance said, putting the knife back in his belt, "and he could come up with something else. If he's right about the knife, and there's no way of asking him to prove it, anything else he says will probably be right."

"You know how many knives there are in Mexico?" Clum didn't sound too hopeful.

"A lot. But this knife isn't in Mexico, it's here in Los Angeles. Another thing, you can see it's no everyday toad-stabber. It's practically new by the looks of it."

Clum tapped ashes out of his pipe and refilled it, tamping in tobacco with his little finger. Lighting the pipe with a sulphurhead, he looked at Sundance. "You figure the killer's a Mexican?"

"Could be. But just because the knife was made in Vera Cruz doesn't have to prove that. An indication maybe, but not hard evidence. You think Cicatrice will come up with anything else?"

"Hard to say. If we were years back I'd say probably.

99

Now he's old and feeble. I'd say the best thing for you to do is go on back to town. I know where you're at."

"If I'm not at the wagonyard," Sundance said, "it's all right to tell Gabriel Feliz anything you know. He'll pass it along to me. You know I'm beginning to think there's hope after all."

"Let's hope so," Clum called out as Sundance rode away.

Riding back to Los Angeles along the old King's Highway, Sundance's hand touched the handle of the knife in his belt. Vera Cruz! Mexico! The two names echoed in his head; he could still hear the old Apache's voice. The knife was very new; there were no signs of wear. Plunging it through Many Horses' heart hadn't left a mark on the blade; throwing it into the soft, rotten wood of a gatepost hadn't scratched it either. What puzzled him was the perfect balance of the knife; someone had gone to much trouble and much expense.

In Mexico, more so than in the United States, there were many hired killers who used the knife, but most of the time the knife never left the killer's hand. At best, knife throwing was a risky business unless you really knew how to do it. Sundance himself could throw a knife better than most men, but even he preferred his Colt or his bow.

During all his years, from British Columbia to the State of Morelos, he had never run across a professional killer who used a throwing knife. Another thought was that once you've pitched a knife into a man's back, there's little chance of getting it back unless it happens in a lonely place. Sundance touched the handle of the knife. What man who loved weapons would throw away a knife like this one? But, as John Clum had said, anything was possible and that was the hell of it.

Still and all, it was a beginning. Sheriff Rowland could probably be persuaded to telegraph the police in Vera Cruz and ask them to question the knife makers in the city. Depending on how they felt that day, they might do it or they might not. The Mexicans took their time, and time was the one thing he didn't have. And then, even if the Mexicans found the knife maker, he might lie out of fear or habit.

Sundance decided to let the sheriff send the telegraph message, but wouldn't count on it. If the Mexicans replied, well and good; if not, to hell with it. What he had to do, Sundance knew, was to find the connection between the knife and some man in a city jammed with tourists. He grinned bitterly and spat. That was *all* he had to do. Damn it to hell! That was just what he had to do anyway. He decided to go back to the wagonyard and see if Gabriel Feliz had learned anything.

It took him about an hour to get back to Calle de los Negros. The night was chilly and the old Mexican had gone into his adobe house; for a rich man it was a very modest place to live. Gabriel Feliz lived there by himself; his sons lived in other small houses behind the wagonyard with their families.

The old man sat at a table, shoveling in chili and peppers with the blade of a knife. A bottle of tequila and a glass stood on the table in front of him.

"Vera Cruz, you say," Gabriel Feliz exclaimed after Sundance had finished telling him about Cicatrice. "For a beautiful knife like that, Vera Cruz would make sense. There they make the best knives in all of Mexico, better than in the capital itself. Three brothers from Toledo started making knives there many years ago. I don't know how long. Two hundred years maybe. There is still a knife called the Vera Cruz knife, as famous in its way as your Bowie."

"I know, I've seen it. But this isn't it. The Vera Cruz knife is like a short-bladed sword, a lot like the Bowie except for the curved-up three inches of tip on the end."

Gabriel Feliz gulped some tequila and offered Sundance a plate of beans.

Sundance said no.

"I am sorry I have nothing to tell you, my friend," the old Mexican bandit apologized. "My sons are dead from lack of sleep and yet they have learned nothing."

"What do you know about a man named Jack Clagett, a big brute of a man. He picked a fight with me today in Cleary's Saloon and I had to settle him down."

Gabriel Feliz's eyes opened wide. "You settled Jack Clagett down!"

"What about him?"

"He used to be one very bad man. He is still a very bad man, but the sheriff has warned him to stay outside the city limits. Always fighting, beating people. Last year he killed a man in a fight, but Matt Cleary persuaded the judge to let him off. He promised to keep him out of town."

"Then he works for Cleary?"

"For Cleary's brother, Con. A blacksmith and wagon builder out in the valley."

"Then Matt Cleary knows him?"

"I just told you Cleary was the one who talked to the judge about the manslaughter charge. Of course he knows him, my friend. If he says he does not, well then he is a liar, and of that I already have no doubt. Mr. Cleary and his

Anglo friends have at times attempted to make some trouble for me. However, after I reminded them of how some of them got their start in life, and how well their dealings with me are recorded, they have ceased to bother me."

"How does Clagett tie in with Cleary?"

"Cleary and his friends at City Hall sometimes employ Clagett and some of his friends to persuade citizens how to vote. And there is talk of other things. A few years ago a young missionary on his way to Hawaii, one of those reformers, met and fell in love with one of Cleary's new prostitutes, a girl from New Orleans. Cleary had marked her for his own, at least until he became tired of her. He warned the young preacher away, but he refused to go. He had asked the young whore to go with him as his wife, and she accepted. Later that night, while the girl was packing in her room, somebody with immense strength broke the young preacher's neck."

"Clagett?"

"He was in Cleary's shortly before the killing. The sheriff asked some questions, but nobody was ever charged. But, as you say, I would bet my money on Clagett."

"That still doesn't explain why he tried to kill or cripple me. I wasn't trying to steal any girls. I never saw the brute before he braced me today."

"I'm just telling you what I'm telling you, my friend. Who can say what reason a savage like that will have!"

Sundance accepted a small drink of tequila. "Maybe he had a very definite reason."

"Which is?" Gabriel Feliz stopped shoveling beans and listened carefully.

"Which is that Cleary has something to do with the

plot against General Crook. He stood there in his fancy saloon and let it happen. How much do you know about Cleary, Gabriel? Was he here during the Civil War?"

The old man nodded. "Yes, he was here, right where he is now on the Plaza. The Plaza was named after Mayor Downey who later became Governor and now is Mayor again. Cleary had a little one-room saloon in those days."

"What about Cleary and Downey?"

"What about them, Sundance?"

"I know Downey was for the South during the War. What about Cleary?"

"That I cannot tell you, but it should be easy to find out. Now you want to ask next if Cleary and Downey are good friends? The answer is yes. They are both Irishmen and very important in Democratic politics. But they are friends anyway. The Mayor's daughter is married to one of Cleary's sons. But what does that prove?"

"Nothing, but I'm thinking about it. If Cleary is somehow involved in the plot to murder General Crook, it's just possible that the Mayor is mixed up in it too. I know two men like Cleary and Downey can't have too much interest in the Indian problem, but who can tell how they are being paid off. The railroads are as opposed to Crook's nomination as the Indian Ring."

"My head is beginning to hurt," Gabriel Feliz groaned, "and it is not because of the tequila. We start with one hired killer and now you are bringing in the Mayor and the railroads. You don't mind if I finish the bottle. I need to get drunk. If you need me just pour a bucket of water over my head. That's what my sons do when there is trouble."

"If I have to I will," Sundance said, and went to his cabin.

It was cold and he started a fire in the cookstove and put on a pot of coffee. Then he found a sheet of paper and began to write down names: Many Horses, Matt Cleary, George Crook, Sheriff William Rowland, John Jacob Cass, John Downey, Captain Jack Crawford, John Greer, Helen Hunt Jackson, Stephen Dobson, John Clum, Cicatrice. Some were involved because they had to be. Wrong! It didn't follow that any of them had to be involved. He continued to write the names in different combinations, then started all over again. He kept at it for hours.

Late that night, he had to admit to himself that he had nothing but a knife and an old Indian's word that it had been made in Vera Cruz in the recent past. Tired, feeling low, he decided to turn in for the night.

Chapter 9

"You mean you want me to send a telegraph message to the Vera Cruz police on the strength of what some old crazy Apache told you. I don't believe it."

Sheriff William Rowland stared over Sundance over the rim of his steaming coffee cup. The sheriff hadn't shaved yet and didn't look as if he had slept well. He was eating ham and eggs and biscuits, and wasn't too enthusiastic about it. Sundance helped himself to coffee at the sheriff's invitation.

"Will you please do it, Sheriff." Sundance persisted. "I know how it sounds to you. I'll pay for it, so what's the difference? If there's nothing to it you won't be made to look foolish."

"Yes, I realize that, but I'll *feel* foolish. I'll do it if you insist. I don't know anybody in Vera Cruz, but I do know the Chief of *Rurales* in Sonora. He was as glad to get rid of Tiburcio Vasquez as I was. I'll send the message to him and ask him to forward it. But for God's sake, don't let it get out that I'm bothering an important man on the say-so of a witch."

Sundance didn't mind the sheriff's disbelieving attitude; most white men had no faith in, or respect for, Indian magic. He could understand that for even among the Indians themselves there were madmen and power-greedy men who had no gifts of any kind.

"If you've finished with that knife maybe you can give it back," the sheriff said crankily, hacking at his overfried slab of ham.

"I'd like to keep it a little longer. It'll get back to you."

"Oh, the hell with the goddamned knife. I just said that to be saying something. I'll just be glad when this town empties and gets back to the normal shootings and cuttings. Those kinds of things I'm well able to handle. I know every bad man in the county by sight. It's the ones I don't know who worry me."

Sundance grinned at the exasperated lawman. "The city fathers wouldn't like to hear you saying that, about the town emptying out. Looks like everybody is raking in a pile of money."

"I don't make anything extra on it," Rowland said. "So I'd just as soon have a quiet town as a noisy one. Damn! Crook and his supporters should get their convention over with and clear out."

"Nobody would like that better than Crook himself," Sundance said. "And I'm right behind him."

"Well, in just two days it'll be all over." The sheriff's big silver watch lay on the table and he tapped it with his finger. "I've been counting the minutes and the hours."

"How many deputies can you spare for the convention?" Sundance asked, gamely trying to finish the

107

sheriff's awful coffee. "I know what you said about not having the money to hire extra men."

"That's what the Mayor said," Rowland said with a grim face. "Not only that, but he made it clear that I'm not to leave the rest of the city without protection just because of General Crook. I guess he's right, what with all the hardcases in town."

Sundance said, "I take it that Mayor Downey isn't too worried about the general's safety."

Sheriff Rowland gave Sundance a quick, sharp look. "You didn't hear me say that. Let me put it this way: the Mayor isn't too sure Crook's campaign manager, Greer, hasn't cooked up this whole thing to pull sympathy in Crook's direction."

"Then why hasn't Greer given the story to the newspapers?"

"Mayor Downey thinks that would be too obvious. The Mayor believes Greer wants the newspapers to find out about the plot for themselves. With a lot of help, naturally."

It wasn't yet eight o'clock in the morning, but the early summer heat beat down steadily and the back of City Hall was washed in blinding sunlight. A faint smell of flowers came from the sheriff's neglected garden below the front porch.

"You know, Sundance," the sheriff said, "as soon as the convention and the Southern Pacific people are gone I'm going to take two weeks off and do something about that garden. And when I'm not digging in the garden I'm going to sit here on the front porch and not do a goddamned thing. And if I get tired of that I'm going to ride down to the railroad depot and buy a whole stock of dime novels. I love those damn fool things. Did you know there was one about me when I brought in Vasquez. Wish I still had a copy."

"How well would you say Mayor Downey likes General Crook?" Sundance asked. "I'm just asking."

"No, you're not," Rowland said. "I'm getting to know a little something about how you think—and you don't just ask anything. How does Downey feel about Crook? How the hell should I know. I'm not one of the inner circle."

"Like Matt Cleary."

"What's that supposed to mean? Confound it, man, can't you ever come out and say anything plain?"

"I can't because I don't know." Sundance told the sheriff about the fight with Clagett in Downey Plaza.

"I guess I was out in the Valley when it happened," the sheriff remarked. "Damn that MacPhail! He never tells me a thing unless I use a hot iron on him. Yes, sir, it's true that Clagett works for Cleary's brother—horseshoeing, helping to build wagons. A mean, miserable son of a bitch. I had to warn him outside the city limits. Looks like I'll have to do it again."

Sheriff Rowland tapped the face of his watch with a fingernail, a nervous action. "Why would Cleary say he didn't know Clagett?"

"Why would he?" Sundance said.

The sheriff tried for an answer, though he didn't look too pleased with it himself. "Clagett has a bad reputation, so maybe Cleary doesn't want to be associated with him in any way."

Rowland was suddenly exasperated. "Oh, all right, that doesn't hold water. Cleary got him off on the manslaughter charge and got him the job with his brother."

Sundance knew that he'd be treading on thin ice when

he asked the next question. "What about the young missionary Clagett is supposed to have murdered?"

Sheriff Rowland's face turned an angry red, and he slapped the table with the flat of his hand. "You've got an awful lot of nerve, you know that. Who the hell are you to ask me a question like that? I've been sheriff of this county for close to twenty years...."

"Please, Sheriff..."

"Please, like hell! Any man that hints that I didn't fully investigate that young preacher's killing is a liar. I know Clagett did it, but what use is that? You want me to frame him up onto the gallows. Give me proof—a witness, something, is all I ask."

Sundance waited until the sheriff's outburst had subsided.

Then Rowland said with a wry grin, "You seem to be catching most of my wrath these days. I know you didn't mean anything by the question. It just galls me that a simple-minded brute like Jack Clagett can commit a brutal murder in my town and get away with it."

Rowland looked at Sundance. "You asked me if Downey liked Crook. The honest answer is I don't know. He was pro-Southern during the War, even had something to do with sending Dr. Marsh to Richmond with the offer of thirty thousand California volunteers, provided the Confederacy footed the bill for their travel, food, and so on. By then Jeff Davis had no more money in the till, so the scheme came to nothing."

Sundance said he knew that John Downey had come from Ireland as a young man and had been a druggist in Cincinnati before he arrived in Los Angeles.

"That first pharmacy he opened on the Plaza made a fortune," the sheriff said. "Later he branched out into land, cattle and fruit growing. He had thousands of acres of oranges and lemons. Now he's got an interest in some oil wells. Yes, you could say the Mayor is fond of a dollar. You want to know if he could be bought?"

Sheriff Rowland smiled to himself.

"What about Cleary?"

"Matt served with the New York Volunteers in the Mexican War. All three thousand of them were discharged here in 1849—one hell of a thing to do to men who had fought well. Uncle Sam just said, 'That's it, lads, the war's over. Make your way home as best you can.' A wild bunch of Irish clodhoppers, I can tell you. Most of them from the Bowery and the Five Points sections of New York. That was more than twenty years ago, so Matt would be somewhere in his forties now."

"Looks like he got over the hard times all right," Sundance remarked.

"Well, they did have hard times," Rowland said, "and they also gave the sheriff a hard time—getting drunk, brawling, shooting off guns. Some of them managed to make their way back to New York, but most of them stayed. Matt Cleary is one that stayed. Now he owns that big moneymaker of a saloon, and a lot of other businesses besides. He has a rancho out in the Valley and is belly deep in Democratic politics."

"What about his brother?"

"Funny kind of a man, younger a few years than Matt, served with him in Mexico. He's lived here most of his life, but I hardly know him. Never married, keeps to himself, and doesn't welcome strangers."

Rowland stood up. "I'd better get that telegraph message off to Mexico. What are you going to be doing?"

"Looking over the convention hall," Sundance said. "I haven't seen it yet. How big is it?"

"Too big. That's the trouble with it. Sure wish I had

111

some more deputies. But like I say, that takes money, of which my office has very little. I've been thinking. Why don't you ask the Crook Committee people to come up with the necessary funds?"

Walking to the gate with the sheriff, Sundance said, "I did and some of them agreed. Then one of them told the general and I got my head snapped off. Hadn't I gone far enough by going behind his back to enlist the help of his own men? To make it short—no special deputies."

At the gate the two men shook hands. "As soon as I hear something from Mexico, if I do, you'll hear about it," Rowland said.

Sundance walked in the direction of the Bella Union Hotel, then past it to what was called the Los Angeles Fair Grounds, ten dusty acres with the spanking new convention hall in the center of it, a tall frame building now being painted a garish blue by a crew of men on scaffolding. It looked forlorn standing there in the middle of all that dun-colored space. The workmen wouldn't hang the enormous WELCOME TO LOS ANGELES GENERAL GEORGE CROOK banner until the paint work was finished.

On the far side of the convention hall Sundance saw the brightly painted wagons of the Captain Jack Crawford Wild West Show. It looked like a small city in itself; everything it needed was carried in those wagons, from a tailor shop to a printing press. Trestle tables had been set up on both sides of the cook wagon; the roustabouts and performers were eating their breakfast. A man in buckskins who didn't look Indian was shooting arrows into a soft, slanted target. He stopped to look at Sundance as he went into the hall.

A thick-bodied man with a dead cigar and a derby hat

was behind a desk reading a newspaper. He looked up with a bored expression on his closely shaved red face. "Something I can do for you?"

"I'd like to talk to John Greer," Sundance said. "I was told he'd be here this morning."

Rustling his newspaper and making himself comfortable again, the doorkeeper said, "Go on in. He's down front by the stage."

The light inside the huge hall was brighter than the sun outside. Gasoliers in two rows hung by chains from the ceiling, and they were all burning. Against one wall hundreds of benches and folding chairs were stacked, waiting to be set up. Up in front of the wide, curtained stage two men were having a furious argument: one was John Greer, the other was Captain Jack Crawford. Captain Jack looked as if he'd been drinking hard the night before.

When Sundance got close they stopped shouting for an instant, then, ignoring him, they began arguing again. Sundance gathered that the row was about how Captain Jack's show should be staged. Finally, Captain Jack turned to Sundance for support.

The old showman's smooth face was red with anger; a whiff of bourbon came from him. "Listen to me, Mr. Sundance. Greer wants me to cut the acts short. I don't want to do that."

"If you don't they'll take up too much time. They'll even take away attention from the convention itself."

"That's right, they will," Captain Jack said defiantly.

"But that's not what you were hired for. The idea was to add a little icing to the cake. The cake is the convention; you're the icing, an extra attraction."

Captain Jack flared up at that. "My Wild West show is

113

never an extra attraction. It is never anything less than *the* attraction!" The old faker's loud voice rolled like thunder. "Are you telling me that I don't know how to provide the most popular entertainment in the land? Why, sir, I have entertained presidents and kings, captains of industry, in North and South America, the length and breadth of Europe, even the great island continent of Australia."

Greer was adamant. He was a smallish man with a thin voice, but he stood up gamely to Captain Jack. "You'll have to do it my way, Captain Crawford," he said quietly, exhausted by all the shouting, "or I'll have to cancel the engagement. The time of each act has to be shortened."

Captain Jack took a silver flask from his back pocket and drank deeply from it. He stoppered it again and put it back. It was hot in the hall and he took off his beautiful Stetson and fanned himself.

"You don't know what you're saying, sir. It isn't that simple. A circus act isn't like a length of board. You don't just say, 'Cut it down a little.' It's all been worked up in rehearsals. Of course I can do it, but it'll take time—and the convention is only two days away. I think it's time I spoke to a lawyer."

Sundance cut in, "Do you mind if I make a suggestion, Captain Jack?"

The showman nodded reluctantly.

Sundance said, "Instead of cutting the time of the acts, why don't you put on fewer acts, the very best acts, of course. That way Mr. Greer gets the time he needs, and your performers go on as usual."

Captain Jack considered the idea, then finally nodded. "I'd rather do it the usual way, but all right, Mr. Greer, I'll work it out and get back to you later."

Greer climbed up on the stage to talk to some men

114

Captain Jack took Sundance by the arm and walked him toward the door. "You'd think a man like Greer would understand that in a good—a great—circus every act is timed to the second. Well, almost. If you didn't work it out like that you'd have complete chaos. Timing is everything in show business."

Captain Jack left to go back to his encampment, and Sundance walked around the vast, echoing hall. Greer had told him that two thousand people could fit in there with ease; another thousand could be squeezed in if necessary. Three thousand people, mostly men, and just one assassin!

Half of the hall was covered by a balcony that slanted upward almost to the roof; on both sides, close to the stage, there were boxes for important guests. So a bullet could come from a darkened box or the uppermost row in the balcony. Or it could come from a catwalk high above the stage. Sundance climbed up on the stage and looked up into the tangle of ropes and pulleys, and raised and lowered the scenery when the hall was used as a theater.

The hall had a short basement, and there was nothing down there but gas and water pipes and a stack of old trunks. Sundance came up from there, satisfied that there was no way to the stage except through the door at the top of the metal stairs.

It was going to be hell trying to guard the general in so large a place. Worst of all, the shot might come right at the moment when three thousand people were yelling their heads off. If it came then, it might not even be heard.

He was up in one of the boxes, looking down sideways at the stage when John Greer came in with a sheaf of papers in his hand.

"What do you think?" he asked Sundance. He sat

down heavily and loosened his collar.

"It's going to be hell. In a smaller hall there would be a chance. Here—none. Even if we could search everybody that came in it wouldn't be much use. A handgun is a small thing in such a big crowd. Anyway, they'd complain, maybe not come in at all. That would only hurt the general's chances. And what about the women? We can't search women even if we wanted to. A woman could bring in a pistol, even a carbine, with no trouble at all."

"But what are you going to do, Sundance? So far all you've been saying is how easy it will be to kill General Crook."

"I'm going to post men with rifles high up. Way up at the back of the balcony, up on the catwalks. Then I'm going to scatter the rest of the men I have throughout the crowd. They're army, but they'll be in civilian clothes, armed with pistols. I'll be close to the stage, so will Major Collinson and Sheriff Rowland and some of his deputies."

"Doesn't sound too bad an arrangement," Greer said, his eyes brightening. "Say! Just imagine the headlines it would make if you could nab this killer when he was about to do his dirty deed. Why, every newspaper in the country would run the story. It would push everything else right off the front pages. I could write a big story on you—the faithful friend who saved the life of America's next Secretary of the Interior, General George Crook."

"No thanks," Sundance said, taking one last look at the stage.

They walked downstairs, Greer still excited about the possibility of catching the killer in the act. "Promise me you'll do your best, Sundance."

Sundance was getting sick of Greer and his nonstop

mouth. "I promise to do my best to kill the son of a bitch," he said. "The first man who points anything at the general will get every bullet in my gun. You want a promise. There it is."

Greer said urgently, "You don't want to kill this man if you don't have to. Take him alive and I'll write a special story in which General Crook commanded you to spare the assassin's life. In the story you're all set to kill him, but the general is a man of compassion and orders you to put up your gun. In fact, Sundance, I'm sure that is exactly what the general would do, should the circumstances arise."

"Probably," Sundance agreed, "that is if he had anything to say about it. But I'm not about to take any chances with his life. His life is more important to me than your newspaper stories."

Greer's face was hostile. "Please explain what you mean by that."

Sundance walked away without answering.

Chapter 10

Sundance was finishing his noonday meal in his cabin in the wagonyard when a young deputy sheriff knocked on the door. He came in, hat in hand. "Sheriff Rowland wants to see you soon as possible, Mr. Sundance. He said to tell you he got an answer to his telegraph."

Leaving the rest of his steak uneaten, Sundance rushed to saddle Eagle. The great stallion didn't understand why he was being left in the stable so much. He whinnied as Sundance slapped the saddle on his back.

Sundance scratched his horse between the eyes, something Eagle liked, and said, "I know how you feel, boy. I'd like to shake this city dirt from my feet as much as you do."

People in the crowded streets yelled angrily as Sundance set Eagle to moving at a light center, heading as fast as he could for City Hall. Time was running out, and he hoped Rowland had something useful to tell him. A name, a description no matter how slight, anything at all. At precisely eight o'clock the next night the convention would begin with a roll of drums and the blare of a brass band. And then...

The sheriff was sitting behind his desk, not looking too happy with himself. A yellow Western Union form lay in front of him. Sighing loudly, he tossed it to Sundance. Vera Cruz, Mexico was the place of origin, and the message was simple:

HAVE IDENTIFIED KNIFEMAKER AS J. GUZMAN. EIGHT KNIVES YOUR DESCRIPTION MADE ON SPECIAL ORDER. NO NAME AVAILABLE THIS DATE. GUZMAN OUT OF TOWN. WHEN MORE INFORMATION AVAILABLE WILL TELEGRAPH.

It was signed Antonio Parral, Chief of Police, Vera Cruz.

Rowland tugged at his beard and slammed the telegraph message into a drawer. "You can't say I didn't get fast action from the Mexicans. The only trouble is, I didn't get much. Eight knives of the same kind! What in hell would any man want with eight knives of the same kind? Unless he's one killer in a thousand who uses throwing knives in his work. But you said yourself you never heard of that."

"That's right. I never have."

"You'd have to get in pretty close to throw a knife accurately." Sheriff Rowland was thinking out loud.

"Not if you're good enough," Sundance answered. "Throwing a knife is like everything else. If you work at it long enough you get to be very good, especially if you

119

have a knack for it in the first place. But I still don't see this man as a knife-throwing professional killer."

"You certainly are hard to convince, Sundance. I'm sorry, but this time I have to go against you. There's going to be somebody in that crowd with one of those knives on him, probably in his hat. He waits until there's a lot of excitement, then out comes the knife."

Sundance had to agree that some of what the sheriff said made sense. "But how does he get away after he throws the knife? The people next to him will see him do it. He can't throw it from the back of the hall, because the distance is too great. That means he will have a packed crowd behind him, and I'll be up front with Collinson and you. So he'll be in a tight squeeze, if that's the way it happens."

"You're right, Sundance. A professional killer wouldn't put himself in a bind like that. Not only that, but he stands a good chance of being shot down the moment he pulls out the knife. I don't know what to think any more. We keep finding out things that look good at first glance, then turn out to be nothing at all. First, you stumble on that old Indian at Cleary's, then this fellow John Jacob Cass tries to kill you, and then Clagett tries to stomp you because of what he thinks Crook did to Cass."

"Wait," Sundance said. "Suppose Clagett never had anything to do with Cass. That might mean something."

"But you said yourself that Clagett served under Cass when he was a cavalry lieutenant."

"That's what Clagett said. That's the reason he gave for starting the fight. I didn't think any special of it until you mentioned it just now."

"What's the difference?"

"If Clagett didn't fight with me because of Cass, then

he had to be doing it for some other reason. You ever hear that Clagett was ever in the military?"

Turning out the light in his dark basement office, the sheriff went outside with Sundance. "Can't say that I have." He shook his head emphatically. "No, I never have, and that's one thing you're always likely to hear about a man, especially a bully and a braggart."

Sheriff Rowland asked Sundance if he wanted to come up to the house and have something to eat.

"Just ate," Sundance said. "I'm going over to the Bella Union to talk to Major Collinson. Let's hope the Mexicans get something from this J. Guzman when he gets back. Of course..."

Sundance didn't finish the sentence, but the sheriff knew what he was going to say. The Mexicans hadn't said when J. Guzman would get back to Vera Cruz. A day? A week? A month?

At the hotel Sundance found Major Collinson eating lamb chops in the Oak Room. A string band was plucking away energetically on a platform. There was the clatter of dishes from the kitchen. Like every other hotel in town, the Bella Union was making money as fast as the management could take it in.

Sundance told Collinson he'd settle for a cold beer. It had been hot walking over from the sheriff's office.

A waiter brought two steins of beer. Between sips, Sundance told Collinson about the telegraph message from Vera Cruz. "But that's not what I wanted to talk to you about. That man I had the fight with in the Plaza—Jack Clagett—how soon can you find out if he was ever in the cavalry? He says he served under Lieutenant John Jacob Cass. The time would be about ten years ago. Around the time of the fight at Branch Crossing."

"Telegraph is the fastest way," Major Collinson said, "but you know how army red tape is. They'd prefer to have the request in writing, with two copies for the files." Collinson smiled nervously. "Of course, I could always send the telegraph out under the general's signature. Can you promise me that I won't get sent to the Dry Tortugas if Old George finds out?"

Sundance laughed. "We may both be doing time on the Florida Keys before this is over. Do your best, Major. That's all any of us can do. How soon do you think you'll get a reply?"

"If it goes out with Old George's signature it'll be back before you know it."

Sundance said, "The question is: was Clagett ever in the cavalry, and did he serve under John Jacob Cass?"

Two and a half hours later Sundance walked in the front door of Cleary's Saloon on Downey Plaza. It was well into the afternoon, and the place could hardly hold any more drinkers. There was no sign of Matt Cleary, and when Sundance pushed his way to the bar on the main floor, one of the bartenders yelled that he would have to talk to Mr. Hutchins before he got to see Cleary himself.

The bartender jerked a thumb at a middle-sized man with heavy shoulders and a thick, graying mustache. "That's him over there by the foot of the stairs."

Hutchins had a New England accent, a pearl stickpin in his tie, and a blank look on his nondescript face. He had the look of a man who had once been a sailor. "You don't want to start any more trouble in here, mister," he said. "I was here when you started the fight with that other fellow."

122

"What other fellow?"

"How do I know? A big fellow."

"I'd like to see Mr. Cleary."

"He's busy, he's always busy."

"Too busy to see me?"

"I think for you he's busier than usual."

"Did you decide that on your own?"

"That's right. Now why don't you about-face and walk out of here."

"I think you better ask Mr. Cleary," Sundance said easily. "You shouldn't make big decisions all by yourself."

Hutchins had seen what Sundance had done to Clagett, so he kept his temper in check. But he clicked his fingers, and two thick-necked bouncers came over and stood on either side of Sundance.

"You still trying to tell me my business?" Hutchins asked, more secure now.

"What business would that be?"

"Looking out for Mr. Cleary's interests."

"Then do it," Sundance said. "Tell Cleary I want to talk to him—if he'd rather not remind him that it's about Clagett's army service."

Watched over by the two roughnecks, Sundance waited while Hutchins went upstairs and came back. He looked disappointed that he hadn't been given orders to throw Sundance out. Sundance knew that, and was glad for Hutchins that he hadn't been given such an order.

"Second floor," Hutchins said. "The door in back marked *Private*."

Sundance went up the broad, curving staircase and found Matt Cleary's office. He knocked and was told to come in.

It was a big room with too much furniture in it. Over

the fireplace hung an oil painting of Cleary. It made him look a lot more honest than he did in the flesh. Cleary's desk was so big and massive it looked as if it had been chopped out of a redwood.

"Sit down," Cleary said, waving at an uncomfortable chair without arms. He rubbed his hands together briskly, an old habit of his, one he had acquired because he thought it looked businesslike.

Cleary said, "I don't know what you want, but you must want something. Otherwise you wouldn't be here."

Only traces of Cleary's New York slum accent was left, but he was still a thug for all his well-tailored broadcloth suit and barbered face. "Now what's all this about Jack Clagett and his army service? All right! All right! I know the man. I got him out of trouble one time, but I want no more to do with him. But what about this army business?"

"Clagett said he had served with the ex-officer I killed. That was before he started the fight."

"What of it?"

"Clagett was never in the military, so he never served with Cass."

"Maybe he heard about Cass and felt sorry for him." Cleary's quick, clever eyes looked up for Sundance's reaction.

"No," Sundance said. "Clagett was very definite about it. Said he had served with Cass before he was cashiered for murdering the Cheyenne at Branch Crossing."

Cleary poured a drink and lit a cigar; Sundance said he didn't want either.

"I still don't know what you want," Cleary said, pulling hard at the whiskey.

"Then I'll make it simple. If Clagett didn't want to kill or cripple me because of Cass, what would you say the

124

reason was? I would say the reason had something to do with the plot to kill General Crook."

With a cry of indignation, Cleary jumped to his feet, his red face redder still with anger. "Goddamn you!" he roared. "I heard something about that and don't believe a word of it. Somebody I trust completely swears it's just one of John Greer's newspaper tricks."

"It's no stunt," Sundance said quietly. "You better get that through your head. Somebody is going to try to kill General Crook. My guess is the final night of the convention."

Cleary lowered himself into his chair by placing his hands on top of the desk. Suddenly he looked tired. Something in Sundance's voice had convinced him that the plot against Crook could no longer be denied.

"Christ, man," he said, "you don't think I'd be a part of a thing like that. I've done a lot of things in my time, but . . ."

"Then why did you set Clagett on me? Was it to get me out of the way so your hired killer could have a clear shot at the general?"

"Don't call him *my* hired killer, for God's sake. I have nothing to do with it. And I didn't set Clagett on you. I would have stopped the fight if it looked like it was going to happen indoors. It didn't so I stayed out of it."

Cleary poured himself another drink, much bigger this time.

"You're lying," Sundance said. "I want to know why you set Clagett on me, and while you're making up your mind I'd like to tell you a few home truths. I have already talked with the military authorities about Clagett."

"Take a look at that if you don't believe me." Sundance threw the telegraph message on the desk. "See whom it's

125

addressed to? General George Crook. I talked to Major Collinson, and he's already making inquiries about you. You lived in New York before you joined the army and landed here. If the police in New York have anything on you, Collinson will find out. Even if they can't arrest you now, it won't look so good when Greer gives it to the newspapers."

"If I tell you the truth, what then?"

"I'll call Collinson off. Your name will never appear anywhere. If you don't, and Crook gets killed, your name will always be mentioned as one of the men who plotted to murder a great man. And not for political reasons, just for money. Make up your mind."

Cleary gave a sour smile. "The answer is so simple it'll make you laugh. Word came to me that you were thick with old Gabriel Feliz, that you were friends from the old days, that you were bunking at his wagonyard. I already knew something about your reputation, and didn't like you taking sides with Feliz. That's what I thought you were planning to do after the convention was over. I knew you were a friend of Crook's, but made your living with your gun. Feliz and I have been butting heads for years. I want to take control of Calle de los Negros and the Mexican quarter, but Feliz keeps getting in my way."

"You sent Cass and the big Mexican, Luis, to kill me that night." Sundance didn't think he had, but he wanted to keep Cleary nervous.

Cleary shook his head. "No, I didn't. I swear it. I never even heard of Cass until you killed him. As to hiring Luis, that wouldn't make any sense at all. Luis hated me more than old Feliz does."

Sundance didn't think he would get anything else out of Cleary, so he stood up. "I want to tell you something, saloonkeeper, so you'd better listen good. I didn't come to Los Angeles to sell my gun to Gabriel Feliz."

Cleary looked relieved. "I'm glad to hear that."

"But now I've decided to give it away free if he needs it. Leave him be, Cleary. That's the best advice I can give you. You're a businessman now. Stay away from gunplay and Feliz."

"I get you," Cleary said, sweating hard. "You sure you'll call off that major?"

"A deal is a deal. I won't go back on my part unless I find you've been lying to me. And then a bad name is the least you can expect."

Sundance was back at the wagonyard talking to Gabriel Feliz. The old Mexican went into his mud-walled house and brought out a bottle of tequila and two glasses. He poured two drinks before he sat. The chair threatened to collapse under his immense weight.

Sitting on a pile of harnesses, Sundance said, "Then you think Cleary was telling the truth?"

"It has some of that sound, my friend."

"What do you mean?"

"Well, when Cleary said he has been feuding with me, that is true, but not altogether. My feuding has been done with that dog Luis, the one you killed. Luis feuded with me while Cleary pulled the strings. Mexican against Mexican with the smart Irishman waiting to take everything when they killed themselves off."

"Cleary said he didn't hire Luis to kill me. I believe him for some reason."

"Why not? Luis hired out his knife and his gun and his strangling rope to many people. Luis would kill man,

127

woman or child for five dollars, may God rest his stinking soul."

Sundance said he didn't want any more tequila. It made his eyes water; it was too hot for drinking. "What did you find out about the knife throwers?"

Gabriel Feliz said, "In a few minutes a man who knows about such things will be here with one of my sons. His name is Esteban Camacho and he is a professional murderer. Don't be alarmed. Esteban murders only Mexicans, his own people. It is a rule he has made for himself. Perhaps for a man in his profession it is a wise rule. The law does not care much or at all when a Mexican is killed, but when a gringo dies the law becomes excited, vengeful. Esteban will know who the knife throwers are in Los Angeles."

They waited for five minutes, talking about many things, until Esteban Camacho arrived, a thin, short man in his late forties. He wore a dark suit and leather ankle-boots instead of sandals. His black hat was flat-crowned and very new. He didn't offer to shake hands; what he did was bow twice with great formality.

"Ah, Esteban," Gabriel Feliz said, "It is good of you to come. My friend here"—the killer bowed again—"wishes to ask you about men in your profession who use the knife."

"There are many, Gabriel."

"Not that way," Sundance said. "I mean knife throwers."

The little killer seemed skeptical. "It is most unusual. Men who carry knives sometimes know how to throw them, but it is a risky way to try to kill a man. I know people talk about it, but I have rarely seen it. I myself can throw a knife, but prefer the gun. If you miss with a knife

128

you are not likely to get a second chance, whereas with a gun you still have five shots left after the first miss."

"But there must be somebody?" Sundance said.

"There is," Esteban Camacho said, "and he is the only one I know." The killer smiled thinly, displaying pearly little teeth, very white. "This man and I are not friends, so it is a pleasure to tell you who he is. He is Jose Milagro, and he has a small cantina at the end of Valdez Street."

Gabriel Feliz frowned. "I have heard the name, but not for many years. Is he of your profession?"

"He is, but he has not worked lately. It has been some years. If he has been working it has not been in Los Angeles. I would know that. Be careful if you go to see him. He is a moody, dangerous man, maybe a little crazy."

"I am in your debt," Gabriel Feliz said. "Would you care for a drink of tequila before you go?"

"No," the little killer said proudly, "I do not drink or smoke. In that way my hand remains steady."

Just like George Crook, Sundance thought. Men did the same things for different reasons.

Esteban Camacho left, again without offering to shake hands.

"That's a strange little man," Sundance remarked.

"Yes, but a man of honor," Gabriel Feliz said. "Before he agrees to kill a man he must know all about him. Esteban believes a man has to deserve to die before he will accept the money. If a wife has been beaten brutally and often by her husband, and for no reason, Esteban will take the job from her even if the payment is small. He is not a greedy man. First, in order to save her the expense, he will enquire if she has no family to kill the brutal husband. If she has not, only then will Esteban take the job. Yes, I would say he is a strange man, but once he gives his word you can always rely on it. If he says this Jose Milagro is the only killer who uses the throwing knife, then it must be so. There is little in his profession that he does not know about, at least in Los Angeles. That is something else about Esteban. He hates to travel in his work. Remaining always in the city he knows what he is talking about."

"How do I get to Valdez Street?" Sundance wanted to know.

Chapter 11

It was getting dark when Sundance made his way through the maze of half-lighted smelly streets and alleys that led to Valdez Street. It was deep in the Mexican quarter that ran down the side of the hill from Calle de los Negros. Sundance, who was already known as the man who had killed Big Luis and his two friends, as well as the gringo who hired them, was watched carefully as he walked silently on moccasined feet toward the cantina kept by Jose Milagro.

The thought that even a savage like Big Luis might have friends remained constantly in his mind, as he walked in the center of the narrow, twisting streets, keeping well away from darkened doorways. Always he quickened his pace when there was light streaming from a window. He carried the throwing knife in his belt, the long-barreled .44 Colt with the rawhide thong off the hammer, for he didn't know how long it might be before he had to start shooting.

131

Two men, very young, almost boys, followed him for a while, but when he stood and waited for them to approach they ducked into an alley. After a while he looked back again; there was nobody in the street. He went on.

Valdez Street was slightly wider than the streets that ran into it. It was longer, too, but there was only one cantina. Evidently, Jose Milagro discouraged competition. The cantina had no name, and even before Sundance reached the door the raucous laughter and the tinkle of a badly-played guitar had stopped.

Pushing his way through the swinging doors, he found himself in a wide, low-ceilinged room lit only by guttering in saucers. The bar was nothing more than two planks laid across three barrels; on the floor the sawdust was thick with spit and slops. The only mirror in the place was thick with grease and starred by an old bullet hole.

There were five tables, and there were Mexicans at all of them. Many had their hats pulled low, but they were all watching carefully. Behind the bar a very fat Mexican with a leather vest and striped trousers looked up, pretending to be pleased and surprised. He set down a bottle of mescal and gulped the drink he had been pouring.

He greeted Sundance in Spanish, then switched to English. He was muscular and fat at the same time. Sundance guessed that he was strong as a bull, though the only exercise he got, probably, was bending his elbow to put drinks in his mouth.

"A drink, yes," Sundance said. "Mescal is all right. Or tequila. Makes no difference. And why don't you have one with me."

"I would rather a cigar," the bartender said.

Sundance drank his tequila, and it was even worse than

132

the kind Gabriel Feliz favored. He put down money for the drink and the cigar.

"It is a nice evening," the Mexican said politely. "The hottest part of the summer has not come yet. It is in July that the real scorching heat comes."

"True," Sundance agreed, ordering another drink and a cigar for the bartender.

Just as politely, the Mexican said, "I have not had the honor of meeting you before tonight."

Sundance nodded as he raised the glass of rotgut to his mouth. "That is so," he said. "I would like, if I may, to speak with Senor Jose Milagro. If tonight is not a good night I can always return."

The bartender's smile was sorrowful. "I am sorry that you have come such a long way for nothing. Someone must have given you wrong information. You see, there is no Jose Milagro here."

Raising his voice, the bartender asked, "Is there, compadres?"

It looked like there wasn't. Like hell there wasn't, but Sundance didn't see any way to push it. A gun and a knife wouldn't do much good against this gang of cutthroats.

"I am sorry too," Sundance said, "because my business with Senor Milagro involves the exchange of money."

"I am sorry," the bartender insisted, "but no man of that name is here."

Sundance was turning to go when an almost inaudible voice told him to stay. He looked around and at first didn't see anyone except the bartender. Then when he looked down toward the end of the bar he saw a man well past middle age, wearing an undershirt and baggy cotton pants. He loved up the bar toward the light, and Sundance saw that he was missing his right ear; a slash

133

across the face gave his mouth a grotesque twist.

"You were looking for Jose Milagro?" His English was heavily accented but good.

"Are you Jose Milagro?"

"I might be. It depends on who wants to speak to him."

"My name is Jim Sundance. I want to pay Jose Milagro for his services, though not in the usual way. I want some advice."

"Sundance!" Milagro repeated the name. "Ah, yes. That is a beautiful knife you carry on your belt. I would like to see it, as a favor, of course."

Sundance handed Milagro the knife. "It was made in Vera Cruz," he said. "By J. Guzman. Does that name mean anything to you."

The knife-throwing killer shook his head. "This is a beautiful knife. Would you like to sell it"

Sundance said no.

"Would you mind if I tried it," Jose Milagro asked. "I am said to be expert with the thrown knife."

"So I've heard. That's why I came to see you. No, I don't mind if you try it."

Jose Milagro ordered the bartender to light a few more candles. When they were burning, Jose Milagro turned to Sundance. "Do you see that cockroach on the post over there?"

"I see it," Sundance said.

Milagro's thin hand moved so fast it was a blur. The knife streaked across the room and pinned the cockroach to the wooden post. A burst of approval ran through the men at the tables.

Smiling modestly, Jose Milagro went to get the knife. "Yes, a beautiful knife," he said for the third time. "How well do you throw it? It is simply a question, a matter of interest to myself."

134

"I'll show you," Sundance said, hefting the perfectly balanced knife. "You see the hole the blade made when it went in. I think I can put it back in the same place."

Jose Milagro said, "If you can do that you will not have to pay for my advice, if advice I can give you. Yes, I would like to see you do what you say you can."

The smoky cantina was absolutely silent as Sundance moved away from the bar. It had to be done casually and yet quickly. His hand flew up and the knife sped from his hand with the speed of an arrow. There was no need for the tremendous force he put behind the throw; he thought it necessary to impress Jose Milagro. The thick blade hit home hard and true, burying itself nearly three inches in the post.

Milagro went to the post to inspect the throw. His face was a mask as he turned to offer congratulations, but Sundance could see the hard jealousy in his eyes.

"What did you want to talk about, Sundance?" Milagro asked.

"About the knife we just stuck in that post," Sundance said.

"You were very good with that knife," Jose Milagro said as he showed Sundance the way into the two stuffy rooms behind the cantina where he lived.

The first room had an old brass bed with two mattresses on it instead of one. The air was gray with the acrid smoke of marijuana, the Mexican weed Sundance sometimes smoked because he had long realized that too much liquor of any kind did not agree with the savage, the Indian side of his nature. He liked the feeling the first few drinks of liquor gave to him, and like most men of Indian blood he liked it too much; after those first few drinks of liquor had been drunk he craved to finish the whole bottle, and then to start on another. When he was a much younger man it had always been his determination to drink as much as he liked and yet manage to control it. Too many fights, vicious saloon brawls, being pitted against a man or men he scarcely knew, finally taught him that his attempted self-control was useless.

Tamping marijuana into a small clay pipe, Jose Milagro asked, "Do you care to smoke a pipe with me."

It would be impolite to refuse, so Sundance said, "A small pipe. I have many things to do."

Milagro said he understood and found a clay pipe for Sundance on the rough pine shelf above his bed. There was a whole box of cheap clay pipes in a wooden box. The Mexican killer was the host, so he filled the pipe for Sundance. He did it slowly, with delicate movements of his frail hands.

"I break so many pipes when the power of the weed is upon me that I have to buy them by the box."

Milagro's smile showed all the teeth he didn't have. "By the box," he repeated.

A small joke had been made; Sundance answered it with his own smile. These Mexicans were touchy as a boil ready to be lanced; if you breached their prideful sense of propriety you could make an enemy for life—or an enemy for the here and now.

Jose Milagro struck a sulphurhead match on the baked mud wall; they smoked silently for a few minutes.

The thin-framed Mexican killer sounded very calm when he spoke next. "What is your interest in this knife, my friend?"

Sundance said, "It was used to kill a friend of mine. I would like to find the man who used it."

Milagro asked Sundance to give him the knife so that he could look at it again.

136

Sundance handed over the knife, wondering if Jose Milagro planned to put it in his heart, his throat, or even his eye. He knew the bare-boned Mexican assassin could do it. He didn't know how fast he could pull the Colt and fire before the Vera Cruz knife flashed across the few feet that separated them. Not fast enough, he decided, but he knew he would give it a try if the knife came up in the other man's hand in a throwing motion.

After a while, turning the knife over in his hand, feeling the weight of the blade, Milagro said, "This is not the knife for a professional killer. There is something wrong with it, yet I cannot say what it is. See how brightly the blade is burnished and there is no guard for the hand."

"Maybe the man who owns it likes fancy things."

Jose Milagro smiled thinly. "You are thinking of gunfighters. Many of them like nickeled guns with pearl or ivory grips. All that is to draw attention to themselves, to let people know who they are. A professional assassin is never like that. Usually he is not even a gunfighter, but a quiet man who works for money and not for glory."

Sundance had to agree that this was true. Well, he thought bitterly, I'm back where I started. Maybe I should have let Gabriel Feliz kidnap the general after all. No matter how angry he got he would be safe out there in the hills. But it was too late now.

When he got back to the wagonyard, deciding that he might as well get some sleep, he found Gabriel Feliz waiting for him in a great state of agitation. There was nobody else in sight, but the old Mexican was waving his percussion Colt, ready to do battle.

"Somebody just tried to kill your general," he said. "The sheriff sent Deputy MacPhail to tell you. I was just going to send one of my sons to find you."

137

"When? How?" Sundance asked, cutting in on the other man's babble of words.

"Less than an hour ago. A shot came through the window at the hotel, severely wounding one of the general's aides. MacPhail thinks the young man may die."

Within minutes Sundance had saddled Eagle and was riding hard for the Bella Union Hotel. Soldiers and sheriff's deputies armed with rifles were on the wide porch of the hotel. Dobson, the newspaperman, tried to grab his arm as he went in. Sundance pushed him aside. "Make way or I'll knock your teeth down your throat," he snapped.

Dobson backed off; his face was very pale. "Look," he protested, "I don't like General Crook's politics, but no decent man wants to see him dead."

Ignoring him, Sundance went upstairs three steps at a time. Sheriff Rowland and Major Collinson were talking in the hallway.

"What happened?" Sundance asked. "Is the general all right?"

The sheriff nodded. "The bullet didn't even come close to him. He was going to bed at the time. I guess the killer mistook the general's aide for the general himself. He was passing by the window on his way out when the shot came at him. The curtains were drawn. All the killer saw was a shadow."

"Where did the shot come from?"

Rowland tugged at his beard. "That's the funny thing, Sundance. Like we checked the other day, there are no high buildings back there. It looks like the shot was fired from a long way back, at ground level. That's the only way it could have been done."

"How is the officer who was shot?"

"Already taken to the hospital. The bullet hit him high

in the chest. It went in low and came out high. He's lost a lot of blood."

The three men knocked on the door of Crook's suite, and went in. The general sat in an armchair in his shirtsleeves, pulling on his boots. His bearded face was set in grim lines, and he chewed savagely on an unlit cigar.

"How is my aide?" he asked Rowland, getting up to throw the cigar into the fireplace.

"No news yet, General. The doctor will let me know as soon as there is anything definite. May I suggest that you go to bed, sir? There's nothing you can do tonight."

"Tarnation, man!" Crook growled. "That bullet was meant for me. Do you think I'm just going to sit here while my man is bleeding to death?"

Sundance interrupted. "What else can you do, Three Stars? The killer isn't waiting out there to be caught."

"That's right," the sheriff said. "My men have searched all the streets and alleys in all directions. Not a sign of him, but we'll keep on looking."

After Rowland and Collinson left, Sundance locked the door and sat talking to Crook. The general took a Havana from his leather-covered cigar case and touched a match to it. "Looks like you were right all the time, Jim," he said. "I feel terrible about that boy. Only three years out of the Point and he gets a bullet that was meant for me."

"I think it was meant for anybody—nobody special," Sundance said.

Crook looked puzzled. "What on earth do you mean? Out with it, man."

"I think that shot was just mean to throw us off. No professional killer would make a shot like that, from ground level at a shadow on the window curtains. I've seen the boy who was shot. He's tall and thin, you're short

139

and stocky. I'm pretty sure that he meant the bullet as a diversion."

"You have no proof of that."

"No, sir, but the convention opens tomorrow night. That's when he'll try to kill you. I feel sure of that. I think he figures that we'll figure he's had his chance and didn't succeed."

"That's exactly what I was thinking," Crook said. "I was thinking he won't make another try. It was different before he actually shot somebody, when some people believed John Greer was up to his P.T. Barnum tricks. Now all that's changed. He won't dare show his face."

Sundance said, "Why not show it? Nobody knows what it looks like. By the way, did the sheriff dig the bullet out of the wall?"

"Just an ordinary .44-40. The sheriff took it with him. Did you want to see it?"

"No, I don't think it makes any difference. I still think it was just an attempt to throw us off the track." Sundance took a deep breath because he knew how Crook would react to what he was about to say. "Maybe you should postpone your appearance at the convention. The convention can proceed without you. It's happened before in politics."

"Not a chance, Jim," Crook said, but he wasn't angered by the suggestion. "A lot of good people have come from all over the country to attend. I can't let them down. And that young man who was shot tonight— that's his blood over there on the carpet—I can't let him down either. No matter what happens I've got to be there. I've got to show those sweaty rats back in Washington that I'm not afraid of them."

Crook grinned suddenly. "Besides, I probably wouldn't get the nomination if I didn't show up. And now

I think I better get some rest. Will you leave word downstairs that they're to wake me any time there's some news about my aide."

John Clum was waiting for Sundance when he returned to the wagonyard. Like Sundance, Clum hated cities and would rather sleep out under a blanket and eat cold beans from the can than stay at the best hotel in New York.

"The old Mexican said I could wait for you in your cabin," Clum said, giving one of his mournful smiles that his drooping mustache almost completely concealed. "I said I was an old friend of yours, but I don't think he believes me. One of his sons is watching the place from under a wagon at the other side of the yard."

Building up the fire in the cookstove with some short pieces of wood, Sundance put on a pot of coffee. While he waited for it to cook, he got the bottle of tequila Gabriel Feliz had brought the first day. He poured drinks for both of them. Clum asked for salt and Sundance gave it to him.

"The police in Vera Cruz says the knife that killed Many Horses was made there," Sundance said. "They didn't see the actual knife, of course, but Sheriff Rowland described it in detail."

"Did they have a name?"

"They had the maker's name—nothing else. But it looks like your Apache was right. Did you learn anything else from him?"

Clum sprinkled salt on the back of his hand and licked it to cut the taste of the tequila. Sundance drank his straight, in sips.

"That's what I came to talk to you about," Clum said. "I don't even know exactly what I have to tell you. I don't

141

think my Apache knew himself. After you left the other night he seemed disturbed by his failure to tell you more about the knife and the man who owned it. He just sat there, not moving, not even blinking. I thought he had decided it was time to die. I spoke to him, but he didn't answer. I don't know how much time passed. It was very late and I had turned in. Suddenly I was awakened by a strange cry."

"The old Apache?"

"His eyes were open, but they were looking at things I couldn't see. I sat across the fire from him; there was plenty of light, but he still didn't see me."

Sundance brought the coffee pot to the table. "What finally happened?"

"He woke up. I guess you'd have to call it that. I asked him if he had been dreaming; he said he didn't know. Then I mentioned the knife from Vera Cruz, and he seemed to know where he was."

"What did he say?"

"He said a soldier, an officer, would be killed by the man who bought the knife in Vera Cruz. Of course, he said it in Mexican Apache."

"Did he describe the man who was to be killed?"

"He didn't describe him, but he was sure he would be killed."

"One of General's Crook's aides was hit by a rifle bullet earlier tonight. He was passing the window. They don't know if he'll live."

"I need another drink," Clum said. "All my life I've been around Apaches, but I've never heard of anything like this."

"About the man from Vera Cruz. Is there anything at all that was said?"

After knocking back almost a full cup of tequila, Clum said, "I couldn't understand some of what the old man said. He rambled on, repeating himself, or maybe trying hard to make things clear to himself. He said the man from Vera Cruz was a double man, two men in one."

"A halfbreed?"

"No, I asked him. Not a halfbreed."

"What else, John?"

"He said this man had two hearts. Of course, to the Apaches the heart and the mind is the same."

"A madman?"

"Beats me, Jim. I'm just telling you what he said. That and mumbling I couldn't understand was all I got out of him. He was very weak when I left. I wouldn't be surprised if he's dead by the time I get back."

Sundance thanked Clum for riding all the way to town. Clum said, "I'd ride farther than that for Three Stars."

Living so long among the Indians, Clum had picked up their name for Crook.

"I'll be getting back to camp if there's nothing I can do for you here in town."

"No, John, you better take care of your people. I'd thank that old Apache, but there's no way he would understand."

"He has lived too long out of the world, his own and the white man's. Take good care of Three Stars. I'll see you at the convention. My, won't it be something if the general gets the job."

Sundance walked to the gate of the wagonyard with his old friend. "It would make a difference to this whole country, and I don't mean just the Indians."

John Clum mounted up and rode away.

Chapter 12

Sheriff Rowland and Sundance passed up breakfast and went to scout the five acres of land owned by some speculator in back of the Bella Union hotel. Once it had been one of the Mexican villages that dotted the countryside now being swallowed up by the same.

"I remember when there were people living here," Rowland said. "Now there's talk of a big hotel being built here to give the Bella Union competition."

Nothing remained of the small village; the houses had been knocked down and the rubble carted away. In the middle of the six acres of desolation there was a big wooden sign advertising "downtown" land for sale.

"Whoever shot at Crook's window had to do it from way out here," Sundance said. "I'll bet we don't find a thing. What would there be to find? At best a spent cartridge, and what good would that be if we did find it?"

"You're still convinced it wasn't a real attempt on the general's life."

Sundance, after thinking about it, told the sheriff about John Clum's visit. "The old Apache didn't say Crook would get killed. He said that an officer is dead."

"Why can't Clum get him to name the killer, describe him?" Rowland looked angry just to be talking about Indian magic, though the business about Vera Cruz and the knife had rattled him.

"Magic doesn't work like a clock," Sundance said. "You don't just wind it up and it ticks away. Maybe that's why they call it magic, because it can't be explained."

Sheriff Rowland gave Sundance a hard look. "You're an educated man. Do you believe in Indian magic?"

"I believe in it when it works," Sundance said, grinning at the dour sheriff.

"That's no goddamned answer," Rowland growled. "It's a hell of a thing when two grown men spend their time talking about Indian magic. Yes! Yes! I know! The Apache was right about the knife. Maybe it was just a lucky guess. Vera Cruz is famous for making good knives. Even I know that. So maybe that's all there is to it."

"I doubt if he even knows where Vera Cruz is. Most Mexican Apaches never get south of the Sierra Madre. No, Sheriff, the knife that killed Many Horses is from Vera Cruz, and so is the man with two hearts."

Rowland asked irritably, "You still haven't figured that out, have you?"

Sundance said no.

"I haven't either. All I get from thinking about it is a pain in the head. Damn! Give me a nice simple bank robbery every day of the week. All you have to do is risk your life. You don't have to hurt your head."

"Your men haven't turned up anything, even a rumor?"

"One thing we've got plenty of is rumors. Would you believe it, one lunatic, otherwise seemingly sane, came to my office and said he was certain Geronimo was behind the attempt to murder General Crook. Crook ran Geronimo ragged in the Mexican mountains and the old fellow is still mad about it."

"What else? I might as well hear them all."

"Another gent says he thinks General Grant is behind it. According to him, Grant is afraid that Crook will run against him in the next election and is afraid of losing his job. So you see what I have to put up with up. Don't ever take up law work in a big town, Sundance. If you're not crazy when you start, it won't be long till you are."

Sundance smiled. "I think we can rule out Geronimo and Grant. I don't say Geronimo isn't capable of killing the general, but he has his own style of doing things. President Grant may have surrounded himself with some pretty shady people, but he won't believe anything bad about them. I'll bet he ends up a poor man while his so-called friends retire with fortunes."

Sheriff Rowland looked thoughtful. "Some of Grant's friends are close to the Indian Ring. Everybody knows that. The Democrat newspapers keep harping on it all the time."

"I don't doubt that the Ring is behind it," Sundance said. "Right now I don't much give a damn who's behind it. I just want to save the general's life. You still don't think Matt Cleary has anything to do with it. I keep thinking of the way he set Clagett on me. His explanation sounded good enough, though I'd say he's had plenty of experience lying."

"It still sounds a mite fishy to me, not that I'm accusing him, you understand. I have to live here after all you people are gone, and I don't want to get on the sour side of

Cleary. He can be a bad enemy, as I happen to know. I don't know, Sundance. Maybe Cleary was telling the truth. Only one thing bothers me."

"What's that?"

"If old Feliz wanted to start a real war with Cleary he could bring in the meanest bunch of pistoleros in northern Mexico. Why would a man like you, a close friend of a famous general, become involved with a bunch of dirty shirt Mexicans?"

"That was one of my own thoughts, Sheriff. Of course, Cleary may just be suspicious of everything and anything. He has that look about him. Could even be that he isn't all that smart."

"He's smart enough or he wouldn't be where he is. On the other hand, there's a difference between crafty and intelligent. Cleary might well have believed that you had come to town to side with Feliz and his sons. That would be all the reason he'd need to set Clagett on you. You know I've been keeping a lookout for that son of a bitch, and there isn't a sign of him."

"Cleary said he warned him to stay away from his place."

"That could be, I suppose, but it isn't like Clagett to stay out in the valley with all the festivities going on in town. I looked for him in the saloons, so did MacPhail, but it seems he hasn't been around since you had the fight with him. If he does turn up and starts to make trouble I may lock him up for thirty days. You two don't want to tangle again."

"I sure as hell don't," Sundance agreed. "Clagett smells bad enough to knock you down with his breath.

For the rest of the day, Sundance moved about restlessly like a great sinuous cat broken loose from its cage. His face wore a drawn, tense look; the increasing strain showed itself in his narrowed eyes.

Several times he returned to the convention hall, going over it. Nothing had changed except that more folding chairs had been brought in. Three fire engines, their steam boilers hissing, clanged their way across the broken ground that led to the hall.

The fire captain, a red-faced man with a thick mustache, went into the hall. Sundance followed him inside; the fireman eyed him suspiciously.

"What might your business be?"

Sundance explained that he was with General Crook.

"Oh sure," he said. "I heard about you. You're the one that beat up that man Clagett in the Plaza. That was a nice bit of work. I had a little trouble with Clagett a while back. The son of a bitch tried to join my company. I said no to the idea. I just hope it doesn't come to real trouble between us."

Sundance wanted to tell the fire captain that Clagett would never bother anybody again; there was no way he could do it.

They got to talking about the possibility of a fire. "It could happen. If it does we can handle it. Those pumpers out there are the latest from St. Louis and we'll have men posted everywhere, watching for the first sign of fire."

"My name is James Mooney," the fire captain said.

They shook hands. Mooney took out a blue bandanna and mopped his face. It was a hot day and the talk of fire was making him hotter.

"They're going to let more people in here than ought to be here. My men will be watching like hawks, but after all, this is an all-wood building. If a fire does break out we'll have to get the crowd out and keep pouring on the water. Just as a precaution we're going to wet down the whole outside of the building before the convention starts. Someday I'd like to see all these buildings made of brick."

"It's pretty bare still," Sundance said. "It's when they put in too much fancy stuff that the danger increases."

The fire captain went outside to talk to his men. After a while they went away, steam boiler hissing, bell clanging.

And still Sundance remained restless. He walked back into the hall and tried to see it as the killer might. Again and again he wondered would it be a shot from high up on the catwalks behind the stage? But that made no sense because there was no way to get up there without being seen. A shot couldn't come from a window because the exterior would be patrolled at all times.

No, the shot would have to come from the crowd. But that would mean instant death for the assassin. If Sundance didn't get him, then Rowland's men would. Or Major Collinson's. There would be men inside and outside the building, all heavily armed.

Sundance went back to the hotel and talked to Collinson, who was on guard with two soldiers at the head of the stairs leading to Crook's suite.

"Anything?"

"No, absolutely nothing. It couldn't be quieter. Nobody has tried to get in to see the general."

"Nobody?"

"Nobody except for that New York reporter—Dobson."

"Did you let him go in?"

"Like hell I did, not after the things he's been writing. John Greer argued with me and said maybe Dobson would come over to Old George's side if I acted more politely toward him."

149

"What did you say to that?"

"I told Greer to go to hell. He went in to see Old George. I expected to get my head handed to me, but nothing happened."

"Good man," Sundance said. "Let Dobson come to the convention if he wants to hear what the general has to say."

Sundance went up and knocked on the door. Mary Crook let him in. "The day is wearing on and I'm wearing out," she said. "George will be out in a minute. He's been trying to take a nap. It isn't easy with all this excitement going."

She lowered her voice and glanced at the bedroom door. "You think it's going to be all right, Jim."

"I'll do my best for him."

"Please do, Jim. We've been together so long, so many years, so many places, I don't know what I'd do..."

"Don't start that again, Mary," Crook growled, coming out of the bedroom and straightening his collar.

"All right, I'm not starting anything, just talking to Jim. You better brush your hair down a bit. It's standing up every which way."

"I'll brush it when I'm ready to brush it, and if I'm not I won't. How does that suit you, woman?"

"One thing you'll never be and that's a diplomat, no matter how long you stay in Washington."

"Glad to hear it."

Crook asked Sundance, "Everything set, I suppose. John Greer says it is."

"As set as it ever will be. I've talked it over with all your people; everybody knows what he's supposed to do. They even have three pumpers standing by in case of a fire."

"Why not a plague of locusts while you're at it? Or a tidal wave."

Sundance could see that Crook was irritable; he was afraid for his wife, not for himself. There wasn't much George Crook was afraid of on earth, but Sundance knew he dreaded the day when it came for the Crooks to part forever.

"Still looking forward to going up in the Sierras, Three Stars?" he asked. "No matter how hot it gets down here, it's always cool up there. Snow still on the peaks and the high places, the smell of tree sap. You still hankering to cook up a mess of yellow perch."

Crook's eyes lit up. "Not just yellow perch, all kinds of panfish. This truck they've been feeding me here could make a man sick. As soon as this blamed convention is wound up, we'll pack our gear and head for the high country. We'll stay up there a whole week. It'll be good to get back to what's real."

"So it will, sir."

"You've been trying to slicker me, haven't you?"

"Sure I have, but I meant it too. I want to go hunting as much as you do."

Crook made a face. "You shouldn't have tried to slicker me, Jim. All that soapy talk about panfish and clear lakes makes me think maybe I don't want to go to Washington, after all."

"The high country won't go away, Three Stars. It'll always be there when you feel like taking a trip. And you can always get up to Maine. They got great hunting up that way, and you can take the railroad all the way. What do you think of that?"

"I think you're still trying to slicker me. But no matter, I feel kind of cheered up."

Chapter 13

Now it was less than twenty-four hours to convention night, and Sundance didn't think there was anything more that could be done in the way of precautions. From now on it was up to fate or luck or whatever you wanted to call it. He kept racking his brain in an effort to put the puzzle together; it didn't work.

That evening, all through dinner, Mrs. Crook had said hardly a word. Sundance and the general tried to keep the conversation going without much success. Crook smoked a lot and Sundance drank a little whiskey.

The general had tried to be jovial. "You sure you don't want a big job in Washington, Jim? Of course you'd have to cut your hair and dress in a black suit."

"No thanks, Three Stars, I already have a job with Captain Jack's Wild West Show. That way I can do without the black suit. When you get to Washington you'll do enough good for both of us."

"It's going to be strange living in the city. Half my life I've been living in tents, eating off tin plates. You think you're going to like Washington, Mary?"

Mary Crook stared at her plate. "I don't know what to think about anything," she said. "I sort of pushed you for this job, didn't I? Yes, if you want an answer, I'd like to live in Washington. Life in the army camps wasn't so bad when we were both younger. Now I wouldn't mind a change. I'd like to go to the theater once in a while and enjoy good restaurants."

She looked up quickly. "But it isn't worth it if anything happens to you."

Crook was annoyed and his face showed it. "You didn't push me for the job. I wanted it, I still want it, and if something happens to me you'll just have to put up with it, just as I would if something happened to you. Do I make myself clear, woman?"

Suddenly she smiled. "I like it better when you shout," she said. "Now if you'll excuse me I have some things to do. You have some spots on the suit you're going to wear. I'm going to try some benzine."

"Not too much, mind. I can't stand the smell of that stuff."

Crook turned to Sundance after his wife left the room. "Well, it's all over but the shouting. This time tomorrow night . . ." The general put his watch back in his pocket.

"We're going to give you the best protection we can," Sundance said. "Sheriff Rowland is a good man. I had some doubts about him when this thing started. Now I trust him completely. He vouches for his men, most of them. Those he isn't absolutely sure of won't be standing guard. Major Collinson's men will back up the sheriff."

Crook lit another Havana and poured some coffee. He

153

handed the cup to Sundance. "I'd just as soon we didn't go on talking about it. For once you're the general, not me. You've made your plan as best you can. You've planned this if that happens, and that if this happens. Now you have to let it alone. I know you'd be rock calm if only your own life was on the block. Let it alone and we'll see what happens. That's how it has to be."

"You're right, Three Stars," Sundance agreed. "There's no use talking it to death. I'm sorry, sir."

"I've been around sudden death most of my life, Jim. I think I'll go to bed now. I haven't been sleeping all that well. This certainly is a noisy town. Funny, I can sleep through cannon fire, but people yelling in the street keep me awake."

It was just after eleven o'clock when Sundance returned to the wagonyard. Gabriel Feliz was on the porch of his adobe house, holding a bottle of tequila and two glasses. He had been drinking.

"Ah, Sundance, my friend," he called out. "I have been waiting for you. What about a drink?"

Sundance didn't want it, but after all, the old Mexican rogue had been a good friend. "A short one," he said. "There is much to do tomorrow, as you know."

They went into the cluttered house and sat down. "I wish I could have helped you more," Gabriel Feliz said mournfully, pouring tequila for both of them.

"You did your best," Sundance said. "I have not been any more of a success. I keep getting to a certain point and then everything stops. A dead-end canyon with no way out but back. All we can do is wait."

"Have you seen the general?"

154

"I just came from him."

"How is he taking it?"

"Calmly. That is Crook's way."

"What he is doing takes more courage than to ride into battle. In my youth I was in many battles, but I would hate to sit around waiting to be killed. You want another drink, my friend. Tonight I feel sad and will drink many drinks." Gabriel Feliz hiccuped loudly. "I have already had many drinks, and now I will have another."

The old man had his back to the window. He stood up with difficulty and reached for the bottle. His legs gave way and he lurched sideways just as a bullet crashed through the window and hit him in the spine. He called out and fell on top of the table; it collapsed under his weight.

The bushwhacker fired one more shot before he ran; Sundance heard him running. Gabriel Feliz was still alive when Sundance turned back from the door. He lay on his back in the wreckage of the table, but Sundance didn't try to move him from where he was. The bottle of tequila, still corked, lay unbroken on the floor.

Sundance poured a trickle of tequila into the old man's mouth, while three of the Feliz boys came in and stood silently, their hats in their hands. Gabriel Feliz coughed and smiled faintly.

"Death comes at last," he said. "After all these years it finally comes."

"You know?" Sundance said.

"Clagett. One of my sons saw him twice today, not far from here. My sons, all of them, warned him to keep away. He left. I thought that was the last of him. I did not tell you about him. You have many things to think about."

155

"I will kill him, Gabriel."

"Let my sons do it."

"Then let me help them."

"Gladly, my friend."

Gabriel Feliz turned his eyes toward his sons, smiled, and died.

The oldest son told the youngest to stay with their father. "Do you think he's on his way back to the valley?"

"We'll check here before we go there," Sundance said. "We have no proof that Clagett did the shooting."

"I do not need proof."

"Neither do I. Come on, let's go."

Travelers were peering fearfully from the cabins in the yard as Sundance and the Feliz boys moved out through the gate into the dark, silent Calle de los Negros. Keeping well apart, they walked down the middle of the street, guns drawn and ready. Sundance didn't know what to make of it. He wasn't even sure that Clagett had meant to kill him. Had Cleary sent him? Had it anything to do with Crook?

They went up the hill from the wagonyard. Nobody was in sight; the only sound was made by crickets in a crumbling adobe wall. Past the ancient cemetery it was still quiet; nothing moved.

"I do not think he is still here, Sundance." This came from Paco Feliz, the oldest son. "He is already on his way to the valley. We must go there now."

"Not yet," Sundance said quietly. "Maybe that's where he thinks we'll go."

"He must not get away, Sundance."

"He won't. Move carefully because he will be in cover, and we are in the street."

They were two hundred yards on the other side of the

cemetery when Sundance heard a faint sound coming from a row of wagons in front of a warehouse. It was very dark under the wide, sloping porch.

"You think?" Paco Feliz whispered.

"It could be just a rat. Don't talk," Sundance said.

Moving on again, they eased their way through the darkness. "Come in from both sides," Sundance said softly. "I'll take him from the front. I know you want to take him alive if he's in there, but don't get yourselves killed just for revenge."

"If just one of us takes him, the rest of us won't mind dying."

"Suit yourselves—they're your lives."

Sundance waited until the Feliz brothers had disappeared into the darkness before he began to edge his way toward the warehouse porch. Suddenly a bullet blasted at him from under one of the wagons. The shot rolled like thunder in the silent street. Two bullets followed the first one, and Sundance felt the hot wind of their passing. He cursed the Feliz boys for not opening fire, but even as he cursed them he understood. They meant to take Clagett alive no matter what happened.

He fired at the last flash of Clagett's gun; the bullet hit the side of a wagon. Then Clagett yelled like a madman as he was dragged out from under the wagon by the heels. "Kill me! Go on, kill me, you lousy stinking greasers! I killed your rotten thieving father. Why don't you kill me! Go on! Get it over with!"

"Bring him along," Sundance said. He knew why Clagett was begging for a quick death. The Feliz brothers wouldn't just use a bullet in the head or the quick thrust of a knife. Nothing that simple, nothing that merciful.

They kicked and dragged Clagett down the hill,

157

making no attempt to keep him quiet. By now the Mexicans of the quarter would know that Gabriel Feliz was dead, and that the Anglo who had murdered him was about to be punished for it. There was no need to gag the condemned man, because nobody would ever remember having seen or heard him.

One of the sons got a lantern and brought it to the old carpenter's shop at the far end of the yard. Clagett was roped to the bench, and a bucket of coals was beginning to glow.

"You can't let them do this to me, Sundance," Clagett begged. "I admit what I did. I meant to get you. Put a bullet in me. Don't let these . . . these . . ."

"Greasers," Sundance said. "Did Cleary send you to kill me?"

Large drops of oily sweat coated Clagett's face. "No! Cleary didn't send me. You made me look like a fool in front of everybody. Cleary warned me to stop coming around. His brother kicked me out. I wanted to kill you, you red nigger bastard."

Clagett's voice rose to a scream. "You hear what I called you, you dog eater. Your mother was a poxy whore. Why don't you kill me?"

"Killing is too good for you," Sundance said, turning away.

There was no sign of Jack Clagett when Sundance got out of his blankets the next morning. Lord knows where the body had gone: buried far out in the desert, maybe even in the cemetery at the top of the hill.

The main room of Gabriel Feliz's little house had been cleaned up and the body of the old Mexican lay in a plain pine coffin which was large enough to accommodate his bulk. The coffin was open; they had shaved him and trimmed his hair. He didn't look dead, but looked as if he was taking a nap after too much tequila.

Sundance shook hands with each of the sons, and said he was very sorry for having caused the death of their father.

Paco said wisely, "His time had come. It could not be put off any longer."

The funeral was to be the following day; Sundance said he would be there. In a little more than twelve hours the convention would begin.

At the hotel Crook poured coffee and listened to what Sundance told him about Clagett. "This place is turning into a slaughterhouse. I'm sorry about your friend Feliz. Do you think Clagett was telling the truth. About Cleary, I mean."

Sundance said he couldn't be sure. "He had no reason to lie. He knew he was going to die, so why would he lie? I really don't know. He said Cleary had kicked him out. For a man like Clagett that might be reason enough. Any problems that you want to tell me about?"

Crook smiled. "Other than Major Collinson, I can't think of a thing. He's driving me crazy, coming in and out every fifteen minutes. If he doesn't stop I'm going to brain him with something. There's a limit, and he doesn't seem to know what it is."

"Is that a hint, Three Stars?"

"It could be, Jim."

"Then I'll take a walk over to the convention hall. The sheriff said he'd be there this morning."

"Why don't you take Collinson with you?"

Sundance went out without answering. Major Collin-

159

son was downstairs in the lobby talking to a young officer Sundance didn't know.

"How does it look?" Sundance asked.

"Not a thing happening. It could be any morning, except the whole town is jammed with people. You going over to the hall?"

"To take another look. I'm going to keep checking that place over right to the last minute. That way nobody sneaks in during the day and gets all set for the kill."

Sundance found Sheriff Rowland up on the stage of the hall, pacing from one side to the other. "I've been over every inch of the place. Not a thing that looks suspicious. No explosives, no hidden cans of coal oil." The sheriff took out his silver watch. "Nine fifteen," he said. "I've had this timepiece for twenty years and I haven't looked at it as often as I have in the last twenty-four hours. I'll wear a hole in the case if I don't stop taking it in and out of my pocket."

Sheriff Rowland gave Sundance a guarded look. "Too bad about old Gabe Feliz getting shot. You wouldn't know anything about that?"

"Say your piece, Sheriff."

"I was talking about Jack Clagett a while ago. How my men are looking all over and still can't find him. That's kind of strange, a big loudmouth like Clagett being so hard to find."

"Maybe he's gone on a long journey."

"Not so long, I'd say. We didn't find Clagett, but we did find his horse stabled at Bymer's. That's about half a mile from Calle de los Negros. Probably just a coincidence, Clagett puttin' up his horse so close to the wagonyard."

Sundance didn't answer; he didn't want to lie to this crusty, honorable man.

160

The sheriff continued with a thin smile. "I told you that a while back Clagett murdered a young missionary who was trying to reform one of Cleary's girls. Broke the young man, snapped him like a twig. I never was able to get Clagett for that killing. Now I get the feeling I won't have to, and that's fine with me. I don't know that I'll ever get Cleary, but then you never know. A man has to bide his time, is what I always say."

"It's going to be a real scorcher of a day," Sundance said with a grin.

Rowland grinned back. "It sure is."

"You feel like a glass of beer?" Rowland asked. "It's too hot and too early for whiskey, at least for me."

"A beer would be fine," Sundance agreed. "The Bella Union?"

"Best bar in town. You can ask for just about any drink—they'll mix it up for you. Me, I favor sourmash and good beer straight from the ice."

They walked back toward the hotel, the sheriff trying to keep up with Sundance's long stride.

"You going to be moving on as soon as this . . . convention . . . is over?" Rowland asked.

"That's the plan. Up north there's an Indian agent who's been having trouble with horse thieves. They come at night and run off the stock. The Indians can't fight back because they were disarmed last year. He thinks some renegade troopers from the closest fort are behind it. They may well be why the army doesn't help. Anyway, that's why I'm going up there to take a look. If General Crook gets to Washington you'll see some fast action on dirty work like that. And, believe me, he won't spend all his time sitting behind a desk. He'll be out there in the field, looking at things with his own two eyes."

161

They went into the hotel bar, a big, cool, high-ceilinged room with a marble bar that ran its whole length. Three bartenders stood behind it. It was early yet, and the place was fairly empty.

A waiter brought two tall bottles of Pearl Beer to their table. It was ice cold; water beaded on the side of the bottle. "This is the real stuff," the sheriff said, wiping a thin line of froth from his mustache. "I don't know that you can get better beer this side of the Mississippi."

Sundance, no great drinker of beer of any kind, said it was very good.

"You've got to show more enthusiasm, Sundance."

Rowland finished his beer and signaled for another. Sundance said he would wait for a while.

"And after you help this Indian agent up north, what then?"

"I'm not rightly sure. I take things as they come to me. Back in Washington I pay a lawyer to fight the Ring as best he can. I can only get as much money together as I can. They're rolling in the stuff. That's one way they've tried to stop. They get a few friendly judges on their side, and a case can drag on for years."

"It looks like you're giving over your whole life to this cause."

"As much time as I can. There's always a need for more and more money, so I have to find work where I can. Mexico, Central America, Canada."

"And this money you make—you give it all away?"

"Lawyers, even honest ones, cost money. If you fall behind with the bills, then you have no more lawyers. I manage to hold up my end most of the time."

"It's a hell of a life, if you don't mind me saying so. Haven't you ever thought that maybe you've done

162

enough? That it's time somebody else took over?"

"Like who?"

"There must be somebody."

"If there is I haven't met him yet. There are good men like Crook. They help in their way, and I help in mine."

"True. But they aren't risking their lives."

"What do you think Crook will be doing when he gets up on the stage tonight?"

Rowland poured the rest of his beer. "What I'm trying to say is, haven't you ever wanted to do something for yourself? Get yourself a ranch, cows, horses? Get married?"

Sundance smiled. "You were married once. Why don't you get married again? You're not so old."

The sheriff gave Sundance a sour look that made him grin all the harder. "I don't feel like getting married. The missus was a great cook, but she nagged the ear off me night and day. I may be a fool in the kitchen, but I can eat what I cook in peace."

"You answered your own question, Sheriff. I'm too set in my ways for settling down and getting married. I like to live my life in my own way, free to wander or stay put, if I feel like it. Wake up in the morning and point my horse in any direction I like. I'm not saying that's the right life for everybody, but it suits me just fine."

"You know what's the matter with you, Sundance." The sheriff was smiling broadly now.

"What?"

"You've got no sense of responsibility."

Chapter 14

"Tarnation, I've been cooped up in that hotel for days, and now when I finally get out, it's only to ride in a closed carriage. I don't know whether you're my friend or my jailer, Jim."

George Crook was grumbling as he climbed in with Major Collinson and Sundance on either side of him. Earlier Sundance had insisted that Mrs. Crook go to the convention hall in a separate carriage. Sundance hadn't explained the reason; there was no need to.

"No need to wipe out the whole family," Crook joked grimly. "Here, take this."

Sundance took the thick brown envelope, but didn't open it.

The carriage began to move. "That's my will," Crook said. "If anything happens to me I want you to look after Mary. Except for the children, neither of us has any family left."

Crook patted Sundance lightly on the arm, "I guess we could call you family, though."

"Nothing's going to happen to you, General," Collinson said with no certainty in his voice. "We'll be watching the crowd, not you. The first man who raises a finger against you will be dead two seconds later."

"There will be no indiscrimate shooting," Crook protested. "I don't want innocent people killed or wounded."

"We won't let you get killed, sir."

"I just gave you an order, Major. I didn't bring these people together to get them shot."

"Please listen to me, Three Stars," Sundance said, wanting to break up the tension between the two men, "if there is any trouble you're to throw yourself flat on the stage. Get down and stay down. The rest of us will take it from there."

Crook made a sour face. "Is that an order, Jim?"

"That's right, sir, and I expect you to obey it."

Crook started to laugh. "How do you like this galoot, Major Collinson? Ordering a full general around like a buck private still wet behind the ears."

"It's good advice, sir."

"Don't be so solemn, Major. I'm not dead yet."

Hundreds of people were in the streets, all moving in the direction of the big hall. It was a warm night, and not yet completely dark. A big yellow moon was taking shape over the rooftops. In front of a noisy saloon an elderly man in ragged clothes was carrying a sign that read: GIVE GENERAL CROOK BACK TO THE INDIANS.

"I'd like to kick that fool's backside out between his teeth," Collinson said angrily.

"Sticks and stones, Major. Let the man have his say. I

sort of take it as a compliment. The time to worry is when they stop talking and start shooting."

Because of the crowds it took the carriage fifteen minutes to reach the hall. Sundance got out first, followed by Crook, then Collinson. They all got out on the same side so as to stay together. Sheriff Rowland and four of his deputies stood at the top of the steps. The deputies carried rifles, the sheriff had his shoulder holster strapped on, and had another six-shooter stuck in the waistband of his pants.

"Everything all right?" Sundance asked.

"Up till now. Maybe nothing will happen, after all."

"That's what we're hoping for."

After giving orders to his men, Rowland led the way into the hall. A wide area in front of the stage had been cleared of chairs. Captain Jack Crawford was there, gaudily dressed in cream-colored buckskins and a high-crowned Stetson of the same color. John Greer watched while Captain Jack made last-minute arrangements for staging his Wild West show.

Captain Jack doffed his hat and the people already there cheered as Crook walked up the center aisle. The general took off his own hat, trying hard to look like a popular politician, but his heart wasn't in it. He shook hands with Captain Jack and nodded to Greer.

Captain Jack was brimming over with good cheer and whiskey. "Ah, my dear General," he boomed, his voice echoing high up into the rafters. "What an evening this is going to be! I see that your lovely lady has already arrived, also the distinguished authoress, Mrs. Jackson. All the finest people are here or will be here to honor one of our nation's bravest warriors."

"Is that me?" Crook whispered to Sundance.

166

Greer was looking at his watch. "We have twenty minutes to go, General," he said. "You better get up there."

Sundance and Rowland watched while Crook went up the stairs at the side of the stage. Collinson went with him. Greer said to Sundance, "First, Mrs. Jackson will introduce the general and make a short speech. That's what she's supposed to do. I just hope she sticks to the schedule. Mayor Downey will then introduce General Crook. At that point the general will make the speech everybody has been expecting."

"So far so good," Sundance said.

Up on the stage Crook was shaking hands with Leland Stanford, president of the South Pacific Railroad. Stanford was a big, smug-looking man with an ample belly. Several punchbowls had been set up at the back of the stage, and an elderly Negro in a white coat was filling glasses with a ladle. Just then, Mayor Downey, a foxy-faced man with ginger hair, arrived with his retinue of politicians. One of them was Matt Cleary.

Sundance drifted back over to where Captain Jack was still giving orders to his roustabouts and performers. Sheriff Rowland said he was going to take a look around outside. Overhead the enormous gasoliers threw down a white relentless light; there wasn't a shadow anywhere.

Captain Jack took off his hat and used it as cover to take two quick drinks from his flask. He wiped his snowy mustache with the back of his hand. "You're going to see a fine show this evening, Mr. Sundance," he boomed. "More's the pity, you won't be able to see it in its entirety. But Mr. Greer says time is of the essence. These city gents don't know when to ease up and have a good time. Still and all, there will be a display of Indian archery, Texas

167

Billy Beaudry will show his skill with the rope, and many other things including a Sioux war dance. I myself will ride my beautiful white steed right down the center aisle and up to the stage, where I will present General Crook with a Comanche war bonnet."

The old showman yelled at one of his men to make sure his horse was "all cleaned out," adding, "and give him very little water until the show is over." Turning back to Sundance, he said, "I don't want him to disgrace himself in front of the ladies." One of his roustabouts called out a question and Captain Jack went over to answer it.

The hall was almost filled now. John Greer, a strained look on his face, said to Sundance, "Ten minutes before we begin."

Sundance walked around behind the stage and saw nothing but one of Rowland's deputies with a rifle in the crook of his arm.

"Everything quiet," he said.

Captain Jack's Genuine German Brass Band, as advertised on the posters outside, filed in and started to test their instruments on a small bandstand on one side of the stage. They were dressed in red and gold uniforms, all healthy-looking except the bassoon player. The leader, a short fat man with a waxed mustache, tapped his baton on the music stand and they launched into a deafening rendition of *Rally Round the Flag*. After that they crashed through *Dixie* for the sake of the Southerners in the audience.

The hall was packed now, so much so that there weren't enough chairs for everybody. A sea of placards and state and territorial flags bobbed up and down. Sheriff Rowland came down the aisle with two of his men. They took up their positions on one side of the stage;

Sundance stayed on the other, watching the crowd.

It was stifling hot in the hall because of the crowd and the flaring gas lights. The band leader was watching John Greer, who had his watch in his hand. Greer nodded and the leader stopped the music in the middle of *The Lane County Bachelor*.

Well here goes, Sundance thought.

Mrs. Helen Hunt Jackson, fat and formidable in a bright green dress with an armor-like corset underneath, walked to the front of the stage and raised her hands to still the light scattering of applause.

"Ladies and gentlemen!" she bellowed in a voice that even Captain Jack might have admired. "Welcome to the General George Crook convention. We are gathered here tonight to honor a great soldier and a great man. This man's life is an open book, and I hardly need to tell you what a fine man he is. George Crook is known from the green forests of Maine to the blue waters of the Pacific Ocean. Men in all walks of life claim his friendship, and he has given it freely and without pause. Above all, he is the true friend of the American Indian, of which he will speak to you later."

Watching the crowd, Sundance didn't see anything out of place except a man trying to sneak a drink from a pint bottle. Rowland whispered to one of his deputies, and the drunk was taken outside without any fuss. Mrs. Jackson went on: "And now, ladies and gentlemen, I give you the Right Honorable John Downey, ex-Governor of California, and Mayor of this fair city. A round of applause, please!"

Mayor Downey came forward and the band broke into a short medley of marching songs.

"Thank you, Mrs. Jackson! Thank you, ladies and

gentlemen!" Downey said, raising both hands above his head after the applause died away. Downey had a faint Irish accent that came faintly through his western twang. "I can't say how delighted I am to be here tonight to take part in these momentous proceedings. As Mrs. Jackson has stated so magnificently, with all her writer's gift for words, General George Crook is a man the whole world admires and respects. And yet, my friends, you have all read about or heard about the dastardly attempt on the general's life. A fine young officer gave his life during the commission of this horrendous deed. Let me tell you here and now that the culprit or culprits will be apprehended and punished. I personally have instructed our fine sheriff to leave no stone unturned in the uncovering of this criminal conspiracy. But, ladies and gentlemen, I did not come here to speak of such things, but to welcome General George Crook."

You fat-bellied hypocrite, Sundance thought. He couldn't see Downey, but he knew the glib politician was well pleased with himself.

The band struck up again, and Crook began to speak. He wasn't anywhere as glib as Downey; his words were blunt and harsh and to the point. There was none of the usual politician's rubbish about growing up on an Ohio farm. Crook spoke briefly of the Civil War and how he had sought to reunite the country after it was over. That brought a roar of applause, and Crook continued. Then he talked about his many campaigns against the Indians.

"I fought them before and after the Civil War. Yes, ladies and gentlemen, and I will fight them again if my superiors order me to. Yet it was always with sadness that I led my men into battle against them. I feel certain that there would be no more useless wars if only we gave them

170

the justice they seek. I know some of you have lost relatives and friends, but so have I. There has to come a time when the killing must stop, and I say that time is now."

Crook's voice rose to a shout, and he clenched his fist in the air. "I want justice for the Indians! And by the God that made us all, that is what they are going to get if I become Secretary of the Interior! However, I would like to remind you that I am just one man and cannot do it alone. I must have your support and most humbly I ask you for it. Together we can do it, you and all the men and women of goodwill who are not present here tonight. We can make this great country a nation of all the people. Thank you."

The applause lasted a full five minutes while the band blared an accompaniment. Then the bandmaster bellowed so hard that the tendons stood out on his neck. "I now give you Captain Jack Crawford, King of the Scouts, and his famous Wild West Show! Captain Jack, ladies and gentlemen, the man you've all been waiting to see!"

Sundance watched while Captain Jack, mounted on a magnificent white stallion, came prancing down the center aisle, waving his cream-colored Stetson while the band played *The Horse Wrangler*. Captain Jack took it slowly, enjoying every minute of it, and when he reached the area where the show was to be staged, the band switched over to waltz time. The big horse sashayed from side to side, keeping perfect time to the three beats of the measure, and while the crowd roared its applause, Captain Jack brought the big stallion to a halt in front of the stage.

"General Crook, Mrs. Crook, I bid you welcome to this evening's entertainment."

Sundance guessed that Captain Jack was slightly drunk.

Captain Jack, carried away by the sound of his own thunder, was about to launch into a speech until a loud cough and a stern look from John Greer brought him up short.

"First you are about to witness a remarkable exhibition of roping by the one and only Texas Billy Beaudry. Watch him as he passes in and out of the whirling loop."

Captain Jack dismounted and one of his men led the stallion outside. Texas Billy Beaudry appeared with his rope and proceeded to dazzle the crowd with his skill. He was a lanky stringbean of a man who took his work very seriously. Captain Jack led the applause when he finished, and left after giving an awkward bow.

Sundance looked around at Crook and saw him sitting with his arms folded, trying to look as if he was enjoying himself. The heat was growing more intense, and the ladies on the stage were fanning themselves vigorously. Mrs. Jackson was sweating like a blacksmith. Mrs. Crook kept looking sideways at her husband.

Sundance felt the tension building inside his head. Despite all hopes, he knew it was going to happen; the question was how soon. Where in hell was the son of a bitch, and what was he waiting for?

After the rope expert left, a bunch of Indians in war bonnets shuffled through a dance that Captain Jack declared was "the genuine Sioux article straight from the grassy plains of South Dakota."

The crowd was growing restless in the heat. John Greer ducked past the front of the stage and whispered something to the Captain, who shook his head at first, then nodded reluctantly.

The so-called Sioux Indians finished their dance and went out. Looking peeved at Greer, Captain Jack announced that the final and most magnificent entertainment of the evening would be an archery display by a young Comanche warrior named Arickaree. "He is truly a great warrior, a legend among his own people, until he chose to follow the way of peace. Skilled in all the terrible instruments of death, he will demonstrate the bow and arrow tonight for your pleasure. However, because of special circumstances need not gone into, and because the hall is so closely packed, he will use a soft target and blunted arrowheads. Arickaree of the Comanche Nation, my friends!"

While two roustabouts dragged a padded target into position, a young Indian came from the back of the hall. He wore a full war bonnet and fringed deerskins; his face was heavily daubed with yellow and blue war paint. He moved as if he didn't hear the applause of the crowd.

One of the roustabouts handed him a bow and a quiverful of arrows. The drummer in the band started a roll as the young Indian readied the first arrow. The target was plain white paper with padding behind it. The drum roll stopped as the first arrow flashed from the bow. It struck the exact center of the target. Then, without pausing, he shot a second arrow beside it and put another arrow right beside the second one.

Sundance looked at him curiously; in spite of the mask of war paint there was something oddly familiar about him. He was about to fit another arrow to the bow when there was a loud explosion behind the convention hall and the gasoliers began to flicker and go out. The light was fading fast when the young Indian flicked up his shirt and pulled out two knives.

"You die, Three Stars!" he shouted in Cheyenne, and

173

threw the first knife. Sundance drew his Colt; the hammer was earing back when the second knife flew from the Indian's hand. The light died suddenly as he fired the first shot. He started to fire again, but there was nothing to see.

Sundance dived at where the Indian had been, but all his body hit was the wooden floor. By now the crowd was in total panic, pushing and yelling as they tried to get out. He heard Rowland shouting at them to keep calm, but it was like trying to stop a maddened herd in full stampede.

A match flared behind him, and when he turned the sheriff was touching a match to a lantern. When the wick was turned up, the floor of the hall was littered with injured men and women.

They went up onto the stage and found Crook still in his chair with one of the knives buried in his chest; the other was buried in the wall.

Mrs. Jackson had fainted, but nobody was paying any attention to her. Crook's eyes were starting to glaze over, but he was still conscious. One of the deputies found another lantern and held it while the sheriff held the other. Mrs. Crook knelt beside her husband, tightly gripping his hand.

Captain Jack lurched up onto the stage with the whiskey flask in his hand. Sundance pushed it away. "He doesn't want it."

Captain Jack finished the rest of the whiskey. "This is terrible," he said in a quavering voice, all the showman's bluster gone from it.

Sundance told him to shut up. "Better hurry with the doctor," he told the sheriff. "He can't be moved until the doctor gets here."

Rowland went out with Downey and Cleary behind him. For some reason, Leland Stanford was nowhere to be seen.

"Did you get him?" Crook asked weakly.

"Not yet, Three Stars, but now I know who he is."

Crook tried to say something else, but wasn't able to do it. His eyes closed and his breathing became quick and shallow.

Mary Crook's eyes bored into Sundance. "Who did this?"

"We won't talk about that now, but I'll find him if it takes me all my life."

"What difference does it make if he dies?"

"It will to me, Mrs. Crook."

The doctor arrived, accompanied by two stretcher carriers. "I better leave the knife where it is until we get him to the hospital. Carry him gently, boys. He's a man we can't afford to lose."

Mary Crook stood up as the men from the hospital lifted Crook onto the stretcher. Her face was completely without expression; only her eyes showed the feelings raging inside her.

"Are you coming, Jim?" she asked dully.

"No," he answered. "You go along with the ambulance. I'll be along later. Right now I have work to do."

Sundance took the lantern from the sheriff and went down in the hall. All the injured had been carried outside; one woman was dead. They hadn't taken the body away yet. Walking around with the lantern, Sundance found what he expected to find—a war bonnet and a deerskin shirts and trousers. Beside them was an oily rag smeared with paint.

"You know who he is?" Rowland said.

Sundance pulled the throwing knife from his belt and matched it with the one he had taken from the back wall of the stage. Both knives were exactly alike.

"Tell me who he is," Rowland said.

Sundance's voice was savage. "Let me alone," he said. "I'll take care of this by myself."

"But he's getting away."

"For awhile maybe. No more questions, Sheriff. Maybe I'll talk to you later. At the moment I don't feel like talking to anybody. See what you can do for General Crook. You can search the circus wagons if you like, but you won't find him there."

"Where then?"

"I have an idea."

Chapter 15

Sundance walked through the dark streets that led to the Mexican quarter. He cursed himself for not having figured the whole thing out sooner. All the information he needed had been there all the time, but he hadn't put it together, and because of that General Crook was badly wounded, maybe dying, maybe even dead.

If Crook died he would blame himself for the rest of his life, for in all his life there had been no finer friend. After his mother and father had been murdered, and he had tracked down the men who did it, there had been an overpowering sense of hopelessness, of not knowing where to turn.

That had been many years before, and at that point in his life he could easily have turned bad, because his mind was numb with the lack of any emotion, any human feeling except hate.

He had loved his English father and his Cheyenne

mother with a fierce love, and now they were gone forever. Rootless, without a place in the white or Indian worlds, he began to drift, to drink heavily in a desperate effort to blot out the past.

Of course, the drinking and the crazed saloon brawls made it worse. Always moving on without purpose, he courted trouble everywhere he went. No matter what the odds, he never walked away from a fight. Instead, he welcomed the pain and the danger as he locked himself in combat with men as desperate as himself.

On many mornings he woke up in a jail cell or in an alley behind some saloon, beaten brutally with boots and fists, sometimes slashed with knives.

Striding fast now, in pursuit of the man who had tried to kill his oldest friend, had perhaps already done it, he knew he would have been dead for many years if it hadn't been for George Crook.

He owed the man his life; he owed him everything.

His friendship with the general began one morning when he woke up in the sweat stink of the guardhouse on an army post in Arizona. The night before there had been a savage brawl with three cavalary troopers in the sutler's store.

He had gone to the sutler's, already half drunk, and demanded a bottle of whiskey. The sutler said he couldn't have it, and the three troopers jumped him when he refused to leave. All three men were badly bloodied before somebody smashed a whiskey bottle over his head.

In the morning he had been dragged, with a throbbing skull, to face George Crook, who was just a brigadier then. "What do you think you're doing?" was Crook's first question. "You look like an intelligent man in spite of your appearance."

Sundance's clothes were soaked with blood and his

face was a mass of bruises. He smelled as badly as he looked.

Crook poured him a drink of water from a jug on his desk. Instead of being turned over to the sheriff in the nearby town, he was hired by Crook as a scout.

"You come to work for me or you go to jail," Crook said. "Take your pick. Just remember one thing—get drunk again while you're on the army payroll and you'll never see the light of day."

And that was how it began. In the beginning he was still bitter; gradually that began to pass. There was no more drinking because he knew Crook meant what he said. Crook always meant what he said.

He worked for Crook after the War, and later still as a scout and hunter on the high plains during the second campaign in the Northwest. They slowly became friends, and had remained friends ever since.

Over the years their paths had separated, but the powerful force of an old friendship was still there.

And now George Crook lay dying in a hospital, dying or dead.

Sundance clenched big fists and quickened his pace. This killer had to die; there could be no chance that the men in Washington who had hired him might bribe a jury and get him acquitted, something that was more than a possibility since their influence was everywhere.

Turning in Calle de los Negros from the south end, he started the long climb to the top of the hill where the old Mexican cemetery was, where Many Horses was buried. He passed the wagonyard and kept going. It was still early, not much more than ten o'clock, but most of the houses were without lights. A starved dog yapped at him, then ran away.

As he got close to the top of the hill he slowed up,

listening for sounds. The moon, full up now, hung over the city like a great orange ball of fire. The wind was blowing the other way, and though he stopped again to listen, he heard nothing.

He was moving silently in the shadow of the cemetery wall when he thought he heard a voice, but when he stopped to listen again there wasn't a sound, nothing but the soft push of the wind. He was close to the cemetery gate when he heard the voice again, a man talking quietly. It was faint, but it was there.

Soundless on moccasined feet, he went into the cemetery with the Colt cocked in his hand. Black clouds rolled across the moon, and for a moment it was difficult to see. He remained still until moonlight shone through again, and then he saw a man's figure standing in the center of the rows of neglected graves and broken headstones.

He got closer, moving an inch at a time; he took another careful step and then another. Suddenly, though Sundance made no sound, the man standing at Many Horses' grave whirled like a cat, his hand snaking down to his belt.

"Drop it," Sundance warned him in a cold, deadly voice. "Then put your hands behind your head."

The throwing knife clattered to the ground.

"Kick it away," Sundance ordered.

The man, standing there in the bright moonlight, hardly looked Indian at all. His black hair had been cut short and was parted at the side like a white man's. He wore a dark shirt and Levi pants. His creased hat had nothing Indian about it. When he spoke, after staring at Sundance for a moment, there was no Indian sound in his voice. It didn't even sound western. It was almost too soft; many born killers had voices like that.

"How did you know I'd be here?" he asked.

"A guess," Sundance said. "When you let out that yell in Cheyenne I knew for sure who you were."

"But you might have figured it out anyway."

"Maybe so. But once I knew, I guessed you'd come here one last time before you left town. You hated Crook because of what happened to Many Horses. You were hired for money, but you also did it for your father. You would have done it without the money."

"Is Crook dead?" Many Horses' son asked. "I hope he is. He should be. I never miss."

Sundance raised the Colt. "Crook is only wounded, but if you say that again I'll kill you."

"I'm not afraid to die. You'll kill me anyway."

"Not if you give me the information I need," Sundance lied. "Like who hired you. I want their names. I want the Indian Ring more than I want you. You're still going to jail, but you can make it easier on yourself. Better make up your mind. By the way, what do you call yourself now?"

"Gordon Gillespie, after the Scotsman who founded the school I attended in Pennsylvania. Ironic, don't you think?"

Sundance had no use for talk like that. "The names of the men who hired you!"

"They were just two men, nobody important I learned later. They work for the Indian Ring in Washington. Somebody decided it was too risky to hire an American killer, so these two men came to Mexico. After I was thrown out of the Mexican army for slapping a superior officer, some ex-Confederate, I worked with a political killer named Estrada. We traveled all over Mexico and South America. Estrada went into hiding after he was badly wounded by the bodyguards of a politician in

181

Tampico. They were looking for both of us, so we split up."

"The names of the two men."

"Morley and Zimmerman."

"Go on."

"I joined Captain Jack's circus in Vera Cruz. We went to Mexico City, then back to Vera Cruz. That was two month's ago. The circus was still in Vera Cruz when the two men from Washington were sent to me by Estrada. They had gone to him first, and he passed them along to me."

"You had the knives made in Vera Cruz?"

"I know how to use many weapons. Captain Jack wanted to add knife throwing. I know how to do that, so I ordered the knives."

"Why did you wait so long to try to kill Crook?"

"It was often on my mind over the years, but I was so far away. My hatred for Crook was cold hatred; it burned bright only when I thought of my father. When the opportunity came to kill Crook, and be paid well for it, I was glad. I would have come to Los Angeles even if the circus had remained in Mexico. When I joined the circus I had no idea that it had been hired to put on a show at the convention."

"Why did you use a knife? Why not a gun? And why at the convention?"

Sundance already knew the answer to the third question.

"I wanted to kill Crook in his moment of glory, and I wanted to do it in front of a crowd with all his bodyguards looking on. I couldn't hope to just kill him and get away, so I blew up the gas pipe with a cigar, a fuse, and a stick of dynamite."

182

"How did you know where Many Horses was? There was no way you could have known. I myself thought he had been dead for years."

"So did I. Then the second day after we arrived in Los Angeles I was in Cleary's Saloon with Captain Jack when I saw my father. It had been well over ten years since I saw him last and I hardly recognized him, the dirty hair, the filthy clothes. He was emptying spittoons, or trying to. Cleary threw him two bits and told him to get out and stop stinking up the place. I followed him out to the shanty where he lived like an animal. I was bitter at what he had become. I became angry when I tried to get him to leave with me, and he wouldn't. He said he wanted to die where he had lived. I said I was going to kill Crook because of what had happened. I said I would come back and force my father to leave."

"You came back and you killed him."

"What else could I do?"

"Sure, what else?"

"When I came back he said he had told you that somebody was planning to kill Crook. He said he hadn't given you my name, but was going to because it was the honorable thing to do."

Sundance shook his head in disbelief. "You killed your own father!" In a minute he would shoot the son of a bitch.

"It made no difference. He was as good as dead."

"How did you get this way?"

"It's easy. All you have to do is to be born a stinking, dog-eating Indian. Then they send you to school, you learn to read and write and you're still a red nigger when you graduate."

Sundance straightened up and Gillespie, who had once

183

borne the proud Cheyenne name of Running Cougar because of his swiftness as a boy, put out his left hand as though to plead for his life. Lithe as the big cat he was named after, Gillespie sprang to one side as Sundance triggered off a snap shot that knocked Gillespie's hat off his head. He fired again as Gillespie threw the knife that was concealed in the sheath at the back of his neck. Sundance's second shot tore through Gillespie's shirt, burning a crease across the muscle of his upper arm.

Sundance grunted as the knife, thrown with savage force, sliced along his ribcage. Because the knife had no guard, it cut through his shirt and fell to the ground behind him. By then Gillespie was coming at him in a zig-zag run with another knife in his hand. Sundance fired again as Gillespie leaped high into the air and struck him solidly in the chest with both feet. He crashed backward, his gunhand came down hard on a sharp rock, and the Colt went spinning away from him.

Turning his head quickly, he looked for the gun, but it had fallen into a tangle of weeds. There was no time to go after it as Gillespie jumped on top of him and tried to hold him firm with both thighs, stabbing at his heart. The third lunge broke the skin over his heart. Getting a stronger hold on Gillespie's wrist, he forced back the glittering blade and punched the other man in the mouth.

Gillespie fell back as Sundance pulled the throwing knife, Gillespie's own knife, from his belt and jumped to his feet. Now they faced each other, feet well apart and right foot slightly advanced, body and head held well back, knife pointing out and upward, thumbs against the side of the blade. The idea was to fence, to catch the enemy's strokes on the back of your own blade, fencing them outward.

Sundance knew a knife fighter when he saw one.

Gillespie wasn't going for his head. The torso from hips to breastbone was his main target; a sideways slash could disembowel a man with one deep stroke.

The moonlight glittered on their long-bladed knives as they sought to kill each other, fighting to maintain balance among the crumbling graves of the forgotten dead. A sudden downward chop tried to sever the tendons of Sundance's wrist, but it was a split-second too late, and all it did was draw a thin line of blood from the back of his thumb.

Sundance responded with an overhand thrust that drove Gillespie back. Every now and again, when hard pressed by Sundance's relentless follow-up, Gillespie raised his knife as if to throw it, but Sundance's bored in, swinging his blade from side to side, always shortening the distance. And every time Gillespie tried to set himself up for a throw, he changed his mind, because he knew that if he missed he was a dead man.

Again and again their blades clanged in the moon-drenched silence of the graveyard. They gave and regained ground, their feet sliding in the sand and gravel. Once Gillespie's feet skittered on a weed-covered rock; he fell and Sundance jumped after him, and almost pinned him to the ground with a straight-down-from-the-hand stabbing motion. Gillespie rolled out from under the blade just in time, and it buried itself in the loose sand. Still rolling while Sundance pulled the blade free, Gillespie got Sundance with a kick in the side of the head. Most of its force was spent because Gillespie had no time to get set; if he had been kicking from a firmly braced position, the fight would have ended right there. Even so, a white light flashed in Sundance's head that threatened to turn into darkness.

He shook his head back to alertness while Gillespie

sprang to his feet once more and assumed a fighting stance. As he came up off the ground, Gillespie's left hand scooped up a fistful of sand. He threw it where Sundance's face had been a moment before.

Since the fight had begun, no words had been spoken. None of the usual taunts or curses came from Gillespie. He fought silently and savagely. Either that was his style, or he knew no amount of dirty-mouth jibes would have any effect on his adversary. Trying for a down-and-sideways deep slash that would render Gillespie's knifehand useless, Sundance knew instinctively that this was the other man's style. Hating him almost as much as the men who had killed his father and rape-murdered his mother, Sundance felt the tug of reluctant admiration for the renegade Cheyenne's skill and courage. He admired him, held him in that strange regard that one killer holds another, and more than anything else in life he wanted to plunge the knife through his heart.

They battled back and forth silently, their knives meeting, their feet rustling in the sand, now and then a grunt of pain or satisfaction. Seldom in his dangerous life had Sundance met a man who could fight so well.

Sundance was one of those professional fighters who could think while he fought. That would be his English father's blood, for there was no one cooler in the midst of mortal danger than the Englishman, ruthless for all his good manners, or ruthless because of his quiet, good manners. The Cheyenne had loved his father because his taciturnity, his silence, was so like their own.

Gillespie didn't look so confident now, but he came at Sundance again with great ferocity. They were about evenly matched, and there wasn't that much difference in their ages. Gillespie was still fighting like a professional,

186

but Sundance could see that he was looking for an opportunity to make a quick finish of it. Sundance wasn't about to give him the chance.

The night was turning cool, but both men were sweating hard. The next time Gillespie attacked there was less style in the way he handled the knife. He started with a straight thrust, like a fencer handling a sword, then changed to a chop without warning. If the blow had landed, Sundance would have had the muscles of his right arm cut completely through. But it didn't land. He brought up his blade and let Gillespie's blade saw across the top of it. Steel cut into steel in spite of the fine Mexican tempering. Gillespie brought his full weight down on the knife. One blade sawed across the other as they struggled for supremacy. Then, little by little, Sundance forced Gillespie's knife upward. Jumping backward, Gillespie pulled his knife free and tried for a sideways slash at Sundance's belly. If it had been three or four inches closer Sundance would have been lying in the dirt, bleeding to death.

Gillespie tried to get out of the way; he had just about made it when Sundance, holding the knife far back on the haft, pushed through the other man's defense and slashed him across the face. He couldn't try for a deeper wound without risking a bad cut on the arm. Gillespie tried anyway, but his blade didn't touch flesh.

The wound on Gillespie's face wouldn't kill him unless he neglected it. Sundance wasn't about to let him live that long. Gillespie's face was expressionless in spite of the wound; blood ran down his face, soaking his shirt.

Sundance wanted to get it over with. All his hatred for this man had passed; now he just wanted to kill him, and have done with it. Gillespie seemed to know what was in

187

his enemy's mind, and he reacted at once with the fiercest attack so far, coming at Sundance in a flurry of blows that moved from his face to his crotch. He forced Sundance back a few paces, then he was stopped by the counterattack.

Now it was starting to really go against him for the first time. So far it had been give and take. Nothing could stop Sundance, neither Gillespie's great skill nor his ferocity. There could be only one end to it, and they both knew what it was. The fight had gone on for a long time; it came to a conclusion with startling abruptness. Giving a wild Cheyenne yell, the only human sound since the fight began, Gillespie rushed at Sundance, all caution gone now.

Moving quickly to one side, Sundance buried his knife in Gillespie's belly. He was already close to death, but this time Sundance found his gun and walked away.

Sheriff Rowland was sitting in the hallway of the hospital when Sundance got there. The sheriff jumped to his feet when he saw the blood on Sundance's shirt. "Good God, man! You're badly wounded."

Sundance shook his head. "How is the general?" The sheriff motioned Sundance to sit down; the doctor would be out in a minute.

"He thinks he has a very good chance, but it will be a long time before he'll be his old self. Here comes the doctor. You better ask him."

The doctor was in his sixties, thin and stooped, with a birdlike nose and a halo of white hair. "I'm Dr. Wallace," he said, shaking hands with Sundance. "You better let me take a look at that wound."

"It's mostly the other fellow's blood," Sundance said. "What about the general?"

"Be patient." The doctor pointed toward a door. "Go in there. I've done what I can for General Crook. I think he's going to live if the bleeding doesn't start again, if no fever develops."

"That's a lot of 'ifs,' Doctor."

"That's how it goes."

Sheriff Rowland had followed them into the dispensary; the doctor frowned at that, but the sheriff stood his ground.

"Did you get him, Sundance?"

"I got him. You'll find the body in the Mexican cemetery at the top of Calle de los Negros."

"Who was he? I talked to Captain Jack, and he didn't rightly know. He told Jack his name was Gordon Gillespie, from Pennsylvania, and though Jack never believed that, he didn't give a damn as long as he did his work. I guess he was pretty good with a knife."

Sundance said, "He was very good."

He explained the rest of it to the sheriff while the doctor washed out the wound in his side with alcohol and wrapped a bandage around his ribs.

Rowland wanted to ask more questions, but the doctor ordered him out. Finding an old faded shirt in a closet, the doctor told Sundance to put it on. "Wash your face in that sink," he said, pointing.

Splashing cold water in his face, Sundance said, "I want to see the general."

Dr. Marston hesitated, then nodded. "All right, but you get out when I tell you to."

"Will he be able to campaign for the Secretary's job?"

"Of course he won't be able to campaign. He'll be a

lucky man if he lives. It'll take months in an army hospital before he returns to duty—light duty, at that. The left lung was pierced and anything can develop from that. I'm going to recommend that he goes to the military hospital at Fort Huachuca, Arizona."

"Can I go in now? And where's Mrs. Crook?"

"I gave her some laudanum and she's sleeping in the next room. Go in now, but don't stay."

Three weeks later, still very pale, General Crook was able to leave the hospital. Sundance and Mrs. Crook rode with him in a carriage to the railroad depot. Dr. Marston had given strict orders that he was to remain in his Pullman berth for most of the trip south and west.

"And no cigar smoking," the doctor added. "You'll die if you do."

On the way to the depot, Sundance asked, "You sure you don't want me to come along, Three Stars? It wouldn't be a bother."

Lying back against a pillow, Crook said, "No need, Jim. You'll be having things to do, and Mary will look after me just fine."

Crook turned his head slightly. "We never did get to go hunting in the Sierras, did we?"

Sundance said no. "Time enough for that when you're well again. It doesn't have to be the Sierras. There's fine hunting all over the West."

"True. A man can always go hunting, but how often does he get the chance of being nominated for a Cabinet post? I hear they're planning to put up Sam Moorhead in my place. Sam isn't too bad, I suppose."

"You'd have been better. Maybe another chance will come."

"I hardly think so, Jim. I've been thinking that perhaps the army suits me better after all. All we can do is keep on fighting for what we believe in."

They reached the depot, and Sundance helped Crook inside to wait for the train.

Crook sat down slowly; more of doctor's orders. "While I was lying in bed for the past three weeks, I thought a lot about Many Horses' son. That boy could have been just about anything if he had been given a chance."

"He got a chance."

"No, Jim, I mean a real chance."

The locomotive bell was clanging in the distance; a blast of steam cut off the cries of small boys selling candy and dime novels.

"You're probably right," Sundance said, helping Crook to his feet.

Mrs. Crook shook hands with Sundance. "Thanks for everything, Jim," she said, and got on the train.

Sundance passed their bags up to the porter, who reached for Crook's arm. Turning with his hand on the rail, Crook said, "Let us know what you're doing, Jim. Don't stay away so long the next time."

"You'll be hearing from me," Sundance said as the train pulled away.

Then, with his pulse quickening at the thought of it, he hurried back to the wagonyard to saddle Eagle.

Soon they would be heading for open country, and tonight they would sleep under the stars.

BOOK TWO

PETER McCURTIN

DOUBLE-BARREL SUNDANCE

THE SAVAGE and GOLD STRIKE

GOLD STRIKE

Chapter One

Sundance was scouring the frypan with rough creek sand when he saw the gold. If he had turned away while he threw out the water he wouldn't have seen it at all. But there it was, just a few flecks in the bottom of the pan, dropping to the bottom as he swirled the water. It was a bright morning in early summer and the Nevada hills were bare in the sun. The creek ran down from the mountain and miles below it emptied into a small blue lake. Rimmed by rocks and spruce, the lake was clear and deep and birds made ripples on the mirrored surface.

Sundance scoured the frypan until it was shining clean and dug the rim into sand and gravel. After picking up the pebbles, he swirled the water in the pan, then tilted the pan and poured it out, and there it was again: gold! The brownish-yellow metal that men dreamed of, killed for. The stuff of murder and betrayal and despair. He emptied the pan and moved up along the creek and tried another panful. Gold glittered again, not in the bright way of the newspaper stories or in the tales of back room prospectors, but there it was. This was just a trace, but it was the heaviest he had seen for a long time. If he had been a white man he might have whooped at his good fortune, but Sundance merely went back to his campfire and drank another cup of coffee.

Eagle grazed along the edge of the creek, tearing at the lank yellow grass, stopping now and then to drink, then moving on. A squirrel ran up a tree and down the other side, ducking its head out to look at the tall, buckskinned man hunkered down by the fire. Sundance dug into his food bag and threw a handful of dried applies to the squirrel.

It was more than a trace. He knew it. If there was gold down here, there had to be more higher up. He looked up at the hills that flanked the creek. Up there, and maybe not so close to the creek. This was no Sutter's Mill and he didn't expect to find any nuggets. But there was gold up there waiting to be taken out. He wondered how they had missed it, for this part of Nevada was gold country. A day's ride from where he was lay Orono, second biggest gold camp in the territory, a tough mining town famous all over the West for the handful of men who had grown rich there.

He tossed another handful of apple slices to the squirrel. Another squirrel showed up and they started to fight. Maybe they had missed the gold here because they hadn't looked in the right place. Gold was everything they said it was: faithless, tricky, elusive as a good woman. You could pan miles of a creek or a shallow river and find nothing, not a speck of color. There were so many stories about gold; even a few could be believed. It was said that old Frank Finney, now a millionaire, was ready to give up prospecting when his ancient dog died. Old Frank dug a hole to bury the dog and found gold. Sure as hell, he had found it somewhere.

Panning the length of the creek wouldn't yield that much, Sundance knew. Working the creek wouldn't pay more than pretty good wages, and maybe not even that. There would have to be a mine, a sluice to be built, a lot of hard work shoveling and dumping. The loudmouths always talked about a vein of gold; how thick the vein was depended on who was telling the story. There were such veins, but he had only heard of them; gold you could pick up off the ground usually wasn't gold. Mostly, gold gathering took time and long months of work, even some money if you wanted to do it right.

It looked like he was going to be in Nevada for a while. There was too much gold to ignore, but that's what he would have done if it hadn't been for the battle he'd been fighting half his life. It took more than bullets and blood to fight for the Indians; some cases couldn't be won with a gun and had to be thrashed out in the courts. That lawyer in Washington was a good man but he couldn't fight the Indian Ring with promises. That took money, always more money, and he hired out his gun to get it. It was an uphill battle and the victories didn't come close to balancing the defeats. Other men spent their lives in the pursuit of money or power or fame. Sundance could have had all three, and more, but getting a square deal for the Indians was what he cared about more than anything else.

"That's all I got left, scrounger," Sundance said to the squirrel. He didn't want to work in any damn gold mine no matter how much he took out of it. It went against the grain to be stuck in any one place for too long. The long days of backbreaking work was the smallest part of it. As soon

9

as he figured where to start a shaft he would have to ride into Orono and register the claim. Then came all the buying of supplies and equipment: lumber, pick-axes, shovels, some dynamite. And as soon as he registered the new claim he could expect the hills to be flooded with prospectors ranging from runaway store clerks to grizzled old sourdoughs who had dug for the yellow metal all the way from Mexico to Australia. If he took the time to listen, they would burden him with offers of partnership backed up by everything but hard cash. It had been his experience that men who talked of fast, easy millions seldom had the price of a night's lodgings.

After he stowed his gear away, Sundance walked up along the creek. Past a solid rock shelf where the creek dropped a few feet, he tested another pan of sand and found nothing and didn't expect to. He climbed a slope that ended in a tall bluff above the creek. It went up fairly straight for about a hundred feet, broken in places and tangled with thorn brush. There had been a rock slide during the last few years and the exposed roots of dead trees stuck out of the side of the bluff.

When he reached the bluff he ran perished rock fragments through his fingers. This was where he would stake his claim; nothing would be lost if it didn't turn out as rich as it looked, as he hoped. He cut a green stick with the Bowie knife, split it partway from the top, then wrote his name and where the claim was on a sheet of paper. It had to have a name so, smiling, he wrote The Three Stars Mining Company. Smiling, he knew that General George Crook, his oldest friend, known to the Indians as "Three Stars," would not be flattered, not even pleased, but he did it anyway. He folded the paper and placed it in the cleft in the stick, then bound up the open end with a strip of rawhide. The ground was hard so he had to anchor the claim marker with a pile of stones.

It was time to go to town.

Orono was in a long, wide valley that ran for miles, and what once had been a river ran through the middle of it. Above the town it was dammed and a steam pumping station had been built for the mines. On both sides of the town the hills were bare and brown where they weren't gouged by the digging of men and machines. The town ran along on both sides of the river, with wooden or iron bridges here and there. The town had two streets or one very wide main street if you didn't consider the river as a divider. Both streets were lined with saloons, boardinghouses, stores, eating places. Some of the buildings were new raw-red brick with the cement showing white in the cracks. The bank was brick and so was the Wells Fargo depot, and out past the town, mostly made up of unpainted frame houses, was the straggle of a tent city. Smoke from the town mixed with the smoke and steam from the mines. The mines dominated the town and the valley; the great squat shapes of the mine buildings dwarfed everything else, even the denuded hills on which they were built.

Sundance didn't like anything about the town of Orono. It was the kind of place he had avoided all his life. An ordinary town was bad enough, with people crowded too close together, all the spite and viciousness, but Orono could hardly be called a town. Other than the gold in the hills surrounding it, it had no reason for being. And when the gold was gone, when the big steam crushers and separators had extracted the last ounce, then the mines would close, the machinery would be moved away, any worth the cost of moving, and the town would die. Iron would rust, wood would rot, and the sun and wind would do the rest.

The thunder of the crushers boomed all along the valley and far into the hills. Sundance heard it long before he caught sight of the town. Powered by steam, the great driving wheels clanked and banged day and night, filling the valley with noise. It would be the same winter or summer, and at night the treeless hills would glare with naphtha lights. It was still morning but the saloons and eating places were crowded with men from the mines, men from everywhere. Mechanical pianos jangled under the burden of noise that seemed trapped between the town and the dirty brown sky that lay over it. Men turned to stare at Sundance as he rode in, at the tall copper-skinned halfbreed with buckskins and yellow hair, shoulder long and stirring in the breeze. The men of the town were drab like the town itself, canvas-coated, wearing muddy miner's boots, sullenly aware that this stranger on the great stallion was like no other man they had seen before. They made way for him and they gaped, a few muttering their resentment of the man and his appearance.

The claims office was beside the bank, a sturdy one-story frame building with a wide porch and a sign over it. Men stood on the porch trading mining talk or arguing in loud voices. Talk stopped abruptly when Sundance climbed down and threw a hitch on the rail and went inside. Before he opened the door the men on the porch were already gathered around his horse, commenting on the saddle, the fact that there was no brand of ownership. Eagle whinnied and Sundance turned to set them straight.

"Don't get too close, men. That animal doesn't take to strangers. Leave him be, a favor."

One of the prospectors was mostly drunk and maybe he considered himself a wag. "What would he do if we didn't let him alone?" Looking into Sundance's hard blue eyes, he added, "Just asking is what I am."

"He be likely to kill somebody," Sundance said. "Be neighborly now. Leave him be."

In the claims office the air was rank with sweat and smoke, and there was one long room with a smaller one behind it. The floor was rough plank, dirty and boot scarred, and on the other side of a long counter two men in their shirtsleeves were yelling for order. One of them wore a green eyeshade to cut down on the glare of the hanging lamps. He was middle aged and fat and short, took himself and his job seriously, and was having trouble making himself heard because he had a high, thin voice.

"I told you and I told you," he piped irritably. "Just because you're in a hurry makes no matter to me. If somebody steals your claim before you get back, that's your business, mister. Every goddamned week you're in here with the same goddamned story, always in the same goddamned hurry. Now line up with the rest of them. Form a line there, you men. No business will be conducted in this office till you fellows form a line."

The man he had been yelling at was old, bent-backed, dressed in a dirty wool coat with patches all over it. The seams on his face were so deep they looked as if they had been done with a knife. His hands had no more shape than lumps of seasoned stove wood.

"Didn't I just tell you I'm sitting right on top of it this time," he bellowed. "If you wasn't such a fool you'd know my business here is mighty pressing. You want to beggar me afore I get started."

"You been a beggar all your life, don't go blaming me for it," the fat man said, winking over the top of the old sourdough's head.

Some of the others joined in, tipping the old man's hat over his eyes, tapping him on one shoulder, then on the other. A big bearded man with a belly like a bass drum elbowed the old prospector away from the counter and banged his fist on it. The old man would have fallen if Sundance hadn't caught him. One of the men reached out to snatch the old man's hat and his laugh died when Sundance caught him by the wrist and held it in midair until the man turned red in the face.

"You don't want his hat, you got a hat of your own," Sundance said. "Now, sir," he said to the fat man behind the counter. "I believe this man has business with you. Do him a favor, see to it."

The fat man sensed the force in Sundance and he retreated into bluster. "He'll have to wait his turn, whoever you are. Don't be telling me my job. Anyhow, no claim of his is worth a damn."

"Break the rules just this once," Sundance said. "He was at the counter, but he got pushed."

The bearded man turned quickly for all his size. "You want to start up with me? You saying I pushed this old rat? That's right, I did."

"That's right, you did, you tub of guts!" the sourdough said.

"I was asking you a question," the bearded man said. "You want to start up with me?"

14

Sundance knew the big man was expecting a punch in the belly. It would be like punching a water barrel. Instead, Sundance hit him in the side of the neck. The sound was like a man whacking a side of cold beef with a pick handle. It didn't take more than an instant. The big man's eyes glazed over and he collapsed against the counter, clawing at it to give him support. Then he slid to the floor and lay still.

"No real damage," Sundance said pleasantly to the claims clerk. "A few minutes and he'll be ready to beat up on some other old man."

"I ain't that old," the old sourdough said, banging on the counter. "Pay attention there, pen pusher. I'm here to register my claim."

Sundance waited behind the old man. Before he left, the old man said, "I ain't about to forget what you done for me, mister."

"Be obliged if you did," Sundance said.

A murmur of voice spread through the claims office when Sundance told the clerk the location he wanted to file on. Then somebody shushed the talkers and they gathered in close to hear the rest of it.

"What're you up to, mister?" the clerk asked, not liking anything about Sundance. "That whole country up there has been walked over. There's nothing up there, am I right, men?"

Sundance laid his hands on the counter and said patiently, "You mind not making this into a town meeting, friend. That's what I'm filing for, so why don't you write it down."

Slamming open a leather-bound claims book, the clerk said huffily, "Waste your time, you want to. No business of mine."

Writing in a crabby hand, the clerk looked up,

"You got the filing fee?"

"I got it," Sundance said. "Anything else I have to do besides hand you the money?"

"You got to work that claim, bad or good, that's what you have to do. Filing a claim's got nothing to do with homesteading. You got to work the claim or get the hell off it." The fat man's curiosity got the better of him. "What did you find up there, if you don't mind me asking."

"Gold," Sundance answered, taking his copy of the claim papers. "I found gold."

There was no point lying about it. A man wouldn't be filing if he hadn't found something. As he turned the claims office emptied out in front of him. Well, there it was, it was starting, and they were on their way. By tomorrow there would be prospectors thick as fleas along that creek.

It was all legal now. The law said he could start digging for gold any time he wanted. What the law didn't tell him was how to keep it, once he got it. When he opened the door, some of those who wanted to take it from him were already waiting.

Chapter Two

By the time Sundance got outside, news of the strike was racing through the town like a wind-driven fire. Horses and mules were heading out; men pulled handcarts loaded with everything they owned. Down by one of the saloons a man with a big wagon was selling rides to those without mounts. Sundance knew that when he got back, he would find the creek and the banks along it crawling with gold-crazed prospectors. It was all just luck, in the end. It took thousands of years for the gold to wash down from the high country. There was no big chunk of gold up there. It flaked away and drifted in the water like wet dust. In the winter when there was a fast-flowing current it moved fast. When it was summer and water was low, it stayed where it was, until the floods came again. The best places to look was where the water slowed or swirled and the gold flakes had a chance to drop to the bottom. That's where his claim was, on the deep side of a sandbar, where the main creek was joined by a smaller one.

Three men hadn't joined the rush, and Sundance got ready to set them straight. Two looked like men who had come up empty on too many rushes. It would be hard to mistake them for anything else. Sundance had seen them before, the men who decided to get smart, become businessmen instead of diggers, let the other man find the gold so they could talk him out of it. One was big and one was small, and he guessed they were uneasy partners. The big one was bearded and burly, dressed in a rusty black suit and greased black boots with mud on them. His partner, sandy eyebrowed and quick in his movements, looked like he couldn't wait to start talking.

Sundance brushed past them without turning. "I'm not interested in selling or going partners," he said. "And I don't want to hear about new methods or how to do it faster. Anything else you can think of?"

The big man laughed in his beard and wasn't a bit put off. "I guess you're wise to the ways of gold towns," he said in a Dutchy accent that might have

17

started in Germany or Pennsylvania. "You'd be a fool to be took in by every mucker that shows up with a get-rich scheme. Believe me, sir, it's nothing like that."

"That's the truth, Mr. Sundance," the small man cut in quickly, thinking himself a better bargainer than his partner. "All we ask is a few minutes of your time, a drink or two among friends, so to speak. It won't take but a minute, Mr. Sundance."

They knew his name. Everybody in town knew it by now, but there was no help for that. It was something he would have to get used to, hard though that might be. "No talk, no drink, no time. I'd be obliged if you'd stand out of my way so I can get to my horse."

The big man thought he was big enough to be bold. "You don't have to talk about tough about it. Businessmen talking business is all we are."

Sundance turned and regarded him with cold blue eyes. There was no point in making enemies, but men without manners had to be told. "Don't talk your business to me. Don't talk at all. Understood?"

Faced with the tall half breed's hard stare, the big man's nerve wavered and broke. "Come on, Regis," he said. "Some men just don't want to get rich."

As he was pulled away by the arm, the little man said, "Maybe we should get out there and give it one more try."

Sundance had been waiting for the third man to speak, and now he did. "I see you are amused by Regis and Gilford," he said in a mincing voice that went well with his gray broadcloth and white silk shirt. He held up an ink-stained hand; a printer, a newspaperman, something like that. "Before you jump all over me, Mr. Sundance, let me explain that I am Henry Weyman, owner and editor of the *Orono Star*. And I'm not here to sell you a thing."

Sundance nodded. As a rule, he didn't like newspapermen, and there was even less to like about this one. "Does that mean you're buying instead of selling? The same answer—no deal."

"You're very direct, Mr. Sundance," Weyman said. "I sell nothing but newspapers. Advertising, of course. Handbills. Tickets to raffles and to our glorious theater. As to buying, I don't buy news expect when it's very special. How is your friend General Crook, by the way?"

"He's fine," Sundance said. "I never talk about the General. You know who I am?"

Weyman walked along with Sundance without asking if he could. "Indeed, I do. Your exploits are known to me. Might I ask what you are doing in Nevada?"

"Digging for gold, Mr. Weyman. Nothing more. Like all the others."

Weyman pursed his womanish mouth in a smile. "Not like all the others, you found it, the gold. You're lucky to get off with just Regis and Gilford. There are many others, but they're on their way out to the creek."

"But you don't run, is that it?" Sundance decided not to tell the scribbler to go to hell. It was better to try to get along; he was going to be around Orono for a while. As little time as he could, he decided, but there would be trips into town when something broke, when something was needed. The first thing he would buy was the lumber for the sluice.

"I've never been tempted, odd as that may seem," Weyman said, offering Sundance a thin black cigar from a leather case. He used a silver tinderbox to light it. "I do what I do and like it well enough. I don't do too badly."

Sundance wondered how many newspapers it would take to pay for the editor's fine suit. Not enough. Weyman was doing well, but it wasn't from newspapers or tickets to the theater. "Looks like the small diggings around here are played out," he said.

"There are a few left but it doesn't mean anything," Weyman said. "A small digger can't make more than Chinaman's pay. Some men prefer that to working for Mr. Selby. You must have seen the name when you came in. No doubt you saw other names, but it's all Mr. Selby now. You might say, sir, that he owns this town. If you don't work for Mr. Jackson Selby, you work for yourself. That's the same as not working at all."

"A big man, is he?" Sundance said, putting more stride into his walk.

Weyman had to step lively to keep up with him. "Big as they come. A fine man is Mr. Selby, good New England stock. He's been described as hard but that's just good business. He's put gold mining on a businesslike level. Most small men sell out to him and are glad to get the money. Machinery is what makes the difference."

At the lumber company an overalled Swede said the foreman would be back in ten minutes. "You better vait, mister," he told Sundance. "Lumber vill be going fast, this new strike in the hills."

20

Wood dust was flying and Weyman used a handkerchief to brush off the shoulders of his suit. "You're causing a lot of commotion, Mr. Sundance. The saloonkeepers are going to hate you for emptying out their places. But they'll be back. I hope you won't be disheartened when I tell you there's very little gold up there."

"Maybe so," Sundance said, wishing the foreman would get back so he could get rid of this sneak. He was beginning to put a few ideas together about Weyman. Newspaper editors in mining towns were usually on the boss's payroll. They aired his views about politics and what a workingman would expect to earn, if he behaved himself. All the mining town, gold or silver or copper, had bootlickers like this one. They weren't so much reporters as spies, using their job to ferret out information for the man in the big house. Sundance hadn't seen any big house, but he didn't doubt that this Jackson Selby had one, and it wouldn't be close to any shantytown.

"You don't sound too enthusiastic about it," Weyman went on. "You're right, it won't be worth the effort. I don't know how much you know about gold. I don't dig for it but I know enough about it. There's some gold just about everywhere, even back East. But it's not the time and trouble to get it out. These small diggers and washers don't come close to earning the money they'd get in the Selby mine."

"Selby short of labor, is he?" Sundance asked. "Some men don't like to work for other men."

Weyman dismissed the thought that Jackson Selby was short of anything. "It's not like that,"

21

he said. "If these men want to go to work there are jobs waiting for them. Mr. Selby would like to see every man working, earning a decent living. Mr. Selby says this town has too many idlers, hangers-on. The day of the independent digger is a thing of the past. Mr. Selby would like to see more teamwork in this town, everybody working together for the common good."

Sundance saw a burly man with a foot measure coming out of a restaurant down the street. "You mean the men dig the gold and Selby collects it?"

Weyman laughed again. "That's how it works, Mr. Sundance. I don't know any other system that does. Each man to his station in life. Don't forget a man like Mr. Selby takes all the risks. Invests huge sums of money in equipment. Don't tell me you have sympathy for these men that call themselves unionists?"

"I mind my own business," Sundance said. "Maybe these unionists have a point. But like I said, it's got nothing to do with me."

Weyman wasn't smiling now. "In his town it's hard to sit on the fence. Mr. Selby has definite ideas about that. You have to be with him or against him. I thought I'd tell you."

Sundance had only been half listening to the editor, but now he spun around. He had been wasting his time trying to be civil. "You've been telling me more than that, Weyman. I think I know what you are and what you do. You say there's no room for independent diggers. That means I ought to sell out when Selby's man comes calling. Selby is too big to come himself. You said I didn't sound enthused about my claim. Wrong—I am now. I'm going to work it and to hell with any man that thinks otherwise."

22

The editor took a step backward in the face of Sundance's cold anger. He wasn't carrying a gun and so he wasn't afraid. "That sort of talk won't work here, Mr. Sundance. This isn't just a town—it's a barony. Mr. Selby is the baron and your fame as an adventurer will mean nothing to him. He doesn't just run the town, I want you to understand. My advice to you, the way you've been talking, is to sell out and keep on going. As for boot licking, as you call it, yes, I pass along information to Mr. Selby. That, Mr. Sundance, is simply good business."

Sundance waited for the foreman to get through yelling at a man who wanted to buy lumber on credit.

"Do me a favor, will you, Weyman?" Sundance said. "Go away and let me get on with what I'm doing."

Weyman made a mock bow. "Certainly, sir. The next man you talk to won't be so polite."

The Swede gestured toward Sundance and the foreman came over to see what he wanted. The first thing he said was, "It's going to cost you a lot more than you thought. Not my doing, mister. I just sell at the price I'm told."

Sundance knew it was useless to argue about the price. In a gold town a thing was worth what you could get for it. Felling trees and adzing planks wasn't worth the time it would take to do it. In the end, there might not be that much gold. All he wanted to do was to get in and out as fast as possible. Already the whole enterprise had put a sour taste in his mouth. Minding his own business wasn't going to keep trouble away. He knew it in his bones, and only the thought of what the gold could buy, at least a better chance for the Indians,

23

kept him from climbing on his horse and riding out of there. Weyman—everything—smelled of trouble to come.

The foreman took the money after he wrote everything down, and when he started complaining of how busy he was Sundance dropped a gold piece in his shirt pocket. No trusting soul, the foreman took the gold piece out and looked at it before he said he'd get the lumber loaded right away.

"I'll ride with it when it's ready to move," Sundance said.

"Don't have to, you don't want," the foreman said. "I'll send the Swede to ride shotgun to discourage borrowing along the way. You know what I'd do if I had the money."

Sundance said no.

"Go into the lumber business," the foreman said. "That's what you should do, mister. You got the money, I got the know-how to make it a going business."

"I already got too much business," Sundance said. "Load the wagons and I'll be along. You've been paid so don't get tempted. I wouldn't like it."

At the general store he bought bolts, nails, hammers and mallets, wire, sheets of tin, dynamite, picks and shovels. Everything he needed to get the gold out. Then he loaded up on supplies, flour, coffee, bacon, dried apples, a whole sack of canned goods. If he wanted to shoot fresh meat, he would have to go far afield to get away from the noise and bustle of the gold seekers—the argonauts —along the creek. They wouldn't all be along the creek. The claims there would go fast, so they'd move away from it, the late comers and the drunks who weren't awake yet. Those who were too late to get at the big creek would fan out along the tributary and when the ground there was taken they would try where there was no water. They might find gold even there. There were rules about gold digging but nature had a way of breaking them. In the end, gold was where you found it.

He bought four boxes of ammunition—the same shells could be used in the Colt .44 and the .44-40 Winchester. When he got back to the lumberyard they were still putting rough planks in the first wagon. He stowed his goods under the seat and the big Swede said he'd watch out for thieves.

"I'll break their heads, they try to steal you," the Swede said, lifting a long plank with two men on the other end of it.

Sundance went into the closest saloon and a fat man with an oiled curl across his forehead glared at him from behind the bar. The place was empty except for a drunk snoring with his head on a table. In the back painted girls in tights were standing around looking glum.

"You sell food here?" Sundance asked. "If you do—a steak and a pot of coffee." One of the girls came over and asked was he hungry for anything else. He gave her a dollar and she went away looking mad. The bartender brought the steak and coffee and went back behind the bar, still staring at this stranger who had killed his whiskey trade for the rest of the day, maybe the rest of the week. Once the diggers got started, they wouldn't give up that easily.

Suddenly the trouble Weyman had promised came in, a tall blacksuited man with a lean hard face and small pale eyes. This wasn't just the law come to ask questions of a stranger. Sundance knew that this man was trouble. How much trouble he would soon find out. He went on eating until the man was standing on the other side of the table. Then he looked up.

"You want something from me?" Sundance said, taking in the round silver badge pinned to the lapel of the man's coat. It said he was the chief of police, a city touch, and maybe that had been Jackson Selby's idea. It sounded a lot more businesslike than plain marshal.

The lanky man's voice was level, sort of dead, and listening to it, it was hard to tell where he was from. "Will Durkin is my name," he said. "You see the badge. That's what I do. Mind if I sit down?"

Sundance didn't mind, knowing that Durkin was just trying to put a legal face on what he did for the mine owner. The bartender brought another cup for the police chief, even poured for him. Durkin waved him away, as if he hadn't seen him.

"We run a nice town here," Durkin said, looking over the rim of his cup. "Not a thing goes on I don't know about. You weren't in the door of the assay office before somebody ran and told me."

"Good news travels fast," Sundance said. "My name is the one they gave you. Jim Sundance. That's my right name. You know where I made the strike so I don't know what else I can tell you."

"Oh, I don't know," Durkin said evenly. "Around here things aren't that simple. A man doesn't just ride in, say who he is, and think that's it. Let me see your claim papers. I'm asking as the chief of police."

Sundance said, "What's the chief of police got to do with gold claims?" It looked like Orono was getting more inhospitable all the time. He guessed he'd show the papers to Durkin.

Durkin said, "I'm a county supervisor as well. Now the two jobs are asking to see your claim papers. You want to see my county badge? It's not as pretty as the one on my coat. I like the police badge best."

This was Durkin's way of telling Sundance what he liked to do to men who got in his way. What he thought was his way—Jackson Selby's way. Durkin was a new name to Sundance, but he was cut from the same cloth as so many other gut-kicking lawmen. Durkin was the same and could be he was meaner and smarter. He looked like a man who had it all figured out. The badge gave him the means and Jackson Selby gave him the power to back it up.

Durkin put the county badge back in his vest pocket. Sundance slid the claim papers across the table. There wasn't much to read but Durkin took his time. Then he held onto the papers and looked up, feigning surprise.

"It says here you're a citizen of this country," he said. "Right here where it says if you're Irish or German or what. How can you be an American. You're Indian, am I wrong about that?"

Sundance found the strength to control his anger. Unlike the editor, this man was wearing a gun, something with a short barrel in a shoulder holster, and no doubt he was fast with it. If he killed him, there went the gold and maybe his life. It would be hard to shoot his way out of a company town, especially this one. None of it was worth it.

Sundance said, "Indians that served in the

Civil War, Union side, were made citizens if they wanted. I guess I'm American enough. The Indian Bureau has it in a book—you can use Western Union. If you want any more references, get hold of General George B. Crook, Military Department of the Missouri. That enough for you?"

"No need to take that tone. Maybe I'll send the telegraph. I hear they're slow to give answers. About Crook, he may command the Missouri. This is Nevada. Wouldn't matter if he commanded here. This has nothing to do with military business."

"Do I get my papers back?"

"Sure you do. Wouldn't be legal if you didn't. I get a bad feeling about you though. Why don't you drop that mine business and ride. I hear you got business all over."

"Abandon the claim?" Sundance said.

"You could do that," Durkin said. "Won't be worth anything, you'll see. Sell the thing and make a few dollars, is my advice. That's good advice. Wouldn't give it if it wasn't."

Sundance gave up on the steak and pushed the plate away. "You got somebody in mind to buy it."

"Nobody special," Durkin said. "It wouldn't be legal for a county supervisor to get mixed up in buying or selling. I wouldn't be surprised somebody didn't come right along and make you an offer. It'll be fair, you'll see. But you better take it, whatever it is. By that I mean you might not get another offer."

Durkin stood up so he could pull his gun fast if he had to. Sundance guessed he was pretty fast. Fast gunmen wore their guns all kinds of ways, belted high, belted low, cross draw, or under the arm like Durkin. The fast ones found a way that suited them best—that was how they killed.

"A parting word to you," Durkin said. "It's important that you listen good. We go by the law in this town. This is no crossroads cow town with a marshal and one or two deputies. Mister, I got ten hard men working for me. The law is me and my men—but mostly it's me. I see that nobody starts trouble. Trouble, I always say, is a man having a wrong slant on things. One man gets the idea he can stand against things as they are, no telling what's going to happen. Other men look to him, get wrong ideas too. I won't have that here. Be advised—get out!"

Durkin turned his back but Sundance knew he was watching in the long mirror behind the bar and his right arm was crooked high, ready to turn and fire. The bartender had moved well away, and so had the girls. The drunk mumbled in his sleep and a glass rolled off the table. Sundance stayed where he was still waiting for Durkin to wheel and fire. Most likely he would pull and drop to one knee. His arm got higher by the time he got to the door, but by then he could no longer see himself in the mirror. He pushed open the door and went out. Welcome to Orono, Sundance thought.

He filled his cup with coffee and waited for them to come. More than ever he wanted to be gone from this town. He didn't stay because later men would say that Will Durkin had made him run. What people said about him didn't matter a damn. And he wasn't even sure that it was stubbornness that kept him there. The claim was his and he was going to work it. It was as simple as that.

Four men came in.

Chapter Three

The claims buyer and his three assistants, Sundance thought, and they all had the look of men who had done this many times before. The three hard cases had been joking on their way in; now their smiles faded as they took the measure of the man they had to persuade, because this was no man who would sign on the dotted line, swallow a nervous drink, and be glad to be gone. But they were tough and there were three of them, and they thought that made a difference. Sundance had never seen any of them, but he had seen their kind in a hundred towns. Men who sold their fists and their guns; he didn't doubt that they were good at what they did for a living.

Seeing Sundance for the first time, the buyer pulled up short, as if he wanted to walk away. Then he put on a smile like a mask and came over to the table. This was his day for visitors, Sundance thought. The buyer wore clothes that were just a bit too big for him, and that must have been a personal quirk; the clothes were new, and if he had been thirty pounds heavier they would have fitted him to perfection. He was about forty-five, with sparse sandy hair and gold-wire spectacles polished to a shine.

He said in a Yankee voice, "My name is Travers. Mind if I sit down a minute?"

Sundance nodded, sick of talk but wanting to get

this over. His wagons would be loaded by now, and he wanted to get back to the claim while it was still day.

Travers put a big leather business wallet on the table and gave Sundance another insincere smile. The hard cases shifted their feet and waited. Behind the bar the barkeep was straining his ears and so were the whores in the back.

"I'll get to the point, Mr. Sundance," Travers said, his quick little eyes hoping for an easy transaction. "Which is, I would like to buy out your claim, I meaning the Selby Mining Company. We are prepared to make what we think is a generous offer, given the circumstances."

The three hardcases stood far apart, an old trick intended to make it hard for him to watch everything at once. So he watched them instead of the jittery claims buyer. The hard case in the middle was the one to kill first, if it came to killing. He hoped it wouldn't because he was holding a bad hand. It would be no trouble to kill one man, maybe even two, but to take on three was pushing his luck. Luck always had something to do with it, no matter how fast you were.

"What circumstances?" Sundance asked.

Travers had done this so often, like an actor too long in the same play, that he forgot that he was supposed to explain. Still, he looked surprised.

"Well, so far it's just a claim, Mr. Sundance. A handful of creek sand doesn't mean very much, does it. Of course not. You'll have to invest a lot of time and money before you even make a living, if that. At best it's unlikely that you'll make more than Chinaman's wages, as we say. Think of it, sir—long hard days of work for very little. We, the Selby Mining Company and myself, are prepared to relieve you of your burden." Travers unfastened the strap of his wallet and pushed a sheet of paper toward Sundance. "I'm a plain man and I don't believe in beating about the bush—what do you say to five hundred dollars for a quit claim?"

Travers wasn't a plain man and beating bushes was his life's work. Sundance had to restrain the urge to slap his drawling Yankee mouth. Not kill, just slap. He wasn't worth killing though it was plain that he had caused other, better men to be killed.

Sundance said, watching the hardcases, "If the claim is no good, why do you want it?"

Only the gunman in the center showed no impatience; the others looked like they wanted to get back to a whore or a card game. Sundance was sure now—the man in the middle would have to die first. In the back of the saloon the whores were giggling and the barkeep was wiping the same spot on the wood.

The buyer smiled ruefully, a kindly teacher forced to explain the obvious to a dull student. "Oh, I don't say there isn't gold where your claim is. You found it, some of it, so it's there. But your creek isn't Sutter's Mill, sir, and you won't just shovel it into a bucket. It's low-grade stuff, calls for machinery to get it out. You don't have machines, Mr. Sundance. I think you should take my offer."

It was too bad it had to come to this, Sundance thought. All he wanted to do was work his claim in peace, take what gold he could get, and then ride on. He felt the weariness that always came when some man crowded him in to a fight. One more time, he thought. It got to be monotonous.

"I don't want your money," he said getting up.

Travers was about to argue, to warn; the look of finality in Sundance's face stopped him. Gathering up his papers, he said, "This is most unfortunate—for you." He walked around the three gunmen as he went out.

"Now you get nothing," the middle hard case said quietly, no bluster, just stating what he thought was fact. "But you can still walk out, if you like. You ought to know who I am—Jesse Ehlers. I know who you are."

Sundance stood easy. "Then you know I won't back down."

Ehlers was just as relaxed, no hate in his eyes. He wasn't the kind that had to get worked up. Sundance had heard his name in a few places, saloon talk, no wild stories. The really fast gunmen didn't have to be flashy.

Ehlers had a grim sense of humor, and maybe he prided himself on always speaking the truth. All killers were strange, or they wouldn't be killers. "These two men aren't as good as I am," Ehlers stated. "But they're good. I don't 'specially want to kill you."

That would be Selby's orders, Sundance knew. To a businessman there was no profit in killing unless there was no other way. It gave a man a bad smell when too much killing was associated with his name.

"You'll have to," Sundance said. "You could drop this and let Travers come back with more papers."

Ehlers smiled again. "You mean you'd take a better offer?"

"I guess not."

"That's what I thought. There won't be one. Travers can't think higher than five hundred. Why

33

don't you walk out, ride out—go! There's no shame in that."

Sundance didn't tense, didn't relax, because either movement of the body would be a dead give-away that he was going to draw. Then a voice said, "There's a shotgun on you, boys. A ten-gauge shorty. Just twitch and you're stewmeat."

Only one voice in the world sounded like that, and it belonged to Tate Yarnell, one of the strangest, most dangerous men who ever lived. Sundance didn't take his eyes away from Ehlers.

"You're bluffing," Ehlers said calmly.

"Sure I am," Yarnell answered. "All you have to do is pull your gun. You there on the end, it's all right for you to take a look. Do it, Dolores, my love."

"Do it," Ehlers ordered, still in an eye-lock with Sundance.

Sundance didn't smile but he felt like it. He hadn't seen Tate for the best part of ten years, but on the face of it he hadn't changed. How could he still be alive, the way he was, the manner in which he courted death? To call a man Dolores, the shameful jail name for men who dropped their pants for other men, was the worst insult around. But that was Tate, always going for the jugular.

A flush spread up from the gunman's neck as he turned to look at the single-barreled English shot-gun resting on the flat piece of wood where the swinging doors came together. The oversized hammer was eared back and Yarnell's thin fore-finger was resting on the trigger. In the cartridge was a lethal load of double-O, and no man could survive that. If it struck you in the arm, you lost the arm; same for a leg. You died no matter how it hit you. No doctoring could save you; trying to bind the wound or staunch the flow of blood was a waste of time.

"He's got it, a single ten," the gunman said.

Yarnell's Southern voice was almost a whisper, yet it reached in and filled the big room with its menace. Sundance knew Yarnell wanted to kill them. Maybe they knew it too. At least Ehlers did because his hard eyes flickered for an instant, a sign that he was thinking past the moment.

"A single ten, only one bitty barrel," Yarnell said, and then came his strange, creaking laugh. Sundance knew that laugh; too often it was the last sound some men ever heard. "Where's your sense of sport, gentlemen? You in the middle, you've been making unpleasant sounds at my friend. How's about you make some in my direction. Be a pal—do it!"

Ehlers said, "I won't pull against a shotgun cocked and aimed."

Yarnell's deadly voice came back. "Suppose I set the hammer down?" The hammer went down with a tiny click. "There now, it's down. Come on now, be the men you think you are."

"We're going out," Ehlers said. "That's all we want to do now. Trip that thing and you'll never get out of this town."

"Hear that, Sundance," Yarnell said, laughing again. "The bad man is going to set the sheriff on me. Imagine a bad man doing that in Texas. Why all the other girls would laugh at him. I mean you, bad man in the middle. What's your name?"

Ehlers said his name.

"I think I'll call you Mary," Yarnell said. "So now again, what's your name . . . Mary? Say it . . . Mary."

Sundance knew that Ehlers would die first; he

was ready to turn and take the shotgun blast in the face. That was where he would get it. It would be shooting fish to kill the other two.

"Let them go, Tate," Sundance said. "A favor to an old friend—let them go."

Ehlers stared at Sundance and his face twitched once before he got himself under control. "I don't owe you a thing."

"Nobody said you did. Leave me be, that's all I ask. You won't do that, will you?"

"Like hell I will! This is just the beginning."

Tate Yarnell pushed the door open without moving the short ten-gauge, and there he stood, all six-two of him, skinny as a rail, black suited and awkward looking, his smile tilting the Mexican cigar in his mouth.

"Don't get your feet wet, girls," he told the gunmen as they walked out under the gaping eye of his gun. Before the double door stopped swinging he went back and looked outside. "They don't make 'em like they used to," he laughed. "The one called Ehlers wasn't too bad, the other two, weak sisters."

Sundance said, "You're a terrible man, Tate."

Yarnell smiled. "Vicious gossip, as the ladies say back in Savannah. What in blazes are you doing in this awful place?"

They shook hands, two men as different as they can could be, and yet there was a bond betwen them that went beyond explanation. In some ways Tate reminded Sundance of Doc Holliday, and they even looked alike, but there the resemblance ended. Holliday claimed to be a Southern aristocrat, but he was just a dentist, and from all reports, not a very good one. Tate Yarnell was the real McCoy, only son of the biggest shipowner in

Savannah, but he never waved the Stars and Bars or mourned the old life that was gone with the wind. Fact was, the Yarnells hadn't lost anything by the war; if anything, they had grown richer by running goods from England through the Yankee blockade. A bullet through the lung had sent Tate West to die in the desert at the end of the war. Dry desert air was his only hope, the doctor said, and not much of that. Tate got ready to die, accepted the fact that he was a dead man, and then his bad lungs doublecrossed him and got well. Another man would have whooped, but Tate felt cheated. Somehow, in his crazy way, he felt he was living on time that didn't belong to him. Nothing could ever frighten him again.

Sundance allowed himself two drinks to celebrate their reunion. Two drinks, his limit. He had his own brand of craziness, and it came with too much whiskey. They had a lot to talk about, this time and that; the night in Abilene they killed all five of the Brady gang.

Tate didn't have to stop with two drinks; liquor had little effect on him. For a killer he had merry eyes, dark and bright, humorous when they weren't killing cold. He started to laugh as he looked at Sundance with a sort of wonder.

"That last I heard of you you were dead in Mexico," he said. "Just a flesh wound in the heart," Sundance said, smiling at his old friend. "That's my story and it isn't true. How come you're still alive?"

"God doesn't like me. Odd thing, the closest brush I had all these years was when a farmer snuck up on me with a pitchfork while I was tending to his wife. Now I couldn't shoot a farmer, could I? I was still trying to talk him out of using

37

that pronger on me when he did."

Sundance said with a straight face, "Is it true that you're as fearless in bed as out of it?"

"More so," Tate said. "It must be my refined manner. I got a very big manner."

Women were another side to Tate's wildness; it seemed that he brought out the wildness in them. Tate didn't chase them too hard; they lay down for him like corn stalks after a strong wind. Women got him into deep trouble, but he never complained.

"You'd do better with the ladies than I do," Tate said. "Only you got this strange notion of one woman at a time. Which doesn't bring us back to where I came in. That business before, what was that all about?"

Sundance told him.

"I should have killed Ehlers," Tate decided when Sundance finished. "That was a mistake. You said don't kill him so I didn't. If I'd known you planned to stay on. Yessir, a mistake. He's not going to let it go. I guess he can't, it's his job. What the hell! Let him come and bring his friends. We'll do them like we did the Bradys."

Sundance told the bartender to get fresh coffee. "I don't want to start a war, Tate. I'd like to work my claim if they let me."

"You really mean to do that? There's a lot more money to be made at the card tables. Forget the god-damned claim. We'll get a good game going and get rich. What have you got against cards?"

"Not a thing. I like a game but I get sick of it. As of now I'm in the gold mining business and that's where I mean to stay." He leaned back and studied the lanky gambler. "You wouldn't be looking for work, by any chance?"

Tate smiled and looked over his shoulder. "I thought you were talking to somebody behind me. Seeing as you're not, by no chance am I looking for work. When was the last time you heard of me working at anything besides cards?"

The bartender brought the coffee and went away. "Never did I hear of such a thing," Sundance said. "Seems to me you must have worked hard enough to tunnel out of that Yankee prison in Illinois."

Tate's face clouded for an instant. The Union prison at Rock Island wasn't Andersonville; it was close enough. The guards there were mostly French-Canadian lumbermen from northern New England, as rough as they looked, and more Southerners died there than in a fair sized battle.

"I did all the digging I ever want to do to get out of there." Tate displayed his slender hands palms up. "See how pretty they are now. Not so when I moled my way out and under the Rock. Besides, I don't know the first thing about gold digging. You're stuck, is that it?"

"I figured to hire a man to help. By now Selby or his police chief will have the word out on me. No man that's worth a damn will come to work for me. Too dangerous."

"That's different," Tate said, helping himself to whiskey. "If that's how it is, I'll do it, be glad to. Lord, won't we have a time."

"I just want you to dig, Tate. Help build a sluice, then dig. We'll stay away from Selby if he stays away from us."

"Maybe he'll be sensible," Tate said. "No sensible man likes to get killed. You think he'll be sensible."

Sundance said no. "You don't have to get mixed

up in this if you don't want to."

Tate paused with the glass halfway to his mouth.
"Don't try to play me like a piano, halfbreed.
You're looking at a genuine war hero." Tate
grinned and bolted the whiskey. "I'll do my best
for you, is all I can say."

Warmed by the whiskey and the reunion with a
good friend, Tate grew enthusiastic about the
claim. "Who knows, we may dig up a fortune."

"You don't dig it up, Yarnell. You dig up the
dirt the gold is in, then you dump it in the sluice
and wash it out. When we hit rock and shale we
render it down with sledges and then wash it. First,
though, we'll work on the creek. That's sand."

"Thanks for the geology lesson," Tate said,
frowning a little. "What do you think they'll try
first?"

Sundance had been thinking about Selby and
Tate knew it. It was too much to hope that Selby
would write off the claim as something he couldn't
have. From the looks of his subordinates, his go-
betweens and gunmen, Selby was the kind of man
who always got what he wanted, no matter what
the price in blood and human suffering. It would
make sense for Jackson Selby to be like that. If one
man could stand up to him, there was no telling
where it would end. Powerful men were all alike;
ranchers, mine operators, railroad tycoons, they
bulled their way through any opposition, and
because they were rich, the law didn't do a thing.
And here Selby was the law.

"It depends on how badly he wants the claim,"
Sundance said. "Be sure of one thing, he won't
give up. Could be he'll dig up some old law nobody
ever heard of. A lot of that in Arizona. That's how
they drove out old Albert Steuben after he struck it

rich in the Pima Mountains. Something about a Spanish land grant."

"That wouldn't be so bad."

"Bad enough if he sends killers with the look of legality. My guess is he'll try that first, and when that doesn't work he'll take off the gloves. We can expect sniping, damage done at night, people turned against us. It will get worse every day we stay. You still want to do it?"

"I said I did. You want me to sign apprenticeship papers?"

Tate had a way of overstating everything; he admitted it, explaining that everything Southern was too lush. "All I want you to sign is the partnership papers," Sundance said. "We go fifty-fifty in this. Maybe it's fifty-fifty of nothing. You got something to write on?"

Tate took an envelope from his coat pocket and unfolded a letter, green ink on pink paper. He spread it on the table and told the barkeep to fetch pen and ink. "This was a letter from a lady I know —knew—down in Denver. I know she'd be pleased to have it used for something like that. You suppose that's legal?"

"Legal enough," Sundance said. He dated the letter of agreement and wrote out the rest of it. There wasn't much to write: the location of the claim and the claim registration number. They were to share equally in the mine and its contents, and if one of them died the other became sole owner.

"If I get killed first, who do you want to leave the mine to?" Sundance asked. "I'm leaving what I don't have yet to the lawyer who works for the Indians in Washington."

"Put me down for the same thing," Tate said.

41

"My father has more money than the Mint."

Sundance called the barkeep over and gave him a dollar for signing as a witness. Then the Swede from the lumberyard came in and asked what was the hold-up.

"We'll be right with you, my good fellow," Tate said, grinning.

"Gude man, my osshole!" the surly Swede said, and everyone laughed even the bartender, though he was itching to run and tell Travers the good news.

Tate had a fine gray gelding and sat his saddle like the Confederate irregular he had been nearly twenty years before. He had the love of horses that is the mark of the true Southern gentlemen. They were watched as they left, riding behind the two heavily loaded wagons. Durkin was one of the men who watched, tall and silent on the boardwalk in front of the city jail. The newspaper editor, recovered now from his fit of temper, came strolling along and doffed his hat as he went by, trying to figure out who Tate was. Travers, the claim buyer, wasn't around. Sundance looked at the blanket of smoke that hung over Orono. It would be good to get back to the clean air of the hills, to set up camp while there was light, and when that was done, to build a fire and cook a big supper. It sounded peaceful but it wasn't going to be, not for long. One of them would have to guard their supplies and their sluice at all times. Selby was the biggest enemy they had to face; he was one of many. Robbers, desperate men, would come and try to make off with everything they owned, and would kill to get it. But that was in the future, and

Sundance never worried about things that hadn't happened yet. You didn't rush into danger or try to bring it to you, not usually; what you had to do was to be ready to face it. And, sure as sundown, it would come.

They wound they way out of town and into the hills. Already the road showed signs of all the men and animals that had passed over it. A mile from town they came on a man who had left late for the rush and they told him he could ride in a wagon. He was a middle aged man who would have been better off behind the counter of a general store, and when they got to talking, he said he had quit his job in an express office and he knew his wife back in town would be mad as hell at him. Before they had gone another two miles, he thanked them for the ride and said he had changed his mind and was going back to face the music.

"That's the smartest man in this country," Tate said. He called the clerk back, gave him a handful of silver, told him to buy something nice for the missus.

They traveled on in silence as the sun began to go west in the sky. Far away the hills were red in the light of the sun. Beyond the hills the mountains stuck up, bare and jagged and cold, winter snow still on the high peaks. All day it had been hot, but now there was an edge to the wind blowing down from the peaks. Sundance climbed up in the second wagon and got a wool lined canvas coat from the supply crate. Tate shook himself into it and buttoned it tight and didn't look half so elegant as in his gambler's black suit.

"I could be in a nice warm poker game," he said.

Sundance knew that Tate wasn't complaining.

Behind the fancy clothes and easy manner, this man was hard as tempered steel, a thin, dangerous blade of a man, loyal beyond the bounds of reason. Once he gave his word he would back a friend to the death. He had all the faults, all the virtues of the Southern gentleman. Pride, honor, friendship came before everything; at the same time, he could be touchy, given to black moods, even unapproachable. Above all he was a man in a land where every man wanted to be a man, and so few were.

"You ever thought you'd find yourself digging for gold?" Tate asked.

Sundance said no. "I'd rather be in a warm poker game. How about you?"

"Oh, I don't know. Wouldn't it be something if we struck it rich—big, big rich—and it got in the papers and my great wonderful father heard about it."

Sundance wondered why Tate hated his father, but didn't know, had never asked. There were so many things he didn't know about Tate. No matter, he was here and he was a friend. By now Tate's name would be in Jackson Selby's head, or in a paper on his desk, and even if Selby didn't know who Tate was, Durkin would. Both of them had killed their share of men, but Tate's count was higher than his. But he didn't think Tate's fearsome reputation as a mankiller would be enough to make Selby back off. The mine operator wouldn't know how. It was as simple as that, and as dangerous. Together, they would have to fight for the right to live and to work.

"Will you look at all those people," Tate said when they caught first sight of the creek.

Chapter Four

As far as the eye could see, the creek was alive with men, and their shouting echoed far into the hills. Watching from a distancce, Sundance was reminded of a huge ant hill that had been overturned, the disturbed insects running back and forth in a frantic attempt to restore order. But there was no community spirit here, nothing but a frenzied mindless search for the yellow metal. Here it was every man for himself; the meek would never inherit this earth unless they had the money to hire other, tougher men to hold onto it. Before it was over there would be shooting and stabbing and maybe a miner's court would be convened to hang or to exile the culprit. And some would find gold, and some would find nothing.

Looking down from the long ridge that overlooked the valley, Tate Yarnell's mouth curled in scorn. "Yonder you see Man at his finest," he said. "They make rodents look good."

Sundance knew that Tate was sometimes given to philosophizing, something he never did himself. Wondering what made men do the things they did was a waste of time. "Speak for yourself, Professor," he said. "I'm going down there and look for gold."

"Me too," Tate said.

In the dying light the creek no longer ran clear as the wild panning continued. Men looked up at the sky and cursed the dying of the light; here and there along the creek oil soaked torches began to burn bright orange in the gathering darkness. Some had come prepared with lanterns and they burned too, and a man with neither torch nor lantern was starting a fire. Woodsmoke drifted and hung over dark creek water, as Sundance and Tate rode down to the creek with the wagons, then along the edge of the creek until the wagons began the uphill climb to the claim.

Sundance had been telling Tate about the claim, the way it was positioned just above the meeting of the creek and the tributary, and now when they topped the long ridge and went over it and down, they could see where they were going to work. Above the claim was a deep but narrow gorge where the water flowed fast, a place that didn't look good for gold and would be hard to work. That meant they would have no close neighbors to the north; past the gorge the creek flattened out again, but the diggers there wouldn't cause them any bother unless they tried very hard. In the gorge the rush of water drowned all other sounds, and Sundance knew they would have to keep a careful watch, day and night, to keep men from creeping up on them unawares.

Sundance told the Swede where to halt the wagons, and they all pitched in to unload the lumber before the light was gone. Men still working along the creek raised their heads as the lumber crashed together and the pile grew higher. A misting rain blew down from the mountains before they got everything out of the wagons.

When he was done the Swede went down to the creek to drink but turned away in disgust when he saw something floating in the water. "Pigs!" he said, and nodded thanks when Sundance told him to help himself to a canteen.

"You batter boil efferyting gude," he said, stoppering the canteen and giving it back. "You catch cholera you don't. The sickness was here when this town first start, it could come back. Dirty pigs! It don't have to."

Cholera was one more thing they would have to be ready for; the threat of cholera hung over gold camps like fog on swamp. Sundance knew the Swede was right: cholera didn't have to break out, it often did. Human dung in the water was what did it; as long as men dropped their pants along the creek there was a good chance of disease.

Sundance smiled at the Scandinavian's contempt for his fellow man, and he guessed it had been well earned. He liked the look of the big gangling man, the way he took pride in what he did. "You get tired of that lumberyard maybe I could use you here," he said.

The Swede waved his hand downstream toward the diggers hunched over in the uncertain light. "I don't root in the dirt," he growled. "The lumberyard is fine by me, clean wood, clean work."

"There's a man that'll never get rich," Tate said after the Swede was gone. "You think he will?"

Rain drummed on store new canvas as they set up the tent and pegged it down. "Not very rich," Sundance said. "What we have to do is set a figure. Unless this claim is different there will come a time when the gold take starts to dwindle. That's when we have to decide to quit or go on."

Tate broke a tent peg and had to get another one from the box. "How much would you say?"

"Too soon to tell. The end of a full day's work will give us some idea."

Sundance went up to the bluff and came back with an armload of deadwood and hunched his back against the rain while he blew life into a small fire. Flame licked up and he built it carefully and though rain hissed on the fire it burned bright after a while. It was full dark now and below them, on both sides of the creek, campfires were orange blobs, and the digging went on even as the rain came down harder. In the rain was the lingering cold of mountain winter, and in the wind that drove it, and they shivered in their wet clothes while they waited for coffee to boil.

Sundance said first thing in the morning he was going to gather all the firewood he could find before it was all gone. As soon as the gold fever dwindled to a dull ache, and men were faced with the reality of daily living, they would strip the hills of every stick of wood they could find. Wood meant cooked food and warmth and light to work late by. But in the end it was more than all that— men liked a fire. A man in a hole in the ground had a home if he had a fire.

Sundance hooked the coffee pot off the fire with a stick and set it in a bed of embers while he greased a skillet and laid two steaks in it. Using the hem of his coat to keep from burning his fingers, Tate poured coffee for both of them, and then sat with a steaming cup in the door of the tent. The rain softened and became drizzle again, and for all that lay ahead of them, there was a feeling of contentment in the wet woodsmoke and the smell of frying meat.

The rain stopped after they ate and they dried out talking in front of the fire, and it got quiet along the creek except for some man yelling far away. So far there had been no shooting; that would come when the whiskey sellers started hawking their wares for twice or three times what they were worth, and while the fever lasted men would pay, because no man trusted his neighbor and if he had a partner he watched him too. The whores wouldn't come until the men had done a few days' work; after that a dollar girl would sell for ten, and with men lined up outside the tents, the pimps would get richer than anyone.

Sundance took the first watch and Tate crawled into a tent and fell asleep with his boots on. The tent was too short for him and his feet stuck out through the flap. Using no more wood than he had to, Sundance built up the fire, shoveling dirt around it to keep it from spreading and burning too fast. He hung his slicker over his shoulders and sat with his back to the stack of boards. In the gorge the water rushed through with a soft thunder, frothing white where it ran over rocks, and down from where he was the fires burned low and some went out, and the noise died away altogether.

At midnight, Tate got up without being called, and the oiled shotgun glistened in his hands as he sat down to watch through the rest of the night.

Before first light, Sundance shaped two young trees and nailed them together to make a skid to haul back the firewood, and while he was gone Tate fried bacon and made coffee. There were clouds but the wind was blowing the sky clear.

"We better get started on the sluice," Sundance said.

"I knew there was a catch to this," Tate said.

Sundance knew that Tate didn't know the first

49

thing about gold mining, so he explained that they weren't going to build anything elaborate. "If we didn't have the money to buy lumber we'd have to do it the old Mexican way. It works well enough but a lot slower and you lose gold. You saw the men two claims down from us. That's what they were using, what they call a Mexican ground sluice."

"Looked more like a ditch to me." ·

"Same thing. Sand and gravel is washed through by water. Riffle bars, cobbles if that's all you have, trap the gold on the way. Gold is heavier than the other stuff, so it drops to the bottom."

Tate grinned. "All you do is collect it."

Sundance grinned back. "If there's any to collect. It takes a lot of shoveling and washing to come up with an ounce of dust. In California there was more gold so they think it has to be the same everywhere. Nothing as rich as California has turned up that I know about."

"Then there won't be any nuggets. I saw a nugget one time, big as a hen egg."

Sundance said, "Could be we'll find one. Don't count on it. Mostly we'll just work and eat and work some more. My guess, it will pay pretty good."

So they began to build a wooden sluice twenty feet long and eighteen inches deep and reinforced at intervals with top and bottom cleats. Spaced apart inside at the bottom were V-shaped riffle bars; the sluice itself was slightly tapered so that other sections could be added on as they dug deeper into the bluff. Leading into the sluice was a wooden flume to carry the water, and the top of the flume was a screened hopper to reject gravel and small rocks. Built beside the start of the flume was a small deck to work on, and both flume and sluice had to be cleared constantly as sand and gravel piled up. The hardest work would be getting the rough pay dirt to the flume, and the shoveling in.

Tate lapsed into silence as he worked, stopping only to ask Sundance about something, and long before they had finished the sluice he was carpentering like an old hand. The sluice took shape and it had to be sturdy because of all the punishment it would take in the weeks to come. Ton after ton of sand and dirt would pass through it, and that had to be disposed of too. Nothing but work, and then more work, until they would lie down at night too tired to talk. It was always like that at first, Sundance knew, and it would take days for their muscles to grow accustomed to the lift and heave of the work.

They worked straight through from dawn until noon, and the day held fine with only a bright sun shower at midmorning. By four o'clock they had finished sluice and flume and walked along the length of the two structures, putting their weight on places that might be weak, and finding nothing wrong, they stood back and admired what they had done. At least, Tate did, saying that he hadn't worked so hard since the time he tunneled out of the Yankee prison. "Hey, partner," he said. "We ought to put up a sign. Sundance and Yarnell."

Sundance smiled. "I already named it after George Crook, but you do what you like. I'm going to make coffee."

They got some work done before it got dark, hauling up creek sand and dumping it in at the top of the sluice. It had rained and at that time of year the creek should have been running full. But it

51

wasn't. Since they got there the day before, it had dropped about a foot, and would drop even more, as the diggers upstream held back water to work their claims.

The sluice was built close to the creek but still close enough to the bluff so they wouldn't have to haul the pay dirt too far when the stream ran out of dust. Sundance still was counting on the bluff as the main source of gold. There was a central pillar of rock running up through the bluff at a slant, but the rest of it wouldn't be too hard to work. They would have to sink a tunnel in the side of the bluff, then shore it well against cave-ins; the ore and dirt would have to be brought out by wheelbarrow or in canvas buckets. A regular mine, even a small one, would use rails and iron trolleys to move the ore. What they had would do well enough, Sundance decided.

But first they started with the creek sand, and when a load was dumped and ready, they had to haul up water. So far the creek level hadn't dropped too far. In the sluice the flow of water had to be even and steady; if the water went through too fast, it would take too much dust with it. They could have used another man on a sluice of this size, because there were so many things that had to be done at the same time. Sundance spilled the water in and Tate worked the long handle of the hopper, the framed screen that held back the rough gravel and rocks, and let the sand and dirt through to be washed. When too much rough gravel accumulated in the hopper, it had to be emptied. The sand and dirt was washed down into the sluice by the action of the water, the lighter sand passing over the riffle bars, the gold dust falling to the bottom.

After the first load had been washed, they went down to the sluice and Sundance traced his finger along the side of one of the riffle bars. Then he held it up so Tate could see the trace of gold glittering on the tip of his finger, dull yellow and wet, hardly impressive—but there it was!

"So that's what it looks like," Tate said. "I thought gold came all ready in little cloth pokes to be wagered in poker games."

"That's how we're going to get it out," Sundance said. "What we just did, you do over and over. This may not look like much to you, but it's a good yield for one load. If we're lucky, it will add up."

They worked on another load. "Funny," Tate said. "I've been betting against gold, dust and nuggets, half my life. Never thought about it much—just gold. I guess it makes a difference when you harvest it yourself."

Tate told about the foxy bartender in an Arizona gold camp. "You know that box they weight the dust in. Sure. Got the balance and the little tray the gold falls in so they can blow away anything that isn't dust. This man I'm telling about had a breath like a bull. You'd think he was blowing suds off his beer, that hard he blew. Plenty complained but all they got out of him was if you don't like it here go somewhere else. Well, one saloon was as crooked as the other, so what could they do. People called this bartender Greasy Jack because his hair was still with the stuff. I used to watch the son of a bitch handling the gold mighty careless and running his fingers through his hair all the time he was doing it. I'm stupid. It took me half a day to catch on what he was doing. That night I followed him to his cabin and found him washing the dust out of his hair. Had a fine-tooth comb by the basin in case he missed any of it.''

Sundance reached into the hopper to grab a rock. "What did you do?"

"Gave him a baldy haircut, right down to the scalp," Tate said. "Then I went around town and gave the gold away, most of it. No way to know who'd been cheated by this greasy man, so I gave it to the neediest. Of course the saloon got it all back, but this time they had to trade whiskey for it."

"Start working that hopper, Robin Hood," Sundance said, and by the time five more loads had been washed it was dark.

They had decided to work only in daylight. Without carbon lights that turned night into day, you missed too much gold. Besides, the day was long enough as it was. But the most important reason was Selby and his gunmen; a man standing in front of light made too easy a target, and it would be a mighty poor rifleman who couldn't hit a mark like that. And it might not just be Selby's men; by gold camp standards they were rich—lumber, supplies, tools, guns, a tent—and just waiting to be robbed by men with enough nerve. All over the West they said miners' courts dispensed better justice than the regulation law. There was some truth in that, though it varied from place to place, and in one California camp the miners had to lynch the members of their own court, to get a fair shake.

That night, Tate took the early watch, and when Sundance came to relieve him at midnight, he found him rubbing the barrel of his English single-barrel with an oiled rag. Fires glowed down in the valley, but the only sound was water rushing through the gorge, and even that wasn't as loud as it had been.

"Quiet as an empty grave," Tate said, stretching his long legs, giving the shotgun one final rub. "Except for the work and wet, your lousy cooking and sleeping in my clothes, I don't mind it so much up here. I'm almost ready to bet friend Selby has forgotten all about us. An important man like that, to him we're just a pair of muckers."

Sundance stood the Winchester against what was left of the lumber, enough to make any repairs needed. "How much you want to bet?"

Tate laughed softly as he headed for the tent. "I was just talking," he said. "I never bet against a sure thing."

Sundance prepared to wait the long hours until morning. Tate was right. It was a sure thing that Selby wouldn't let it pass. What he had to do, to be ready for Selby, was to take a look at the other diggings, in the morning. No one had approached them, even called a hello, and they had been there for two full days. If some of the other diggings proved to be rich, it would take away some of the attention they expected to get from Selby. This wasn't naturally gold-rich country; the gold was there but it didn't come easy. If the other diggings looked even fair, Selby would send his persuaders to buy them out. The most land a man could claim was two hundred feet, and that meant a lot of claims up and down the river; there was a good chance that some claims wouldn't show more than the faintest trace of gold, and even now experienced diggers would be ready to pull out. In just a few days the population of the valley would dwindle; the exodus would swell as disappointment set in. By the end of the week, Selby's persuaders and disappointment would empty out two thirds of the valley. Some men would hang on, unwilling to believe that they hadn't struck it rich; had all their dreams in plain sight. Those who did find gold would sell out for the most they could get; if not, they would have to face Selby. Sundance knew the law, such as it was, wouldn't be much help. The side of right was the side with the most money; good intentions usually got an honest man killed.

Sundance listened to the creek and waited for morning. Overhead, the blue-black cushion of the sky was stuck with bright stars. During the night he added wood to the fire so there would be good hot coals to cook on in the morning. A chunk of wood crackled like a small-bore pistol and the crick-click of the shotgun hammer came right on top of it. If it had been a man instead of a chunk of wood he would have been dead an instant later.

Tate squatted in the door of the tent with the outsized hammer eared back. There would be no need to aim with that thing. "You make more noise than a buffalo," he said, easing down the hammer.

"Go back to sleep," Sundance said. "Next time I'll try to get quieter wood."

"Anything for a quiet life," Tate said, dropping the tent flap. In a moment Sundance heard him breathing heavily, already asleep, his fingers resting on the stock of the gun. Tate used to say that women got nervous sleeping with a man and a shotgun. Sundance smiled. He could see where it might.

Tate was right about life being quiet. If Selby's men came in the night, they wouldn't make a sound.

Chapter Five

Sundance knew that Tate was beginning to feel at home when he unwrapped his long-barreled twelve-gauge Fox double-barrel while breakfast was on the fire. It was in a guncase of wool-lined leather, and when Tate was on the move he wrapped everything in a waterproof cover and tied it tight with rawhide thongs. It was a beautiful gun, slim and well balanced; the beauty of its design and manufacture made it seem lighter than it was. Tate had two other shotguns, a four-gauge and a ten, but the Fox was his favorite.

While Sundance was turning the bacon, after dropping egg shells in the coffee to improve the taste, Tate broke the gun and sighted through the barrel for signs of rust. There wouldn't be any, for Tate was as fussy about his shotguns as Sundance was careful with his own weapons. The sun edged up weak and runny as gruel, but then it firmed up and gathered strength. Sundance forked the slab bacon off the skillet and put it on a tin plate to stay hot while he fried up a second batch.

Tate cleaned the Fox though it didn't need cleaning, and when he finished, he pushed in two cartridges and snapped it shut. The stock and barrel came together with a solid sound; a shotgun that didn't make that sound was no good.

"I see them," Sundance said. "Is that what the early shoot is all about?" Two men were walking toward the ridge then ran up to the claim. They weren't Selby's men, or they wouldn't be on foot. Maybe they were Selby men—Selby had men all over.

"I was going to do it anyway," Tate said, hefting the shotgun, sighting along the barrel. "An early shoot sharpens the eye for the rest of the day." Tate didn't snoot off the gun. "What do you figure they want?"

"Maybe nothing. Neighbors coming to bid us good morning." The skillet wasn't sitting right on the fire and Sundance raked the coals under it. The bacon spattered grease.

"You think that's what it is?" Tate sighted at nothing.

"Not likely," Sundance said. "You want me to throw for you?" It was as good a time as any to show the other diggers what they could do with their guns. Nobody had seen it yet. Anything that happened here would get back to Selby.

"Too bad you didn't make biscuits, we could use them," Tate said. "Corn dodgers will do."

"A bad waste of food," Sundance said, getting up to get the bag of hard-baked dough balls. "You sure you don't need glasses after all these years of squinting at cards?"

"I'll manage," Tate said. "Come on now, they're getting closer." Tate had eyes like a hawk.

Sundance called a throw and then he threw, the dodger sailing up high and at a fair range. Tate was so good that he didn't need to hold the shotgun clapped to his shoulder, the usual way to shoot on the wing. He followed the flight of the corn dodger and broke it easily. He made it look so simple but there were so many things to be considered. The target wouldn't be where it was when the shooter aimed. It keeps falling and the shooter has to place the charge of shot where the target will be in a second. And the speed of the shot was nothing like that of a rifle—it had to get there. Not so oddly, many a good rifleman didn't do well shooting a shotgun on the wing—velocity made the difference.

"You don't have to give me odds," Tate said, knowing that Sundance hadn't. "This time throw it out far."

"Eighty feet ought to hold you," Sundance said, getting ready to throw. The two strangers hadn't come all the way up the slope; now they stood watching.

Sundance threw and Tate broke the target without an effort. He broke the shotgun and pushed in fresh cartridges. The second echo took a time to roll away in the morning silence of the hills. "Two together this time," Tate said. "One right after the other, fast as you can make it. How are our two friends doing?"

"I think they're impressed—go!" The second target left his hand a split second after the other. He threw for eighty feet and overshot by a good eight or ten feet. The two dodgers went up and fell at different speeds. Tate fire, broke one, fired again, broke the other.

Grinning, Tate thrust the shotgun at Sundance and picked up the sack of dodger. "You do it now."

The crump-crump sound of the shotgun rolled in the hills. Sundance didn't miss once. It was funny how any kind of shooting came back to you.

"Like riding a bicycle," Tate said, breaking the

gun to clean it.

The men were coming up the hill. "You ever ride a bicycle?" Sundance asked. The clothes they wore said the men were diggers like all the others.

"They didn't have bicycles when I was young," Tate said. "Damn you, Sundance—what did you do to that bacon! It's all burnt."

The second batch of bacon was nothing but a few slabs of blackened meat. "Next time don't ask me to throw targets when I'm cooking breakfast." He took the smoking skillet off the fire and portioned out equal shares of the bacon on the plate. One of the men called for permission to come into camp.

One was a short thick man with a square beard and a new canvas coat and miner's boots. He had a black crew jersey under the coat and a yellow scarf wound twice around his neck. Looking at him, Sundance was reminded of the stump of a tree, but his bright blue eyes said he had more brains than a treet. The man with him was about the same age, late thirties or forty, and wore a scarred leather Montana coat and soft black knee boots. A long Remington .45 stuck out of the thick man's cavalry holster, and the flap of the holster had been cut off, the lighter color of the cut showing dark against the rest of it.

The other man spoke first when they were closer than shouting distance. He jerked his thumb to one side. "His name is P.J. Grimes, I'm William Rance —that was some shooting a minute ago."

When the names were out of the way, Tate said, "I got a four-gauge and a ten-gauge too."

"That's some family of shotguns you have," Grimes said. "You hardly ever see a four-gauge. What do you use it for?" They both nodded

60

thanks when Sundance told them to sit down and share the coffee. He had to get new cups from the food box before he could pour for them.

Tate said, "I use all my guns to do the same thing—keeping the peace."

"Does that mean you're a lawman?" Rance wasn't as bright as Grimes, or was new to the gold camps, or he would never have asked such a question. Grimes, sipping coffee, grunted his annoyance.

"I speak of my personal peace, sir," Tate said.

"Just thought we'd shag along up here and say how-do," Grimes said.

Tate looked at Sundance. "There was bacon but it got ruined. How's it going down where you are?" That was a very general question, more a casual remark than a question.

Grimes turned and pointed far down to where the creek made a bend. "That short S there, that's where we are. The current's slow where the creek turns. Not a bad trace there, what we got thus far."

Sundance knew the S was a good place; at any turn of a river or creek, usually there was a swirl to the water. Sand was held in the same place, turning in the swirl of the water, while what gold there was dropped to the bottom.

"Not a bad place," Rance said. "But didn't we have a time getting there before the others."

"How'd you manage that?" Tate asked.

"Lit out with nothing but two pans and two shovels," Grimes said. "We just ran like the hammers of hell when we heard where you was. Didn't carry a thing but pans and shovels. That way we got our claim marker in the ground before some of them left town. Same night I went back to town and was ready when the claims office opened in the morning."

"That you did," Rance agreed. "Only you had to pay triple the true cost of the supplies."

Grimes didn't look pleased at having his judgment questioned in front of strangers. "You can't have it both ways, William. The claim has to come first." Then to Sundance, "How are things with you?"

"Got a good trace, the first we washed," Sundance said. "That was creek dirt and it will stay rich for a while. I got down to bedrock, the fifth load I took out."

Grimes said, "We hit bedrock faster than that. We're down lower so we did. What did you get, you don't mind me asking."

"About fifteen dollars for a full say," Sundance said. "The claim is two hundred feet like all the others. Figure fifteen dollars for, say ten feet, and you have as much as we're going to get in the creek."

Rance took a fistful of coarse brown sugar from his coat pocket and dropped it in his coffee. "Got a sweet tooth. Ain't it funny though how everything changes. Back in Illinois a man making fifteen dollars a day would count himself rich. Fifteen hell! He'd be doing well at five. What was you making before you came out here from Ohio? You did mention Ohio, P.J."

"What was I making?" Grimes said. "Nothing, that's what I was making. Same as you or you wouldn't be here. You're a farmer, ain't you."

Rance didn't miss the way Sundance looked at the sun. Time was money, especially in a gold camp. "Don't mean to keep you from your work," Rance said. "We'd like to talk to you a minute."

"Here let me say it," Grimes said, refusing any more coffee. "You two have the look of men that don't need any help from nobody. Word is out how you stood up to Selby's thugs. Maybe you can do that and get away with it."

"We'll get away with anything we try," Tate said, informing rather than taking offense.

Sundance cut in with, "You're expecting trouble and you want us to join up with you."

Grimes waved Rance into silence. "That's why we're here. Not to beg or borrow or dig for information. I figure Selby's men will be here sometime today. Not this early. What I'm saying is, Selby isn't just one man. Hell! I don't hardly know if there is a Selby. I guess there must be, signs all over the place saying he owns everything. But he's not like a man you can face up to. There's I don't know how many men between him and you. My point, Mr. Sundance, he's got the power to run off any man—even you."

"You've talked to some of the others. That's a risky thing to do, Mr. Grimes."

Grimes shrugged his heavy shoulders, a gesture of resignation. "Starving to death is a worse risk. It's starve or go to work in his goddamned mines. Mines hell! They're just like the cotton factories back East. You work dawn to dusk or you work all night. Same thing—you never see the sun."

"What about the other diggers?" Sundance asked. More or less, he knew what the answer would be.

"They're just diggers like us," Grimes said. "From all over. Name a trade and a man down there has done it. Farmers, run-off apprentices, old soldiers. But we're all diggers now. Like any bunch, some scared, some not so scared.''

Rance said, "They're looking to you, Mr. Sundance.''

Grimes glowered at his partner. "That's what I was about to say. If you stand in with us we'll stand against Selby. Not enough of us, a number of us. You think they won't come after you when they're done with us? No offense, all that fancy shooting won't do much good when they decide to run you off. They've got too many men.''

Sundance said, "We don't plan to stay here that long. All we want to do is take what we can get. Selby can have what's left.''

Grimes put his cap on the ground and stood up. So did Rance. "Then you won't side with us,'' Grimes said. "They'll be here soon.''

"Least you might do is think about it,'' Rance said irritably.

"Don't press the man,'' Grimes said, turning away.

Tate looked at Sundance and shrugged. "I don't want to get into it,'' Sundance said at last. "When you dig too close to a man like Selby you have to be prepared for trouble. A hard fact, but still a fact. If Selby makes trouble for us we'll do the same for him. I don't know any other way to say it.''

Rance wanted to get in a last shot. "You'd help us quick enough if we was Indians. We heard a few things about you, how a man has to be red instead of white to get a kind word from you. There's such a thing as the human race, Mr. Sundance.''

Grimes pulled him away, apologizing as he did it. "William's just mad and new to the life,'' he said. "I can see some sense in what you say. Thanks for the coffee—we'll make out some way.''

Sundance began to throw the cooking things together. "Let's get some work done. All that talk. I'd be obliged if you didn't talk at all for a while."

Sundance looked at the two men going away from the bottom of the hill. After he finished at the fire, he went to the sluice, and from there he could see the water in the creek. It had dropped by a few inches, all the more reason to get on with the work, to keep out of other people's business. What Rance had said still rankled a little. It wasn't true that he made distinctions between men. Rich or poor, white or red or black made no difference to him, but a man had only so many years to live, and he couldn't fight all the world's battles. No man would ever see the end of injustice; he had narrowed his concern to the Indians, and that was more than enough.

They had been working in silence for almost an hour when Tate said, "Riders heading down toward the creek."

Sundance had seen them. "Could be anyone."

Tate worked the long handle of the hopper. "Those two diggers were right. Selby won't stop with them."

"That's not what you're thinking about."

"You're right. Selby doesn't bother me, not that way. I don't like it when those men can't do their work in peace."

Sundance helped Tate to lift the hopper from its position. They turned it over and banged out small stones that had stuck in the screen. "Since when did you start taking up for gold diggers? A few days ago they made rodents look good."

Tate said, "I like to take down the high and mighty. It's a fault I have."

"It's got you into plenty of trouble." Sundance didn't know what Tate had been doing lately; in the old days he was always sticking up for people he thought were being pushed around. Tate was a puzzle. On the face of it, he seemed to care for nothing, not even his life, especially his life, yet his anger broke through his indifference when he saw something that had to be set straight. Some of it made no sense, not if you went past the moment. Tate would kill a man who beat a woman and never consider that the man he killed might have children somewhere depending on him. It was like the story about the crooked gold-weighing bartender. One out of two bartenders was a crook, so how many bartenders did that make.

"If we go down there we'll be starting something we have to finish," Sundance said. "We could wait and let trouble come to us."

Tate fitted his end of the hopper back at the top of the sluice. "We could do that."

It looked as if the four riders were heading straight for the S shape in the creek. Sundance wished he had never had seen this place. "If we get into this we'll have to stay in. The gold won't come as fast."

Tate let go the handle of the hopper. "You decide. I'm just the hired man."

"Get mounted," Sundance said, and as he made the decision he felt good about it. The moment they interfered with Selby's buyers, there would be no turning back. It was one thing to get tough about holding onto their own claim—even a man like Selby could understand that—but now they were shouldering their way into something that was strictly none of their business. No wary truce was possibly now, and he still felt good about it.

"Anything beats working," Tate said, breaking the single-barrel to check the loads. "Don't fret it, partner, I won't start any trouble till you do it first."

Sundance touched his heels to Eagle's flanks and the big stallion shot forward like a bolt. He was in the lead for a minute or two until Tate's horse closed the gap between them. Wind hit their faces and Tate's wide-brimmed gambler's hat was turned up in front like a cavalryman's, and then they cleared the end of the slope and were down on the flat, galloping past startled diggers who looked from their work open-mouthed or cursing. They reined in just before Travers and his hardcases reached the bend in the creek.

Grimes nodded and Sundance said, "You don't have to sell if you don't want to."

"We don't want to," Rance said, taking an old five-shot revolver from his pants pocket and sticking it in the waistband of his pants.

Travers, a poor horseman, jolted in the saddle as he rode up close, trailed by Ehlers and the two gunmen. One of the gunmen carried a sawed-off shotgun, but not just any sawed, and Sundance had seen few like it in his life. It wasn't quite a foot long and the barrel had been cut off behind the front end of the stock, and the stock itself had been cut off behind the pistol grip. The barrel was so short that the hard-paper ends of the cartridges stuck out of the muzzle. It was good for nothing but killing at close range, and for that there was nothing better. Everything got killed except the man behind it, because with nothing to contain the shot, it spread at the same instant it was fired. A man with a ten-gauge like that stood behind a wall of lead.

Travers mopped his face though a chill wind blew along the creek. He ran a handkerchief around the inside of his too-large collar and put it away. Tate smiled at the hardcase with the queer looking shotgun. Ehlers, with a score to settle, watched Sundance.

"Something I can do you for?" Grimes said to Travers.

Instead of answering, Travers spoke to Sundance. "We don't want any trouble with you."

Sundance nodded. "Don't make any."

"This is a business matter," Travers said. "I'd be obliged if you'd let us talk in private."

"No need for that," Grimes said. "The claim is not for sale, if that's what you came about."

Travers didn't like to talk business from the back of a horse, but he stayed there because he didn't know how it was going to go. His fidgety face took on an aggrieved look, as if he couldn't see why people wanted to change the old rules. The old rules had paid him well—so why did this halfbreed and this gambler have to turn up.

Tate nudged his horse away from Sundance, calculating how far the buckshot would fan out if the gunman fired the stubby gun. The man with the one-handed shotgun looked sideways at Ehlers, who continued to stare at Sundance.

The stubby gun didn't mean anything to Rance, and maybe he didn't even know what it was, because nothing like it had ever been seen on a farm. "You can just turn around and ride out," he told Travers.

Travers was about to answer when Ehlers rode his horse alongside and told him to get out of the way. "Save your breath, they came here loaded for trouble. You want to join in I'll give you a gun. Move over or go on back. Talking's done with."

"Listen . . ." Travers licked his lips and turned

pale.

"Scat!" Ehlers said. "You two diggers do the same. You ought to have more sense than listen to these two."

Grimes stood like the tree stump he looked like. "There's no law we have to—well, you have no right."

"Might is right," Ehlers said with a faint smile. Sundance knew the gunman would go through with it. There was no shame in backing down in the saloon—his gun was in his holster and there was a cocked shotgun pointed at his back—but this time was different. Ehlers was a professional gun, with all that was bad and good about the murderous breed. Sundance knew the quiet gunman was a proud man, accepting himself for what he was, a paid killer with his own twisted code of honor. If a gunman backed down too often he found work hard to get; self respect flew away and usually he got killed by a younger man who wanted to get his own career started.

"I backed down for you. You want to do the same for me?" Ehlers smiled again. "You could. My friend there knows how to use that thing."

"I got one too," Tate said, bringing up the English single-barrel.

"Not like that one. You only got one barrel and his two will do more damage than four of yours. Go to it or get out!"

That was supposed to make them think that Ehlers would wait for them to make the play. Ehlers was saying something else, but the shotgun man's finger was closing on the trigger as he spoke. Sundance drew and fired and the stubby gun exploded in the man's hands. The bullet exploded the first cartridge, splitting the gun, ripping the gunman's hands to bits. The second cartridge exploded and blew off half his left hand. Tate's shotgun blasted the second gunman out of the saddle as Sundance swung his own gun on Ehlers. Ehlers horse jerked back with the explosion of the short gun and Ehlers missed the two quick shots he got off at Sundance. If the horse hadn't moved Sundance would have died. Both shots were aimed at his heart. Sundance fired three times and put all three in Ehlers' chest. The horse ran into the creek and the body fell off and streaks of blood appeared in the water. Knocked off his horse by the explosion of the short gun, the last gunman rolled on the ground trying to hold his ruined hand together. Rance pulled his old five-shooter and emptied it into him. Travers was galloping away from the creek holding on to the saddlehorn.

Grimes gave Rance a shove that nearly knocked him down. "There was no need to do that. He couldn't have shot anybody."

Pleased with himself, Rance proceeded to reload his old pistol. "A sheep as a lamb if Selby catches us. Ain't that right, Mr. Yarnell?"

Tate smiled at the farmer's sudden outburst of ferocity. "You speak the truth, Mr. Rance. We're in as deep as we can go." Tate got down and picked up the dead man's short gun and turned it over with professional interest. "It's an interesting idea. You ever see anything like it, Sundance?"

"Twice, both times in a city. In New York they call that a 'room cleaner.' Heard of a man that pushed one of those through a window and killed all five men in a poker game."

Tate threw away the shattered metal and wood. "Can't hardly call that a gun. You have a lot of confidence in yourself, my friend, trying for a shot like that. They'd have to pick us up in a basket if you'd missed."

Grimes, still shaken by the three sudden deaths, was trying to explain it away by quoting the law, what he thought was the law. "It wasn't murder. They forced their way in here and wouldn't leave. Against a gun like that, what else could you do. It was self defense."

Still keyed up by his murder of the wounded man, Rance walked around in a sort of strut that got on Sundance's nerves. Tate, the peculiar bastard, was enjoying the skinny farmer's moment of glory.

"Self defense my cornhole!" Rance said. "It was a straight man to man shootout. They asked for it and they got it, am I right, Mr. Yarnell"

"You were like a tiger, Mr. Rance," Tate said, sticking the single-barrel through his belt.

Rance looked at the dead men, but kept away from them. "I was just a little too fast for him. Sneak guns, that's what you have to watch for. I'll bet you . . ."

Grimes told him to button his goddamned mouth. "What's going to happen?" he asked Sundance. "How will it go with the law?"

Sundance had been thinking about the law. Durkin was chief of police in nowhere but Orono and—legally—he had no jurisdiction over what happened out in the hills. There would be a county sheriff, but the law was spread thin in this wild country and killings were common; how much interest the sheriff took was probably up to Selby.

"We're not going to take the bodies into Orono, if that's what you mean," Sundance said. "Best we can do is plant them and let the sheriff dig them up if he comes around. About the law in general, I know as much about that as you do. You still want to stick?''

Grimes stared at the dirty water, sluggish in the creek. "I never thought it would get this far. I didn't think they would face up to men like you."

"You don't sound as determined as you were," Tate said coldly. "What you're trying to say is you tried to use us as a bluff. It got called and you don't want to pay up. Don't try to be too smart, my friend. You'll hurt your head."

Grimes grew sullen, knowing that Tate was right. Selby's wrath loomed larger than his determination to hang onto his claim. His hairy face took on the look of a man who had placed a big bet he couldn't cover, and pretty soon he would have to pay up.

"I'll stick," he said.

A few diggers drifted by to gape at the dead men; most worked away, as if it hadn't happened, wanting no share in the blame when Selby called a reckoning. Sundance and Tate made them uneasy; two men beyond their understanding, men who walked tall where they crawled. They were jealous as the weak are of the strong. Not all, of course, Sundance knew; there would be quiet, dependable men among the others. There would be spies, men who would do it for money, others merely to bask in the warmth of the big man's power. For the moment, the spies didn't matter; later they would have to be flushed out and done away with.

"Call a meeting of the men for tonight," he told Grimes.

Chapter Six

Sundance and Tate worked on through the rest of the morning, keeping the noon break short to make up for lost time, and for hours the yield from the creek sand wasn't too bad, and it wasn't until late afternoon that they started to come up with nothing but sand and gravel.

Sundance finished clearing the end of the sluice with a shovel. "It's happening faster than I thought," he said.

"There's still a light dusting," Tate said, checking the row of riffle bars.

"Not worth it when you figure the labor. Maybe the whole creek isn't played out. Our two hundred feet is. Time we got started on the bluff. This is where the real work begins."

Tate was rubbing the blisters on his hands with bacon grease; the fat and grease cured the hands like cowhide. "You mean what we've been doing wasn't work?" After the second day, Tate had traded his soiled black suit for a canvas coat and pants, and his ruffled shirt, torn and dirty, made a strange contrast with the miner's clothes. Their weapons leaned against the legs of the sluice.

"You just hope there isn't too much sledge work," Sundance said. "That's the real back breaker."

They carried picks and shovels up to the bluff

and the late afternoon sun was hot on their backs. During the day, they had seen men and horses and mules pulling out, heading back toward Orono, and upstream beyond the gorge other diggers were calling it quits—the level of the creek had been rising for hours. Tomorrow, more miners would go, and so on in the days ahead until only the lucky ones or the diehards were left.

Sundance went back down to get a crowbar, a massive bar of steel weighing fifty pounds, with a tapered point; and if the picks ran into rock, the bar would serve as a drill to make holes for a dynamite charge.

Tate threw away the bacon rind and scooped up a handful of sand so he could get a grip on the pick handle. The side of the bluff was faced with loose sand and shale left there by the old slide, and the bare roots of trees hung out of it, dying for lack of water. The camp squirrel, as Tate called it, had followed them to the bluff and ran up the side of it, twittering at the top. Sundance dug his hand in his pocket and found a slice of dried apple among the rifle cartridges. The squirrel followed it when he threw it.

"That son of a bitch is smarter than we are," Tate said, hefting the pick.

Timing their swings they dug into the side of the bluff, bringing down a shower of dry sand with the first few blows, and then they shoveled the dirt into the canvas buckets they had lined up behind them. When they were finished loading they carried the buckets, one at a time, down to the sluice and dumped them. Next water had to be hauled up and spilled after the dirt had been worked through the hopper. Tate spilled more water while Sundance moved down along the sluice pushing the dirt along with a piece of board. Slowly, as more and more water was spilled, the dirt was washed to the end of the sluice. The dirt from the bluff took more work, more water, than the easy-to-handle creek sand.

"Well look at that now!" Tate said, holding up his fingertip which was coated with coarse dust, heavier than anything they had taken from the creek. "I didn't even try hard to get that much." Tate picked up the smooth leather dust bag and rubbed his finger inside the neck and closed it again.

In spite of himself, Sundance felt something of Tate's excitement as he looked at the second pinch of gold from the sluice. Money or gold meant little to him outside the Indian cause, but maybe Tate was right—it was different when you found it yourself. There was, he thought, more excitement in the finding than the spending. No wonder men had been fascinated by gold at all times and in all ages. Gold would wear away but couldn't be destroyed; powerful acids had no effect on it—nothing changed it.

"I think this changes everything," Sundance said. "Selby won't walk away from this."

"That good?"

"Better than most. Could be this bluff is rich in gold, and that's it."

They walked along the sluice collected the gold flakes from the bars, and there was so much that it could be taken up a pinch at a time and dropped into the bag. Load after load was taken from the bluff; they worked until dusk and the yield remained good. Now, in spite of the rule they had established, they wanted to work on after dark.

"Better not," Sundance said. "Soon as they eat their suppers those diggers will be here. We better talk over a few things before they get here."

Supper for them was pork and beans, a lot of pork and beans, boiled black coffee, two big cans of peaches. Darkness brought a chill and they sat close to the fire, Tate with a cigar, Sundance with another cup of coffee. The firelight threw their shadows on the side of the tent. Down below the fires of the diggers were fewer and smaller.

"It's time we set a figure," Sundance said. "I'm ready to settle for ten thousand. Unless the gold yield gets bigger as we go in—not likely—that's enough for me."

Tate regarded the long ash of his cigar, a habit he had picked up from deadpanning it in poker games. Then he seemed to remember that he didn't have to be foxy with Sundance. "If another man told me that I'd figure he wanted me to leave so he could sneak back in."

"You don't have to leave when I do," Sundance said. "If there's gold left, you're welcome to it."

"Then you could get more than ten thousand?"

"By the look of the place, maybe twice that."

"Then why?"

"Two reasons. I have things to do far from here. The second reason—how do you feel about taking on some men?"

Tate didn't show any surprise. "You mean partners?"

"No, men working for shares," Sundance said. "I'm guessing there isn't much gold except right here. Selby will be coming at us and we could use men to dig and shoot. I wasn't thinking of men who just want to dig."

Tate knocked the end off his cigar; he did that in poker games when he was ready to make a move. "Grimes and Rance? I don't know that you could count too much on Rance. I like the little bugger—wasn't it a caution how he did for that shotgun man!—but he's a bundle of nerves. Grimes is cautious but he's all right.''

"I meant more men than Grimes and Rance."

"How many more?"

"I'd say two but you got to agree on it. If you want to go it as we are, then say so."

Tate stretched his long legs and massaged the muscles in his thighs. "Call me a partner if you like. Fact is, I'm hired help, like I said. Do what you think right. Come to think of it, with extra men I could get to sleep through one whole night once in a while."

"It will mean more than that," Sundance said. "Together, five or six of us won't be such a bad little army. If some of them are new I'll have to lay it out for them. They'll make money, good money, but they'll have to risk their lives for it."

Tate bit the end off a fresh cigar and lit it with a stick from the fire. Sundance thought he looked a little like the Devil when he blew on the burning end of the stick. "I don't think I'd ever risk my life for money," he said.

"That sounds like you," Sundance said. "You'd risk it for nothing."

Fifteen men gathered to hear what Sundance had to say. Grimes and Rance came up before the others. Rance wasn't looking as peppery as he had been that morning; thoughts of the dead gunman and the consequences to follow had caught up with him. Grimes was the same, plainly averse to gunplay but ready to do his part. Twelve men arrived in three groups, and one man, a cadaverous Irishman, came by himself. Sundance bid them welcome and they drew close to the fire, rubbing their hands against the cold.

"Nothing happened all day," Grimes said. "But you know that."

"All that's coming is here," Rance said, trying to recapture some of his earlier jauntiness.

"It's enough." Sundance wanted them to know what they were getting into. "You men are all strangers to me, I don't know a thing about you. We're all here for the same thing—gold. It will take too much time to ask each of you how he's doing. What one thinks is good won't be good for another. So here it is, I won't hedge with you. Our end of the creek is coming up empty. That bluff you can see from down below, that's where the gold is. Today we found a good yield in there."

"Good luck to you!" the Irishman said without much enthusiasm. His belly rumbled as he looked at the empty skillet.

Sundance went on. "If you're coming up short, I have a deal for you. Take it or leave it, no bargaining."

Rance had a question but Grimes told him to shut up.

Sundance said, "By now you've heard about the trouble with Selby. It hasn't come yet. It will. I need extra men because it's hard to dig gold and watch for bushwhackers at the same time. I'll be straight. I wouldn't invite you in if I didn't need you. I'm speaking for my partner when I say that. Who can speak for you? It will save time if there is one man who can say what you all think."

Grimes spoke up. "I'll talk for them if they have no objections. Any that has say them now."

"All right," Sundance said. "I want five men

who are willing to work as hard as me and my partner. Dawn to dusk, two meal breaks. We'll decide to work at night after you're in or out.''

"You'd want fighting men, of course,'' the Irishman named Finnerty said. "I did six years in the infantry, but I ain't got a gun. A pick and shovel, to be sure, but no gun.''

"You haven't found a crock of gold, is that it?'' Tate said.

"Not even a crock of shit,'' Finnerty said.

Sundance said, "You'll get a rifle.'' Finnerty had the look of a sorehead, a born complainer, which didn't men that he wouldn't work or fight. Some of the worst soldiers made the best fighting men. Best of all, the gloomy Irishman had an air of desperation about him; a man looking for one last chance.

"I'd rather start with a can of beans,'' Finnerty said.

Sundance reached into the food box and gave him a quart can of navy beans.

A man who called himself Strydom had a question. He was an ordinary looking man of about fifty, wearing patched boots and a home-spun coat. "You talk like they'll be as much fighting as digging,'' he said. "It's true what you said. My claim's not worth the effort, no better than a kid's plaything, if you know what that is.''

Sundance said he did. In abandoned gold camps, children spent their Sundays searching for traces of dust. "It could be like that,'' he told St dom. "Most likely some of us will be dead when it's over. I can't even promise you we'll win.''

"Then I'll say good night to you,''   ydom said, and three men whispered together and went after him.

"But what about the law?" Grimes said. "Is there-nothing you can do. This is 1885, for God's sake! Wouldn't it be the smart thing to send a man to fetch the county sheriff, explain the trouble to him?"

"That might work fine back where you come from," Sundance said. "Out here I'd have to say no. Our best chance is to take all the gold we can get before Selby falls on us like a wall. Could even be he'll be the one to bring the sheriff in."

One of the other men, Rafer Longworth, had begun to fidget when talk started about the sheriff, and to Sundance he had the look of a wanted man. Not a desperado, a train robber, anything like that; more like a man who had murdered his wife and kids in a fit of rage. Worst of all, though he didn't stink of liquor, he was unmistakably a drunk.

"I'll say good night too," Longworth said. He got up and so did his two partners. Suddenly, it was clear what they were—escaped convicts. They had guns but made no attempt to use them; all they wanted to do was be gone before the sheriff arrived.

"We're dwindling down," Tate said, offering the Irishman a cigar.

"Yer a real gentleman," Finnerty said.

And then, finally, only five men were left: Finnerty, Bascom, Fuller, Grimes and Rance. Bascom and Fuller, both from New York State, had been partners since they got sick of being hired men on a farm near Albany. In their late twenties, they had wandered from camp to camp before sending up in Orono. Both had worked in the Selby mines for three months; since quitting they had been hounded by Durkin's city police, casual labor in town was closed to them, and like Finnerty, they were close to starvation.

"That doesn't mean we're begging for grub," Bascom said, glaring at the Irishman who was grunting happily over his can of cold beans.

"I am," Fuller said. "But I won't beg too hard."

"No need for that," Tate said, getting up to open the food box. "God help you, my friend, you're going to work for it."

Tate was the worst cook Sundance ever saw; years of eating in four-stool restaurants made it hard for him to fry an egg. But it didn't matter how bad a cook he was—the new men would have eaten a boiled boot. Tate scraped the mess he had made onto three plates. "You make the coffee," he said to Sundance.

Before he made the coffee, Sundance got a new Winchester for Finnerty and watched how he handled it. You learned a lot about a man by watching him handle a horse or a gun. He handed Finnerty a box of shells and he thumbed them in with practiced ease. The Irishman might be a deserter, but he knew guns.

"You're a scholar, a gentleman and a judge of good whiskey," Finnerty said.

"No whiskey, not here," Sundance said. "Later you can take a bath in it."

Finnerty said he wanted to open a saloon in Joplin, Missouri, giving no explanation of why he had picked that particular town. Most Irishmen wanted to open saloons. "It's the best business in the world bar none," Finnerty said. "How can you fail in it, for Jaysus' sake! All you do is get in a stock and open the bloody doors and let the sons of bitches lap it up."

"I admire your public spirit, Mr. Finnerty,"

81

Tate said, grinning at the others.

"They'll pay well for my public spirits," the Irishman said, attacking his ham and eggs.

Bascom and Fuller planned to buy a farm back home. The deal to work the mine was ten per cent for each of the five men; Sundance and Tate would split the other fifty per cent.

"We'll be rich or we'll be dead," the Irishman said before he realized that it was the wrong thing.

Tate, crazy beyond knowing, was the only one who smiled.

Chapter Seven

In the morning they started work they might never get to finish. There would be no more talk of death unless Selby forced them to fight. Sundance knew he would but said nothing about it. He had a feeling about Jackson Selby that refused to go away. If danger had a smell, then there was a strong smell of danger all round him. Most of it came from the Indian side of his nature. An Indian lived with death every day of his life: famine, plague, wars with other tribes and, for years now, the Indian-killing calvary. There was never a moment when the Indian could feel truly free of the threat of death. So, in time, he got used to it; the feel of danger became part of his being.

And so Sundance knew there would be killing. It would come as surely as the seasons. Here and now, it would come a lot quicker. He had warned the others what to expect; they had made their decisions. They were well into the morning's work when a lone figure appeared at the far end of the valley, and even at that distance Sundance could see that he was waving a flag of truce.

"Kill him! Give me the Remington. I'll do it."

Sundance told him to wait. He picked up the field glasses and it was Weyman, editor of the Orono newspaper, hardly a killer. Sundance picked up a white rag and waved back and after some hesitation Weyman rode down into the valley. They let him get close.

When he did he asked permission to reach into his pocket. Sundance nodded and Weyman took out a letter in an envelope stamped SELBY MINING COMPANY. He handed it to Sundance. All it said was: "Mr. Sundance. We have to talk about this. Important that we do. I guarantee safe passage to and from my house. Come tonight." It was signed, "J. Selby."

"Tell him I'll think about it," Sundance told the editor.

"You're not going to take him up on this, are you?" Tate said. "Do I have to ask you that?"

"I want to hear what he has to say," Sundance said, knowing what Tate was going to say. "No harm in that."

"The harm is if you get killed." Tate scratched the thick black stubble on his face. "How will we get the gold out with you gone?"

Sundance smiled at his old and dangerous friend. "Just go on digging and washing. I don't need an obituary just yet."

Finnerty said gloomily, "What's to stop him from shooting you in the back? Not him personal, I mean having it done. That's how they do it in Ireland, how my brother Finbar got dead. They had me marked too, but I run over here where it's nice and peaceful."

Grimes wanted to do nothing. "Best idea is make out you never got the message. That's the way to handle it."

Finnerty said, "Kill Selby is the best way."

"I'm with you, me boy," Tate said.

Sundance looked at him. "The best way is to see what he has to say. That's what I'm going to do."

84

Sundance drew his Colt and checked the loads in the cylinder.

Tate frowned angrily. "You're always telling me not to be so fond of death."

"This is business," Sundance said. "I've been in tight places before."

"You didn't just walk in, there's a difference," Tate argued. "I don't get this sudden trust in Selby. What do you know about the man?"

"Not a thing. Never had a chance. Now I do."

"Why does it have to be his house?" Finnerty asked. "If he wants to talk why can't it be neutral ground? I'm a fair hand with a long gun. Change the meeting place and I'll be glad to murder him for you."

Tate clapped the bony Irishman on the back. "You've got a treacherous heart, Finnerty, but you're absolutely right. Make that two long guns—we'll murder him together."

Looking nervous, Rance said, "I don't know what to say."

"Hasn't there been enough killing?" Grimes said in a hopeless voice.

"More than enough," Sundance said. "There hasn't been more because Selby hasn't made up his mind. There's just a chance he'll hold off after I talk to him."

"You said he wouldn't hold back," Tate said. "That's what you've been saying. What's the real reason you're going?"

It was time to level with them, Sundance decided. Not so much Tate, who probably had it half figured, but with the others. "All right," he said. "I'm going to talk to Selby because I want to know what the man is like. So far all I know is what I've heard. I know he has to be a tough hard man or he wouldn't be where he is. But I want to know more than that. Will he go all the way, is what I have to know."

"Sure," Tate said slowly. "If he's ready to do anything, then we have to be worse."

Sundance slid the .44 back in its holster. "That's what I'm saying. That's what we'll do, if that's what it takes. As to whether I can trust him. I think for now I can. There are witnesses to the giving of his word. That's one reason I'm going in. The other reason, just as important, I think Selby believes he can settle anything and everything his way, no matter how tough. That could be his weakness. I can't tell you what to do if anything happens to me. I don't expect to be gone much longer than any trip to town. Now why don't you men do something useful instead of staring at me. Last I heard we were still in the gold mining business."

Riding away from camp, Sundance knew his life depended on the strength of Selby's word, the hold he had over his men. Even if Selby kept his word, it was possible that someone, hoping to please the big man, would disobey orders and act on his own. It was a risk he didn't have to take, but he figured it was worth it. He was curious about Jackson Selby, his enemy. He smiled briefly. Call it professional interest. Know your enemy, Three Stars said, and what was true in a military campaign held true in a face-off between two men. He had the feeling that Jackson Selby wasn't going to be any ordinary man, and not because he was rich and powerful, walled off by guns and cushioned against shock by money. It was just a feeling, of course, but there was a lot to be said for instinct, or whatever you wanted to call it. Sundance sensed great force in

Selby that had nothing to do with his money and influence, and he hadn't spoken of it to the others, because he knew they wouldn't understand. Even Tate, strange as he was, would find it hard to believe; and the others would put it down to Indian superstition, if they thought about it at all. But the feeling remained and he wasn't going to fight it. He smiled again. Tate wasn't the only one who was drawn to danger. Selby had to be faced. Once he talked to Selby he would become a man instead of a name, and that might give Sundance the advantage he needed. Other men might scoff that such things made no difference. Sundance disagreed. He would meet Selby, talk to him, and listen; then decide what had to be done.

Riding away from the creek toward the road to Orono, he caught the flash of sun on binoculars in a grove of trees about a mile away. Of course they were watching him; he would be watched all the way. He rode without bracing himself for the shock of a bullet. He was riding into danger: a calculated risk. The sun was going down, but he would make Orono before it got dark. He guessed he was safe enough for now; it was the ride back he had to think about.

The light was going fast when the road climbed one last slope and the town of Orono lay below him, washed a smoky red by the dying sun. Carbon lights blazed on the hillsides above the town; in the town itself lamps were lit and the lights seemed to quiver in the thunder of the ore crushers that echoed far beyond the valley. The river that divided the town was dull like dirty silver. Sundance followed the road past the biggest of the three Selby mines and it took him over a hill and into a small valley from which the mines or the town could not be seen; and that at least made Selby different, for most powerful men liked to look at the source of their power. The valley was separated from the town by less than mile but here were no signs of industry. In the center of the valley, green and well-watered, stood the mine owner's two-story brick house with white windows doors and flagged walks. It was a big solid house without the usual ornamentation of houses owned by men who got rich in a hurry. Sundance rode right up to the front door without being challenged, and when he let the brass knocker drop just once the door was opened by a stooped old man in a plain black suit.

"Come right in, sir," he said, holding the door open. "I'll show you where to go."

That too was different; most servants in big houses bowed and scraped. Already, Sundance was forming an opinion of Selby, and for what it was worth it was favorable, yet it made no difference—Jackson Selby was his enemy. They would talk but he would remain the enemy.

Selby opened the door at the end of the long hall before they got to it, and Sundance wasn't surprised to see a smallish man framed against the light behind him. Big men often were small. Napoleon inspired short soldiers; Carnegie was the model for businessmen.

Light shone through the fringe of white hair on Selby's otherwise hairless head; and he was thick without being fat. His black suit coat cost more than the manservant's, but it was just as plain. He wore a starched linen collar and a black tie with a big knot. Oddly, his watchchain was silver instead of gold. Sundance was glad he didn't offer to shake hands.

"Glad you could come," he said. "I know you don't drink so I ordered coffee. Come on up to the fire.

"I don't drink either," Selby said. "I have a taste for it, or maybe it has a taste for me. My father was a drunk. Shiftless, foolish, his whole life a waste. Mine is not."

The old man brought the coffee sitting in a larger silver pot heated by a spirit lamp. "Coffee's no good if it isn't close to boiling," Selby said. "I know you don't use sugar so there isn't any."

"Am I right-handed or left-handed?" Sundance asked, sitting down. The coffee smelled good after the ride from camp.

"I know that too," Selby said with a brief smile. "You can shoot left-handed if you have to. In '78 in Arizona you suffered a broken finger on the right hand. How's the finger?"

"Never better," Sundance said. "And I can still shoot with either hand. Anything else you'd like to know about me? There must be something your agents left out."

Selby said, "No doubt they did, but you don't have to tell me. I'll find out as we go along. That's why you're here and wanting to know about me is why you came."

"Among other things," Sundance said. "Fact is, I don't know much about you."

"You will," Selby said.

A big fire of seasoned logs blazed without sparks in the high stone fireplace. The heavy furniture was as sensible as the house itself; and no oil portrait of Selby glowered down from the mantelpiece. Instead, there was a panoramic photograph of a shabby little coal town apparently taken in

89

midwinter. It had been photographed from different positions, the parts fitted together to give a wide view of the place. The frame houses in the picture were built on a hill, rickety on thin supports. Dirty snow had frozen around the bottom of the supports; and there was the usual clutter of washtubs, broken furniture, rusting buckets. Looming over everything was the tall hoist wheel of a coal mine, a slag heap high as a small mountain.

Selby looked at it too. "That's where I was born, where I grew up," he said. "Evanstown, Pennsylvania. What they call a mining patch back there. I want to remember that place."

Sundance poured his own coffee. "What you've made of Orono doesn't look so very different."

Selby accepted the truth of the statement. "There's a difference—some," he said. "I pay fair wages, take care of my people. When a man works for me he isn't dumped in the street if he gets sick. If he's really sick I take care of him until he's well enough to work again. That's not to say I'll support him for the rest of his life. But I do give loyalty for loyalty."

Sundance nodded. "You see that as good business."

"None better," Selby said. "You see me as a hard man, don't you. I am. I'm in business to make money, but that's not all of it. I made this town and that's just a start. The gold mining won't last forever. That's why I want to turn this town into a real manufacturing town. Maybe the first of its kind in the West. There's no future here without it. I ask you, what would these men be doing if I didn't offer them work. Most would be starving. A hard fact but still a fact."

Sundance could see that everything Selby said was considered logical and fair-minded.

"They don't have much of a choice in this town," Sundance said. "They work for you or they don't work at all."

Selby poured fresh coffee and looked hard at Sundance. Not a menacing look, simply the look of a man who is determined to make the other man see his point.

Selby said, "Is that my fault? I hardly think so. What am I expected to do, grubstake them in a lot of useless ventures? Set them up in farms and stores? You know as well as I do that most men are no good at business."

Selby paused to allow Sundance to answer. "You're not saying anything new."

Jackson Selby smiled. "You're not one of these share-the-wealth people, are you? It's been tried in Europe. Hasn't worked there."

Sundance smiled. "It works for the Indians. But they have less and less to share."

Selby remained patient. "We're not talking about Indians here. You say you've heard my arguments before. Maybe you have, or think you have. But not the way I'm going to talk now."

"No point," Sundance said, getting more from Selby's words than Selby knew. "You didn't ask me to come here to discuss your business philosophy."

"Wrong," Selby said. "It's important that you understand the kind of man I am."

"Is it that important?"

"As can be. You know the trouble with most men? They never think things out to the end. I do. Think what you like of me, I'm no hypocrite. I have a great deal of money, not as much as I'd like to have, but that will come. I want it and I'm going to get it."

"Meaning you're an honest business pirate," Sundance said, knowing enough about Selby to know he wouldn't take offense. Sundance didn't know what to make of Selby. Through General Crook he had come to know a few big men in business. In his capacity of top-ranking general, Crook was compelled to deal with manufacturers: hard, smug, ruthless men who made no secret of their contempt for men with less power and money. Selby reminded him of none of them. Not that it mattered. He and Selby were on opposite sides and no amount of talk would ever change that. Oddly though, he didn't flaunt his wealth and power; all he did was to state the facts. and in that he was different from most businessmen. It could, Sundance knew, make him a lot more dangerous.

"I think I'm an honest man," Selby said quietly. "Facts are facts. In this town men want work and I have the money to pay for their work. Has any other system ever worked. I think not. Someone has to be in charge, somebody has to give the orders. That's me."

"It's how you give the orders," Sundance said.

Selby waved away the interruption. "There's no easy way to give an order. Men don't like to obey orders, which is natural enough. In my time I have worked in the mines, gold, silver and—first of all—coal. I didn't like it. How pleasant it would be to live without working. Eat, drink, sleep. That's not possible except on some cannibal island in the South Seas."

"It's still how you give the orders."

"The best way to give an order it to give it once and see that it's obeyed. True, I work the men hard but make up for it by paying good wages.''

"But not as much as they want.''

Selby's smile was real. "No man ever gets as much as he thinks he's worth. It's a fair wage for the work they do. They have a choice. They can move on. Go West and make your fortune, they used to say when I was a very young man. Now I'm no longer young and neither is the West. The West stops at the sea.''

"Men like to be free,'' Sundance said.

"You mean you like to be free,'' Selby said, smiling. The mine owner had a curious smile. It wasn't the fake smile of the smooth-talking businessman. It was real and yet it wasn't. It started at his mouth, which wasn't set in the grim line of the man who thinks he has to look tough all the time. He doesn't have to look tough because he is tough, Sundance thought. Selby's smile never seemed to reach his eyes. They remained expressionless, almost mild. Some businessmen were avid readers and quoters of the Bible: a way to justify their greed, the cruelty that was passed off as a firm hand.

"You're free as the wind,'' Selby said. "It's all right for you to talk. You don't just talk about being free—you are free! But I ask you this. Except for what Mr. Horace Greeley said, did the West ever exist. These days—go West . . . to what?''

"The West lives on. Everything changes but the West lives on.''

"For men like you.''

"It's still a good idea.''

"While it lasted it was. But to come back to the trouble with men. They want to have it both ways. They want things to change and they want them to stay the same. First, there was nothing but prairie, desert and mountain. But now the prairie has been slashed through by the railroads, the mountains breached by the rails. You lose your privacy—your freedom—when civilization comes. In a few years the West as we know it will be gone. Too bad, you say. Maybe so. But you can't argue with the facts. Accept it, Mr. Sundance, the future is here now."

"Meaning you own this town."

"Most of it. What I don't own doesn't matter. That's the way it works. I'm in charge and intend to stay in charge. What I do for these men is to take the uncertainty from their lives. I could abandon the town, let it die, when the gold is gone. I won't let that happen."

"What has all this got to do with my two-bit mine?" Sundance said. He knew the answer but wanted Selby to give it, so that later there wouldn't be any misunderstanding when the trouble got bad.

"Your mine has everything to do with it," Selby said. "You must know that by now."

"I know it," Sundance said.

"It's very simple," Selby said. "I can't let you oppose me and get away with it. By itself, your mine means nothing to me. It's not even that some of the others will follow your example. That's part of it, of course, but a small part. I could make an exception in your case."

"Why don't you?"

"Because I can't."

Selby thanked his man servant for bringing in more coffee. "I can't because I made my rules a long time ago and have lived by them ever since. A sort of personal constitution, if you like."

"But no bill of rights, is that it?"

"None needed. Good work, good pay. Some of my business associates don't agree with me.

They're wrong. There is no need for warfare between worker and employer."

"Then why do you need all those gunmen passing as police?"

Selby shrugged. "I see a time when they won't be needed anymore. They are now—another fact." Selby's dry voice became almost enthusiastic. "This town can become a model for all the towns in the West."

"But it will remain your town?"

"What should I do with it? Give it away?"

Sundance said, "I don't know what you should do with it? I'll ask you again—what about my mine?"

Selby said, "Before we get down to the hard part of our talk, how much do you figure to take out of it?"

Sundance told him what he hoped to gain by working the claim.

Selby nodded. "You might be able to make that much money even sharing with the other men. Think on this for a moment. I'll double your figure and throw in an extra five thousand. Let's not mention good will or luck. We're both hard men in different ways so let there be no hypocrisy. Agreed?"

"Agreed," Sundance said.

"Sign the claim over to me and I'll give you twenty-five thousand in cash. Gold, if you like. How much you give your partners is your business. I'm making you an offer and you know it. It's the only offer you'll get and if you say no, that's it. Say no and there won't be any more talk. You need time to think it over?"

Sundance looked at the man standing in front of the fireplace. Some of what Selby said had been just as he expected. The man wasn't a liar; that much was clear. Hardest to swallow was that much of what he'd said was true. It was true that men were stupid, cruel, greedy, lazy, ill-willed. Jackson Selby thought he had found a way to change all that. To put man in a stall and feed him well, hoping that his wild, animal nature could be subdued. Selby wanted to replace the lash with the full dinner pail; and maybe to a hungry man that was better than pie in the sky. Even so, it wasn't that much better than slavery. Some of the old Southern gentry had treated their slaves just fine. Still, it was wrong. Man was meant for something better than being simply being a well-fed animal.

Selby was waiting without impatience.

"I won't sell," Sundance said at last. "Twice the offer wouldn't make any difference."

"I said there wouldn't be."

"So where does that leave us?" Sundance asked.

"Where does that leave you?" Selby said. Selby had nodded his confirmation of Sundance's refusal. He displayed no anger, not even in a narrowing of the eyes, a tightening of the mouth. "Once again, because I know who you are, I am going to state some facts. I have everything that you haven't got: money, gunfighters. If I need more gunfighters I can use the telegraph. I have men now working in the mines who will fight you for double what they're getting now. The law listens when I talk. But finally it all comes down to having the money. If money can buy governments, it can buy a small mining town. So you don't have a chance. You have to give way, Mr. Sundance. If you don't you'll be fighting an unequal battle."

Sundance stood up and drank the rest of his coffee standing up. Oddly, he didn't hate Selby, the way he had hated other men. Maybe it was the man's twisted notion of honor. He put down the cup.

"We're equal in one way," he said.

"Selby showed real interest. "And what is that?"

"Both of us has one life to lose. Ask yourself, is it worth it? To risk your life for something that doesn't mean much. Why not bend, Mr. Selby. It's been done. We all have to do it at times."

This was Sundance's appeal to reason.

"Am I risking my life?" Selby said. "I hardly think so. You could have killed me anytime you walked in here. Look around you. Do you see any hidden riflemen waiting to kill you the first move you made. There are none. So you see I'm not afraid of losing my life. A man can't live if he's too afraid to die. Besides, I know the kind of man you are. It's a pity it has to come to this. You are determined to fight me, aren't you?"

"If I have to."

"You'll have to."

"You won't like the way I fight, Mr. Selby."

"I suppose I'll have to get used to it. What does it matter—you can't win. You think you can?"

"I'll have to think about that."

"That's what you've been doing since you came in here."

"You're right but now I know for sure."

Sundance turned to go and Selby called him back. "Why?" he said with real puzzlement in his face. "After all I've said—why? All you can accomplish is to get those men killed, yourself killed. Then your Indians get nothing. Tell me—why?"

"Because you don't own the world," Sundance

said. "The claim is legal but more than that it belongs to us. A halfbreed, a gambler, a few down in their luck drifters. That's what we are. But we're men and even if you kill us other men will fight you. Maybe not tomorrow or the day after or next week. Just the same, it will happen. And then you'll have to kill them too."

"No doubt," Selby said. "You just could be wrong about that."

Sundance opened the door, and it was like Selby had said. No rifles or shotguns were waiting to blast him. Once again, he felt the cold, honest ruthlessness of Jackson Selby's nature. No doubt about it, he was in for one of the worst fights of his long career as a professional fighting man.

"I know I'm right about one thing," he said.

Selby walked with him to the front door and opened it himself.

"What are you right about?" he asked.

"You'll have to kill me first," Sundance said. "A lot of men have tried that and I'm still walking around."

"There's a first time for everything," Selby said with a brief smile. "You think I'm going to call for the militia, aren't you? I could and they'd come. Ordinarily, that's what I'd do. Not this time though. That would be the sensible thing to do, but I'm not going to do it. You said it yourself: a halfbreed, a gambler, a handful of drifters. I don't need the militia to run you off or bury you. No sir, this is my town and I'll handle things in my own way."

"I know you'll try hard," Sundance said before he rode away.

Chapter Eight

Most of the diggers along the creek had left by the next morning. Sundance was glad to see them gone, but it wasn't just a sign of the gold giving out. Even the miners who could have stayed and made enough to feed a Chinaman had cleared out because of the trouble to come. But for the moment, it was good to look down from the heights along the length of the creek and hear nothing but silence. Soon the debris and filth left by the diggers would be washed away; the creek would run clear again.

They were eating a big meal at first light, fried meat and potatoes, coffee black enough to use as ink. Finnerty, still half-starved, ate ravenously. Only Tate was in a good mood. Sundance glanced at him; the crazy son of a bitch was looking forward to the fight with Selby.

Finnerty was mild mannered but had a murderous soul. "All this man of honor bullshit is going to get you killed one of these days," the gaunt Irishman said through a mouthful of potatoes. "You should have killed him when you had the chance."

Rance, not so brave now, fidgeted with his plate of food. "Don't be a damn fool, Finnerty. If Sundance had killed Selby he wouldn't have got ten feet from the house. Am I right, Sundance?"

"That wasn't the reason," Sundance said,

looking at the creek, thinking that the creek got to be a river before it reached Orono. The big creek and its smaller tributary were the source of all the water in Orono. What they called "working water" in mining country. For drinking water there would be a few deep driven wells in town. Nothing more than that.

"That wasn't the reason I didn't kill him," Sundance said. "He gave me safe passage to and from the house. He could have had me ambushed going in or out."

Tate wasn't much of an eater. Too many years of black coffee, strong cigars and whiskey had taken away his appetite. "I felt sure he'd try to bushwhack you on the way out," he said. "Selby hates to be told no."

Sundance said, "He took it well enough when I said no."

Grimes, the cautious one, stopped poking aimlessly at the cook-fire. "Maybe you should have said yes, Sundance. That was a lot of money he offered."

Finnerty flared up at that. "Maybe he should have kissed Selby's hind end while he was at it. You seem to be forgetting something, Grimes. Nothing here belongs to you. Nor to me. Nor to you and you." The Irishman pointed his fork at Longworth and Fuller.

Longworth and Fuller, the New Yorkers, had been hired men all their lives. It wasn't in their nature to enter into business discussions.

Longworth, tougher of the two, glared at Finnerty. "You're the one doing all the talking."

"What do you know about mines and mining?" Fuller said to the Irishman. "The only mines you ever worked in was a potato mine. You're just a foreigner in this country."

Finnerty grabbed up the coffee pot still half full of boiling coffee. "You want your dirty face washed, you Yank son of a bitch. You people started the Civil War—begging your pardon, Tate, the War Between the States—but it took the Irish and the Germans to win it for you. Am I right or wrong, Tate?"

Sundance grinned. Tate and Finnerty had formed one of those odd friendships: the fierce-tempered clodhopper and the Southern aristocrat. Sundance had been through the War and knew the Rebs had more respect for the Irish than they had for the Yankees. The night before the two men had been talking about the bloody battle of Mary's Heights. Both men had been in the fight. At one point Tate said, "You wiped out the First Alabama in that one, and they were the best men we had."

"None better," Finnerty had said. "Three times they tried to storm the heights and three times we drove them back. Ah yes, it was a glorious slaughter."

"Of course you had artillery," Tate had said.

Now it was morning and the war was with Jackson Selby. Sundance guessed they would be nothing like the First Alabama or the Fighting 69th. They'd be bad enough. There would be no cheering for a foe bravely beaten, no flags of truce under which to bring in the wounded. Selby would send his best, meaning his worst, men against them. While he half listened to the others, he looked down at the creek and the country beyond. The valley they were in was miles wide and long, steep hills on both sides. A valley that big would hold a lot of water.

101

Tate had heard the story of the meeting with Selby, but he wanted to hear it again. "You think he's that bad?"

"Never met a harder man in my life," Sundance said. "He's more dangerous than most because he thinks he's right."

Tate laughed as he reached into his shirt pocket for a cigar. "He thinks God is on his side."

Sundance shook his head. "He didn't drag God into it. He just knows what he wants to do and means to do it. To keep it simple—we're getting in his way."

Tate smiled. "At least we know what to expect."

Sundance said, "We can expect the worst. How it will start I have no way of knowing."

Tate blew cigar smoke into the clear morning air. Tate smoked cigars as if he expected the one in his mouth to be his last. "How soon do you think?"

Sundance said there was no way to tell. "I don't think more than some long-range sniping at first. Maybe not even to kill, but if he has to kill he'll kill without mercy. But I think the sniping will come first. Some of us will run after the first few bullets start flying, is what Selby figures."

Sundance knew he could count on Tate and Finnerty; unlike as two men could be except for their love of fighting, first and last, they were men. Still, he couldn't single out this man or that when he asked the question.

"Anybody feel like quitting? There's still time."

Loading his plate again, Finnerty said, "Mister, you'll have to drive me out of here at the point of a gun. You're the first man that's treated me decent in a dog's age. I'll stick with you to the last bullet and then I'll throw rocks at the bastards."

Tate laughed and clapped the Irishman on the

shoulder. "We'll show them what Mary's Heights was like, Finnerty. Only this time we'll be on the same side."

"Anybody else have anything to say?" Sundance said.

Longworth spoke first. "I won't go back to working as a hired man. Fuller is of the same mind."

Fuller nodded unhappily, but Sundance didn't mind that. Fighting and killing was something you had to get used to. Fuller might be all right, at least for a while. He had some doubts about Fuller, but for now he would have to take the man at his word. Take him at his word and watch him carefully. Selby had money to throw around and Fuller had the look of a man who had been poor too long.

Grimes said, "There must be some way out of this."

"Jesus Christ!" Finnerty said angrily. "Are you in or out?"

"I wasn't talking to you," Grimes said.

Tate didn't like Grimes. "What's the difference? The question is still the same."

"I'll stick," Grimes said.

"Me too," Rance said.

Sundance wondered about Rance. The killing of the wounded gunman hadn't won him any favor in Sundance's eyes. It was just as well that he had killed the shotgun man, but there had been something cowardly and hysterical in the way it had been done. Rance would have to be watched as closely as Fuller.

"Time to go to work," Sundance said.

Finnerty complained when Sundance ordered

103

him to go up to the top of the bluff with the field glasses and the Big Fifty Remington. The top of the bluff was the highest point in the valley and a man watching carefully with glasses could spot about anything for miles in any direction.

"You're sending me because I don't look strong enough to work," Finnerty said. "Well, mister, me lad, I can pull my weight with any man walking. You don't have to do me no favors."

Sundance thrust the heavy rifle at him. "You'll do what I tell you or get the hell out of here. Or maybe you're not the marksman you say you are."

Finnerty's bony face grew red with anger. "I never said I was a fast shot. I said I could hit what I shoot at."

"Prove it," Sundance said, pointing to an empty bottle glinting in the sun in the grass two hundred yards away by the side of the creek.

"I see it," Finnerty said.

"Break it," Sundance said.

"Child's play," Finnerty said. He thumbed back the hammer to full cock, rolled the breechblock back, exposing the breech. Then he pushed a shell into the chamber and flipped the block back into place. He steadied the big rifle on top of the lumber pile, sighted for a moment, and fired. Two hundred yards away the bottle exploded.

"Not bad," Sundance said.

The Irishman's anger flared up again. "Shit! If I had a tube sight for this weapon I could hit at twice that distance. Aye, and maybe more than that."

Sundance crawled into the tent and came out again. "You have one now. Now get up on the bluff and keep your mouth shut. I'll tell you when you're strong enough to work. Watching for Selby's men is a lot more important than digging in the side of a hill. Even a thick-headed Irishman ought to know that."

Finnerty smiled, or tried to. Hard luck for too long had set his face in a melancholy mask. "What do I do up there besides keep a lookout for Selby's bastards? They'll have to be Selby's bastards if they come into this valley. Do I just start killing or just see what happens? Makes no difference to me which way it is. I'd as soon kill them as spit."

Sundance said, "If you see a man trying to get into a sniping position—kill him. Don't call down to us because sound carries a long way. Shoot to kill."

"That's what the army trained me to do."

Grimes, ever cautious, looked alarmed. "Can't he just shoot to scare them off? That way they'll know we mean business."

Sundance was getting tired of Grimes and his bush beating. "No more talk, I said. Grab your pick and shovel and go to work."

Nothing happened as the sun came up, weak and lacking in heat at first. Then the sun grew hot and the sky was a bright, hard blue. The wind coming down from the mountains wasn't so cold. They put their weapons in places where they could get them in a hurry. After a while the soreness of their muscles from the work the day before had worked itself out. They took turns with the work, digging or washing out the sluice. The yield of gold was still holding up; if anything, it was better. Little by little the leather bag was beginning to fill with the dull yellow dust. Hefting the bag, Rance yelled that they were getting rich in a hurry until Sundance reminded him that everything in the bag wasn't pure gold.

"There's some fine sand, almost powder in with

the gold," he said. "That'll have to come out before we know how much we have."

But Rance refused to be discouraged. "I don't care what you say. It's heavier than it was. How much do you figure?"

"Not nearly enough," Sundance said.

Swinging the pick, Sundance wondered when they would try for the first shot. Up on the bluff, Finnerty lay flat on his belly hidden by a clump of brush. Sundance walked away from the mine, past the stack of lumber, and down along the creek. The only reason he did it was to see if Finnerty could be seen. He couldn't. He had climbed up before there was enough light to be seen from a distance. He had dried meat and bread and a canteen of water to last him for hours, all day if necessary.

Sundance figured they would try for the first sniping shot during the midday meal break. They would be bunched up around the fire, eating and resting after a hard morning's work. That would be the way to do it. Six men sitting together—a sniper would have his pick of targets. If he was any kind of shot, he should be able to kill somebody. Kill or cripple. It came to the same thing. They were a working team and a crippled man was a dead man. Worse than dead: they would have to look after him.

Not a sound came from the top of the bluff, no rustling of brush, no scatter of falling gravel. Finnerty, whoever he was or had been, sure as hell knew his business. Overhead the sun was a ball of brass in the sky. It was noon and they had been working steadily since six that morning. Longworth and Fuller, hired men since boyhood, worked without effort. Grimes was too thick-bodied to be agile, but he did his share. Tate, wiry and long-limbed, did more than his share. Only Rance, smallest man of the lot, showed real signs of fatigue. He would have to toughen up or drop out, Sundance decided. There was no place in camp for chief cook and bottle washer.

They had dug far enough into the bluff to make it necessary to shore it up or risk being buried in a fall. Easy digging was dangerous digging. Sundance wondered if maybe another man shouldn't be posted to guard the approach by the creek; the lookout on the bluff couldn't see everything at the same time. If he could then he wasn't doing it right. Once they got deep into the bluff they would be in real danger, not from bullets but from a dynamite charge thrown at the entrance to the shaft. The bluff, except for the vein of rock in the center, was dry and crumbling. A few sticks of dynamite, maybe even one well aimed stick, would seal them up forever. A Selby man could do that if he managed to sneak up along the creek, a small man who moved carefully and kept to the overhang of the bank. If they were trapped in the shaft death would not come quickly. They would wait in the darkness waiting for the air to give out. It was something he would have to think through.

Rance, glistening with sweat, was making for the mouth of the shaft when Sundance called him back. The small man was exhausted enough to be rebellious. "It's time to eat," he said.

Sundance told him to shut up and listen. "I get the feeling they're going to try something right now. We'll be bunched up and that's as good a chance as any. Maybe I'm wrong."

"We've been out in the opening half the day," Rance said. "In and out of here. Why didn't they

107

try it then?"

"How do I know why they didn't?" Sundance said. "We weren't all out there at the same time. Those that were outside were moving about. That doesn't make for such an easy target."

Rance said, "Then why don't we bring our food into the shaft?"

A sudden hard look from Sundance shut him up. "We'll build up the fire and cook our grub. But keep moving around and when we sit down to eat keep well apart. Not in a circle or a line. If they start sniping don't run back in the mine. If they can come at Finnerty from behind they can blow the tunnel. Right now we have to count on Finnerty."

Fuller's face was sullen, resentful of the respect Sundance and Tate showed the Irishman who was by any standards just a wandering tramp. "You sure we can depend on that clodhopper?"

A dark shadow seemed to pass across Tate's lean face. "Call him that again and you'll wish you were farting beans back in Yankeeland. You get that, plowboy?"

"More out and save the fighting for Selby," Sundance ordered.

Tate gave a mock salute. "Sorry, Colonel. It gets me mad to hear a good man dowgraded by white Yankee trash. All right! I'm going—the Civil War is over."

After the gloom of the mine shaft the sunlight was blinding. Shading his eyes with his hat, Sundance looked down the creek to the end of the valley. Not a digger in sight. The brown hills that ringed the valley were bare in the sun and birds flew along the creek foraging for scraps of food left by the diggers. During the night coyotes had ranged along the creek trying to dig up a dead mule. They were gone now, waiting for night to return so they could start again. Soon the deer scared off by the diggers would be back; Sundance knew there wouldn't be any chance to go hunting fresh deer meat.

It was Fuller's turn to cook up the noonday meal and he did it quickly, burning the beans and frying the meat too hard. Even so, the food smelled good after six hours of moving rock and dirt. Sundance threw a handful of dried apples to the squirrels while Fuller doled out the food on tin plates. The coffee was the only thing he hadn't spoiled.

Then from atop the bluff Finnerty's Remington boomed a split second before a bullet blew Rance clear off his feet. They threw themselves flat as five more long-range rifles fired right after the first one. Finnerty was a fast reloader and he fired again. Rolling away from the fire and behind the stack of lumber, Sundance yelled at Fuller to stay out of the mine shaft. Fuller ran in anyway. A bullet smacked the rock near his head but nothing but rock fragments dug into his sweating flesh. Longworth and Grimes got behind the lumber with Sundance. Heavy caliber bullets thunked into the wood. Tate stayed where he was behind a rock, with his head down. Sundance looked over at him and Tate was grinning.

Finnerty's Remington boomed again and now the hidden snipers turned their fire on him. Sundance inched up his head and saw the flash of field glasses on the crest of a hill on the far side of the creek. Selby's men must have thought they were pretty good to be firing from more than three hundred yards. Bullets ripped into the top of the bluff and for a moment Sundance thought the mad Irishman had been hit or killed. Then Finnerty's rifle boomed again and a faint scream came from the far away hill. "I got two of the bastards!" Finnerty yelled down from the bluff.

The top of the bluff was flat, with no cover except for the brush. Sundance called out to Tate as the other snipers opened fire again. "They'll kill him sure if we don't do something. They got his muzzle flashes spotted by now."

"We're going into the creek," Sundance yelled up at Finnerty. "Throw as much lead as you can."

"Stay out, you crazy bastard," the Irish shouted back. "You've got no range with the repeaters."

"Are you loaded?" Tate yelled. "All right, here we go!"

"You stay here," Sundance ordered Longworth and Grimes who hadn't made any move to join the attack on the hill. "Open up when Finnerty does."

Tate looked at Sundance. "You ready?"

"You left, me right," Sundance said. "We'll have cover if we make the far bank. Then we'll move along till we're out of range. After that we'll make for the hill from both sides."

Tate grinned with the sheer joy of danger. "Keep your head down, halfbreed."

Sundance grinned back. "You too, tinhorn. Go!"

Finnerty fired from the bluff as they ran down the hill toward the creek. Bullets from the hill came at them as they ran. Finnerty fired again. Longworth was faster with the Winchester than Grimes. Sundance reached the creek seconds before Tate, but didn't turn to see what was happening to his friend. Then he heard Tate dive into the water beside. A bullet splashed water in Tate's face. The wet cigar was still in his mouth and he chomped on it with a savage grin. Big bullets still came from the hill, but by then they had reached the far high bank of the creek.

"Let's do some killing," Tate said as he moved off to the left, waist deep in the fast flowing water. He carried the long-barreled Fox shotgun, with a Winchester stuck in his belt and his handgun holstered at his side.

Sundance had to push hard against the current as he headed for the narrow gorge just north of their claim. The sniping from the hill started again, but he knew they were just hoping for a lucky shot. He reached the gorge and had to hang onto the outgrowing bushes to get through. The rushing water in the gorge drowned out everything but the occasional boom of Finnerty's rifle.

Past the gorge the banks of the creek were so high he couldn't see the hill where the snipers were. There was a bend in the creek before it ran through the gorge; he had no idea what Tate was doing. When he was a good quarter of a mile from the gorge he climbed out of the creek and was able to see the hill, the top of the hill, through a stand of pines. He went through the pines at a run and nobody shot at him. Past the pines and down and up again from a hollow a long ravine snaked its way up the north side of the hill. Again, he wondered how Tate was doing. Behind him Finnerty's rifle stopped firing. That could mean three things: Finnerty was dead, out of ammunition, or there was nothing to shoot at. A fourth possibility was the remaining snipers were laying low waiting for a last chance to do Selby's killing.

There wasn't a sound in the ravine except birds twittering nervously at his passing. He stopped when he was close to the top, then he went through the ravine until he was on the back side of the hill. He was moving again when a man rose up from behind a rock and fired point-blank at him. He shouldn't have missed but he did. Maybe he fired so fast because he had the surprise and thought he couldn't miss at that range. If the bullet had struck Sundance in the belly it would have blown his spine out through his back. Sundance fired the Winchester from the hip and then fired again from the same position. The first man was still spilling blood from his mouth when another ambusher broke from cover and began to run. Sundance shot him in the back and put another bullet through his skull when he got closer. A shotgun blasted lead about a half mile away. Tate! The shotgun blasted again, and after that there was no more shooting.

Sundance made his way along the back of the hill until he found Tate standing over the bodies of two snipers. He reached down and took a cigar from the shirt pocket of one of the corpses, a big youngish man with a carefully trimmed mustache. The other dead man was a few years older, about forty, and the little finger was missing from his left hand.

Tate lit the cigar and made a face. "Hell! This smells and tastes like mattress stuffing." But he continued to puff on the cheap cigar. Same old Tate, Sundance thought. Comes through something as bad as this and all he can do is complain about a dead man's cigars.

"Sounded like you had some good luck back there," Tate remarked.

"I did all right," Sundance said.

"I didn't doubt you for a minute," Tate said. "Looks like we got all six of them. Finnerty's two are over there in the brush." Tate gave a low whistle. "Six of us and six of them. We'd all be goners if you hadn't put Finnerty up on the bluff. I tell you, my friend, I could kiss that ugly Hibernian."

Sundance grinned. "Don't try it while he's wearing a gun. The two I killed didn't have police badges on them. Not pinned in the open or hidden."

Tate threw away the half smoked cigar. "I checked the others before you got here. No badges. Anyway, they wouldn't have that many snipers in Durkin's police force. Don't bother looking at the ones Finnerty killed. I did that already. No badges, nothing to tie them to Durkin or Selby. You know what I think?"

"What?"

"It was all some terrible mistake."

"Sure," Sundance said. "Best part of it is they won't make it again."

Chapter Nine

They buried Rance and Grimes made the headboard for his grave. Tate spelled Finnerty on the bluff while the Irishman climbed down and ate a hot meal. Fuller, shamefaced with cowardice, stood around doing nothing. Sundance knew he was waiting to be told to leave. Longworth had nothing to say to him. Finnerty looked at Fuller and spat.

Rance's death didn't mean much to anyone, not even to Grimes, who had been his partner. The two men hadn't been real friends. There was no point in making a coffin. Lumber was scarce and it really didn't make any difference how a man got planted.

In a way, Sundance was glad that Rance was dead; yet the death of this man who didn't work, who wasn't liked much, had to be avenged. Like him or not, Rance had been one of them. To Sundance, it was simple and inevitable as death itself—Selby would have to pay for it. He wanted a war and he was going to get it, and it would be a bigger and longer war than he expected.

Grimes dug the grave too because it was his place to do it. You can have no use for a partner, but you are expected to bury him when he dies. No one offered to help; that also was part of the code. The hole in Rance's back was as big as a dinner plate; even the entry wound was bigger than an ordinary rifle would make.

Sundance had been through this scene, or scenes like it, so many times before. Finnerty went on eating without a word. The killing of Rance hadn't spoiled his appetite; and for all the expression on his face he might have been witnessing the burying of a dog. He refused to look at Fuller, the man who ran.

Then all was ready and Longworth helped to lower the blanket-wrapped corpse into the grave. Rance had been a small man so they didn't have to heave and puff. That done, Longworth stood back while Grimes shoveled sandy dirt on top of his partner. After that, Grimes said a few words about ashes to ashes. It was over once he set the headboard in place. Watching, Sundance promised that it wasn't over for Selby.

After the grave mound was finished, Grimes piled rocks on top of it to keep the coyotes away. They would come at night but wouldn't work too hard for their meat. Fuller's rifle still stood where it had been when he ran, and he made no attempt to claim it, as if by doing so he would remind himself and the others of his cowardice.

Fuller walked down by the stream and Sundance followed him. Below them the valley looked empty and peaceful. The only movement was the flapping of buzzards on the hills far up from the creek. The dead snipers were getting their own form of burial; their bodies would be bones long before the worms worked on Rance. Grimes, Longworth and Finnerty had gone back to getting out the gold.

Fuller heard Sundance coming up behind him. "I'll be gone in a minute," he said. "I'm just thinking where to go."

"That's what you want to do?"

"The only thing I can do. The others stayed, I ran."

"You think you'd run again? You didn't get Rance killed but you did run. What about the next time? There's going to be a next time. No way this thing with Selby will stop. You can talk straight to me. I've seen all the sides of men to be seen."

"You haven't called me a coward."

"There are born cowards. Some men accept the fact as part of their nature. Most men are a mixture of fear and courage. The sane ones are."

Fuller looked at Sundance. "You don't have problems like that."

If there had been sarcasm intended, Sundance would have punched Fuller to the ground. But there was none: the other man just wanted to know, to ask a question he always had wanted to ask someone.

"I try to keep from dying," Sundance answered. "But wanting to stay alive too hard is often the quickest way to get killed. If they had dropped a charge on that shaft you'd be in there now sucking your last breath. You think that's better than a quick bullet? One time in Mexico I dug out men who'd been buried in a mine fall, all were dead, but one had tried to cut his throat with a sharp rock."

Fuller shuddered. "You saying you'll give me another chance?"

Sundance said, "No more than one. Tell me this. You ever been under fire before today?"

"Not a once," Fuller said.

Sundance nodded, though still unsure about this Yankee. "Men do the damnedest things when they're under fire for the first time. It never stays the same. One time I saw a full colonel shit his pants during a skirmish. That man had been through the whole War. Something happened that day. That's all. Later he was killed leading a charge against a Reb stronghold that couldn't be taken. No man is the same all the time."

Fuller stared into space. "That's not much consolation to me."

Sundance's usually quiet voice became harsh. "I'm not here to give you consolation. I'm asking you what you want to do?"

"How can I stay after what I did?" Fuller asked. "Even my friend Longworth looks away from me. The Irishman spits when he sees me. The only one who hasn't treated me any different is your friend Tate."

"Tate doesn't give a damn about you," Sundance said. "He's seen too much death to care about what one man does. If it was up to Tate you'd be dead right now. Nothing personal. He'd see you as a danger to what we're doing."

Fuller said after thinking about it, "I'll stay if

116

you make a deal with me?"

"What is it?"

Fuller was no show-off. "Promise you'll kill me if I turn yellow again."

Turning away, Sundance said, "You didn't have to ask me that. I planned to do it. Now get back to work. Remember what I said. Run off again and I'll drop you without a word."

On his way to the bluff, Sundance said to Finnerty, "You spit too much. Fuller stays for now. If you don't like that you're welcome to haul freight."

The Irishman was dumping ore into the sluice. "Anything you say. Just don't ask me to wipe his eyes if he breaks out crying."

"You talk too much, too," Sundance said.

Up on the bluff, Tate said casually, as if nothing had happened, "You know this lookout stuff won't work a second time. They know we have a man up here. If they circle wide they can come at us from behind. What do you think they'll do next?"

"A night attack maybe," Sundance said.

"That's what I was thinking," Tate said. "At night when there is no moon, they'll come up the creek, most of them. They'll leave their horses, the far end of the valley, and wade up the creek."

"That wouldn't be a bad way to do it," Sundance agreed. "First, they'd start an attack from some other point. But you're right about the creek. The water would cover any noise they made, the banks would give them cover. On a dark night you could bring fifty men up that creek."

"You think we should fire the grass and brush along the banks? That would cut down on the cover."

"On a dark night that wouldn't mean much. If

they wear dark clothes you wouldn't see them at all.''

Tate chomped angrily on his cigar. "You're the one with the crystal ball. What would you do? How would you stop them.''

"Petroleum.''

"Petroleum? You mean that stuff they make into coal oil?''

"Same thing,'' Sundance said. "All the big mines use it. Selby must have plenty of it.''

"You mean use it for light when the attack comes.''

Sundance said no. Selby wanted to fight dirty, so dirty it was going to be. "Not for light—to burn men alive. Listen and don't ask so many questions. Petroleum burns even on water. Back in Pennsylvania where they drill for it some of it leaks off and the rivers catch fire. It burns until it burns itself out. Any man that comes up that creek will be burned to ash. They can run out of the creek but they'll keep on burning.''

Take liked the idea of shooting at lighted targets. "Why, Mr. Sundance, we can just lay back and kill them like ducks.''

"Easier,'' Sundance said. "Men are bigger than ducks.''

Tate liked that too. "But how are we going to get it from Selby? Walk up to his front door and ask if we can buy a few extra barrels he isn's using?''

Sundance looked down at the valley. Fuller and Longworth were at the sluice. Everything looked so peaceful. Sundance didn't like the gold mining business, but he was getting used to it. Too bad Selby wouldn't let them work out the piddling little mine and move on.

"I don't know how we're going to get it," he said.

Tate's new beard made him look like a flimflam itinerant preacher. "That's what I like about you, halfbreed. You start off talking all-wise, then you say you don't have the real answer."

"Steal it, I guess. I hope we can steal it."

Tate's dark eyes glittered with a murderous idea. "If we can get that close to it, why not blow the whole thing?"

"Your answers are worse than mine," Sundance said. "You want to burn the whole town just to get at Selby?"

"It's Selby's town."

"People live there."

"All of them Selby bootlickers."

"Working people mostly. I won't burn a whole town just to hold onto a hole in the ground. Besides, what do you think would happen if we did that? Kill and cripple hundreds of people? We can't send them warning that we're going to do it. If we burn a town we'll be hunted men for the rest of our lives. Women and children are in there, too."

"All right. But how are we going to steal it. You know Selby will have it guarded like gold. And if we do steal it, don't you think he'll figure what we're going to use it for?"

Sundance nodded. "He'd know right off. What we have to do is steal a supply that's coming in. A mine uses a lot of it, so a supply has to be coming all the time. It has to come by wagon because the railroad is a good fifty miles away. I figure six big barrels to a wagon. No more than that, it's too heavy. It'll take at least two of us."

"What happens to the mine while we're gone."

"While I'm gone," Sundance said. "Finnerty

goes with me, you stay."

Tate didn't like the idea of being left out of it. "Why Finnerty? A good man to be sure, but why him instead of me?"

"Finnerty's a good man when it comes to some things. The real reason—half the wagon drivers in the West are Irishmen. You have a shifty look especially with that new beard. You'd ever take you for a teamster?"

Tate smiled. "They'd believe me for a teamster before they'd believe you."

"That's why it has to be Finnerty," Sundance said. "We'll clean him up to make him look less like a tramp. Then we'll head for the railroad. If we're lucky there will be a supply of petroleum waiting at the depot. I'm betting there is."

"What if you run into some of Selby's men at the rails?"

"No reason Selby should be watching the depot. By now Selby knows we have dynamite. I bought it in plain sight before this trouble started. Coal oil he won't figure on. I hope he won't."

Tate looked at Sundance's copper skin and shoulder-length yellow hair, his pale blue eyes and rangy look of suppressed violence. "What part are you going to play in this melodrama? No freight agent in his right mind will believe you have anything to do with wagon driving."

"I'll be offstage but not too far off," Sundance said. "Finnerty will be the principal player. If he plays his part right we'll have a whole wagon of petroleum."

Tate scrubbed his hand across his wiry black beard. "You want to tell me the plot?"

Sundance looked at the sky. It would be dark before long and time to move out. "I don't want to spoil the ending for you. I can't tell you what to do if a night attack comes before we get back."

"No need," Tate said. "We'll be dead."

They didn't shake hands. "If we don't get back you better pull out," Sundance said.

Tate raised the field glasses to scan the quiet valley. "Like hell, my friend! I got a half interest in a gold mine to protect."

Sundance went down and called Finnerty out of the mine. "I'm not spitting and I'm not talking," he said.

"Forget that. You know where the railroad stop is?"

Finnerty said, "Sure I do, fifty or sixty miles down the road from Orono. It's not a depot exactly, just a stop. You figure to go for a train ride."

Sundance looked the Irishman over. "Get rid of that hat. The rest of you doesn't look too bad now that you've been filling your belly. Keep your dirty shirt on; you've more than earned your ham and beans."

Sundance called out the others and hats were tried on Finnerty. Rance's hat was a bit too large, but it didn't look too bad. Sundance gave him his own extra canvas coat. Both were rangy men, so it fitted fine. Now the Irishman looked more like a teamster with a job.

"You know how to handle a team?" Sundance asked.

Finnerty said, "I've drive everything there is to drive in my time. You want to tell me what this is all about?"

Sundance wanted to take a look around before they left. "We'll talk on the way," he said. He knew there might be no one left alive when he got back. If he got back. The force defending the mine was down to four men, maybe three. How Fuller would act under fire was still a question. As riflemen, Fuller and Longworth couldn't be called anything but poor. Grimes could shoot but wasn't any kind of natural rifleman. That left Tate, merciless and accurate. Still, one man couldn't hold off an army of killers. What he and Finnerty were setting out to do was dangerous; if they didn't do it, he knew they were whipped.

They started out in the dark, crossing the creek and the hills to the west. There was a moon but most of the time it was hidden by clouds drifting across its face. As they crossed the crest of the first hill, they turned for a last look at the camp. The cookfire burned bright in the darkness. After that they crossed the hill and hills beyond the first one. Thirty minutes after they started they rode into a stand of stunted trees and waited in the darkness with rifles ready. If they were being tracked then the trackers were good. Night-hunting animals skittered in the dry leaves under the trees. Otherwise—nothing.

They moved ahead when the moon clouded over again. This wasn't farming country so there were no barking dogs to look out for. Now with the sun gone and the earth giving back little of the day's heat, the wind blew cold. In a few hours they would skirt the town of Orono but keep well away from it. On the far side of the town they would pick up the road going to the railroad. There might be killing to do if Selby had posted guards along the road. Sundance's guess was that he hadn't. But if it came to killing they would do it and move on.

To stay on the road was a risk they had to take. Traveling through the hills would have taken them to the railroad just as surely as the road. But there wasn't time for that. Back at the mine four men waited in the darkness, waited to be attacked at any minute.

Finnerty huddled inside the lined coat as the wind blew harder and colder. This was semi-desert country; it got cold at night in the hottest months of the year.

"Thanks for the loan of the coat," Finnerty said. "A good coat on my back, a horse under me! Makes me feel like a man again."

Sundance told him to keep the coat. "You can buy a better horse when you get your share of the gold."

"I'll never forget you for this," the Irishman said. "You sure you don't have some Irish in you, Sundance?"

Sundance said his father Nicholas had been an Englishman, and they laughed about that. "Well, sir, there must be one good Englishman in this whole wide world," Finnerty said.

Several hours had passed and they could see the lights of Orono from far away. The thump of the ore crushers came faintly on the wind. Finnerty spat, but Sundance knew he wasn't thinking of Fuller. The Irishman, like Tate, was something of a philosopher, though his thoughts didn't range so far or so deep.

"Tell me," he said quietly. "Why do men try to set themselves up as kings?"

"Because other men let them do it," Sundance said. "It's time to talk about what you have to do."

"Name it," Finnerty said.

123

"We have to go over it good so you won't make any mistakes. Early in the morning, soon as it's light, you have to go to the rail stop and find out if there is a wagonload of petroleum—coal oil—waiting to be driven to the Selby mine. We have to hope there will be."

Finnerty got part of the idea. "But I can't just pass myself off as a Selby teamster. I don't have a wagon and they'd ask me to show some kind of a letter from the company. Mind you, I'll do anything you say. I'm just asking."

The lights of Orono were fading as they rode through a shallow valley. "You're right, that wouldn't work," Sundance said. "What you have to do is find a teamster who's sleeping it off after a night with the bottle. If I know teamsters they make a trip that long in one day, stay overnight, come back the next. That sound right to you?"

"Right as rain," Finnerty answered. "I've done it many a time myself. A trip of fifty or so miles would use up most of a day in a heavy wagon. As to the drinking, I never knew a teamster that didn't drink when he was out from under the boss's eye. Nobody minds too much, long as they get the wagonload back on time. But we'll have to get there right early. Half drunk or not, they all start out early."

"You know the stop we're going to?" Sundance asked.

"I ought to. That's where they threw me off the train. A brakeman—mean son of a bitch—conked me with a billy and pitched me off the roof about a mile outside town. When I come to I was fixing to hop to another freight when this woman I begged a meal from said there was plenty of work in Orono."

124

Sundance looked at Finnerty, somewhat filled out with food, wearing a hat and a brand new lined coat. The fact that he had a horse was just as important. "You think they'll remember you?"

The Irishman scoffed at the idea. "Nobody ever remembers a hobo. They don't like to look at you even when they're doling out charity. You, sir, are looking at a man of means."

Sundance said, "This teamster you're hoping to find. If he's coming out of a nightlong drunk your job is to get him back on." Sundance dug into his pocket and handed Finnerty greenbacks and Mexican gold coins. "Get him drunk again and keep him drunk, so drunk he won't know what day it is."

Finnerty pocketed the money. "So far so good, but what am I supposed to be doing at the train stop?"

"You're on your way to a new gold strike close to the California line. Pretend to be as drunk as he is. It's a secret but you'll stake him to the train fare because you've taken a fancy to him. Give him a bottle, maybe two, and get him on the next train going that way. By the time he wakes up he won't know where he is. Don't be stingy with the money. My guess is he'll drink up the rest of it, then find himself another job."

Finnerty said casually, "Maybe it would be simpler if I smothered him with a pillow, then splash whiskey all over him. Do it that way and there's no chance he'll use the telegraph to warn Selby that something is going on."

Sundance thanked the Irishman for his kind thought. "The man just works for a living. Why kill the poor bastard?"

"Just a suggestion," Finnerty said mildly.

"It's important that you show him off while you're getting him drunk. The freight agent has to see him barely able to walk. You be talking sense to him, at the same time getting him drunker. Then when he fails to show up to get the loaded wagon, the freight office won't think too much about it. They'll be glad to get rid of him and the wagon."

They reached the road to the railroad and put distance behind them. As they rode, Finnerty said, "What you said sounds pretty good. Course you know Selby is going to find out about the missing wagon at some point."

"I'm hoping it's later than sooner," Sundance said. He had to restrain Eagle from breaking into a gallop that would have left Finnerty's horse far behind.

Finnerty laughed wildly. "Meaning you don't want him to hear about it until we have our fish fry."

Sundance rode ahead without answering. He found nothing to joke about in the burning of other men. The hell of it was, the Irishman was right. If it worked right, Selby's men would fry in their own fat.

Chapter Ten

Hours later, passing no one on the road, they saw the railroad tracks gleaming dully in the gray morning light. The town was nothing but a freight office, a water tower, a scatter of houses and shacks. In the freight office the light still burned; the rest of the place was asleep. Smoke curled from the chimney of the freight office and a dog barked and the rails stretched into nowhere. The railroad freight office was the biggest building there, built to last. The water tower stood taller than everything else.

Lying on the crest of a hill off the road, Finnerty handed the field glasses to Sundance. "See that frame building painted yellow. They sell drinks there and in back are beds for people that have to wait over for trains. If he's there he'll be sleeping off last night. It's best I go in right now. Once he gets his head under cold water it may not be so easy to get him rummed up again."

Sundance nodded. "Sorry you have to do this by yourself."

"Don't forget about me," Finnerty said. "I've had every hard knock there is. If something happens, it's been a pleasure knowing you."

"Same here, Irishman. I'll cover you best I can with the Remington. If it looks fishy get out fast."

Sundance, the Remington ready and both shirt pockets filled with shells, watched the strange Irishman ride back onto the road. He smiled when he heard Finnerty's tuneless whistle start up. There was no little music in it, it might have been a hymn or a dirty cantina song. Now and then there had been doubts about the war with Selby. Now they were gone as Finnerty rode away. If a poor down and outer like Finnerty was willing to risk his life to stand up to Selby, then who was Jim Sundance to even consider quitting?

Sundance was no more than two hundred yards from the freight office; with a Remington fitted with a sharp-shooter's tube sight that was no distance at all. At that distance he didn't even need the sight, and with the tube there was no way he

127

could miss.

Beside the freight office was a corral with work horses and wagons in it. His heart quickened when he moved the field glasses to the last wagon in the row. Whatever was in the last wagon stood up high and was covered with a sheet of tarpaulin held down with ropes. But then as the light grew stronger he could see the circular shapes under the taut wagon cover. Yes, he thought, and they could be barrels of nails for some hardware store.

He watched while Finnerty rode to the freight office and hitched his horse to the post. Then he went inside and after a few minutes a sleepy looking man came out with him and pointed to the yellow painted building. He went back inside and slammed the door. Nothing moved on all the endless miles of track.

Finnerty rode down to the yellow building and went in. A few shacks on both sides of the rails had cookfires going by now. The dog kept barking until a fat man came out of the yellow house and threw a bottle at him. The dog dodged the bottle and ran away, then continued barking from a safe distance.

About an hour later, Finnerty and a thick-set man in his fifties came out of the yellow house and went down past the freight office to the corral. The teamster had a red shirt, a bulging belly, and a bottle in his hand. As they passed the freight office, the agent came out and looked after them.

When they came out of the corral the freight agent was waiting on the porch. Glassing the porch, Sundance couldn't hear a word. He knew the freight agent was urging the teamster to be on his way. Instead of answering, the teamster took a swig from the bottle and offered a drink to the agent. The teamster opened his pants and pissed against the side of the freight building. While he was doing it the agent exchanged a look of disgust with Finnerty. Finnerty shrugged at the agent, as if to say, What the hell do you want me to do? Angered, the agent went back into his office.

Finnerty was doing fine. He took a comradely drink from the bottle after the agent was out of sight. Then they went back to the yellow house, and the fat man and two whores came out onto the porch to welcome them. They went inside and the door closed. It stayed closed for almost another hour, then Finnerty came out by himself. Sundance watched while the Irishman went back to the freight office and came out with the agent. Finnerty stood a foot taller than the freight agent and was talking a lot. Finally, the agent shrugged and came out with papers that Finnerty had to sign. Finnerty turned away with the angry air of a man with important things on his mind and went to the corral. The agent shrugged and went into his office.

But Sundance kept the Remington sighted on the freight office until Finnerty had hitched up the team and pulled away. Fifteen minutes later, after rounding a bend in the road, Finnerty drove the wagon up and into the stand of trees.

Finnerty climbed down and showed Sundance the receipt the freight man had given him for Selby's manager. "Not six barrels—eight!" Finnerty said. "Look at the size of that wagon!"

"But what about the driver?" Sundance said. "You were supposed to put him on the next train. What happened to that?"

"A wreck down the line," Finnerty said. "One of the whores told me. She's all packed and waiting for it. She put some knock-out drops in the driver's whiskey and he won't wake up for hours. When he does she'll give him another dose. I gave her money for everything. She'll get that teamster all the way to California."

"She didn't think something was going on?"

"Sure she did. Then I said I wanted him gone because he'd been studding my wife. So it was kill him or get rid of him. If I killed him I'd have to do some time in the penitentiary. Meanwhile, the wife and kids would starve."

"You think she believed you?"

"Could be she didn't. Money talks though," Finnerty said. "So does this." He yanked his belt gun. "I said if she ever came back to this country I'd blow her knees and her titties off. As far as the freight agent knows or cares, he's just another drifting teamster making off for greener pastures with a whore. How did I do?"

Sundance looked at the ugly, mash-fashed Irishman. "You should have been on the stage, Finnerty."

The Irishman felt the jagged, hollow place in the jaw that must have been caused by a bullet or a shell fragment. "You may be joking but there was a time in my long-ago youth the ladies thought I was one fine-looking lad."

"Let's go," Sundance said.

This time they had to stay off the road all the way back, because there was no telling when some of Selby's tough nuts would come along on fast horses. Loaded as it was, the wagon would make too much dust; they'd be spotted long before they got it off the road. Besides, just one bullet through a barrel would blow them sky high.

"The boys could be making their last stand right about now," Finnerty said, gloomy again now that his moment of triumph had passed.

"No use thinking about it," Sundance said. "All we can do is make the best time we can."

For a long time traveling wasn't too bad; a long valley between low hills ran parallel to the road. It was well-grassed and the wagon didn't raise much dust. It was still early when they started back, but the day seemed to drag on forever. At the far end of the valley, about ten miles from where they started, a bad patch of country had to be crossed. In one place the only way they could cross a narrow ravine was to fill it with rocks, dead trees, anything they could find. And even so the wagon wobbled precariously on the makeshift bridge. Finally, using ropes to steady the wagon, they got it across. Then there was another dangerous stretch littered with rocks of all sizes; a broken wheel would doom them quicker than anything else. Finnerty set his bony jaw and started through and an hour later they were through the worst part of it. They rested the horses, ate jerked meat and drank water, and moved on again. If they were lucky they would arrive back at the mine not long after midnight.

Another long valley made for easy traveling. There was one bad moment when a rattler, hidden by grass, struck at one of the horses but got only the hoof. Finnerty's hand streaked for his gun, but before he could draw it, Sundance's throwing knife was buried in the snake's head.

Finnerty holstered his pistol again. "Wasn't thinking when I did that," he said. "A shot would have been heard for miles. That was some throw you made just now."

Sundance just grunted as he wiped the blade clean and put it away. It was close to dark so Orono wasn't that far away. They saw the lights of the town after a while, winking on in the gathering darkness. The ore crushers, working night and day, thumped in the silence of dusk.

Then they turned west from the town and made their way through the hills. It had been one hell of a day. Hot food and black coffee would be good to come back to. Every mile of the way they watched for Selby's guards, but the hills were dark and silent. The mine-owner's hardcases would be guarding his vital parts: the machines, mine shafts, dynamite houses. His big square house would be ringed with guards, waiting to kill on command. Still, it would be wrong to decide that Selby had what General Cook called "the fortress mentality," meaning men who holed up in what they thought were impregnable positions. The attack by the six snipers was proof that Selby could strike out when he felt like it.

When they got about two miles from the camp, Sundance rode ahead to check the west side of the creek. He dismounted and left Eagle to follow at a distance while he went ahead on foot to scout the creek. But a careful search along the banks, east and west, turned up no Selby spy. On the far side of the creek, high up by the mine, the fire still burned and he could see the tent and the stack of lumber. If there had been an attack everything would be burned by now. If they intended to make a night attack, they still were making plans about how and when to do it.

The best place to cross was at the sandbar below the gorge, at the place where the tributary ran into the main creek. He knew Tate would be awake and waiting no matter what the hour and, knowing Tate, he approached the creek cautiously. When he got to the sandbar he whistled like a night loon, doing it so that it couldn't pass as real for anyone but a greenhorn. A whistle came back and Tate's voice called out, "You better be Jim Sundance, friend."

Sundance crossed on the sandbar so firmed with up sand and so high that he hardly got his feet wet. Tate stood up and lowered the Fox shotgun. "We had a quiet day here, old friend. How did it go with you? I don't see the Irishman."

Sundance said, "We got what we wanted. I figured on six barrels—we got eight."

"Jesus Christ! I'll be disappointed if they don't come. What a sight that would be."

"You won't like it when you see it."

"Like hell I won't. I just wish we could fry Selby along with the rest of them."

"No chance of that. Durkin maybe."

Sundance stamped his moccasined feet on the sand-firm sandbank. "It feels hard enough but it won't support a loaded wagon."

Tate looked up at the camp. "We could use the lumber to lay out a bridge."

"Maybe," Sundance said. "But they'll catch on if some of the boards tear loose and float away downstream. They'll see the marks of the wheels and put it together. No other way but unload the wagon and drag out one barrel at a time. We'll unload the wagon and turn it on its side, then put the barrels in again. On their side, with the stoppers loosened but firm enough so nothing leaks out before it's time. The sandbank is the best place because it's high and slows the flow of the water. Once we open the stoppers the petroleum will flow out and go downstream nice and easy."

"Not too easy I hope."

Sundance dipped his hand in the water where it

flowed over the sandbar. "It's flowing fast enough. If you mean can they get out before it hits them—the answer is no. They'll be waist deep in a river of fire."

Even Tate was awed. "I never heard of such a thing in my life."

Sundance said, "I told Selby I fight dirty, fight to kill. That's what we're going to do. Come on now, let's get to work. They could get here at any time."

Tate stared at Sundance. "Why do you think it's going to be tonight?"

"I feel it. The moon is down, but that's not the reason I think they're going to attack. Selby will figure that the dead hour of the night will be the best time. The Indians have a saying that four o'clock in the morning is when a man's spirit is at its lowest. Did you know that most sick people die at that hour? They know they're going to die so they die when there's nothing left but silence and darkness."

Tate smiled. "It's going to be different for Selby's men. They're going to have the brightest deaths since Creation."

Sundance went back and told Finnerty to bring up the wagon. Then Sundance sent Grimes down along the creek to watch for any sign of Selby scouts. "If you spot any, don't do any shooting," Sundance said. "Just try to get back here without being seen."

They unroped the barrels and got them out of the wagon. They were heavy and it took four men to move a barrel. They stood them side by side on the river bank. Finnerty went up the camp and got a wrench to loosen the metal stoppers. As soon as he did, the stink of raw petroleum mingled with the clean night air. Finnerty unhitched the team and led the horses to the far side of the creek and around behind the bluff. If they whinnied, the gorge water would kill the sound. When he came back Sundance, Tate and Longworth were pulling the wagon down onto the sandbar. Once on its side it stayed there; the current passing over the bar wasn't enough to move it. But just to make sure, they rolled rocks down the slope and lined them in front of the overturned wagon. One by one, they rolled the barrels down the bank onto the sandbar and set them in position in the wagon, turning them so the metal caps were on the bottom and the petroleum would flow out fast, emptying every last drop. The weight of the barrels held them firm, but Sundance said to rope them anyway. Then he told Fuller and Finnerty to jack up the back of the wagon with rocks so the flow from the barrels would be faster.

"What now?" Tate said, chewing a dead cigar.

"We wait in position," Sundance said. "I figure they'll start shooting at us from the sides while the main force comes up the creek. You Fuller, you Longworth, take up positions where you can fire back. It won't be too bad. I hope it won't. Blaze away, try to make yourself more than you are."

Finnerty was eating a slice of ham steak between two slabs of bread. "What am I supposed to be doing?"

"You stay here with the wagon. Grimes will be with you. You have to get the barrels opened fast. Grimes will give you a hand."

Tate said, "What do we do—start the fire?"

"That's what we do. If they come they won't be bunched up, depend on that. They'll be close enough so they can throw enough force into the attack. We find the best cover we can, then wait."

"How do we do it, strike a match?"

"We wait with rocks wrapped in oil-soaked rags. Then we strike the match."

"That'll bring a fine storm of lead," Finnerty remarked.

"We'll keep our heads down when we do it," Tate said.

"They won't be shooting for long," Sundance said. "But don't try to follow and finish them off. The fire will do that. Some will get out but they won't have the same bodies they started out with. If Selby attacks us tonight, the way I figure, he's going to lose most of his men."

Longworth picked up his rifle. "He could still send for a force of militia."

Sundance said there would be no militia.

Longworth looked puzzled. "Why are you so sure of that?"

"Because he sdaid he wouldn't and I believe him. Selby is too proud and that's why we're going to beat him."

Just then Grimes came splashing up the creek, heavy-footed and awkward.

"That can't be Grimes," Finnerty growled. "Nothing but a bull buffalo could make that much noise."

Sundance told Finnerty to shut up.

Grimes, unused to running, threw himself down in the sandbar shallows gasping for breath. "They're moving into the far end of the valley," he said.

Sundance glared at Fuller and saw that the man's face was tight with fear. Fuller looked back without saying anything. Maybe he'll be all right, Sundance thought. He had no special feeling about Fuller. He didn't like him or dislike him. He was needed, the only reason he was there. But this wasn't the time for soul searching. It wasn't time for anything but prepare for the attack that was to come. It would be a big one.

"He's going to throw everything he has at us," Sundance said. "If we come through this we'll have a chance of beating him." He didn't look at Fuller. "Every man here will have a job to do. See that you do it right."

Chapter Eleven

"They're coming in slow," Grimes said. "Both banks of the creek and coming this way. There's a lot of them. You told me not to hang around and try to count. At a guess, fifty men. Jesus! It looked like they had their faces blacked over. Dark clothes, you could hardly see a one of them in that light."

"You called it right, crystal gazer," Tate said, finishing wrapping the oiled rocks in rags, leaving a long tail on all of them.

Earlier, Sundance had made all the fire arrows he needed. He slung the quiver over his shoulder and picked up the great ash bow. The great bow was the first weapon he had been taught to use as a boy among the Cheyenne, and though he was expert with all weapons, the bow was the one he liked best. The powered steel shaft of an arrow could penetrate a man's skull as surely as a bullet. Best of all, it was silent and there was no give-away sound like a gun.

It was about three miles to the far end of the

valley; it wouldn't take him that long to get there. First, they would come along the banks of the creek, then when they were closer they would get down into it.

"You go up with Fuller and Longworth," he told Grimes. "You sure the dynamite is safe?"

Longworth said it was where no bullet could get at it, in the mine shaft.

Sundancce had to keep Tate from springing at Longworth. Tate was cursing a blue streak, mad enough to kill. "I told you a safe place, you god-damned fool. That meant bury it behind a rock, then pile rocks on top of it. You ever hear of a richochet, or are you dumber than most Yankees? That whole shaft could come down with one bullet."

Sundance kept his hand on Tate's arm. "No time to move it now. You all set, Finnerty?"

"Ready to do the honors," the Irishman said, slapping the wrench against the palm of his hand. "Soon as you fire the first arrow by the wagon I'll turn this stuff loose."

"Good," Sundance said. "You stay to the right of the wagon. The arrow will come to the left. Then open the barrels fast as you can and get the hell out of there. Even an empty barrel will have gas in it. That can blow too if a bullet hits it."

Tate clapped Finnerty on the shoulder. "Run like the dickens, Irish."

Finnerty grinned at the man he had fought so long before at Mary's Heights. "Imagine me taking orders from a Johnny Reb. I'll run faster than the wind, Tate."

"You're a poet and don't even know it," Tate said.

Sundance and Tate waded into the creek, slowed even more by the wagon lying atop the sandbar. Tate had his pockets full of fire-starting rocks. They had to whisper because sound carried so far on water. "The S bend where Grimes and Rance had their claim," Sundance said. "Water slows and swirls there, deeper than most places."

Tate said, "There's no way they won't smell it."

"We'll have to chance that. It's never been done so I'm hoping they won't figure until it's too late. Even if it doesn't catch them it'll break any attack. They'll figure maybe there's a worse surprise up ahead."

After that they moved in silence, and they were having an easier time: they didn't have to wade against the current. They stayed to the sides of the creek as the attackers would be doing, all but covered by the overhang of grass and brush. Now and then the moon showed through the clouds, faded, throwing weak light. Sundance looked back along the creek and could barely see the dark outline of the wagon. There might not be any light when it came time to loose the warning arrow, so he fixed the place he was going to fire at in his head. He had done it before, killed a man in total darkness; hitting a wagon ought to be easier. But this one had to be right. If he overshot the wagon and hit the water behind it, Finnerty might not hear the splash. An arrow slicing through water didn't make much noise. All his years of experience had to count now. If they didn't . . .

They crawled out of the water at the S bend. Sundance stayed at the first part of it. For a moment, the moon went out like a doused lamp; there was nothing but running water and the darkness and cold wind. From where he was, he couldn't see Tate lying in the brush on the far side of the creek. That was good. He wasn't supposed to be seen. Nothing more could be said or done until the time came to kill.

Minutes passed and then they heard them coming.

Pale moonlight glinted on their rifles held above their heads. Their faces were smeared with black oil, even their hands. Silent, faceless, they moved like a small army of ghosts. Not such a small army. Grimes had been wrong in his estimate of fifty men. It was more like a hundred and they couldn't all be hired gunmen. Selby had theatened to use miners for double, maybe triple pay. No doubt they had been promised better jobs, easier jobs in the mine, maybe jobs outside the tunnels. It was too bad that none of them would ever get to be foremen. After this night there would be widows and orphans. It was too bad but when a man joined an army, any army right or wrong, he had to expect to get killed.

Sundance had the first arrow nocked and ready. He turned and could just about see the wagon on the sandbar. Then the moon went behind the clouds and the wagon melted into darkness. There was no time to wait for the light to come again. It had to be now: they were starting to come into the deep pool at the S bend where the water turned black and deep.

Sundance steadied, seeing the wagon in his mind's eye. That's all he had to go by. Too much wind came from the east and he moved the bow inches into the wind. He took a breath and let it out slowly. Then, to make the arrow fight the east-blowing wind, he put all the force he could into the shot. The steel tipped shaft left the bow with the speed of a bullet. A small cracking sound came from the darkness. It wa barely audible above the sound of the wind and water, the rustling of the dry grass along the banks.

He waited, and then it began to come, the smell of petroleum. Floating on top of water, mixed with water, it didn't smell as strongly as he had expected. But it was there and he smelled it. The moon gleamed again and he could see the oiliness of the water as it flowed past his hiding place. By now the attackers were well into the S bend, some past it, the rest in the deepest part of the pool. He heard men muttering at the smell of the water, then a whispered voice ordered them to be quiet.

It was time! Hunched low, Sundance struck a flint to the first fire arrow as bullets sang all around him. A rough voice yelled, 'Get out quick! Out of the water—quick!"

Sundance loosed the fire arrow into the deepest part of the pool and the creek was instantly sheeted from end to end with flames. Bullets still came but they were fired in panic. Men began to scream as the upper half of their bodies burst into flames. Tate was throwing fire-starters from the far side of the creek, and every time a rock with a tail of fire hit the water, there was another spread of flame. Upstream, Finnerty was yelling, the damn fool, and as more and more petroleum poured into the creek the flames grew higher. The fire arrows gone, Sundance grabbed up the Winchester and began to kill men who didn't need killing. Some were trying to climb the high banks, their flaming clothes setting the grass and brush on fire. Sundance and Tate shot at them from both sides. Tate's sawed-off boomed and killed four men at the same time. It was a single shot but he used it like a repeater. It boomed again and again. Men burning to death tried to return the deadly fire. Some firing came from up by the mine; it was just a light scatter of shooting.

Sundance dropped the Winchester and started to use the long-barreled Colt. The stench of burning flesh sickened him as he fired round after round. Men screamed and died and the deep pool of the S bend was thick with bodies, thick as a poolful of dynamited fish. Some sank and some drifted, still burning. Tate was using the Fox shotgun now killing anything that showed a sign of movement. Men trying to run back from the burning pool were followed and enveloped by flames. Up at the mine the firing had all but stopped, but even as he killed, coldly and efficiently, Sundance listened for the dynamite to go up. Even if the mine shaft blew they could start digging again, but he had other uses for the dynamite. He hadn't told the others about it. The dynamite, if he had to use it for the purpose he had in mind, would be their last hope.

He fired, reloaded and fired again, kept on killing, until his weapons grew hot in his hands. There could be no mercy. Selby would show none if given the chance. The worst possible damage had to be inflicted here tonight. Force was all Selby understood.

The creek was choked with bodies by the time the flames started to lick out. Two men managed to scramble out and roll themselves, their shirts burning, in sand and grass. Tate shot them while they were still smoking. One man managed to rip off his burning clothes and stood naked with his hands up. Tate blew him in half with the Fox. Sundance saw a man running, screaming at the same time, and brought him down. In all his life he had never seen such a slaughter.

Then it was over and the moon came out bright and clear. Sundance wished the wind would blow up hard, to blow the stink away. But it didn't. Suddenly, the night was peaceful again. Many years before, during the War, Sundance had walked across a battlefield after all the fighting was done, the enemy driven back. This was in the last days of war when the North was using Negro regiments. The Confederates had spared no one. Blacks not dead had been bayoneted, some mutilated. Not a single black soldier remained alive. The sight had sickened Sundance as nothing before in his life, and the same feeling came back now. There was no need for the Civil War, no need for this one. Walking along the creek and looking at the blackened faces of the dead men he was reminded of the massacred Negroes. But still he looked for men with the breath of life in them; when he found them he killed them. Some, their eyes pale in their blackened faces, begged to be shot. He shot them with no feeling of hate, no feeling of any kind. He felt tired but it wasn't a physical tiredness. A sane man could take only so much killing before he began to go mad.

Across the creek, Tate had no such feeling. He walked along the edge of the water loading and firing the long barreled Fox. He might have been shooting dodgers, a diversion before breakfast. Sundance didn't try to stop him. It had to be done, so let it be done. The moon grew brighter, as if the lights had been turned up at the conclusion of some body-strewn melodrama. Except the actors weren't playing dead. No one stood up and took a bow. They drifted with the current, or sank. Steam and smoke and stink hung over the creek water in a stomach-turning mist.

Standing still, Sundance reloaded the Colt and the Winchester and waited for Tate to get done with killing the wounded. He had enough of it. Let Tate see it through to the end. The Fox fired again and, listening in the abrupt silence, Sundance heard a tiny clink as the spent cartridges fell among small stones. An instant later the shotgun was snapped shut with a solid thud. But it didn't fire and no more firing came from the mine. For now, the dynamite was safe.

Sundance crossed to Tate's side of the river. Tate, unperturbed, was feeling the barrel of his shotgun, "Someday they're going to come up with an alloy, steel and something else, that will stay cooler when you have to do a lot of shooting."

Sundance didn't answer. All the killing had put Tate in high good humor. Killing was as much a part of life as death. In his time he had killed as many men as Tate, probably more; that didn't mean you had to joke about it. Selby's men had to be killed without mercy, because in Selby's world to show mercy was to show weakness, a sure sign that you didn't have the necessary ruthlessness. He had it, he knew, and it was nothing to be proud of. For him fighting professionally was a business like any other, and in the business of killing you didn't get to be second best—you got dead.

"It'll be cool enough before you have to use it again," he said quietly.

Tate had a fierce temper but he seldom showed it to Sundance. He showed it now. "Burning those men was your idea, my friend. I just finished what you started."

Sundance knew that was the truth. "You're right," he said. "They're working on a new alloy in England right now. In this country a man named John Browning thinks he's found a way to cool gun barrels using air. He's also fooling around with a thing he calls a 'silencer.' An extension of the barrel filled with wire wool, something like that. Deadens the sound when you fire the rifle."

As Sundance intended, the gun talk wiped away Tate's anger, and they made no apologies for the flareup between them.

"Does this silencer, so called, hide the flash of the rifle?" Tate asked.

"Browning says it does. It doesn't kill all the sound and it won't work on a revolver. Can work only on a closed magazine so the gas can't escape through the barrel."

Tate said, "Well, I'll be damned! Anybody else told me a tale like that I'd say he was crazy. I'm going to find this Browning where ever he is."

"Not right now you're not," Sundance said.

None of the other men had been hit during the diversionary skirmish at the mine. "That was just a sideshow," Finnerty said, coming out from behind a rock on the riverbank. "Soon as the river caught fire they just melted away. How many did you get?"

Fuller and Longworth came down from the hill. "Just about every last man," Sundance said.

Finnerty whooped and threw his borrowed hat in the air. "God bless Titusville, Pennsylvania!" he yelled.

Longworth didn't get it. "Where the hell is that?"

Finnerty looked at him with scorn. "That, sonny boy, is where petroleum comes from. Don't you Yankees know anything?"

"Everybody shut up," Sundance ordered. "We're going to move back and blow the sandbar to bits. Once the sandbar and the wagon is gone you'll get a faster flow of water. Longworth, you put the dynamite in the shaft. Go fetch a stick and we'll get it done."

Sundance attached a long fuse and put the dynamite stick on the side of the wagon. "Get the hell away from here," he ordered. "Less you want to get a chunk of barrel iron through your head." When they heard that they ran for cover, even Grimes, slowest of the lot.

Knowing he was offering himself as a target, Sundance snapped a wood match to the dry side of the wagon and lit the fuse. It caught immediately and hissed its way toward destruction. He was hunkered down behind a rock when the sandbar blew. The wagon disappeared and so did the wide bar of sand. Wood, metal and sand showered down on all sides of him. A sliver of barrel shaped like a twisted ax head chipped the rock not far from his face. The rain of wet sand was the last to fall, then all was quiet. No longer blocked by the sandbar, the river ran faster.

Tate stood up brushing sand from his beard. "You want to get Selby's loved ones back to town as fast as you can. I can see the sense of that. On the other hand, you'll be given him a greater supply of water for his placers."

"He deserves something for his efforts," Sundance said.

Finnerty's humor was as bitter as Tate's. "How do you think Selby will take it when eighty or a hundred bodies come floating into town? If that don't make him mad then nothing will."

Sundance said no. Selby wouldn't get mad. It wasn't in his cold nature to get mad. "All he'll do is sit and think of something worse to drive us out."

Tate said, "How much worse can he get?"

Sundance was tired and needed at least a few hours sleep. Three hours would do, four would be a luxury. "How do I know?" he said, tired in mind and body. "You went to school, Mr. Yarnell. Try to figure it out for yourself."

Tate yawned. "All I ever learned at school was to play poker. Come to think of it, that's not such a bad training for life. Come on, you red rascal, what are you really thinking about. What's up your sleeve besides a throwing knife."

Sundance looked at the gambler scrubbing at his mangy beard. Once this was over he was going to pull a gun on Tate and make him shave. "You're right," he said. "Life is like poker. What happened tonight won't stop Selby. He'll just raise the odds. There's no way we can bluff him."

"How do we do that?"

"I told you I have to sleep on it."

Finnerty thought Sundance was the greatest man who ever lived. He had given him back his life, his self respect. "See," he said, "Sundance can sleep and think at the same time."

Sundance prepared to roll himself in his blankets. "You may not like what I wake up with."

Chapter Twelve

The look on Sundance's face warned them to be silent, and even the ever-talkative Finnerty had no comment to make. They knew Selby had them beaten if Sundance didn't come up with one last desperate plan. The thought of killing Selby at long-range was a waste of time. As far as they knew he hadn't stirred from his squat stone house, which was itself like a fortress. A long-range marksman, even a man like Sundance, couldn't get him with a rifle.

Sundance handed the field glasses to Tate and pointed to the far end of the valley. "See where the creek widens and goes between those high hills?"

Tate used the glasses and held them in his hand. A look of understanding swept over his face. "You've been thinking about that all along, haven't you? I knew there was something. But there's no use talking to you when you're in one of your Indian moods."

Finnerty felt it was all right to crack a joke. "Is this a private conversation, or can anybody join in. Begging your pardon, gents—what in hell are you talking about?"

Tate smiled and gave the field glasses to the Irishman. "We're going to dam the river, my friend. Blow those two hills right into the river. This valley is big enough to hold half the water in the world."

"Holy Christ! With the river dammed the whole town will come to a stop. Selby's whole operation is set up for placering. No water, no placering, no mines."

Grimes looked nervous. "And no work for the town. The town has stayed neutral so far. We cut off their water they'll hate our guts."

Turning away to dig up the dynamite, Sundance said coldly, "Selby can have his water back any time he wants. While he's making up his mind we'll turn this valley into the biggest lake in Nevada. Plenty of snow water still coming down from the mountains. And there's another creek that runs in at the end of the valley."

Grimes said, "What you're planning to do is—what's the word?"

"Insurrection. Maybe high treason," Tate said.

Sundance had stopped listening to their talk. He dug up the box of dynamite from the soft dry sand and unwrapped the oilcloth covering. Except for the stick they had used to blow the sandbar everything else was packed as it had been. Stick after stick of glistening tubes of destruction. It was new dynamite without a drop of nitro sweat on any part of it. He had made sure of that when he bought it. Two boxes would be better, but then so would three. One was all they had, one would have to do. A single box would be enough if they placed the explosive sticks in the right places. The valley wouldn't fill up as if they were damming a big river. It would take time to fill, and while that was happening the Selby mines would come to a halt. Placering on a big scale required a great pressure of water; once they blew the dam into place Selby wouldn't have enough water to fill a bucket.

Sundance examined each stick before he refilled the box. Then he checked the fuses for breaks and found none. Only then did he look up at the others.

"Anybody got a better idea?"

"I like it," Tate said.

Finnerty said it was a dandy idea, but he scowled at Grimes. "Our friend here is right about one thing. The whole town is going to be mad at us. Me, I don't give a shit how mad they get. But they will try to get their water back and Selby won't have to pay them to fight for it."

Sundance put the lid back on the dynamite box. "That means we have to keep them occupied while the valley fills up. When there's enough water behind the dam they won't dare blow it. Neither will Selby."

"Be like the Johnstown Flood," Finnerty said. "No town, no mine."

This time Tate didn't smile. "And no people. They'd be hit with a wall of water fifteen feet high."

"Maybe higher than that," Finnerty said. "How do you figure to beat off the first attacks they make before the valley fills up?"

"I don't know," Sundance said.

Tate tugged at his ratty beard. "And I thought I had nerve. How soon do you figure to do it?"

"Tonight," Sundance said. "The middle of the night when even the saloons are closed. The mine has holding tanks so the pumps will work away for hours without anything being noticed. The rest of the town won't know."

Grimes said, "They'll know something is going on when they hear the explosions."

"We'll see," Sundance said, as tired of Grimes as he had been of Rance. "While we're waiting for dark we'll work the mine the way we always do."

The day passed wtihout incident and by nightfall they were ready to move. "We'll be leaving the mine undefended," was the last thing Grimes said before Sundance told him to shut up. Then, one by one, they drifted away from the cookfire after the evening meal and made their way down along the side of the creek. They rode for most of the distance, then led their horses the rest of the way. Fuller and Longworth were left behind to do what they could if an attack came. Sundance knew they would be killed if an attack did come.

When they got to the end of the valley and crossed the second tributary, Sundance told Grimes to stay there and look after the horses. "If anything happens to us up there, get back to the mine and all of you clean out. Go north and keep on going. I'm not faulting you when I say that you won't stand a chance against Selby. Take the gold and go!"

Grimes was a cautious man, but there was a stubborn streak in him. "I want no more than my share. I'd like you and Tate to be there when we divvy up."

"Thanks for the thought, Mr. Grimes," Tate said. Sundance just nodded.

Beyond the tributary the creek became a river once it passed between the two tall clay hills. The twin hills stood up tall and treeless; they would have long been washed away by the action of the water if they hadn't stood on a rock base. They moved silently in the darkness, stopping to listen for sounds. They heard nothing and Sundance guessed he had been right all along. Selby had a far-ranging mind; evidently, it didn't go as far as a damming of the river. It would raise hell in the town, but that was something they would have to face. A plan was forming in his mind; this wasn't the moment to go in to it. First, dam the river and then damn the consequences.

Tate scouted one hill, Sundance crept up and over the other. "Nobody here," Tate said in a whisper. "You figured there wouldn't be."

"No figuring," Sundance answered. "The answer came from my gut. Here's how we do it." He pointed. "See how the water has cut into the side of the hills above the rock base. That happens in times of flood. When the water runs at this level the hills stand firm. Someday a big enough flood will take them down. We're going to do it now."

"I don't know a damn thing about it."

Sundance led the way along the side of the creek, then they climbed down to the hollow place grooved by flood water. "Most of the charges go here and across on the other side. Smaller charges go on the back of the hills. It's like pull and push. No matter how right we do it, it won't be as high as a regular earth dam. High enough for what we want to do."

Tate nodded. "You say when."

They crossed the fast flowing creek to the other side. "If something happens get the hell away from here," Sundance said.

"Maybe I will."

"You'll do what I tell you."

Tate nodded. Sundance didn't believe the nod; there wasn't time to argue about it. They crouched under the overhang of the stream and Sundance dug into the soft clay with the blade of his big Bowie

151

knife so the sticks would stay in place. He went along, placing one stick after another. The fuses hung down, ready to be fired.

"You see how it's done?" Sundance said.

Tate said he could place the charges on the back of the hill. Sundance said, "Climb up about fifteen feet before you place the sticks. Place them close together. Now we move back to the creek and get set. You'll be able to see me from where you set. Start with the last fuse and I'll do the same. As soon as I light a cigar and touch off a fuse you do the same. If a fuse refuses to catch don't fuss with it. Move on to the next one. Then run like hell to the back of the hill and set the last two off. You know what to do after that."

Tate grinned, a man in love with danger. "I think I'll probably run like hell. Don't fall over your feet, halfbreed."

Back across the stream and under the lee of the tall hill, Sundance struck a match to a cigar and sucked fire into it. Tate's match flared on the other side. If bullets came they could come. Moving steadily but quickly, Sundance went along the line of fuses. Every fuse caught and began to hiss. He looked over and one of Tate's fuses hadn't caught. Sundance yelled at him to get the hell away from there. The next fuse began to hiss and then they were away from the creek and running hard.

In back of the hill, Sundance lit the last two fuses and ran upstream along the river. He looked over and didn't. see Tate. Then he saw him running, too. The explosion, when it came, blew them off their feet. They were struck by a gust of hot wind and sent rolling in the grass. Sundance rolled up on his feet and dived into the creek and made it to the other side. Tate lay in the grass with blood oozing from a deep cut in his head. Sundance lifted him as if he had no weight and started away from the creek. Behind him tens of thousands of pounds of rock and clay were crashing down with the sound of thunder, damming the river completely. It looked as if both clay hills had been shorn off at their base. The rumble of the landslide continued for a few minutes and then it got quiet.

Grimes jerked nervously when he saw Sundance carrying Tate. Sundance pushed him aside and carried Tate down to the edge of the creek, already deeper than it had been moments before. In a few minutes it would begin to overflow its banks.

Sundance turned Tate over on his back and splashed water in his face. Tate groaned and his eyes opened. He tried to touch the wound in his head, but Sundance pulled his hand away.

"Hold still," Sundance said, tying his bandanna around the wound. "We'll doctor you later."

Tate tried to raise himself off the ground. "Be still," Sundance ordered. "We'll get you back. Can you stand?"

Tate cursed. "Course I can stand. I been hit harder than that in a saloon. Did we do it, old friend?" Tate turned and squinted. Not much blood was seeping through the bandanna. "Funny thing, I can't see no good."

"A knock on the head will do that," Sundance said. "We did it just right. By tomorrow we'll have our own private lake."

By now the creek was overflowing its banks, seeping into the grass on both sides, yet no more than a few minutes had passed. "I wish the hell I could see it," Tate complained as Sundance hefted him up on his horse. "It's like the light is being turned up and down."

The valley was starting to fill up as they made their way back to camp. They couldn't move fast because of Tate. Sundance looked and saw the sheet of water behind him. It would follow them, deepening every minute. As the night wore on the water would creep up toward the encircling hills. It would be at least a few hours before the water in the mines began to give out. By then they would have to be back at the dam, to defend what they had created.

They rode away from the creek and along the side of the hills. Once the valley was filled the only safe place would be the mine. Sundance grinned savagely. At least they would have more than enough water to wash the gold. He knew that would have to wait. He wondered if they'd ever get back to washing gold. If they didn't, the hell with it. Even if Selby beat them—somehow beat them—then to hell with that too. They have given the son of a bitch a good run for his money. In the end, that was what mattered most—to let no man walk all over you. It was the only way to live and it got you killed, at least you died like a man and not like a whipped dog.

Finnerty ran down the hill to catch Tate before he slid off his horse. "Sweet Savior! You did it. Mr. Grimes, if ever I gave you a dirty look, I'm downright sorry for it."

"Mutual," Grimes said.

They carried Tate into the tent and put a match to the lamp. Sundance told Finnerty to hold the lamp closer. He untied the bandanna and the wound didn't look too bad. A deep gash about two inches about the right eye. There wasn't much blood.

"Turn up the damn light," Tate said though the lamp was only a few inches from his face.

Sundance made him lie back and covered him with

a blanket. "We can't turn up the light," he said. "You want to make a target out of us? Finnerty here will give you a snort of whiskey, then get some sleep."

"Right you are," the Irishman said.

He was holding the bottle to Tate's lips when suddenly the gambler closed his eyes and lay still. The last thing he said was, "We beat him. We beat him, the dirty smug-faced son of a bitch."

Sundance turned down the lamp and stared out into the darkness. The moon rippled on the lake that had been a valley and there was nothing else to be said.

Chapter Thirteen

"Look after him, Finnerty," Sundance said after they went outside and looked down the valley at the sheet of water that covered it. The water hadn't reached the rim of the hills, but it was getting there. It would be there in a few hours.

"How bad is the wound in the head, do you think?" Finnerty asked.

"No way to tell. We can't get a doctor up here now. We'll just have to doctor him ourself and see what happens."

The Irishman gripped the stock of his rifle. "If anything happens to Tate I'll get Selby some way. They may drive us out but I'll camp in the hills as long as it takes. Till the day comes I'll trap rabbits and eat snake meat. Then will come the day when I get him in my rifle sights. Maybe I can even take him alive and do a little work on him."

Sundance looked at the mad Irishman, knowing he meant every word he said. "I'll do it with you—if we live that long."

The sheen of spreading water was all over the valley. Finnerty said, "You know your business better than I do. So don't mind me saying this. That water isn't backing up fast enough to be a real danger to the town."

Sundance nodded and pointed to the dynamite box. "I have four sticks left in there. Where do you think the water in the main creek comes from?"

Finnerty's eyes lit up with excitement. "I've trapped over this country. Where else—a crater lake with a spilloff. Christ, man, if you could blow that, this valley would fill in no time. Water will back clear up to where we are. How far up you think the lake is?"

Sundance put the dynamite sticks and fuses in his pockets. "Not that far. I skirted it on the way down here."

"But a crater lake has rock sides. You know that," Finnerty said. "It's not like blowing clay hills, soft ground. Begging your pardon, you may not be able to do it."

"Can you think of anything else?"

"When they're nothing else to be done, then you do that."

In the tent Tate groaned and Longworth came out to get clean water. Blood was in the pail of water he threw away. "Looks like he's got some kind of fever," he said.

Sundance waved him away. "Do the best you can. Keep his head raised and cool as you can."

Sundance turned back to Finnerty. "The only chance is to blow the lake where the water spills over. There has to be a break there or the water wouldn't come through. That's where I'll place the charges.

Before I leave, move everything up the bluff, close to it."

Finnerty looked about, figuring how long it would take them to do that. "No way to move the sluice less we take it apart."

"We can always build another sluice with the gold we have. You know how to make a raft?"

"I guess I can. We going for a voyage on our new lake?"

Sundance nodded. "The rest of you are. Water isn't deep, still too deep to get back to the dam."

"What about Tate?"

"If he dies it might as well be with the rest of us. Get everything on the raft and pole your way down to the dam. Pull the raft up as high as it will go. If it's too heavy, the hell with it. I have a feeling this is our last go-round in this fight. Flank the dam, don't stay on top of it. It may crumble when the lake water comes. I'm guessing Selby's people won't be there yet. That business with the petroleum will make them think."

Finnerty said, "Selby should have thought to leave us be. How soon before we hear the dynamite going off?"

Sundance looked up at the dark hills. "No more than an hour."

Finnerty smiled. "Then it's gold or glory. I been thinking. I been thinking what Selby said about not calling in the militia. That's not to say he can't get the loan of some artillery, men to use it. You ever hear of a dynamite gun?"

"Saw one once. Used to fire dynamite to bring down dangerous sections of cliff. Fires a stick by compressed air. Carries a long way, they tell me."

"Right they are, good as artillery, some ways better," Finnerty said. "They could lay off and use that

157

on the dam. No more town."

"And no more town, no more Selby mine. If there's enough water behind that dam they won't dare bust it open. Now start moving the stuff and making the raft. The next two hours will tell the story."

Sundance mounted up and left without looking at Tate. If he died Selby would pay for it, for there was no right or wrong in this. For all his highfalutin' ideas, Jackson Selby was dead wrong. He didn't care what Finnerty did: Selby would die if Tate died. Everything else would have to wait.

There wasn't much room. He waded Eagle through the gorge and then took the big stallion out of the water, then followed the creek by its sound. If he blasted out the side of the deep crater lake, he would have to keep to the high ground all the way back. It was quiet in the lines, with a warm night breeze; definitely not a night to be setting out to wreak death and destruction. That was the trouble with men like Jackson Selby: they gathered information about a man and thought that was all there was to know. Sundance thought that so many other men had made the same mistake about him. To underestimate the enemy was a mistake he never made. At heart, for all his ruthlessness, Jackson Selby was just a businessman. Smarter than most, a better judge of men than most—yet still a businessman. His money was his power and his downfall. It was one thing to order death; another thing to face it. Twenty or thirty years before he might have found it possible to bend to the situation, but buying governors and senators, telling whole towns how to jump, had dulled his workingman's canny sense of self-survival. What he faced now was not just some business rival but a professional fighting man. It was a hell of a thing that it had to come to this, Sundance thought.

Less than an hour, following the creek, Sundance spotted the high walls of the crater lake in the almost moonless darkness. On a bright clear day it would be a deep blue clear lake, changing from blue to green as the sun moved across it. Now it was just deep, smooth and dark; it had a bottomless look. Sundance followed the creek right to the spilloff point, a sort of V shape with stunted pines growing on both sides. The water flowed through swift and clear. It was spring fed for nothing flowed into it. If he could blow it, it would fill again, spill over again. Like most volcanic lakes it was hundreds of feet deep. There was so much water in it that he wondered if the clay dam would hold when the torrent of water released by the dynamite hit the far end of the long valley. But like Finnerty had said, when they're nothing else to be done, that's what you do.

The creek ran down sharply from the spilloff, so he had to place the charges as low as possible. The rock near the spilloff was fissured and hundreds—thousands—of years old, crumbling under the billions of gallons of water that had poured through it for time beyond counting. The rock walls on both sides were crumbling too, though they looked as solid as the walls of a castle in the dim light. It was too bad that he didn't have more dynamite; but the dam in the valley had to come first.

It took him a while to decide where to place the only two charges he had. At first he thought of blowing a wider hole in the spillover place, then decided against that. No doubt that would increase the flow of water; what he wanted was to empty the lake as much as possible. What he had to do was to split the fragile rock shell of the crater and count on the enormous pressure of the water to do the rest.

He inspected both sides of the spilloff and his heart quickened when he found a narrow crack where another spilloff had started. Not much water seeped through but the rock fissure ran deeper than the spilloff opening itself. In the darkness he dived into the deep lake and swam deep under the bone-chilling water. Sucking in air, he edged his way down the inside of the crater feeling for the fissure as it went down beyond his capacity to breathe. Unless he was wrong, the fissure ran all the way to the bottom. Forget about the spilloff opening—this was the place to plant the two charges. Out of the water again, shivering in the wind, he pulled brush and grass away from the fissure. If there had been time to dig deeper that's what he could have done. He was counting on Finnerty and the others to be halfway to the dam by now.

He placed one charge above the other and brought Eagle close before he fired the long fuses. Once the charges blew they would ride west into the hills and hope they were quicker than rushing water. Likely, if the fissure cracked wide open, deep and wide, a good part of the lake would empty in seconds. He could have started as soon as he touched a match to the fuses. But it had to be done right and he had to wait. He touched the match to the second fuse and vaulted onto the stallion's back. Water seeped from the fissure and he had wrapped fuse and charge in oiled paper. In the darkness he saw the white smoke hissing from the fuse and touched his heels to Eagle's flank. They were most of the way up the hill when the lake cracked wide open. The fissure split and there was the roar of pent-up water. It looked as if the fissure had opened up clear to the bottom and the lake began to empty with the rumble of a waterfall. The fissure split wider and part of the wall of the high lake began to topple. Millions of gallons of water roared down from the heights, the edges of the flood following them up the hill as they rode, splashing at Eagle's heels as he galloped to escape the deluge. And then they were high enough to be out of danger and the flood roared downward following the old creek bed, covering it completely, uprooting trees and tossing huge boulders about as if they were empty baskets. The flood, once released, moved at incredible speed, faster than any spring freshet Sundance had ever seen. The thin rock walls of the ancient lake were cracking in other places, and even for Sundance, long accustomed to the unusual, it was a sight that he would remember to the end of his life.

He rode to higher ground while the flood thundered by without cease. Along the creek the banks were torn away completely, as if there never had been a creek. He wondered how long it would take to reach the high bluff where the mine was. He thought the bluff would stand against the force of the water. Most of it would because of the rock vein that ran up through its center. Naturally, there would be some tearing away at the sides. It was hell to think what would happen to Finnerty, Tate and the others if the wall of water caught up with them in the center of the valley. If he had been a man who prayed he would be praying that they had reached the dam by now. No matter how heavy the raft, they would be swept away like sodden cloth dolls; with the first onslaught the raft would turn to matchwood.

He rode high on the hills above what once had been a creek. The creek, what he could see of it, had been swept bare to the bottom. He rode fast but the flood had reached the gorge and the bluff long before he did. The flood ran over the gorge instead of through it; the west side of the bluff had crumbled into the water. Most of the landfall had been swept away by the onrushing water. Water lapped at the entrance to the mine shaft, now the only sign that they ever had been there, had lived and worked there, joked and quarreled. No matter; they were playing out their hand, all brave men could do.

Once the flood hit the valley its force began to soften. Some force was behind it; now it was spreading out, calming its rush, filling the valley from end to end. A guess said the valley was under twenty feet of water; a lot deeper toward the south end. By moonlight he used the field glasses; nowhere was there a raft or anything floating besides uprooted trees. The water was well up the hillsides on both sides of the valley. From very far away he heard the sound of a steam whistle, a sign that the Selby holding tanks were empty.

Right after that he heard gunfire and urged the stallion to a gallop. No more gold would be taken out that night unless Jackson Selby scrounged up a few gallons of well water and did it by hand. He rode and circled until he came to the dam. The new flood had brought the water level dangerously close to the top, but the dam was holding. It was a good thing for Orono that the dam was holding. As Finnerty had said, no dam, no town. He gave out a whoop to let them know he was coming, and they held their fire when he rode up, dismounted and led his horse along the high ground.

Grimes, Fuller and Longworth looked as if they would rather be anywhere else. Sundance didn't blame them; they hadn't done so badly. Only Finnerty was jubilant, lying on his belly in a clump of brush with the tube sighted Big Fifty Remington poking out. Tate lay not far away with the long-barreled Fox shotgun in his hands. His face was pale and bandaged with a strip of shirt. One of his eyes had been fitted with a makeshift patch, a round piece of leather and a strip of rawhide.

Before Sundance could ask why, Tate said, "I came to all right, but the eye with the wound over it doesn't see so good. It was fuzzy and was affecting the other eye. This way I can shoot better."

"What about pain?"

"Some pain, nothing worse than a bad hangover. They're down there shooting up at us, but they haven't rushed us. Finnerty says they have a dynamite gun down there, are ready to start blasting at the dam. Finnerty asked them if they wanted another Johnstown Flood. After they were was a lot of palavering down there and they didn't fire the gun. So for now it's just shooting back and forth. I think you got those poor folks all nervous, Jim."

Finnerty laughed with the joy of battle. "I told them we had that whole lake behind us now. Didn't they hear the boom-boom back in the hills. Some of them have been on the high ground to the east and they know that's no horsecock. After that there was no more talk about the dynamite gun. I did some talking of my own about dynamite. Said he had the whole dam planted with lovely little sticks of the stuff. If they try to rush us we'll wipe the town off the map."

"You ever hear such a liar?" Tate said.

"God forgive me," Finnerty said. "But what happens if they call our bluff?"

"They won't," Sundance said. "Town is right downhill from this end of the valley."

Grimes said, "Now's the time to make a deal with Selby. What can he do?"

"Make a deal, then go back on it," Sundance said.

163

"He said he was going to run us out and he will. We let the water spill over at the right place, a week from now he'll come at us again."

Grimes said, "I thought you said you trusted the man."

Sundance said, 'I trust him to do what he says—run us out, kill us off. He can't let us get away with that. Not because of the town. Because of himself."

Finnerty crawled close to Sundance. "Not too much chance of them shooting at you since I told them about the dynamite. They have it down there in a clump of brush. Kind of looks like a cannon with a long thin barrel. Don't know the exact working of it. Guess there's a compressed air chamber at the back made to take plenty of pressure. Guess they pump it up. They got off one stick but it overshot us and made a big splash in the lake. Threw water a hundred feet high. That was the only shot they made."

Sundance could barely make out the slender shape of the dynamite gun far below the dam. With the field glasses he saw the shapes of men moving in the semidarkness. He didn't shoot and ordered the others to hold their fire. "Some hothead could cut loose with that cannon," he said.

He called down the slope for Durkin; he knew he wouldn't get to talk to Selby at first. He was right: Durkin answered. Durkin had the nerve of the truly hard man.

"You've gone and done it now, Sundance," he called back. "You'll hang for this." Durkin raised his voice. "The rest of you men can still get out. Safe passage all the way."

Finnerty was moving the tube sight of the Remington. "I think I can get the bastard. Think I should try for him, Sundance?"

Sundance pushed the Remington aside. He called back to Durkin, "We can all go together anytime you like. You don't believe we can blow the dam. Then show some guts—open fire on it. Blast it with that gun if you like. Same thing happens."

Durkin was silent for a moment. "We have this valley ringed end to end. You can't wait too long."

"Same thing goes for the dam. Water's filling into the valley all the time. Put enough pressure on that dam and she'll pop like a cork. It won't just take the town, the mines will go at the same time. You'll be dead and so will most of the people still in town. How long do you think it will take Selby to rebuild? How much money? With the flood will come the fever."

Durkin yelled, "This is rebellion. No man has the right to do what you're doing."

"Defending my property," Sundance said. "All we wanted to do was work our mine, bother nobody. Selby said it couldn't be allowed. Where's Selby? I want to talk to Selby, not you."

"Mr. Selby isn't here," Durkin yelled back. "You'll have to settle for me. I'm the law here. I have full authority. You want to talk to the county sheriff?"

"Why isn't he here by now?"

Durkin answered in his slow touch voice. "Sheriff's been busy with other matters. He's getting here fast as he can."

Sundance yelled, "No sheriff, no bought-and-paid for law."

Durkin's voice was hard and sarcastic. "How about the governor? He big enough man for you? He knows what you've done by now. Telegraph wires been clicking the news all over the country."

"First I want to talk to Selby."

"He won't come, Sundance. What are you going to do now?"

Sundance wasn't bluffing. If he had to die there, then so be it. It had to come sometime along the road. One thing was sure: he wouldn't knuckle under to Selby. They had come too far, suffered too much.

"I'm going to wait for Selby to change his mind," he called back to Durkin. "Maybe you can't hear the shifting of the dam from where you are. If you shut up and listen you'll hear it again. There's no central core of rocks to the thing. Just two hills of clay, one piled on top of the other. It will give way in the middle and everything will go at once. Go get Selby."

Durkin's voice had some panic in it at last. "Mr. Selby won't deal with you."

Sundance paused. "Then say goodbye to a town. The rest of us here, we're as ready as we'll ever be."

Chapter Fourteen

Jackson Shelby's voice answered instead of Durkin's. The mine owner had been there all the time, not far back either; if there had been shooting he could have caught a bullet as quickly as one of his men. At the moment he heard Selby's voice Sundance knew they had won. But there had to be guarantees; the biggest problem on his mind was—would the dam hold?

Nobody talked but Selby; his voice was clear with authority. Sundance didn't know how big Selby's fortune was, but he guessed most of it was tied up in Orono. That had to be why he wanted to have complete control of the town and everything else. Already his spotters had reported that the valley was a huge lake hanging over his town, his mines, even his fine house. Yet his voice remained calm; that was the toughness in the man. He knew, too, what Sundance was thinking.

"Looks like we're at a standoff," Selby said.

"How do we fix it?" Sundance asked. He couldn't see Selby. "This time I won't take your word for anything. It wouldn't be good business for you to keep it. Same thing goes for your tame sheriff and paid-for politicians."

What Selby said next came as a surprise. "Would you take the world of your friend General Crook?"

"The General is a long way from here," Sundance said. "Last I heard he was in St. Louis. Bringing a telegraph with his name on it won't work either. Even if he did come this dam won't hold that long."

"You're wrong about St. Louis," Selby said. "News of our . . . disagreement . . . has spread a long way from Nevada. There's a telegraph message if you want to read it. I can make out some of what's in it. The rest of it has no meaning to me. You willing to let our newspaper editor, Mr. Weyman, come up there with the message and a copy of our newspaper?"

Sundance said, "All right with me if he comes by himself. You can come yourself if you like, Selby."

The mine owner's voice remained calm. "This is no time for joking, sir."

"You started the fun," Sundance called back. "Tell Weyman to climb up and over."

Sundance knew they had nothing to fear from Weyman. The newspaperman wouldn't have the guts to try anything. There seemed to be an argument going on down below under the trees. Sundance guess Weyman was sorry for the first day he took Selby's

167

bribe money. Then he was pushed out from the shadow of the trees, about as nervous a man as Sundance had ever seen. It was a far cry from writing lying editorials to walking up a steep hill under the guns of desperate men.

"I'm unarmed," Weyman said with a wobble in his voice.

"You better be," Sundance said. "I told you to come ahead."

Weyman's fine suit got plenty of mud on it on the way up. It was good to see the bastard fall and then crawl in the mud. But it was a bad sign that the face of the dam was so waterlogged. Weyman got over the top of the dam and Sundance pulled him to one side. Weyman was trembling and his eyes widened when he saw the expanse of water that threatened the town. Finnerty pushed him down and held a gun on him.

Sundance struck a match and read the telegraph message first. YOU CAN'T DO THIS, JIM. NEVADA IS TERRITORY. HAVE REQUESTED PERMISSION TO ARBITRATE. COMING SPECIAL TRAIN FROM CARSON CITY. BE THERE MORNING. IF YOU HAVE TO RELEASE WATER DO IT. WILL SEE JUSTICE DONE.

Crook's name was at the bottom of the telegraph message, but it wasn't until he saw the other additional words that Sundance knew it could have come from no one but his old friend Three Stars. What clinched it was a name known only to both of them; that of a highly placed army officer they had forced to resign because of his involvement with the Indian Ring. In private, their name for him was Boston Bull because he had a face like that famous fighting dog.

Sundance told Weyman to remain while he looked at the front page of the Orono newspaper. The headline read INSURRECTION IN ORONO! Sundance was described as the notorious halfbreed renegade. Tate got some bad press too: gambler and killer. According to the paper they were holding the town of Orono for ransom. The second biggest story on the page was that the Civil War hero, General George C. Crook, was rushing to the scene by special train from Carson City, where he had been staying on army business.

Sundance kept newspaper and telegraph message and told Weyman he could go.

Weyman went down the dam and back to the cover of the trees. Then Selby's voice came from the darkness. "You ready to believe me now?"

"I guess it's from Crook," Sundance answered, knowing that it was, but in a game this big you gave away as little as possible. "I want to deal with him, nobody else."

For the first time Selby's normally calm voice displayed some apprehension. "But he said to release some of the water if it looks dangerous. It's dangerous now, past dangerous. let some of my men come up and cut a slot in the top to take off some of the pressure. They can side it with heavy timbers so it won't cave in when the water comes through."

Sundance turned to the others before he answered Selby. After all, it was their fight too. Except for Tate they were all strangers to him, and Tate was a man no man could ever hope to understand. Yet they had fought alongside him, done their jobs.

"He's right about the dam not holding till morning," he said. "He wasn't lying about Crook, but if he gets at us before Crook gets here there isn't much Crook can do. What do you have to say?"

Tate looked at Sundance with his one good eye. "I say don't trust the bastard one inch. If the dam goes it's Selby's doing."

Finnerty hefted the Remington. "I'm for trusting none of that pack of town rats down there. But you led us all right thus far. Anything you decide is all right with me."

Grimes nodded. "Release some of the water, is my opinion."

"Some water anyway," Longworth said, and Fuller said he was for that too.

Sundance looked down from the dam. "Six men, Selby. No more than that. They come up one at a time so we see what they look like. I know a mine worker from a gunman. Send up a gunny and you'll get more water than you want. Start them coming right now and tell them extra pay isn't worth dying for. Right now we don't care how many widows and orphans we leave in Orono."

Sundance and the others moved to the side of the dam and watched the first man start out from the trees, a bulky man in a plug hat and canvas pants. The dam creaked and the man stood for a moment before he started to climb the muddy face. Once over the top, they searched him for weapons and found only an old clasp knife.

"I forget that," he said in a German accent. Sundance threw the knife in the water.

The five men who were to breach the dam climbed up covered from both sides. It wasn't likely that Selby would try anything, but you never knew. Bending, even for his own good, would come hard to a man like Selby.

When the men and the equipment were on top of the dam Sundance told them what to do. "Make the V and line it with heavy timber, then secure them good. After that I want a drop-gate so I can cut off the flow any time I want."

The German nodded. "We do anything you say."

Sundance asked, "You got your families moved to high ground?"

"First thing we do, we hear about this," the German said. "You mind I say one other thing?"

"Say it while you're working," Sundance ordered.

Digging with powerful strokes, the German said, "No matter what happen after this night Orono won't be the same. You made Selby bend his knee. Nobody ever do that till now."

A mutter of approval came from some of the men working on the dam. Maybe they hated Selby as much as the German; he watched carefully just the same.

They started at the outer edge of the dam and worked back from there. Then they cut the V at a downward slant and secured it by driving in balks of wood. After that they braced the opening at top and bottom until it was as solid as they could make it. As they worked the dam creaked again, tens of thousands of tons of clay moving under the pressure of the water.

Last came the building of the dropgate and that took more time than anything else because Sundance wanted it to be strong. Selby was a resourceful man and even now he might be thinking up some sort of complicated doublecross. It was in Selby's nature to have to win, no matter what the cost. Sundance didn't know what to expect when Crook came except that the shooting would stop. Even a man like Selby wouldn't dare stand against a man like Crook. Three Stars was a man slow to anger, but when it came, it was terrible.

Less than an hour later the opening and the dropgate were finished. The German had used planed wood in the thick double dropgate and greased the slots so that it would fall at a touch. It would hold, it would hold for a while.

171

The bulky German was the last man to go down the hill. "Good luck," he said. "This General Crook will make things right in this town, you think?"

"I don't know what he can do," Sundance said. "Go on now. Thanks for making the dropgate so good. Selby tell you to do that?"

"What do you think?" asked the German. "I would have brought dynamite if I could have." The thick-bodied German had nerve. "You don't have one stick up here, do you?"

"How do you know?"

"Because you would have used it against the dynamite gun down there. Don't worry, mister, I don't tell Selby a thing."

Tate raised the sawed-off English shotgun. "Damn right you won't, Fritz."

Sundance grabbed the gun and wrestled it from Tate's hands. Tate let him take it. "Lucky you're who you are, halfbreed," he said. "If that German tells what he knows we're as good as dead. They'll come swarming up that hill."

Sundance eased down the outsized hammer and gave the gun back to Tate. "You can't kill everybody. Here goes the water."

Sundance lifted the first dropgate and Finnerty raised the one beyond it. Immediately, the pent-up water surged into the V opening and spilled down the face of the dam into the dry riverbed. They lifted the dropgates all the way and secured them with wooden pegs driven into auger holes on both sides. The tap of a rock would send them sliding back into place.

"There's your water, Selby," Sundance shouted. He turned and saw Tate staring at him, sure that an attack would come within minutes. None came and Tate's face sagged in the lines of a sick man. He raised his hand to his eye.

172

The water was rushing through, filling the riverbed below. "How's your eye?" Sundance asked.

"Not so good," Tate said. "It's like I said. The light comes and goes." He took the patch off the other eye. "This one is blind. That stone cut a nerve, something like that. I guess the other one is going the same way. You ever hear of a blind poker player. Maybe I can get a little orphan girl to sit in the games with me. Whisper to me the cards I'm holding."

"Soon as Crook gets here we'll get you to a doctor."

"Don't think that's going to do any good, old friend," Tate said. "Maybe there was a chance if it had been looked at right away."

Sundance knew that was true. It was possible that the doctor in Orono had taken his black bag and headed for the railroad. "You sorry you got into this game, Tate?"

Tate laughed. "Hell no. When you play for the big stakes you have to expect to get hurt. I got hurt. What galls me is nothing is really going to change after your friend Crook settles this matter. Maybe we can go back to working the claim. Selby will own the town like always."

Sundance knew Tate was speaking the truth. He would still own the town, still boss it from his big house. "We start out to work a claim and that's what we're going to do."

"You mean you are," Tate said. "Who's going to lead me in and out of the shaft—Finnerty?"

Finnerty looked away from Tate, knowing nothing could be said that would make it any better. The Irishman was a hard bitter man and knew that any offer of charity, of help in the future would be out of plae. Like the others, he knew that Tate Yarnell had come to the end of the line.

Grimes looked up at the sky. "It won't be too long till morning. Too bad there isn't a railroad direct to Orono."

"Don't worry about George Crook," Sundance said. "He'll get here faster than any man you ever knew."

No one spoke after that. All that could be done had been done. From now on it was all up to Crook. It would be strange, Sundance thought, to have to face Three Stars in this way.

"You're not letting enough water through," Selby called up from the bottom of the hill. "I tell you, that dam won't hold."

"It better hold," Sundance said. "Want to know something else? The water level in the valley isn't going down that much." Sundance wasn't lying. Water was still coming into the valley from the crater lake and the tributary creeks.

"You sure General Crook knows how to get here when he comes to Orono?" Sundance shouted above the noise of the water.

"Men are waiting for him at the railroad, in the town," Selby answered. "They'll send up flares when he gets to town."

"I want to see Crook, not flares," Sundance said. "You want some advice, Selby?"

"What's that?"

"Don't talk to Crook the way you talk to your miners. You might get knocked down. Knocked and kicked."

Selby said nothing after that. For hours there was nothing but the rush of the water and the creaking of the dam. They waited by the dam, tired, dirty, but determined to see it through.

Then at last the light began to thin out. First light came dirty and gray in the east. Behind them the morning wind rippled the sheet of water in the valley. They chewed on jerked meat and waited for the light to grow stronger. On this morning, perhaps the last morning of their lives, it seemed to come so slowly. Tate had his eyes closed but Sundance knew he wasn't asleep. Finnerty stared down the barrel of the Remington, a hard man to the end. Fuller and Longworth whispered. Grimes sat by himself.

The sun was breaking through when the first flare went up. It was hard to see it against the glare of the sun. Then another flare went up right after it. The flares went up and hung suspended for an instant before they burst apart and trailed back to earth.

Finnerty rubbed at his red-rimmed eyes. "By Christ! The general got here after all."

"Maybe," Sundance said.

Chapter Fifteen

But there was no mistaking George Crook's tall figure when it finally came into view at the head of a company of regulars. Sundance heard them coming long before he saw them skirting the creek that ran down toward the town. They must have pushed it hard to get there so early from the railroad, but Crook, in spite of his age, rode ramrod-straight in the saddle.

The sun was up bright when Crook's column reached the bottom of the dam. Crook dismounted but ignored Selby's proferred hand. The regulars sat their horses, rifles at the ready. Ignoring the mud, Crook began the climb to the top of the dam. Halfway up, he turned and ordered Selby to stay where he was. Two of the troopers had thrown ropes on the dynamite gun and were pulling it away from the dam.

Crook looked at the valley of water before he turned to Sundance. He didn't offer to shake hands. "Looks like you stirred up a little fuss here, Mr. Sundance," he said.

"Just defending out lives and property, General," Sundance said.

"So I see." Crook looked at Finnerty, Tate and the others. "You'll have to let the water through, Jim. They wanted to send the militia against you and you know what they'd be like. Half of them drunkards never did a day's work in their lives."

Sundance hated to go against his old friend, this tough old campaigner who had given him back his life. Crook had found him a wandering halfbreed drunk half crazy with grief after the murder of his parents by white and Indian renegades.

Still, they had fought so hard against Selby. A few things had to be said, even to George Crook. Mostly he was angry that Jackson Selby was still alive.

"We could wash away the militia as fast as Selby."

Crook searched for a match to light one of his ever-present Havana cigars. He didn't drink or swear but he smoked like a chimney. Sundance gave him a match and he grunted thanks.

"I took over from the militia," Crook said, blowing smoke into the morning air. "I had to take a lot on myself to go that far. There's going to be some caterwauling in Washington when the politicians get hold of the President's ear. No matter. I've been in hot water before."

Sundance said he was sorry Crook had to get involved in the fight with Selby. It was the wrong thing to say.

"To Hades with Selby and your apologies. Since

when did you start talking out of the side of your mouth? Listen to me. When I countermanded the militia orders I had to guarantee to get you off this dam. That's what I'm going to do, old friend. You can't destroy a whole town because of a fight with one man."

"It comes to the same thing. Selby *is* the town."

"You don't listen too good, Jim. Some of the people in Carson City gave me plenty of detail on Selby and that gunman he calls a police chief. How he's been kicking people around all these years, running them out, killing them if he has to. Still makes no difference at this very moment. You have to get off this dam and let the water flow."

"Then what happens, Three Stars? That means Selby will go on doing what he's always done. Nothing will have changed."

Crook snapped his cigar in momentary irritation and put a fresh one in his mouth. Sundance gave him a match.

"First things first, that's all I can tell you," Crook growled, tired after his breakneck journey from Carson City. "I don't know what can be done about Selby. I'll do what I can in Washington. Now will you get the hell off this dam. By the way, where's all the dynamite they're talking about down there?"

Sundance said there was none.

Crook shook his head in wonderment. "If you had any more nerve you'd be a fool." Crook placed his hand on Sundance's arm. "I'll have to send my regulars against you if you don't give up. If I have to attack I won't let them take you alive, Jim. You fight the regulars and that's making war on the United States. That's a hanging offense and I won't let them hang you."

"I know you wouldn't," Sundance said. "What

happens after we give up the dam?"

"Selby's men will breach the dam more than it is. They'll shore it up at the same time so it won't break. Then we'll have some kind of hearing in town. I can order that, as temporary military commander of this district. If enough truth comes out I'll push to get this business into the courts. More than that I can't do for you."

Sundance turned to the others. "We're giving up the dam," he said. "It's that or fight the regular army. General Crook says we'll get a fair shake and that's all I want to hear."

Sundance had to speak sharply to Tate before he lowered his shotgun. "I'm not giving up my weapons until this is settled. I don't want to walk around like a target for one of Selby's snipers."

It was plain that Crook didn't like Tate. A lot of people didn't. "Everybody can hold onto their weapons. My regulars will have the lot of you covered. First man that fires off a shot will get riddled. That goes for everybody."

"Meaning me, in particular," Tate said. "Did you give the same warning to Selby?"

"You could use some manners, my friend," was all Crook said.

Then, covered by the carbines of the regular cavalrymen, Sundance and the others climbed down from the dam. Sundance looked at the regulars. Crook had picked a good bunch of men, experienced soldiers who wouldn't hesitate to open fire on their commander's orders.

Selby came out of the grove of trees and his face remained impassive. He had lost and won at the same time. Durkin was the only man with a smile. The men who were to breach the dam were ready to go to work. But no one moved until Crook gave the order.

"Go to it," he said. "Only the work crew stays. The rest of us go back to town. There are questions to be asked and answered."

Selby watched his workmen climbing the dam. "I'll be along in a little while, General. I want to see this done right."

Crook turned his hard eyes on one of the most powerful men in Nevada, maybe in the West. "You'll come when I tell you—and that means now. You too, Durkin." Crook pointed his cigar at Weyman, the newspaper editor. "You can gather your news later. You had no small part in stirring up this trouble."

Selby and his people mounted up and went ahead with one detachment of troopers. Sundance, leading his own men, was escorted to town by the rest of the regulars. Crook rode by himself, puffing smoke and looking gloomy.

The dam was the end closest to Orono and it didn't take much more than an hour to get there. The river was running high, clean for a change, but the streets were empty. The people from the shantytown had moved all they owned far up on the hills. Some of them began to come down when the first party rode into town. They were streaming along the main street as Sundance and his men came in.

Crook turned to Selby. "Is that your courthouse over there?"

The two tough men locked eyes for a moment. "Not my courthouse, General Crook," Selby said. "It belongs to the county."

Crook grunted. "Call it what you want. That's where we'll hold the hearing."

It looked like the courthouse hadn't been used for a while. Selby's law was informal. He decided what should be done to a man, and Durkin did it. One of

179

Crook's sergeants pushed open the doors and they filed into the big dusty room. The United States flag and the Nevada Territorial flag were as dusty as the rest of the place. But except for the dust it was just like any other courtroom.

Crook didn't dust off the judge's chair before he sat in it. His regulars, carbines ready, lined both sides of the room. Crook was no lawyer but he knew what was right. He said, "Everybody shut up till I finish talking. Then everybody gets a chance to talk. We're going to try to get at the truth." Crook paused to light a cigar. "As close to it as we can."

Having said that, Crook outlineed the situation as it had been told to him. One Jim Sundance, a citizen of the United States, had found gold and legally registered his claim. Thereupon, he had been warned, threatened, and finally attacked. This Jim Sundance, acting with Tate Yarnell, had killed deputy sheriffs who had attempted to force two men known as Grimes and Rance to sell their claim. Later the Sundance-Yarnell mine had been fired on from men in concealment and the man known as Rance had been killed. Jim Sundance and Tate Yarnell had killed the ambushers. The dead ambushers had not been identified as members of the Orono police force. Later, fearing for their lives, Jim Sundance and Tate Yarnell and others not identified had dammed the river as a way of making the aggressors come to terms.

Crook looked down at Selby. "You can talk now if you like."

Selby stood up. "I'd prefer to speak last, General, since I didn't meet Sundance until he had been here for some time."

Crook nodded. "Who do you have in mind?"

"Mr. Weyman, editor of our newspaper, was one

of the first men to have words with Sundance."

"Step forward, Weyman," Crook ordered.

Weyman was nervous but he had his testimony ready, like an actor who had gone over his lines many times in his head.

Weyman said, "As an editor it's my business to gather news. I had heard of Sundance and thought there might be a story for my paper. I approached him in the most civil manner. Instead of answering my questions or declining to answer, Sundance became loud and threatening, placing his hand on his gun as he did so. He called me a number of obscene names and vowed that he was going to make a lot of changes in Orono. The land here rightfully belonged to the Indians and he was going to see that they got it back. The land and the gold. Knowing his reputation, I informed Chief Durkin."

Durkin was called next and he took the witness chair with the assurance of the born liar. "I'd been told of a fight Sundance had with a miner in the claims office. It didn't seem like much damage was done. Still, that and what Mr. Weyman told me made it my business to have a talk with Sundance. I told him Orono was a well run town and he was welcome to stay as long as he didn't make trouble."

"What did he say to that?" Crook asked.

Durkin said, "He said he'd do as he pleased."

Crook said, "You didn't try to persuade him to sell his claim to the Selby Mining Company?"

Durkin pretended to look surprised. "Me do that? I'm a lawman. I got nothing to do with buying and selling."

"What happened then?" Crook asked.

"I warned him again," Durkin said. "Then I left. Later I heard there was more trouble with Mr. Travers, purchasing agent for the Selby Mines. As is his custom, he came to the saloon where Sundance was. The idea, same as always, was to make him an honest offer for his claim. Making an offer is standard custom whenever a new claim if filed."

"Why did this Travers take deputies along with him?" Crook asked.

"Simple. He was afraid of Sundance. An argument developed, more like a fight. My men were about to arrest Sundance for disturbing the peace when that man over there, Tate Yarnell, held them up with a sawed-off shotgun. Knowing Yarnell's reputation as a killer, they tried to let it go, but he tried to force a fight on them. Kill them, in fact."

Crook stared at Durkin with undisguised contempt. "Where were you while all this was going on?"

Crook's attitude didn't bother Durkin. "I had to leave town for about an hour."

Travers was called after that and he backed up the story about the trouble in the saloon. "I thought they were going to kill all of us. I was afraid for my life like never before. I knew from the tone of Yarnell's voice that he wanted to kill us."

Crook growled, "Never mind the tone of his voice. What about the killings out in the valley?"

Travers, sweating hard, said he wanted no more to do with Sundance and Yarnell. They could keep their claim—and welcome to it. "I went out to the valley to ask Grimes and Rance if they wanted to sell. My offer was the standard one, quite generous."

Crook scratched a match on the judge's desk. "Why did you need deputies to talk to Grimes and Rance. Were you afraid of them, too?"

Travers wiped his face. "Of course not, General. But I knew Sundance and Yarnell were fairly close-by and was afraid of trouble. There was trouble, sir.

They murdered those deputies in cold blood. I heard later that the man Rance, now deceased, murdered one of the wounded deputies after he had thrown down his gun."

The testimony went on and on; Sundance knew there wasn't a chance of ever getting Selby into a real court of law. Selby was laying out a lot of money, making a lot of threats, to build a story as solid as this one.

Sundance was questioned and admitted everything he had done: the stealing of the petroleum—everything. He knew it was a waste of time and Crook knew it, too. Selby watched and listened with absolutely no expression on his face. Then, finally, it was his turn to give his testimony.

Once again, Sundance wondered at the strangeness of the man. In his own mind, he wasn't lying, just doing what had to be done, and for a man so powerful there was nothing threatening about him. His voice remained reasonable, calm, matter-of-fact.

Selby appealed to reason. With all the holdings he had, why go to so much trouble to gain control of a piddling little gold claim? It didn't make sense, he said.

He didn't deny that he had asked Sundance to come to his house for a man-to-man talk. "What was to prevent me from having him killed then?" he asked. "A single shot from ambush and he'd be dead. No, General, I asked him to come so we could straighten out the bad feeling that seemed to be developing. I'll be completely honest, sir. I feared that Sundance would rally troublemakers around him. There are men like that in every mining town, General. Fools! Men who talk of labor unions and strikes that can lead to nothing but bloodshed. To head that off I offered Sundance much more than his

183

claim was worth. Ask him, sir, if that is the truth."

Sundance stood up at Crook's order and said it was. He didn't say anything else. Anything he said would be a waste of time. He had won and yet he had lost.

Selby went on smoothly. "Sundance refused my offer, said he was going to fight me in a way I wouldn't like. Well, sir, I'm no brawler or bandit, and I hardly knew what to expect. But I knew there was going to be trouble—and there was."

Crook raised his hand to stop Selby's flow of words. "I don't want to hear anymore about this. What I am going to do is make a full report to the Governor of this territory, also a report to the Secretary of the Interior. This is no court of law, simply a hearing. I have no power to decide anything. It will have to be settled in court."

Selby turned his smooth face toward Crook. "As far as I'm concerned this matter is over. I want no part of legal proceedings. I don't know what Sundance and his partners want to do. If I may say so, they have no case against me. You heard the testimony of my fellow citizens."

Crook asked Sundance what he wanted to do. Sundance said nothing. It was over for him, too.

"So be it," Crook said. "My report goes in just the same. And now a word to everyone. I came here to restore peace and, by God, it will be done. If there is any more bloodshed I will be back. Work your mines, Selby, and let Sundance and his people do the same. It will go badly for anyone who makes any more trouble. Impress that on your 'fellow citizens,' Selby."

Selby gave his assurance that the trouble was ended.

"This hearing is concluded," General Crook

declared.

Sundance's face was expressionless as they filed out of the courtroom. General Crook walked with him. "I did the best I could for you, Jim," Crook said. "But you heard what the witnesses said. You started the trouble. You went into partnership with a known gambler and killer. You can't deny Tate is a killer. I know something about him but that isn't the point."

"Tate's a good man," Sundance said. "Somebody should have killed the men he killed. He just happened to be the one."

Crook said, "That won't matter if this comes to a regular trial. I have only so much influence. It won't come to a trial, not in this territory. Face the facts, it's over and you beat Selby. He won't bother you again. He knows I say what I mean. At least you can go back and work your claim in peace."

Sundance shook his head. "I've had a bellyful of gold mining, Three Stars. I'm going to take my share and get away from here. Finnerty and the others can have the mine. Tate's the only one I'm thinking about. He's close to blind."

"There must be doctors. San Francisco maybe."

"I told him that. He feels it's over for him."

"I don't know. I can't see Tate sitting on the porch and have an old black man lead him around."

Crook's regulars were mounted on their horses waiting for the general to get started. "I can't tell you what to do about Tate," Crook said. "Thousands of men were blinded in the war. You can't weep for the whole world."

"Tate doesn't feel sorry for himself," Sundance said.

"Here he comes now," Crook said, and they both turned to look as Tate came out of the saloon with a bottle in his hand, the short English shotgun stuck in his belt. He took a final swallow from the bottle and threw it away. The eyepatch covered his bad eye and he was squinting hard with the other one.

Sundance called over to him, "Let's go see a doctor, gambling man."

"In a minute, halfbreed," Tate said, and something in his voice made Sundance's body grow rigid with danger. Selby and Durkin were coming out of the courthouse, smiling, talking quietly.

Sundance knew what was going to happen and his first impulse was to call out. But he didn't do anything. In a way he was betraying the best friend he'd ever had; in another, helping another old friend to ease his way out of life. He would never tell Crook about it.

Tate's sawed-off was still stuck inside his belt, the hammer down. "That you, Selby?" he asked quietly, turning his head to one side so he could see better.

Durkin said, "Mr. Selby has nothing to say to you, Yarnell. This business is finished."

Tate pulled the stubby gun, cocked it and fired all in one motion. Standing close together, Selby and Durkin were blown to bits by the single blast. Sundance didn't yell not even when Tate whirled and pointed the empty single-barrel at the line of troopers. The hail of bullets from the trooper's pistols knocked Tate all over the street; and when he died he didn't even twitch.

General Crook looked at Sundance before he climbed on his horse. There was a suspicion of a smile playing about his hard mouth. "I think somebody ought to go find the county sheriff. I have to get back to Carson City, then north from there. Where were you going when you got into this mess?"

"Mostly south."

General Crook pointed. "South is that way. The next news I hear from you is that you're running a hardware store."

Sundance smiled at his old friend of so many years. "That'll be the day, Three Stars."

"Don't I know it," General George C. Crook said.